SPECIAL MESSAGE TO READERS

This book is published under the auspices of

THE ULVERSCROFT FOUNDATION

re ses.

c/o **The Royal Australian and New Zealand
College of Ophthalmologists,
94-98 Chalmers Street, Surry Hills,
N S W 2010 Australia**

Alistair MacLean, the son of a Scots minister, was born in 1922 and brought up in the Scottish Highlands. In 1941 at the age of eighteen he joined the Royal Navy. After the war he gained an English Honours degree at Glasgow University, and became a schoolmaster. In 1983 he was awarded a D. Litt from the same university. He is now recognized as one of the outstanding popular writers of the twentieth century. Many of his bestsellers have been filmed, including *The Guns of Navarone*, *Where Eagles Dare*, and *Ice Station Zebra*. Alistair MacLean died in 1987 at his home in Switzerland.

PARTISANS

World War II rages, and while Tito's rebel
forces resist occupation, the Germans
infiltrate and plan their destruction.
Yugoslavian Peter Peterson and his team
of compatriots set out from Rome to relay
the German battle plan — but where do
their loyalties lie? Aboard a damaged
motor torpedo boat, in bitter winter
conditions, it's a dangerous journey with
dangerous companions, where no one is
who they seem . . . and where the three
men find intrigue and betrayal around
every corner.

ALISTAIR MacLEAN

PARTISANS

Complete and Unabridged

ULVERSCROFT
Leicester

First published in Great Britain in 1982 by
William Collins Sons & Co. Ltd.
London

First Large Print Edition
published 2012
by arrangement with
HarperCollins*Publishers*
London

British Library CIP Data

MacLean, Alistair, *1922 – 1987*
    Partisans.
    1. World War, *1939 – 1945-* -Fiction. 2. War stories.
    3. Large type books.
    I. Title
    823.9'14–dc23

    ISBN 978–1–4448–1321–0

Published by
F. A. Thorpe (Publishing)
Anstey, Leicestershire

Set by Words & Graphics Ltd.
Anstey, Leicestershire
Printed and bound in Great Britain by
T. J. International Ltd., Padstow, Cornwall

This book is printed on acid-free paper

To Avdo and Inge

1

The chill night wind off the Tiber was from the north and carried with it the smell of snow from the distant Apennines. The sky was clear and full of stars and there was light enough to see the swirling of the dust-devils in the darkened streets and the paper, cardboard and assorted detritus that blew about every which way. The darkened, filthy streets were not the result of the electrical and sanitation departments of the Eternal City, as was their peacetime wont, staging one of their interminable strikes, for this was not peacetime: events in the Mediterranean theatre had reached a delicate stage where Rome no longer cared to advertise its whereabouts by switching on the street lights: the sanitation department, for the most part, was some way off to the south fighting a war it didn't particularly care about.

Petersen stopped outside a shop doorway — the nature of its business was impossible to tell for the windows were neatly masked in regulation blackout paper — and glanced up and down the Via Bergola. It appeared to be deserted as were most streets in the city at that time of night. He produced a hooded torch and a large bunch of peculiarly shaped keys and let himself in with a speed, ease and dexterity which spoke well for whoever had trained him in such matters. He took up position behind the opened door, removed the hood from the torch, pocketed the keys, replaced them with a silenced Mauser and waited.

He had to wait for almost two minutes, which, in the circumstances, can be a very long time, but Petersen didn't seem to mind. Two stealthy footsteps, then there appeared beyond the edge of the door the dimly seen silhouette of a man whose only identifiable features were a peaked cap and a hand clasping a gun in so purposeful a grip that even in the half-light the faint sheen of the knuckles could be seen.

The figure took two further stealthy steps into the shop then halted abruptly as the torch clicked on and the silencer of the Mauser rammed none too gently into the base of his neck.

'Drop that gun. Clasp your hands behind your neck, take three steps forward and don't turn round.'

The intruder did as told. Petersen closed the shop door, located the light switch and clicked it on. They appeared to be in what was, or should have been, a jeweller's shop, for the owner, a man with little faith in the occupying forces, his fellow-countrymen or both, had prudently and totally cleared all his display cabinets.

'Now you can turn round,' Petersen said.

The man turned. The set expression on the youthful face was tough and truculent, but he couldn't do much about his eyes or the apprehension reflected in them.

'I will shoot you,' Petersen said conversationally, 'if you are carrying another gun and don't tell me.'

'I have no other gun.'

'Give me your papers.' The youngster compressed his lips, said nothing and made no move. Petersen sighed.

'Surely you recognize a silencer? I can just as easily take the papers off your body. Nobody will know a thing. What's more to the point, neither will you.'

The youngster reached inside his tunic and handed over a wallet. Petersen flicked it open.

'Hans Wintermann,' he read. 'Born August 24, 1924. Just nineteen. *And* a lieutenant. You must be a bright young man.' Petersen folded and pocketed the wallet. 'You've been following me around tonight. And most of yesterday. And the evening before that. I find

3

such persistence tedious, especially when it's so obvious. Why do you follow me?'

'You have my name, rank, regiment — '

Petersen waved him to silence. 'Spare me. Well, I'm left with no option.'

'You're going to shoot me?' The truculence had left the youngster's face.

'Don't be stupid.'

★   ★   ★

The Hotel Splendide was anything but: but its dingy anonymity suited Petersen well enough. Peering through the cracked and stained glass of the front door he noted, with mild surprise, that the concierge, fat, unshaven and well stricken in years, was, for once, not asleep or, at least, wide enough awake to be able to tilt a bottle to his head. Petersen circled to the rear of the hotel, climbed the fire escape, let himself in to the third-floor passage, moved along this, turned into a left-hand corridor and let himself into his room with a skeleton key. He quickly checked cupboards and drawers, seemed satisfied, shrugged into a heavy coat, left and took up position on the fire escape. Despite the added protection of the coat his exposed position was considerably colder than it had been in the comparative shelter of the streets below and he hoped he would not have to wait too long.

The wait was even shorter than he had expected. Less than five minutes had passed when a German officer strode briskly along the corridor, turned left, knocked on a door, knocked again, this time peremptorily, rattled the handle then reappeared, frowning heavily. There came the creaking and clanking of the ancient elevator, a silence, more creaking and clanking, then the officer again hove into sight this time with the concierge, who had a key in his hand.

When ten minutes had passed with no sign of either man Petersen went inside, eased his way along the passage and peered round the corner to his left. Halfway along the corridor stood the concierge, obviously on guard. Just as obviously, he was an experienced campaigner prepared for any contingency for, as Petersen watched, he produced a hip flask from his pocket and was still savouring the contents, his eyes closed in bliss, when Petersen clapped him heartily on the shoulder.

'You keep a good watch, my friend.'

The concierge coughed, choked, spluttered and tried to speak but his larynx wasn't having any of it. Petersen looked past him and through the doorway.

'And good evening to you, Colonel Lunz. Everything is in order, I trust?'

'Ah, good evening.' Lunz was almost a look-alike for Petersen himself, medium height, broad shoulders, aquiline features, grey eyes and thin black hair: an older version, admittedly, but nevertheless the resemblance was startling. He didn't seem in any way put out. 'I've just this moment arrived and — '

'Ah, ah, Colonel.' Petersen wagged a finger. 'Officers, whatever their nationality, are officers and gentlemen the world over. Gentlemen don't tell lies. You've been here for exactly eleven minutes. I've timed you.' He turned to the still red-faced and gasping concierge who was making valiant efforts to communicate with them and clapped him encouragingly on the back. 'You were trying to say something?'

'You were out.' The convulsions were easing. 'I mean, you were in, but I saw you go out. Eleven minutes, you said? I didn't see — I mean, your key — '

'You were drunk at the time,' Petersen said kindly. He bent, sniffed and wrinkled his nose. 'You still are. Be off. Send us a bottle of brandy. Not that tearful rot-gut you drink: the French cognac you keep for the Gestapo. And two glasses — *clean* glasses.' He turned to

Lunz. 'You will, of course, join me, my dear Colonel?'

'Naturally.' The Colonel was a hard man to knock off balance. He watched Petersen calmly as he took off his coat and threw it on the bed, lifted an eyebrow and said: 'A sudden chill snap outside, yes?'

'Rome? January? No time to take chances with one's health. It's no joke hanging about those fire escapes, I can tell you.'

'So that's where you were. I should have exercised more care, perhaps.'

'No perhaps about your choice of lookout.'

'True.' The Colonel brought out a briar pipe and began to fill it. 'I hadn't much choice.'

'You sadden me, Colonel, you really do. You, obtain my key, which is illegal. You post a guard so that you won't be discovered breaking the law yet again. You ransack my belongings — '

'Ransack?'

'Carefully examine. I don't know what kind of incriminating evidence you were expecting to find.'

'None, really. You don't strike me as the kind of man who would leave — '

'And you had me watched earlier tonight. You must have done, otherwise you wouldn't have known that I had been out earlier

7

without a coat. Saddens? It shocks. Where is this mutual trust that should exist between allies?'

'Allies?' He struck a match. 'I hadn't thought about it very much in that way.' Judging by his expression, he still wasn't thinking very much about it in that way.

'And more evidence of mutual trust.' Petersen handed over the wallet he had taken from the young lieutenant, together with a revolver. 'I'm sure you know him. He was waving his gun around in a very dangerous fashion.'

'Ah!' Lunz looked up from the papers. 'The impetuous young Lieutenant Wintermann. You were right to take this gun from him, he might have done himself an injury. From what I know of you I assume he's not resting at the bottom of the Tiber?'

'I don't treat allies that way. He's locked up in a jeweller's shop.'

'Of course.' Lunz spoke as if he had expected nothing else. 'Locked up. But surely he can — '

'Not the way I tied him up. You not only sadden me, Colonel, you insult me. Why didn't you give him a red flag to wave or a drum to beat? Something that would really attract my attention.'

Lunz sighed. 'Young Hans is well enough

in a tank but subtlety is not really his métier. I did not, by the way, insult you. Following you was entirely his own idea. I knew what he was up to, of course, but I didn't try to stop him. For hardly won experience a sore head is little enough to pay.'

'He hasn't even got that. An ally, you see.'

'Pity. It might have reinforced the lesson.' He broke off as a knock came to the door and the concierge entered bearing brandy and glasses. Petersen poured and lifted his glass.

'To Operation Weiss.'

'*Prosit.*' Lunz sipped appreciatively. 'Not all Gestapo officers are barbarians, Operation Weiss? So you know? You're not supposed to.' Lunz didn't seem at all put out.

'I know lots of things that I'm not supposed to.'

'You surprise me.' Lunz's tone was dry. He sipped some more brandy. 'Excellent, excellent. Yes, you do have a penchant for picking up unconsidered — and classified — trifles. Which leads to your repeated use of the world 'ally'. Which leads, in turn, to what you possibly regard as our undue interest in you.'

'You don't trust me?'

'You'll have to improve on that injured tone of yours. Certainly we trust you. Your record — and it is a formidable one — speaks for itself. What we — and especially myself — find difficult to understand is why such a man with such a record aligns himself with — well, I'm afraid I have to say it — with a quisling. I do not hurt your feelings?'

'You'd have to find them first. I would remind you that it was your Führer who forced our departed Prince Regent to sign this treaty with you and the Japanese two years ago. I assume he's the quisling you're talking about. Weak; certainly, vacillating, perhaps cowardly and no man of action. You can't blame a man for those things: nature's done its worst and there's nothing we can do about nature. But no quisling — he did what he thought was best for Yugoslavia. He wanted to spare it the horrors of war. *'Bolje grob nego rob'*. You know what that means?'

Lunz shook his head. 'The intricacies of your language — '

''Better death than slavery'. That's what the Yugoslav crowds shouted when they learned that Prince Paul had acceded to the Tripartite Pact. That's what they shouted when he was deposed and the pact denounced. What the people didn't understand was that there was no 'nego', no 'than'. It was to be death *and* slavery as they found out when the Führer, in one of his splendid rages, obliterated Belgrade and crushed the army. I was one of those who were crushed. Well, nearly.'

'If I might have some more of that excellent cognac.' Lunz helped himself. 'You don't seem greatly moved by your recollections.'

'Who can live with all his yesterdays?'

'Nor by the fact that you find yourself in the unfortunate position of having to fight your own countrymen.'

'Instead of joining them and fighting you? War makes for strange bed-fellows, Colonel. Take yourselves and the Japanese, for instance. Hardly entitles you to a holier-than-thou attitude.'

'A point. But at least we're not fighting our own people.'

'Not yet. I wouldn't bank on it. God knows, you've done it enough in the past. In any event, moralizing is pointless. I'm a loyalist, a Royalist, and when — and if ever — this damned war is over I want to see the monarchy restored. A man's got to live for something and if that's what I choose to live for, then that's my business and no-one else's.'

'All to hell our own way,' Lunz said agreeably. 'It's just that I have some difficulty in visualizing you as a Serbian Royalist.'

'What does a Serbian Royalist look like? Come to that, what does a Serbian look like?'

Lunz thought then said: 'A confession, Petersen. I haven't the slightest idea.'

'It's my name,' Petersen said kindly. 'And my background. There are Petersens all over. There's a village up in the Italian Alps where every second surname starts with 'Mac'. The remnants, so I'm told, of some Scottish regiment that got cut off in one of those interminable medieval wars. My great-great-great grandfather or whatever, was a soldier of fortune, which sounds a lot more romantic than the term 'mercenary' they use today. Like a thousand others he arrived here and forgot to go home again.'

'Where was home? I mean, Scandinavian, Anglo-Saxon, what?'

'Genealogy bores me and, not only don't I care, I don't know either. Ask any Yugoslav what his ancestors five times removed were and he almost certainly wouldn't know.'

Lunz nodded. 'You Slavic people *do* have rather a chequered history. And then, of course, just to complicate matters, you graduated from Sandhurst.'

'Dozens of foreign countries have had their officers graduate from there. In my case, what more natural? My father was, after all, the military attaché in London. If he'd been the naval attaché in Berlin I'd probably have ended up in Kiel or Mürwik.'

'Nothing wrong with Sandhurst. I've been there, as a visitor only. But a bit on the conservative side as far as the courses offered are concerned.'

'You mean?'

'Nothing on guerrilla warfare. Nothing on espionage and counter-espionage. Nothing on code and cypher breaking. I understand you're a specialist on all three.'

'I'm self-educated in some things.'

'I'm sure you are.' Lunz was silent for some seconds, savouring his brandy, then said: 'Whatever became of your father?'

'I don't know. You may even know more than I do. Just disappeared. Thousands have done so since the spring of '41. Disappeared, I mean.'

'He was like you? A Royalist? A Četnik?' Petersen nodded. 'And very senior. Senior officers don't just disappear. He fell foul of the Partisans, perhaps?'

'Perhaps. Anything is possible. Again, I don't know.' Petersen smiled. 'If you're trying to suggest I'm carrying on a vendetta because of a blood feud, you'd better try again. Wrong country, wrong century. Anyway, you didn't come here to pry into my motives or my past.'

'And now *you* insult *me*. I wouldn't waste my time. You'd tell me just as much as you wanted me to know and no more.'

'And you didn't come here to carry out a search of my belongings — that was just a combination of opportunity and professional curiosity. You came here to give me something. An envelope with instructions for our commander. Another assault on what it pleases you to call Titoland.'

'You're pretty sure of yourself.'

'I'm not pretty sure. I'm certain. The Partisans have radio transceivers. British. They have skilled radio operators, both their own and British. And they have skilled code-crackers. You don't dare send secret and important messages any more by radio. So you need a reliable message boy. There's no other reason why I'm in Rome.'

'Frankly, I can't think of any other, which saves any explanation on my part.' Lunz produced and handed over an envelope.

'This is in code?'

'Naturally.'

'Why 'naturally'? In *our* code?'

'So I believe.'

'Stupid. Who do you think devised that code?'

'I don't think. I know. You did.'

'It's still stupid. Why don't you give me the message verbally? I've a good memory for this sort of thing. And there's more. I may be intercepted, and then two things may happen.

14

Either I succeed in destroying it, in which case the message is useless. Or the Partisans take it intact and decipher it in nothing flat.' Petersen tapped his head. 'A clear case for a psychiatrist.'

Lunz took some more brandy and cleared his throat. 'You know, of course, of Colonel General Alexander von Löhr?'

'The German Commander in Chief for southeastern Europe. Of course. Never met him personally.'

'Perhaps it is as well that you never do. I don't think General von Löhr would react too favourably to the suggestion that he is in need of psychiatric treatment. Nor does he take too kindly to subordinate officers — and, despite your nationality, you can take it that he very definitely regards you as subordinate — who question far less disobey his orders. And those are his orders.'

'Two psychiatrists. One for von Löhr, one for the person who appointed him to his command. That would be the Führer, of course.'

Colonel Lunz said mildly: 'I do try to observe the essential civilities. It's not normally too difficult. But bear in mind that I am a German Regimental Commander.'

'I don't forget it and no offence was intended. Protests are useless. I have my

15

orders. I assume that this time I will not be going in by plane?'

'You are remarkably well informed.'

'Not really. Some of your colleagues are remarkably garrulous in places where not only have they no right to be garrulous but have no right to be in the first place. In this case I am not well informed, but I can think, unlike — well, never mind. You'd have to notify my friends if you were sending in a plane and that message could be just as easily intercepted and deciphered as any other. You don't know how crazy those Partisans could be. They wouldn't hesitate to send a suicide commando behind our lines and shoot down the plane when it's still at an altitude of fifty or a hundred metres, which is an excellent way of ensuring that no-one gets out of that plane alive.' Petersen tapped the envelope. 'That way the message never gets delivered. So I go by boat. When?'

'Tomorrow night.'

'Where?'

'A little fishing village near Termoli.'

'What kind of boat?'

'You do ask a lot of questions.'

'It's my neck.' Petersen shrugged his indifference. 'If your travel arrangements don't suit me, I'll make my own.'

'It wouldn't be the first time you'd

16

borrowed shall we say, a boat from your — ah — allies?'

'Only in the best interests of all.'

'Of course. An Italian torpedo boat.'

'You can hear one of those things twenty kilometres away.'

'So? You'll be landing near Ploče. That's in Italian hands, as you know. And even if you could be heard fifty kilometres away, what's the difference? The Partisans have no radar, no planes, no navy, nothing that could stop you.'

'So the Adriatic is your pond. The torpedo boat it is.'

'Thank you. I forgot to mention that you'll be having some company on the trip across.'

'You didn't forget. You just saved it for last.' Petersen refilled their glasses and looked consideringly at Lunz. 'I'm not sure that I care for this. You know I like to travel alone.'

'I know you *never* travel alone.'

'Ah! George and Alex. You know them, then?'

'They're hardly invisible. They attract attention — they have that look about them.'

'What look?'

'Hired killers.'

'You're half right. They're different. My insurance policy — they watch my back. I'm not complaining, but people are always spying on me.'

'An occupational hazard.' Lunz's airily dismissive gesture showed what he thought of occupational hazards. 'I would be grateful if you would allow those two people I have in mind to accompany you. More, I would regard it as a personal favour if you would escort them to their destination.'

'What destination?'

'Same as yours.'

'Who are they?'

'Two radio operator recruits for your Četniks. Carrying with them, I may say, the very latest in transceiver equipment.'

'That's not enough, and you know it. Names, background.'

'Sarina and Michael. Trained — highly trained, I might say — by the British in Alexandria. With the sole intent of doing what they are about to do — joining your friends. Let us say that we intercepted them en route.'

'What else? Male and female, no?'

'Yes.'

'No.'

'No what?'

'I'm a fairly busy person. I don't like being encumbered and I've no intention of acting as a shipborne chaperon.'

'Brother and sister.'

'Ah.' Petersen said. 'Fellow citizens?'

18

'Of course.'

'Then why can't they find their own way home?'

'Because they haven't been home for three years. Educated in Cairo.' Again the wave of a hand. 'Troubled times in your country, my friend. Germans here, Italians there, Ustaša, Četniks, Partisans everywhere. All very confusing. You know your way around your country in these difficult times. Better than any, I'm told.'

'I don't get lost much.' Petersen stood. 'I'd have to see them first, of course.'

'I would have expected nothing else.' Lunz drained his glass, rose and glanced at his watch. 'I'll be back in forty minutes.'

★　★　★

George answered Petersen's knock. Despite Lunz's unflattering description George didn't look a bit like a killer, hired or otherwise: genial buffoons, or those who look like them, never do. With a pudgy, jovial face crowned by a tangled thatch of grey-black hair, George, on the wrong side of fifty, was immense — immensely fat, that was: the studded belt strung tightly around what used to be his waist served only to emphasize rather than conceal his gargantuan paunch.

He closed the door behind Petersen and crossed to the left-hand wall: like many very heavy men, as is so often seen in the case of overweight dancers, he was quick and light on his feet. He removed from the plaster a rubber suction cap with a central spike which was attached by a wire to a transformer and thence to a single earphone.

'Your friend seems to be a very pleasant man.' George sounded genuinely regretful. 'Pity we have to be on opposite sides.' He looked at the envelope Petersen had brought. 'Aha! Operational orders, no?'

'Yes. Hotfoot, you might say, from the presence of Colonel General von Löhr himself.' Petersen turned to the recumbent figure on one of the two narrow beds. 'Alex?'

Alex rose. Unlike George, he had no welcoming smile but that meant nothing, for Alex never smiled. He was of a height with George but there any resemblance ended. His weight was about half George's as were his years: he was thin-faced, swarthy and had black watchful eyes which rarely blinked. Wordlessly, for his taciturnity was almost on a par with the stillness of his face, he took the envelope, dug into a knapsack, brought out a small butane burner and an almost equally small kettle, and began to make steam. Two or three minutes later Petersen extracted two sheets of paper from the opened envelope and studied the contents carefully. When he had finished he looked up and regarded the two men thoughtfully.

'This *will* be of great interest to a great number of people. It may be the depths of winter but things look like becoming very hot in the Bosnian hills in the very near future.'

George said: 'Code?'

'Yes. Simple. I made sure of that when I made it up. If the Germans never meant business before, they certainly mean it now. Seven divisions, no less. Four German, under General Lütters, whom we know, and three Italian under General Gloria, whom we also know. Supported by the Ustaša and, of course, the Četniks. Somewhere between ninety thousand and a hundred thousand troops.'

George shook his head. 'So many?'

'According to this. It's common knowledge of course that the Partisans are stationed in and around Bihać. The Germans are to attack from the north and east, the Italians from south and west. The battle plan, God knows, is simple enough. The Partisans are to be totally encircled and then wiped out to a man. Simple, but comprehensive. And just to make certain, both the Italians and Germans are bringing in squadrons of bomber and fighter planes.'

21

'And the Partisans haven't got a single plane.'

'Even worse for them they don't have anti-aircraft guns. Well, a handful, but they should be in a museum.' Petersen replaced the sheets and re-sealed the envelope. 'I have to go out in fifteen minutes. Colonel Lunz is coming to take me to meet a couple of people I don't particularly want to meet, two radio operator Četnik recruits who have to have their hands held until we get to Montenegro or wherever.'

'Or so Colonel Lunz says.' Suspicion was one of the few expressions that Alex ever permitted himself.

'Or so he says. Which is why I want you two to go out as well. Not with me, of course — behind me.'

'A little night air will do us good. These hotel rooms get very stuffy.' George was hardly exaggerating, his penchant for beer was equalled only by his marked weakness for evil-smelling, black cigars. 'Car or foot?'

'I don't know yet. You have your car.'

'Either way, tailing in a blackout is difficult. Chances are, we'd be spotted.'

'So? You've been spotted a long time ago. Even if Lunz or one of his men does pick you up it's most unlikely that he'll have you followed. What he can do, you can do.'

'Pick up *our* tail, you mean. What do you want us to do?'

'You'll see where I'm taken. When I leave find out what you can about those two radio operators.'

'A few details might help. It would be nice to know who we're looking for.'

'Probably mid-twenties, brother and sister, Sarina and Michael. That's all I know. No breaking down of doors, George. Discretion, that's what's called for. Tact. Diplomacy.'

'Our specialities. We use our Carabinieri cards?'

'Naturally.'

⋆   ⋆   ⋆

When Colonel Lunz had said that the two young radio operator recruits were brother and sister, that much, Petersen reflected, had been true. Despite fairly marked differences in bulk and colouring, they were unmistakably twins. He was very tanned, no doubt from all his years in Cairo, with black hair and hazel eyes: she had the flawless peach-coloured complexion of one who had no difficulties in ignoring the Egyptian sunshine, close-cropped auburn hair and the same hazel eyes as her brother. He was stocky and broad: she was neither, but just how

23

slender or well proportioned she might have been it was impossible to guess as, like her brother, she was clad in shapeless khaki-coloured fatigues. Side by side on a couch, where they had seated themselves after the introductions, they were trying to look relaxed and casual, but their overly expressionless faces served only to accentuate their wary apprehensiveness.

Petersen leaned back in his arm-chair and looked appreciatively around the large living-room. 'My word. This is nice. Comfort? No. Luxury. You two young people do yourselves well, don't you?'

'Colonel Lunz arranged it for us,' Michael said.

'Inevitably. Favouritism. My spartan quarters — '

'Are of your own choosing,' Lunz said mildly. 'It is difficult to arrange accommodation for a person who is in town for three days before he lets anyone know that he's here.'

'You have a point. Not, mind you, that this place is perfect in all respects. Take, for instance, the matter of cocktail cabinets.'

'Neither my brother nor I drink.' Sarina's voice was low-pitched and quiet. Petersen noticed that the slender interlaced hands were ivory-knuckled.

'Admirable.' Petersen picked up a briefcase he had brought with him, extracted a brandy bottle and two glasses and poured for Lunz and himself. 'Your health. I hear you wish to join the good Colonel in Montenegro. You must, then, be Royalists. You can prove that?'

Michael said: 'Do we have to prove it? I mean, don't you trust us, believe us?'

'You'll have to learn and learn quickly — and by that I mean now — to adopt a different tone and attitude.' Petersen was no longer genial and smiling. 'Apart from a handful of people — and I mean a handful — I haven't trusted in or believed anyone for many years. Can you prove you're a Royalist?'

'We can when we get there.' Sarina looked at Petersen's unchanged expression and gave a helpless little shrug. 'And I know King Peter. At least, I did.'

'As King Peter is in London and London at the moment isn't taking any calls from the Wehrmacht, that would be rather difficult to prove from here. And don't tell me you can prove it when we get to Montenegro for that would be too late.'

Michael and Sarina looked at each other, momentarily at a loss for words, then Sarina said hesitatingly: 'We don't understand. When you say it would be too late — '

'Too late for me if my back is full of holes.

Bullet wounds, stab wounds, that sort of thing.'

She stared at him, colour staining her cheeks, then said in a whisper: 'You must be mad. Why on earth should we — '

'I don't know and I'm not mad. It's just by liking to live a little longer that I manage to live a little longer.' Petersen looked at them for several silent moments, then sighed. 'So you want to come to Yugoslavia with me?'

'Not really.' Her hands were still clenched and now the brown eyes were hostile. 'Not after what you've just said.' She looked at her brother, then at Lunz, then back at Petersen. 'Do we have any options?'

'Certainly. Any amount. Ask Colonel Lunz.'

'Colonel?'

'Not any amount. Very few and I wouldn't recommend any of them. The whole point of the exercise is that you both get there intact and if you go by any other means the chances of your doing just that are remote: if you try it on your own the chances don't exist. With Major Petersen you have safe conduct and guaranteed delivery — alive, that is.'

Michael said, doubt in his voice: 'You have a great deal of confidence in Major Petersen.'

'I do. So does Major Petersen. He has every right to, I may add. It's not just that he knows the country in a way neither of you ever will. He moves as he pleases through any territory whether it's held by friend or enemy. But what's really important is that the fields of operations out there are in a state of constant flux. An area held by the Četniks today can be held by the Partisans tomorrow. You'd be like lambs in the fold when the wolves come down from the hills.'

For the first time the girl smiled slightly. 'And the Major is another wolf?'

'More like a sabre-toothed tiger. And he's got two others who keep him constant company. Not, mind you, that I've ever heard of sabre-toothed tigers meeting up with wolves but you take my point, I hope.'

They didn't say whether they took his point or not. Petersen looked at them both in turn and said: 'Those fatigues you're wearing — they're British?'

They both nodded.

'You have spares?'

Again they nodded in unison.

'Winter clothing? Heavy boots?'

'Well, no.' Michael looked his embarrassment. 'We didn't think we would need them.'

'You didn't think you would need them.' Petersen briefly contemplated the ceiling then returned his gaze to the uncomfortable pair on the couch. 'You're going up the mountains, maybe two thousand metres, in the depths of winter, not to a garden party in high summer.'

Lunz said hastily: 'I shouldn't have much trouble in arranging for these things by morning.'

'Thank you, Colonel.' Petersen pointed to two fairly large, canvas-wrapped packages on the floor. 'Your radios, I take it. British?'

'Yes,' Michael said. 'Latest models. Very tough.'

'Spares?'

'Lots. All we'll ever need, the experts say.'

'The experts have clearly never fallen down a ravine with a radio strapped to their backs. You're British-trained, of course.'

'No. American.'

'In Cairo?'

'Cairo is full of them. This was a staff sergeant in the US Marines. An expert in some new codes. He taught quite a few Britishers at the same time.'

'Seems fair enough. Well, a little coopera-tion and we should get along just fine.'

'Cooperation?' Michael seemed puzzled.

'Yes. If I have to give some instructions now and again I expect them to be followed.'

'Instructions?' Michael looked at his sister. 'Nobody said anything — '

'I'm saying something now. I must express

myself more clearly. Orders will be implicitly obeyed. If not, I'll leave you behind in Italy, jettison you in the Adriatic or just simply abandon you in Yugoslavia. I will not jeopardize my mission for a couple of disobedient children who won't do as they're told.'

'Children!' Michael actually clenched his fists. 'You have no right to — '

'He has every right to.' Lunz's interruption was sharp. 'Major Petersen was talking about garden parties. He should have been talking about kindergartens. You're young, ignorant and arrogant and are correspondingly dangerous on all three counts. Whether you've been sworn in or not, you're now members of the Royal Yugoslav Army. Other rankers, such as you, take orders from officers.'

They made no reply, not even when Petersen again regarded the ceiling and said: 'And we all know the penalty for the wartime disobedience of orders.'

★ ★ ★

In Lunz's staff car Petersen sighed and said: 'I'm afraid I didn't quite achieve the degree of rapport back there that I might have. They were in a rather unhappy frame of mind when we left.'

'They'll get over it. Young, as I said. Spoilt, into the bargain. Aristocrats, I'm told, even some royal blood. Von Karajan or something like that. Odd name for a Yugoslav.'

'Not really. Almost certainly from Slovenia and the descendants of Austrians.'

'Be that as it may, they come from a family that's clearly not accustomed to taking orders and even less accustomed to being talked to the way you did.'

'I daresay they'll learn very quickly.'

'I daresay they will.'

★   ★   ★

Half an hour after returning to his room, Petersen was joined by George and Alex. George said, 'Well, at least we know their name.'

'So do I. Von Karajan. What else?'

George was in no way put out. 'The reception clerk, very old but sharp, told us he'd no idea where they'd arrived from — they'd been brought there by Colonel Lunz. He gave us their room number — no hesitation — but said that if we wanted to see them he'd have to announce us, ask permission and then escort us. Then we asked him if either of the rooms next to the number he had given us was vacant and when he told

30

us those were their bedrooms we left.'

'You took your time about getting back.'

'We are accustomed to your injustices. We went round to the back of the hotel, climbed a fire escape and made our way along a narrow ledge. A very narrow ledge. No joke, I can tell you, especially for an old man like me. Perilous, dizzying heights — '

'Yes, yes.' Petersen was patient. The von Karajans had been staying on the first floor. 'Then?'

'There was a small balcony outside their room. Net curtains on their French windows.'

'You could see clearly?'

'And hear clearly. Young man was sending a radio message.'

'Interesting. Hardly surprising, though. Morse?'

'Plain language.'

'What was he saying?'

'I have no idea. Could have been Chinese for all I knew. Certainly no European language I've ever heard. A very short message. So we came back.'

'Anyone see you on the fire escape, ledge or balcony?'

George tried to look wounded. 'My dear Peter — '

Petersen stopped him with an upraised

hand. Not many people called him 'Peter' — which was his first name — but, then, not many people had been pre-war students of George's in Belgrade University where George had been the vastly respected Professor of Occidental Languages. George was known — not reputed, but known — to be fluent in at least a dozen languages and to have a working knowledge of a considerable number more.

'Forgive me, forgive me.' Petersen surveyed George's vast bulk. 'You're practically invisible anyway. So tomorrow morning, or perhaps even within minutes, Colonel Lunz will know that you and Alex have been around asking questions — he would have expected nothing less of me — but he won't know that young Michael von Karajan has been seen and heard to be sending radio messages soon after our departure. I do wonder about the nature of that message.'

George pondered briefly then said: 'Alex and I could find out on the boat tomorrow night.'

Petersen shook his head. 'I promised Colonel Lunz that we would deliver them intact.'

'What's Colonel Lunz to us or your promise to him?'

'We want them delivered intact too.'

George tapped his head. 'The burden of too many years.'

'Not at all, George. Professorial absent-mindedness.'

2

The Wehrmacht did not believe in limousines or luxury coaches for the transportation of its allies: Petersen and his companions crossed Italy that following day in the back of a vintage truck that gave the impression of being well enough equipped with tyres of solid rubber but sadly deficient in any form of springing. The vibration was of the teeth-jarring order and the rattling so loud and continuous as to make conversation virtually impossible. The hooped canvas covering was open at the back, and at the highest point in the Apennines the temperature dropped below freezing point. It was, in some ways, a memorable journey but not for its creature comforts.

The stench of the diesel fumes would normally have been overpowering enough but on that particular day faded into relative insignificance compared to the aroma, if that was the word, given off by George's black cigars. Out of deference to his fellow-travellers' sensibilities he had seated himself at the very rear of the truck and on the rare occasion when he wasn't smoking, kept himself busy and contented enough with the contents of a crate of beer that lay at his feet. He seemed immune to the cold and probably was: nature had provided him with an awesome insulation.

The von Karajans, clad in their newly acquired winter clothing, sat at the front of the left-hand unpadded wooden bench. Withdrawn and silent they appeared no happier than when Petersen had left them the previous night: this could have been an understandable reaction to their current sufferings but more probably, Petersen thought, their injured feelings had not yet had time to mend. Matters were not helped by the presence of Alex, whose totally withdrawn silence and dark, bitter and brooding countenance could be all too easily misinterpreted as balefulness: the von Karajans were not to know that Alex regarded his parents, whom he held in vast respect and affection, with exactly the same expression.

They stopped for a midday meal in a tiny village in the neighbourhood of Corfinio after having safely, if at times more or less miraculously, negotiated the hazardous hairpin switch-backs of the Apennine spine. They had left Rome at seven o'clock that morning and it had taken over five hours to cover a hundred miles. Considering the incredibly dilapidated state of both the highway and the ancient Wehrmacht truck — unmarked as such and of Italian make — an average of almost twenty miles an hour was positively creditable. Not without difficulty for, with the exception of George, the passengers' limbs were stiff and almost frozen, they climbed down over the tailboard and looked around them through the thinly falling snow.

There was miserably little to see. The hamlet — if it could even be called that, it didn't as much as have a name — consisted of a handful of stone cottages, a post office store and a very small inn. Nearby Corfinio, if hardly ranking as a metropolis, could have afforded considerably more in the way of comfort and amenities: but Colonel Lunz, apart from a professional near-mania for secrecy, shared with his senior Wehrmacht fellow-officers the common if unfair belief that all his Italian allies were renegades, traitors and spies until proved otherwise.

In the inn itself, the genial host was far from being that. He seemed diffident, almost nervous, a markedly unusual trait in mountain innkeepers. A noticeably clumsy waiter, civil and helpful in his own way, volunteered only the fact that he was called Luigi but thereafter was totally uncommunicative. The inn itself was well enough, both warmed and illuminated by a pine log fire in an open hearth that gave off almost as much in the way of sparks as it did heat. The food was simple but plentiful, and wine and beer, into which George made his customary inroads, appeared regularly on the table without having to be asked for. Socially, however, the meal was a disaster.

Silence makes an uncomfortable table companion. At a distant and small corner table, the truck-driver and his companion — really an armed guard who travelled with a Schmeisser under his seat and a Luger concealed about his person — talked almost continuously in low voices; but of the five at Petersen's table, three seemed afflicted with an almost permanent palsy of the tongue. Alex, remote and withdrawn, seemed, as was his wont, to be contemplating a bleak and hopeless future: the von Karajans who, by their own admission, had had no breakfast, barely picked at their food, had time and opportunity to talk, but rarely ventured a word except when directly addressed: Petersen, relaxed as ever, restricted himself to pleasantries and civilities but otherwise showed no signs of wishing to alleviate the conversational awkwardness or, indeed, to be aware of it: George, on the other hand, seemed to be acutely aware of it and did his talkative best to dispel it, even to the point of garrulity.

His conversational gambit took the form of questions directed exclusively at the von Karajans. It did not take him long to elicit the fact that they were, as Petersen had guessed, Slovenians of Austrian ancestry. They had been to primary school in Ljubljana, secondary school in Zagreb and thence to Cairo University.

'Cairo!' George tried to make his eyebrows disappear into his hairline. 'Cairo! What on earth induced you to go to that cultural backwater?'

'It was our parents' wish,' Michael said. He tried to be cold and distant but he only succeeded in sounding defensive.

'Cairo!' George repeated. He shook his head in slow disbelief. 'And what, may one ask, did you study there?'

'You ask a lot of questions,' Michael said.

'Interest,' George explained. 'A paternal interest. And, of course, a concern for the hapless youth of our unfortunate and disunited country.'

For the first time Sarina smiled, a very faint smile, it was true, but enough to give some indication of what she could do if she tried. 'I don't think such things would really interest you, Mr — ah — '

'Just call me George. How do you know

what would interest me? All things interest me.'

'Economics and politics.'

'Good God!' George clapped a hand to his forehead. As a classical actor he would have starved: as a ham actor he was a nonpareil. 'Good heavens, girl, you go to Egypt to learn matters of such importance? Didn't they even teach you enough to make you realize that theirs is the poorest country in the Middle East, that their economy is not only a shambles but is in a state of total collapse and that they owe countless millions, sterling, dollars, any currency you care to name, to practically any country you care to name. So much for their economy. As for politics, they're no more than a political football for any country that wants to play soccer on their arid and useless desert sands.'

George stopped briefly, perhaps to admire the eloquence of his own oratory, perhaps to await a response. None was forthcoming so he got back to his head-shaking.

'And what, one wonders, did your parents have against our premier institute of learning. I refer, of course, to the University of Belgrade.' He paused, as if in reflection. 'One admits that Oxford and Cambridge have their points. So, for that matter, does Heidelberg, the Sorbonne, Padua and one or two lesser educational centres. But, no, Belgrade is best.'

Again the faint smile from Sarina. 'You seem to know a great deal about universities, Mr — ah — George.'

George didn't smirk. Instead, he achieved the near impossible — he spoke with a lofty diffidence. 'I have been fortunate enough, for most of my adult life, to be associated with academics, among them some of the most eminent.' The von Karajans looked at each other for a long moment but said nothing: it was unnecessary for them to say that, in their opinion, any such association must have been on a strictly janitorial level. They probably assumed that he had learned his mode of speech when cleaning out common rooms or, it may have been, while waiting on high table. George gave no indication that he had noticed anything untoward, but, then, he never did.

'Well,' George said in his best judicial tones, 'far be it from me to visit the sins of the fathers upon their sons or, come to that, those of mothers upon their daughters.' Abruptly, he switched the subject. 'You are Royalists, of course.'

'Why 'of course'?' Michael's voice was sharp.

George sighed. 'I would have hoped that

that institute of lower learning on the Nile hadn't driven all the native sense out of your head. If you weren't a Royalist you wouldn't be coming with us. Besides, Major Petersen told me.'

Sarina looked briefly at Petersen. 'This is the way you treat confidences?'

'I wasn't aware it was a confidence.' Petersen gestured with an indifferent hand. 'It was too unimportant to rate as a confidence. In any event, George is my confidant.'

Sarina looked at him uncertainly, then lowered her eyes: the rebuke could have been real, implied or just imagined. George said: 'I'm just puzzled, you see. You're Royalists. Your parents, one must assume, are the same. It's not unusual for the royal family and those close to them to send their children abroad to be educated. But not to Cairo. To Northern Europe. Specifically, to England. The ties between the Yugoslav and British royal families are very close — especially the blood ties. What place did King Peter choose for his enforced exile? London, where he is now. The Prince Regent, Prince Paul, is in the care of the British.'

'They say in Cairo that he's a prisoner of the British.' Michael didn't seem particularly concerned about what they said in Cairo.

'Rubbish. He's in protective custody in

Kenya. He's free to come and go. He makes regular withdrawals from a bank in London. Coutts, it's called — it also happens to be the bank of the British royal family. Prince Paul's closest friend in Europe — and his brother-in-law — is the Duke of Kent: well, he was until the Duke was killed in a flying-boat accident last year. And it's common knowledge that very soon he's going to South Africa, whose General Smuts is a particularly close friend of the British.'

'Ah, yes,' Michael said. 'You said you're puzzled. I'm puzzled too. This General Smuts has two South African divisions in North Africa fighting alongside the Eighth Army, no?'

'Yes.'

'Against the Germans?'

George showed an unusual trace of irritation. 'Who else would they be fighting?'

'So our royal family's friends in North Africa are fighting the Germans. We're Royalists, and we're fighting with the Germans, not against them. I mean it's all rather confusing.'

'I'm sure *you're* not confused.' Again Sarina's little smile. Petersen was beginning to wonder whether he would have to revise his first impression of her. 'Are you, George?'

'No confusion.' George waved a dismissive

hand. 'Simply a temporary measure of convenience and expediency. We are fighting *with* the Germans, true, but we are not fighting *for* them. We are fighting for ourselves. When the Germans have served their purpose it will be time for them to be gone.' George refilled his beer mug, drained half the contents and sighed either in satisfaction or sorrow. 'We are consistently underestimated, a major part, as the rest of Europe sees it, of the insoluble Balkan problem. To me, there is no problem just a goal.' He raised his glass again. 'Yugoslavia.'

'Nobody's going to argue with that,' Petersen said. He looked at the girl. 'Speaking — as George has been doing at some length — of royalty, you mentioned last night you knew King Peter. How well?'

'He was Prince Peter then. Not well at all. Once or twice on formal occasions.'

'That's about how it was for me. I don't suppose we've exchanged more than a couple of dozen words. Bright lad, pleasant, should make a good king. Pity about his limp.'

'His what?'

'You know, his left foot.'

'Oh, that. Yes. I've wondered — '

'He doesn't talk about it. All sorts of sinister stories about how he was injured. All ridiculous. A simple hunting accident.'

Petersen smiled. 'I shouldn't imagine there's much of a diplomatic future for a courtier who mistakes his future sovereign for a wild boar.' He lifted his eyes and right arm at the same time: the innkeeper came hurrying towards him. 'The bill, if you please.'

'The bill?' Momentarily the innkeeper gave the impression of being surprised, even taken aback. 'Ah, the bill. Of course. The bill. At once.' He hurried off.

Petersen looked at the von Karajans. 'Sorry you didn't have a better appetite — you know, stoked the furnaces for the last part of the trip. Still, it's downhill now all the way and we're heading for the Adriatic and a maritime climate. Should be getting steadily warmer.'

'Oh, no, it won't.' It was the first time Alex had spoken since they had entered the inn and, predictably, it was in tones of dark certainty. 'It's almost an hour since we came in here and the wind has got stronger. Much stronger. Listen and you can hear it.' They listened. They heard it, a deep, low-pitched, ululating moaning that boded no good at all. Alex shook his head gravely. 'An east-north-easter. All the way from Siberia. It's going to be very cold.' His voice sounded full of gloomy satisfaction but it meant nothing, it was the only way he knew how to talk. 'And when the sun goes down, it's going to be very very cold.'

'Job's comforter,' Petersen said. He looked at the bill the innkeeper had brought, handed over some notes, waved away the proffered change and said: 'Do you think we could buy some blankets from you?'

'Blankets?' The innkeeper frowned in some puzzlement: it was, after all, an unusual request.

'Blankets. We've a long way to go, there's no heating in our transport and the afternoon and evening are going to be very cold.'

'There will be no problem.' The innkeeper disappeared and was back literally within a minute with an armful of heavy coloured woollen blankets which he deposited on a nearby empty table. 'Those will be sufficient?'

'More than sufficient. Most kind of you.' Petersen produced money. 'How much, please?'

'Blankets?' The innkeeper lifted his hands in protest. 'I am not a shopkeeper. I do not charge for blankets.'

'But you must. I insist. Blankets cost money.'

'Please.' The truckdriver had left his table and approached them. 'I shall be passing back this way tomorrow. I shall bring them with me.'

Petersen thanked them and so it was arranged. Alex, followed by the von Karajans, helped the innkeeper carry the blankets out to the truck. Petersen and George lingered briefly in the porch, closing both the inner and outer doors.

'You really are the most fearful liar, George,' Petersen said admiringly. 'Cunning. Devious. I've said it before, I don't think I'd care to be interrogated by you. You ask a question and whether people say yes, no or nothing at all you still get your answer.'

'When you've spent twenty-five of the best years of your life dealing with dim-witted students — ' George shrugged as if there were no more to say.

'I'm not a dim-witted student but I still wouldn't care for it. You have formed an opinion about our young friends?'

'I have.'

'So have I. I've also formed another opinion about them and that is that while Michael is no intellectual giant, the girl could bear watching. I think she could be clever.'

'I've often observed this with brother and sister, especially when they're twins. I share your opinion. Lovely and clever.'

Petersen smiled. 'A dangerous combination?'

'Not if she's nice. I've no reason to think she's not nice.'

'You're just middle-aged and susceptible. The innkeeper?'

'Apprehensive and unhappy. He doesn't look like a man who should be apprehensive and unhappy, he looks a big tough character who would be perfectly at home throwing big tough drunks out of his inn. Also, he seemed caught off-balance when you offered to pay for the meal. One got the unmistakable impression that there are some travellers who do not pay for their meals. Also his refusal to accept money for the blankets was out of character. Out of character for an Italian, I mean, for I've never known of an Italian who wasn't ready, eager rather, to make a deal on some basis or other. Peter, my friend, wouldn't even you be slightly nervous if you worked for, or were forced to work for the German SS?'

'Colonel Lunz casts a long shadow. The waiter?'

'The Gestapo have fallen in my estimation. When they send in an espionage agent in the guise of a waiter they should at least give him some training in the rudiments of table-waiting. I felt positively embarrassed for him.' George paused, then went on: 'You were talking about King Peter a few minutes ago.'

'You introduced that subject.'

'That's irrelevant and don't hedge. As a

47

departmental head in the university I was regarded — and rightly — as being a man of culture. Prince Paul was nothing if not a man of culture although his interests lay more in the world of art than in philology. Never mind. We met quite a few times, either in the university or at royal functions in the city. More to the point, I saw Prince Peter — as he was then — two or three times. He didn't have a limp in those days.'

'He still doesn't.'

George looked at him then nodded slowly. 'And you called me devious.'

Petersen opened the outer door and clapped him on the shoulder. 'We live in devious times, George.'

★   ★   ★

The second half of the trip was an improvement on the first but just marginally. Cocooned, as they were, to the ears in heavy blankets, the von Karajans were no longer subject to involuntary bouts of shivering and teeth-chattering but otherwise looked no happier and were no more communicative than they had been in the morning, which meant that they were both totally miserable and silent. They didn't even speak when George, shouting to make himself heard above the fearful mechanical din, offered them brandy to relieve their sufferings. Sarina shuddered and Michael shook his head. They may have been wise for what George was offering them was no French cognac but his own near-lethal form of slivovitz, his native plum brandy.

Some twelve kilometres from Pescara they bore right off the Route 5 near Chieti, reaching the Adriatic coast road at Francavilla as a premature dusk was falling — premature, because of gathering banks of dark grey cloud which Alex, inevitably, said could only presage heavy snow. The coastal road, Route 16 was an improvement over the Apennines road — it could hardly have failed to be otherwise — and the relatively comfortable though still cacophonous ride to Termoli took no more than two hours. Wartime Termoli, on a winter's night, was no place to inspire a rhapsody in the heart of the poet or composer: the only feelings it could reasonably expect to give rise to were gloom and depression. It was grey, bleak, bare, grimy and seemingly uninhabitated except for a very few half-heartedly blacked-out premises which were presumably cafés or taverns. The port area itself, however, was an improvement on Rome: here was no blackout, just a dimout which probably didn't vary appreciably from the normal. As the truck stopped along a wharf-side there was more than enough light from the shaded yellow overhead lamps to distinguish the lines of the craft alongside the wharf, their transport to Yugoslavia.

That it was a motor torpedo boat was beyond question. Its vintage was uncertain. What was certain was that it had been in the wars. It had sustained considerable, though not incapacitating, damage to both hull and superstructure. No attempt had been made at repair: no-one had even thought it worthwhile to repaint the numerous dents and scars that pockmarked its side. It carried no torpedoes, for the sufficient reason that the torpedo tubes had been removed; nor had it depth-charges, for even the depth-charge racks had been removed. The only armament, if such it could be called, that it carried was a pair of insignificant little guns, single-barrelled, one mounted for'ard of the bridge, the other on the poop. They looked suspiciously like Hotchkiss repeaters, one of the most notoriously inaccurate weapons ever to find its mistaken way into naval service.

A tall man in a vaguely naval uniform was standing on the wharf-side at the head of the MTB's gangway. He wore a peaked badgeless naval cap which shaded his face but could not conceal his marked stoop and splendid snow-white Buffalo Bill beard. He raised his hand in half-greeting, half-salute as Petersen, the others following close behind, approached him.

'Good evening. My name is Pietro. You must be the Major we are expecting.'

'Good evening and yes.'

'And four companions, one a lady. Good. You are welcome aboard. I will send someone for your luggage. In the meantime, it is the commanding officer's wish that you see him as soon as you arrive.'

They followed him below and into a compartment that could have been the captain's cabin, a chart-room, an officers' mess-room and was probably all three: space is at a premium on MTBs. The captain was seated at his desk, writing, as Pietro entered without benefit of knocking. He swung round in his swivel-chair which was firmly bolted to the deck as Pietro stood to one side and said: 'Your latest guests, Carlos. The Major and the four friends we were promised.'

'Come in, come in, come in. Thank you, Pietro. Send that young ruffian along, will you?'

'When he's finished loading the luggage?'

'That'll do.' Pietro left. The captain was a broad-shouldered young man with thick curling black hair, a deep tan, very white teeth, a warm smile and warm brown eyes. He said: 'I'm Lieutenant Giancarlo Tremino. Call me Carlos. Nearly everyone else does. No discipline left in the Navy.' He shook his head and indicated his white polo neck jersey and grey flannel trousers. 'Why wear uniform? No-one pays any attention to it anyway.' He extended his hand — his left hand — to Petersen. 'Major, you are very welcome. I cannot offer you Queen Mary type accommodation — peacetime accommodation, that is — but we have a very few small cabins, washing and toilet facilities, lots of wine and can guarantee safe transit to Ploče. The guarantee is based on the fact that we have been to the Dalmatian coast many times and haven't been sunk yet. Always a first time, of course, but I prefer to dwell on happier things.'

'You are very kind,' Petersen said. 'If it's to be first name terms, then mine is Peter.' He introduced the other four, each by their first name. Carlos acknowledged each introduction with a handshake and smile but made no attempt to rise. He was quick to explain this seeming discourtesy and quite unembarrassed about doing so.

'I apologize for remaining seated. I'm not really ill-mannered or lazy or averse to physical exertion.' He moved his right arm and, for the first time, brought his glove-sheathed right hand into view. He bent and tapped his right hand against his right leg, about halfway between knee and ankle. The unmistakable sound of hollow metal meeting hollow metal made the onlookers wince. He straightened and tapped the tips of his left fingers against the back of his right glove. The sound was again unmistakable although different — flesh meeting metal. 'Those metal appliances take some getting used to.' Carlos was almost apologetic. 'Unnecessary move-ment — well, any movement — causes discomfort and who likes discomfort? I am not the noblest Roman of them all.'

Sarina gnawed her lower lip. Michael tried to look as if he weren't shocked but was. The other three, with eighteen months of vicious and bitter warfare in the Yugoslav mountains behind them, predictably showed no reaction. Petersen said: 'Right hand, right leg. That's quite a handicap.'

'Just the right foot really — blown off at the ankle. Handicap? Have you heard of the English fighter pilot who got both legs destroyed? Did he shout for a bath-chair? He shouted to get back into the cockpit of his Spitfire or whatever. He did, too. Handicap!'

'I know of him. Most people do. How did

you come by those two — um — trifling scratches?'

'Perfidious Albion,' Carlos said cheerfully. 'Nasty, horrible British. Never trust them. To think they used to be my best friends before the war — sailed with them in the Adriatic and the Channel, raced against them at Cowes — well, never mind. We were in the Aegean going, as the lawyers say, about our lawful occasions and bothering no-one. Dawn, lots of heavy mist about when suddenly, less than two kilometres away, this great big British warship appeared through a gap in the mist.'

Carlos paused, perhaps for effect, and Petersen said mildly: 'It was my understanding that the British never risked their capital ships north of Crete.'

'Size, like beauty, is in the eye of the beholder. It was, in fact, a very small frigate, but to us, you understand, it looked like a battleship. We weren't ready for them but they were ready for us — they had their guns already trained on us. No fault of ours — we had four men, not counting myself, on lookout: they must have had radar, we had none. Their first two shells struck the water only a few metres from our port side and exploded on contact: didn't do our hull much good, I can tell you. Two other light shells, about a kilo each, I should think — pom-poms, the British call them — scored direct hits. One penetrated the engine-room and put an engine out of action — I regret to say it's still out of action but we can get by without it — and the other came into the wheelhouse.'

'A kilo of explosives going off in a confined space is not very nice,' Petersen said. 'You were not alone?'

'Two others. They were not as lucky as I was. Then I had more luck — we ran into a fog bank.' Carlos shrugged. 'That's all. The past is past.'

A knock came at the door. A very young sailor entered, stood at attention, saluted and said: 'You sent for me, Captain.'

'Indeed. We have guests, Pietro. Tired, thirsty guests.'

'Right away, Captain.' The boy saluted and left.

Petersen said: 'What's all this you were saying about no discipline?'

Carlos smiled: 'Give him time. He's been with us for only a month.'

George looked puzzled. 'He is a truant from school, no?'

'He's older than he looks. Well, at least three months older.'

'Quite an age span you have aboard,'

Petersen said. 'The elder Pietro. He can't be a day under seventy.'

'He's a great number of days over seventy.' Carlos laughed. The world seemed to be a source of constant amusement to him. 'A so-called captain with only two out of four functioning limbs. A beardless youth. An old age pensioner. What a crew. Just wait till you see the rest of them.'

Petersen said: 'The past is past, you say. Accepted. One may ask a question about the present?' Carlos nodded. 'Why haven't you been retired, invalided out of the Navy or at very least given some sort of shore job? Why are you still on active service?'

'Active service?' Carlos laughed again. 'Highly inactive service. The moment we run into anything resembling action I hand in my commission. You saw the two light guns we have mounted fore and aft? It was just pride that made me keep them there. They'll never be used for either attack or defence for the perfectly adequate reason that neither works. This is a very undemanding assignment and I do have one modest qualification for it. I was born and brought up in Pescara where my father had a yacht — more than one. I spent my boyhood and the ridiculously long university vacations sailing. Around the Mediterranean and Europe for part of the time but mainly off the Yugoslav coast. The Adriatic coast of Italy is dull and uninteresting, with not an island worth mentioning between Bari and Venice: the thousand and one Dalmatian islands are a paradise for the cruising yachtsman. I know them better than I know the streets of Pescara or Termoli. The Admiralty finds this useful.'

'On a black night?' Petersen said. 'No lighthouses, no lit buoys, no land-based navigational aids?'

'If I required those I wouldn't be much use to the Admiralty, would I? Ah! Help is at hand.'

It took young Pietro an heroic effort not to stagger under the weight of his burden, a vertically-sided, flat-bottomed wicker basket holding the far from humble nucleus of a small but well-stocked bar. In addition to spirits, wines and liqueurs, Pietro had even gone to the length of providing a soda syphon and a small ice-bucket.

'Pietro hasn't yet graduated to bar-tender and I've no intention of leaving this chair,' Carlos said. 'Help yourselves, please. Thank you, Pietro. Ask our two passengers to join us at their convenience.' The boy saluted and left. 'Two other Yugoslav-bound passengers. I don't know their business as I don't know yours. You don't know theirs and they don't know yours. Ships that pass in the night. But such ships exchange recognition signals. Courtesy of the high seas.'

Petersen gestured at the basket from which George was already helping the von Karajans to orange juice. 'Another courtesy of the high seas. Lessens the rigours of total war, I must say.'

'My feeling exactly. No thanks, I may say, to our Admiralty who are as stingy as Admiralties the world over. Some of the supplies come from my father's wine cellars — they would have your three-star somme-liers in raptures, I can tell you — some are gifts from foreign friends.'

'Kruškovac.' George touched a bottle. 'Grappa. Pelinkovac. Stara Šljivovica. Two excellent vintages from the Neretva delta. Your foreign friends. All from Yugoslavia. Our hospitable and considerate young friend, Pietro. Clairvoyant? He thinks we go to Yugoslavia? Or has he been informed?'

'Suspicion, one would suppose, is part of your stock-in-trade. I don't know what Pietro thinks. I don't even know if he *can* think. He hasn't been informed. He knows.' Carlos sighed. 'The romance and glamour of the cloak-and-dagger, sealed-orders missions are not, I'm afraid, for us. Search Termoli and you might find a person who is deaf, dumb and blind, although I much doubt it. If you did, he or she would be the only person in Termoli who doesn't know that the *Colombo* — that's the name of this crippled greyhound — plies a regular and so far highly dependable ferry-service to the Yugoslav coast. If it's any consolation, I'm the only person who knows *where* we're going. Unless, of course, one of you has talked.' He poured himself a small scotch. 'Your health, gentlemen. And yours, young lady.'

'We don't talk much about such things, but about other things I'm afraid I talk too much.' George sounded sad but at once refuted himself. 'University, eh? Some kind of marine school?'

'Some kind of medical school.'

'Medical school.' With the air of a man treating himself for shock George poured some more grappa. 'Don't tell me you're a doctor.'

'I'm not telling you anything. But I have a paper that says so.'

Petersen waved a hand. 'Then why this?'

'Well you might ask.' Momentarily, Carlos sounded as sad as George had done. 'The Italian Navy. Any navy. Take a highly skilled mechanic, obvious material for an equally highly skilled engine-room-artificer. What does he become? A cook. A cordon bleu chef?

A gunner.' He waved his hand much as Petersen had done. 'So, in their all-knowing wisdom, they gave me this. Dr Tremino, ferryman, first class. Considering the state of the ferry, make that second class. Come in, come in.' A knock had come on the door.

The young woman who stepped over the low coaming — she could have been anything between twenty and thirty-five — was of medium height, slender and dressed in a jersey, jacket and skirt, all in blue. Pale-complexioned, without a trace of make-up, she was grave and unsmiling. Her hair was black as night and swooped low, like a raven's wing, over the left forehead, quite obscuring the left eyebrow. The pock-marking, for such it seemed to be, high up on the left cheekbone, served only to accentuate, not diminish, the classical, timeless beauty of the features: twenty years on, just as conceivably thirty, she would still be as beautiful as she was at that moment. Nor, it seemed certain, would time ever change the appearance of the man who followed her into the cabin, but the sculpted perfection of features had nothing to do with this. A tall, solidly built, fair-haired character, he was irredeemably ugly. Nature had had no hand in this. From the evidence offered by ears, cheeks, chin, nose and teeth he had been in frequent and violent contact with a variety of objects, both blunt and razor-edged, in the course of what must have been a remarkably chequered career, It was, withal, an attractive face, largely because of the genuine warmth of his smile: as with Carlos, an almost irrepressible cheerfulness was never far from the surface.

'This,' Carlos said, 'is Lorraine and Giacomo.' He introduced Petersen and the other four in turn. Lorraine's voice was soft and low, in tone and timbre remarkably like that of Sarina: Giacomo's, predictably, was neither soft nor low and his hand-clasp fearsome except when it came to Sarina: her fingers he took in his finger and thumb and gallantly kissed the back of her hand. Such a gesture from such a man should have appeared both affected and stagey: oddly enough, it did neither. Sarina didn't seem to think so either. She said nothing, just smiled at him, the first genuine smile Petersen had seen from her: it came as no surprise that her teeth would have been a dentist's delight or despair, depending upon whether aesthetic or financial considerations were uppermost in his mind.

'Help yourselves,' Carlos gestured to the wicker basket. Giacomo, leaving no doubt that he was decisive both as to cast of mind and action, needed no second urging. He poured a glass of Pellegrino for Lorraine, evidence enough that this was not the first time he had met her and that she shared the von Karajans' aversion towards alcohol, and then half-filled a tumbler with scotch, topping it up with water. He took a seat and beamed around the company.

'Health to all.' He raised his brimming glass. 'And confusion to our enemies.'

'Any particular enemies?' Carlos said.

'It would take too long.' Giacomo tried to look sad but failed. 'I have too many.' He drank deeply to his own toast. 'You have called us to a conference, Captain Carlos?'

'Conference, Giacomo? Goodness me, no.' It didn't require any great deductive powers, Petersen reflected, to realize that those two had met before and not just that day. 'Why should I hold a conference? My job is to get you where you're going and you can't help me in that. After you land I can't help you in whatever you're going to do. Nothing to confer about. As a ferryman, I'm a great believer in introductions. People in your line of business are apt to react over-quickly if, rightly or wrongly, they sense danger in meeting an unknown on a dark deck at night. No such danger now. And there are three things I want to mention briefly.

'First, accommodation. Lorraine and Giacomo have a cabin each, if you can call something the size of a telephone box a cabin. Only fair. First come, first served. I have two other cabins, one for three, one for two.' He looked at Michael. 'You and — yes, Sarina — are brother and sister?'

'Who told you?' Michael probably didn't mean to sound truculent, but his nervous system had suffered from his encounter with Petersen and his friends, and that was the way it came out.

Carlos lowered his head briefly, looked up and said, not smiling, 'The good Lord gave me eyes and they say 'twins'.'

'No problem.' Giacomo bowed towards the embarrassed girl. 'The young lady will do me the honour of switching cabins with me?'

She smiled and nodded. 'You are very kind.'

'Second. Food. You could eat aboard but I don't recommend it. Giovanni cooks only under duress and protest. I don't blame him. He's our engineer. Everything that comes out of that galley, even the coffee, tastes and smells of oil. There's a passable café close by — well, barely passable, but they do know me.' He half-smiled at the two women in turn. 'It will be a hardship and a sacrifice but I think I'll join you.

'Third. You're free to go ashore whenever you wish, although I can't imagine why anyone should want to go ashore on a night

63

like this — except, of course, to escape Giovanni's cooking. There are police patrols but their enthusiasm usually drops with the temperature. If you do run into any, just say you're from the *Colombo*: the worst that can happen is that they'll escort you back here to check.'

'I think I'll take my chance on both weather and the police,' Petersen said. 'Advancing years or too many hours in that damned truck or maybe both, but I'm as stiff as a board.'

'Back inside an hour, please, then we'll leave for the meal.' He looked at the bulkhead clock. 'We should be back at ten. We sail at one o'clock in the morning.'

'Not till then?' Michael looked his astonishment. 'Why, that's hours away. Why don't we — '

'We sail at 1.00 a.m.' Carlos was patient.

'But the wind's getting stronger. It must be rough now. It'll be getting rougher.'

'It will not be too comfortable. Are you a bad sailor, Michael?' The words were sympathetic, the expression not.

'No. Yes. I don't know. I don't see — I mean, I can't understand — '

'Michael.' It was Petersen, his voice gentle. 'It really doesn't matter what you can't see or can't understand. Lieutenant Tremino is the captain. The captain makes the decisions. No-one *ever* questions the captain.'

'It's very simple, really.' It was noticeable that Carlos spoke to Petersen not Michael. 'The garrison that guard such port installations as they have at Ploče are not first-line troops. As soldiers go, they are either superannuated or very very young. In both cases they're nervous and trigger-happy and the fact that they have radio notification of my arrival seems to have no effect on them. Experience and a few lucky escapes have taught me that the wisest thing is to arrive at sunrise so that even the most rheumy eyes can see that the gallant Captain Tremino is flying the biggest Italian flag in the Adriatic.'

★   ★   ★

The wind, as Michael had said, had indeed strengthened, and was bitingly cold but Petersen and his two companions were not exposed to it for long, for George's homing instinct was unerring. The tavern in which they fetched up was no more or less dingy than any other dockside tavern and it was at least warm.

'A very short stroll for such stiff legs,' George observed.

'Nothing wrong with my legs. I just wanted to talk.'

'What was wrong with our cabin? Carlos has more wine and grappa and slivovitz than he can possibly use — '

'Colonel Lunz, as we've said, has a long arm.'

'Ah! So! A bug?'

'Would you put anything past him? This could be awkward.'

'Alas, I'm afraid I know what you mean.'

'I don't.' Alex wore his suspicious expression.

'Carlos,' Petersen said. 'I know him. Rather, I know who he is. I knew his father, a retired naval captain but on the reserve list: almost certainly on the active list now, a cruiser captain or such. He became a reserve Italian naval captain at the same time as my father became a reserve Yugoslav army colonel. Both men loved the sea and both men set up chandlers' businesses: both were highly successful. Inevitably, almost, their paths crossed and they became very good friends. They met frequently, usually in Trieste and I was with them on several occasions. Photographs were taken. Carlos may well have seen them.'

'If he has seen them,' George said, 'let it be our pious hope that the ravages of time and the dissipation of years make it difficult for Carlos to identify Major Petersen with the carefree youth of yesteryear.'

Alex said: 'Why is it so important?'

'I have known Colonel Petersen for many years,' George said. 'Unlike his son, he is, or was, a very outspoken man.'

'Ah!'

'A pity about Carlos, a great pity.' George sounded, and may well have been, profoundly sad. 'An eminently likeable young man. And you can say the same about Giacomo — except, of course, not so young. An excellent pair to have by one's side, one would have thought, in moments of trouble and strife, which are the only ones we seem to have.' He shook his head. 'Where, oh where, are my ivory towers?'

'You should be grateful for this touch of realism, George. Exactly the counter-balance you academics need. What do you make of Giacomo? An Italian counterpart of the British commando?'

'Giacomo has been savagely beaten up or savagely tortured or perhaps both at the same time. Commando material unquestionably. But not Italian. Montenegrin.'

'Montenegrin!'

'You know. Montenegro.' George, on occasion, was capable of elaborate sarcasm, an unfortunate gift honed and refined by a lifetime in the groves of academe. 'A province in our native Yugoslavia.'

'With that fair hair and impeccable Italian?'

'Fair hair is not unknown in Montenegro and though his Italian is very good the accent overlay is unmistakable.'

Petersen didn't doubt him for a moment. George's ear for languages, dialects, accents and nuances of accent was, in philological circles, a byword far beyond the Balkans.

★   ★   ★

The evening meal was more than passable, the café more than presentable. Carlos was not only known there, as he had said, but treated with some deference. Lorraine spoke only occasionally and then to no-one except Carlos, who sat beside her. She, too, had, it seemed been born in Pescara. Predictably, neither Alex nor Michael nor Sarina contributed a word to the conversation but that didn't matter. Both Carlos and Petersen were relaxed and easy talkers but even that didn't matter very much: when Giacomo and George were in full cry, more often than not at the same time, even the possibility of a conversational hiatus seemed preposterous: both men talked a great deal without saying anything at all.

On the way back to the ship they had to face not only a perceptibly stronger wind but a thinly driving snow. Carlos, who had drunk little enough, was not so sure on his feet as he thought or, more likely, would have others think. After the second stumble he was seen to be walking arm in arm with Lorraine: who had taken whose arm could only be guessed at. When they arrived at the gangway, the *Colombo* was rocking perceptibly at its moorings: the harbour swell responsible bespoke much worse conditions outside.

To Petersen's surprise and an ill-concealed irritation that amounted almost to anger, five more men were awaiting their arrival down below. Their leader, who was introduced as Alessandro, and for whom Carlos showed an unusual degree of respect, was a tall, thin, grey-haired man with a beaked nose, bloodless lips and only the rudimentary vestiges of eyebrows. Three of his four men, all about half his age, were introduced as Franco, Cola and Sepp, which names were presumably abbreviations for Francesco, Nicholas and Giuseppe: the fourth was called Guido. Like their leader, they wore nondescript civilian clothes. Like their leader they gave the distinct impression that they would have been much happier in uniform: like their leader they had cold, hard, expressionless faces.

Petersen glanced briefly at George, turned and left the cabin, George following with Alex, inevitably, close behind. Petersen had barely begun to speak when Carlos appeared in the passage-way and walked quickly towards them.

'You are upset, Major Petersen?' No 'Peter'. The trace of anxiety was faint but it was there.

'I'm unhappy. It is true, as I told Michael, that one never questions the captain's decisions but this is a different matter entirely. I take it those men are also passengers to Ploče?' Carlos nodded. 'Where are they sleeping?'

'We have a dormitory for five in the bows. I did not think that worth mentioning, any more than I thought their arrival worth mentioning.'

'I am also unhappy at the fact that Rome gave me the distinct impression that we would be travelling alone. I did not bargain for the fact that we would be travelling with five — seven now — people who are totally unknown to me.

'I am unhappy about the fact that you know them or, at least, Alessandro.' Carlos made to speak but Petersen waved him to silence. 'I'm sure you wouldn't think me such a fool as to deny it. It's just not in your nature to show a deference amounting almost to apprehension towards a total stranger.

'Finally, I'm unhappy about the fact that they have the appearance of being a bunch of hired, professional assassins, tough ruthless killers. They are, of course, nothing of the kind, they only think they are, which is why I use the word 'appearance'. Their only danger lies in their lack of predictability. For your true assassin, no such word as unpredictability exists in his vocabulary. He does precisely what he intends to do. And it is to be borne in mind, when it comes to the far from gentle art of premeditated and authorized murder, your true assassin never, never, never looks like one.'

'You seem to know a lot about assassins.' Carlos smiled faintly. 'I could be speaking to three of them.'

'Preposterous!' George was incapable of snorting but he came close.

'Giacomo, then?'

'One is left with the impression that Giacomo is a one-man panzer division,' Petersen said. 'Cold-blooded stealth is not his forte. He doesn't even begin to qualify. You

71

should know — you know him much better than we do.'

'What makes you say that?'

'Because acting isn't *your* forte.'

'So our school drama teacher said. Lorraine?'

'You're mad.' George spoke with conviction.

'He doesn't mean you are.' Petersen smiled. 'Just the suggestion. Classically beautiful women almost never have gentle eyes.'

Carlos confirmed what seemed to be the growing opinion that he was indeed no actor. He was pleased, and not obscurely. He said: 'If you're unhappy, then I apologize for that although I really don't know why I'm apologizing. I have orders to carry out and it's my duty to follow orders. Beyond that, I know nothing.' He still wasn't a very good actor, Petersen thought, but there was nothing to be gained in saying so. 'Won't you come back to my cabin? Three hours before we sail yet. Ample time for a nightcap. Or two. Alessandro and his men, as you say, aren't so ferocious as they look.'

'Thank you,' Petersen said. 'But no. I think we'll just take a turn on the upper deck and then retire. So we'll say goodnight now.'

'The upper deck? This weather? You'll freeze.'

'Cold is an old friend of ours.'

'I prefer other company. But as you wish,

gentlemen.' He reached out a steadying hand as the *Colombo* lurched sharply. 'A rather rough passage tonight, I'm afraid. Torpedo boats may have their good points — I may find one some day — but they are rather less than sea-kindly. I hope you are also on friendly terms with Father Neptune.'

'Our next of kin,' George said.

'That apart, I can promise you a quiet and uneventful trip. Never had a mutiny yet.'

★ ★ ★

In the lee of the superstructure Petersen said: 'Well?'

'Well?' George said heavily. 'All is not well. Seven total strangers aboard this boat and the worthy young Carlos seems to know all seven of them. Every man's hand against us. Not, of course, that that's anything new.' The tip of his nauseous cigar glowed redly in the gloom. 'Would it be naïve of me to wonder whether or not our good friend Colonel Lunz is acquainted with the passenger list of the *Colombo*?'

'Yes.'

'We are, of course, prepared for all eventualities?'

'Certainly. Which ones did you have in mind?'

'None. We take turns to keep watch in our cabin?'

'Of course. If we stay in our cabin.'

'Ah! We have a plan?'

'We have no plan. What do you think about Lorraine?'

'Charming. I speak unhesitatingly. A delightful young lady.'

'I've told you before, George. About your advanced years and susceptibility. That wasn't what I meant. Her presence aboard puzzles me. I can't see that she belongs in any way to this motley bunch that Carlos is transporting to Ploče.'

'Motley, eh? First time I've ever been called motley. How does she differ?'

'Because every other passenger on this vessel is up to no good or I strongly suspect them of being up to no good. I suspect her of nothing.'

'My word!' George spoke in tones of what were meant to be genuine awe. 'That makes her unique.'

'Carlos let us know — he could have been at pains to let us know — that she, too, came from Pescara. Do you think she comes from Pescara, George?'

'How the devil should I tell? She could come from Timbuktu for all I know.'

'You disappoint me, George. Or wilfully

misunderstand me. I shall be patient. Your unmatched command of the nuances of all those European languages. Was she born or brought up in Pescara?'

'Neither.'

'But she is Italian?'

'No.'

'So we're back in Yugoslavia again?'

'Maybe you are. I'm not. I'm in England.'

'What! England?'

'The overlay of what it pleases the British Broadcasting Corporation to call Southern Standard English is unmistakable.' George coughed modestly, his smugness could occasionally verge on the infuriating. 'To the trained ear, of course.'

3

Both Alex and Carlos had made predictions and both had turned out to be wrong or, in Alex's case, half wrong. He had said, gloomily and accurately, that it was going to be very very cold and at three a.m. that morning none of the passengers on the *Colombo* would have disagreed with him. The driving snow, so heavy as to reduce visibility to virtually zero, had an uncommonly chilling effect on the torpedo boat, which would have been of no concern to those in an adequately central-heated boat but on this particular one the central-heating unit, as became practically everything else aboard, was functioning at about only one-third degree efficiency and, moreover, had been of a pathetically ancient design in the first place so that for the shivering passengers — and crew — the snow had become a matter for intense concern.

Alex had been wrong, even if only slightly — and what he had said had been a statement, really, not a fact — when he spoke of an east-north-east wind. It was a north-east wind. To a layman or, indeed, anybody not aboard an elderly torpedo boat, a paltry twenty-three degree difference in wind direction might seem negligible: to a person actually aboard such a boat the difference is crucial, marking, as it did for those with inbuilt queasiness, the border-line between the uncomfortable and the intolerable. Had the *Colombo* been head-on to wind and seas, the pitching would have been uncomfortable: had the seas been on the beam, the rolling would have been even more uncomfortable: but, that night, with the seas two points off the port bow, the resultant wicked corkscrewing was, for the less fortunate, the last straw. For some people aboard the torpedo boat that night, the degree of sea-sickness ranged from the unpleasant to the acute.

Carlos had predicted that the trip would be quiet and uneventful. At least two people, both, at least outwardly, immune to the effects of sea and cold, did not share Carlos' confidence. The door to the bo'sun's store, which lay to the port hand of the stairway leading down to the engine-room, had been hooked open and Petersen and Alex, standing two feet back in the unlit store, were only dimly visible. There was just enough light to see that Alex was carrying a semi-automatic machine-pistol while Petersen, using one hand to steady himself on the lurching deck had the other in his coat pocket. Petersen had long ago learned that with Alex by his side when confronting minimal forces, it was quite superfluous for him to carry a weapon of any kind.

Their little cabin, almost directly opposite them on the starboard side of the ill but sufficiently lit passage-way, had its door closed. George, Petersen knew, was still behind that door: and George, Petersen also knew, would be as wide awake as themselves. Petersen looked at his luminous watch. For just over ninety minutes he and Alex had been on station with no signs of weariness or boredom or awareness of the cold and certainly with no signs of their relaxed vigilance weakening at any time: a hundred times they had waited thus on the bleak and often icy mountains of Bosnia and Serbia and Montenegro, most commonly for much longer periods than this: and always they had survived. But that night was going to be one of their shorter and more comfortable vigils.

It was in the ninety-third minute that two men appeared at the for'ard end of the passage-way. They moved swiftly aft, crouched low as if making a stealthy approach, an attempt in which they were rather handicapped by being flung from bulkhead to bulkhead with every lurch of the *Colombo:* they had tried to compensate for this by removing their boots, no doubt to reduce the noise level of their approach, a rather ludicrous tactic in the circumstances because the torpedo boat was banging and crashing about to such a high decibel extent that they could have marched purposefully along in hob-nailed boots without anyone being any way the wiser. Each had a pistol stuck in his belt: more ominously, each carried in his right hand an object that looked suspiciously like a hand-grenade.

They were Franco and Cola and neither was looking particularly happy. That their expressions were due to the nature of the errand on hand or to twinges of conscience Petersen did not for a moment believe: quite simply, neither had been born with the call of the sea in his ear and, from the lack of colour in their strained faces, both would have been quite happy never to hear it again. On the logical assumption that Alessandro would have picked his two fittest young lieutenants, for the job on hand, Petersen thought, their appearance didn't say too much for the condition of those who had been left behind. Their cabin was right up in the bows of the vessel and in a cork-screwing sea that was the place to be avoided above all. They halted outside the door behind which George was lurking and looked at each other. Petersen waited until the boat was on even keel, bringing with it a comparative, if brief, period of silence.

'Don't move!'

Franco, at least, had some sense: he didn't move. Cola, on the other hand, amply demonstrated Petersen's assertion that they weren't hired assassins but only tried to look like ones, by dropping his grenade — he had to be right-handed — reaching for his pistol and swinging round, all in what he plainly hoped was one swift coordinated movement: for a man like Alex it was a scene in pathetically slow motion. Cola had just cleared the pistol from his left waistband when Alex fired, just once, the sound of the shot shockingly loud in the metallic confines. Cola dropped his gun, looked uncomprehendingly at his shattered right shoulder then, back to the bulkhead, he slid to the deck in a sitting position.

'They never learn,' Alex said gloomily. Alex was not one to derive childish pleasure from such childishly simply exercises.

'Maybe he's never had the chance to learn,' Petersen said. He relieved Franco of his armoury and had just picked up Cola's pistol and grenade when George appeared in the cabin doorway. He, too, carried a weapon but had had no expectation of using it: he held his semi-automatic loosely by the stock, its muzzle pointing towards the deck. He shook his head just once, resignedly, but said nothing.

Petersen said: 'Mind our backs, George.'

'You are going to return those unfortunates to the bosom of their family?' Petersen nodded. 'A Christian act. They're not fit to be out alone.'

Petersen and Alex moved back up the passageway preceded by Franco and Cola, the former supporting his stricken comrade. They had taken only four steps when a door on the port side, just aft of where George was standing, opened and Giacomo stepped out into the passage-way, brandishing a Biretta.

'Put that thing away,' George said. His machine-pistol was still pointing at the deck. 'Don't you think there has been enough noise already?'

'That's why I'm here.' Giacomo had already lowered his gun. 'The noise, I mean.'

'Took your time, didn't you?'

'I had to get dressed first,' Giacomo said with some dignity. He was clad only in a pair of khaki trousers, displaying a tanned chest rather impressively criss-crossed with scars. 'But I notice you are fully dressed, so I take it you were expecting whatever did happen.' He looked in the direction of the quartet making their slow way along the passage-way. 'What exactly did happen?'

'Alex has just shot Cola.'

'Good for Alex.' If Giacomo was moved by the news he hid it well. 'Hardly worth wakening a man for.'

'Cola might view matters differently.' George coughed delicately. 'You are not, then, one of them?'

'You must be mad.'

'Not really. I don't know any of you, do I? But you don't *look* like them.'

'You're very kind, George. And now?'

'We won't find out just by standing here.'

They caught up with the others in just a matter of seconds which was easily enough done as the now moaning Cola could barely drag his feet along. A moment afterwards a door at the for'ard end of the passage-way opened and an armed figure came — or lurched — into view. It was Sepp and he wasn't looking at all like the ruthless killer of a few hours ago. It required no imagination to see the slightly greenish pallor on his face, for slightly green he indisputably was: time and the seaway had wrought its effect. It was not difficult to understand why Alessandro had selected Franco and Cola for the mission.

'Sepp.' Petersen's tone was almost kindly. 'We have no wish to kill you. Before you can reach us, you would have to kill your two friends, Franco and Cola. That would be bad enough, wouldn't it, Sepp?' From Sepp's pallor and general demeanour of uncertainty it seemed, that for him, things were quite bad enough as they were. 'Even worse, Sepp, before you could get around to killing the second of your friends, you yourself would be dead. Drop that gun, Sepp.'

Whatever other parts of Sepp's physiology were in a state of temporary dysfunction there was nothing wrong with his hearing. His elderly Lee Enfield .303 clattered to the deck.

'Who fired that shot?' Carlos, his habitual smile in momentary abeyance, had come limping up behind them, a pistol in hand. 'What goes on?'

'It would help if you could tell us.' Petersen looked at the gun in Carlos' hand. 'You don't require that.'

'I require it as long as I am the master of this vessel. I asked' — he broke off with an exclamation of pain as George's massive hand closed over his gun-wrist. He struggled to free his hand, an expression of incomprehension spread over his face and he bit his lips as if to hold back another cry of pain. George removed the gun from the suddenly nerveless fingers.

'So that's it,' Carlos said. His face, not without reason, was pale. 'So I was right. *You* are the assassins. It is your intention to take over my vessel, perhaps?'

'Goodness gracious, no.' It was George who answered. 'Your forefinger has gone white at the knuckles. Precipitate action isn't going to help anyone.' He handed the pistol back to Carlos and went on pontifically: 'Unnecessary violence never helped anyone.'

Carlos took the pistol, hesitated, stuck it in his waistband and began to massage his right wrist. The demonstration of pacific intentions had had an unsettling effect. He said uncertainly: 'I still don't understand — '

'Neither do we, Carlos,' Petersen said, 'neither do we. That's what we're trying to do at this moment — understand. Perhaps you could help us. Those two men, Franco and Cola — Cola, I'm afraid is going to require your peacetime professional skills quite soon — came to attack us. Perhaps they came to kill us but I don't think so. They bungled it.'

'Amateurs,' George said by way of explanation.

'Amateurs, agreed. But the effect of an amateur bullet can be just as permanent as a professional one. I want to know why those two came for us in the first place. Perhaps you can help explain this, Carlos?'

'How should I be able to help you?'

'Because you know Alessandro.'

'I do but not well. I have no idea why he should seek to do you harm. I do not permit my passengers to carry out guerrilla warfare.'

'I'm sure you don't. But I'm equally sure that you know who Alessandro is and what he does.'

'I don't know.'

'I don't believe you. I suppose I should sigh and say how much trouble it would save all round if you were to tell the truth. Not, of course, that you are telling lies. You're just not telling anything. Well, if you don't help us, I'll just have to help myself.' Petersen raised his voice. 'Alessandro!'

Seconds passed without reply.

'Alessandro. I have three of your men prisoner, one of them badly injured. I want to know why those men came to attack us.' Alessandro made no reply and Petersen went on: 'You don't leave me any option. In wartime, people are either friends or enemies. Friends are friends and enemies die. If you're a friend, step out into the passage-way: if you're not, then you'll just have to stay there and die.'

Petersen didn't show any particular emotion but his tone sounded implacable enough. Carlos, his pain forgotten, laid a hand on Petersen's forearm.

'People don't commit murder aboard my ship.'

'Haven't committed. And murder is for peace-time. In wartime we call it execution.' For those listening inside the cabin the tone of his voice could have lent little encouragement. 'George, Alex. Help Franco and Sepp into the cabin. Keep out of any line of fire.'

Franco and Sepp didn't need any kind of helping. Execution chamber or not they couldn't get inside it fast enough. The door banged shut and a watertight clip came down. Petersen examined the pear-shaped object in his hand.

Carlos said apprehensively: 'What's that?'

'You can see. A hand-grenade of sorts. George?' George didn't need telling what to do. He never did. He took up position by the cabin door, his hand reaching up for the closed watertight clip. With one hand Petersen took a grip on the door handle, with the other he pressed a lever on the bottom of the grenade as he glanced at George who immediately opened the clip. Petersen jerked open the door the requisite few inches, dropped the grenade inside and banged shut the door as George closed the clip again. They could have rehearsed it a hundred times.

'Jesus!' Carlos' face was white. 'In that confined space — ' He stopped, his face puzzled now, and said: 'The explosion. The bang.'

'Gas-grenades don't go bang. They go hiss. Reactions, George?' George had taken his hand away from the clip.

'Five seconds and then whoever it was gave up. Quick-acting stuff, is it not?'

Carlos was still almost distraught. 'What's the difference? Explosives or poison gas — '

Petersen spoke with patience. 'It was not poison gas. George.' He spoke a few words in the ear of his giant Lieutenant, who smiled and moved quickly aft. Petersen turned to Carlos. 'Is it your intention to let your friend Cola die?'

'He's not my friend and he's in no danger of dying.' He turned to the elder Pietro who had just arrived on the scene. 'Get my medicine box and bring along two of your boys.' To Petersen he said: 'I'll give a sedative, a knockout one. Then a coagulant. A few minutes later and I'll bandage him up. There'll be a broken bone or bones. It may be that his shoulder is shattered beyond repair, but whatever it is there's nothing I can do about it in this seaway.' He glanced aft, passed his hand over his forehead and looked as if he would like to moan. 'More trouble.'

Michael von Karajan was approaching them, closely followed by George. Michael

87

was trying to look indignant and truculent but succeeded only in looking miserable and frightened. George was beaming.

'By heavens, Major, there's nothing wrong with this new generation of ours. You have to admire their selfless spirit. Here we are with the good ship *Colombo* trying to turn somersaults but does that stop our Michael in the polishing of his skills? Not a bit of it. There he was, crouched over his transceiver in this appalling weather, headphones clamped over his ears — '

Petersen held up his hand. When he spoke his face was as cold as his voice. 'Is this true, von Karajan?'

'No. What I mean is — '

'You're a liar. If George says it's true, it's true. What message were you sending?'

'I wasn't sending any message. I — '

'George?'

'He wasn't transmitting any message when I arrived.'

'He would hardly have had time to,' Giacomo said. 'Not between the time I left our cabin and when George got there.' He eyed the now visibly shaking Michael with open distaste. 'He's not only a coward, he's a fool. How was he to know that I wasn't going to return at any moment? Why didn't he lock his door to make sure that he wasn't disturbed?'

Petersen said: 'What message were you going to transmit?'

'I wasn't going to transmit any — '

'That makes you doubly a liar. Who were you transmitting to or about to transmit to?'

'I wasn't going to — '

'Oh, do be quiet. That makes you three times a liar. George, confiscate his equipment. For good measure confiscate his sister's as well.'

'You can't do that.' Michael was aghast. 'Take away our radios? They're our equipment.'

'Good God in heaven!' Petersen stared at him in disbelief. Whether the disbelief were real or affected didn't matter. The effect was the same. 'I'm your commanding officer, you young fool. I can not only lock up your equipment, I can lock you up too, on charges of mutiny. In irons, if need be.' Petersen shook his head. ''Can't', he says, 'can't'. Another thing, von Karajan. Can it be that you're so stupid as not to know that, in wartime at sea, the use of radio by unauthorized personnel is a very serious offence.' He turned to Carlos. 'Is that not so, Captain Tremino?' Petersen's use of formal terms lent to his enquiry all the gravity of a court-martial.

'Very much so, I'm afraid.' Carlos wasn't

too happy to say it but he said it all the same.

'Is this young fellow authorized personnel?'

'No.'

'You see how it is, von Karajan? The Captain would also be justified in locking you up. George, put the sets in our cabin. No, wait a minute. This is primarily a naval offence.' He looked at Carlos. 'Do you think — '

'I have a very adequate safe in the office,' Carlos said. 'And I have the only key.'

'Splendid.' George moved off, a disconsolate Michael trailing behind him, passing by Pietro, bearing a black metal box and accompanied by two seamen. Carlos opened the medicine chest — it appeared to be immaculately equipped — and administered two injections to the hapless Cola. The box was closed and removed: so was Cola.

'Well, now,' Petersen said. 'Let's see what we have inside.' Alex, not without considerable effort, managed to free the watertight clip — when George heaved a watertight clip home it tended to stay heaved — then levelled his machine-pistol on the door. Giacomo did the same with his pistol, clearly demonstrating that whoever's side, if any, he was on it clearly was not that of Alessandro and his henchmen. Petersen didn't bother about any weapon, although he had a Luger on his person: he just pushed the door open.

The guns were unnecessary. The four men were not unconscious but, on the other hand, they weren't very conscious either, although they would be very soon. No coughing, no spluttering, no tears running down their cheeks: they were just slightly dazed, slightly woozy, slightly apathetic. Alex laid down his machine-pistol, collected the several weapons that were lying around, then searched the four men thoroughly, coming up with two more hand-guns and no fewer than four very unpleasant knives. All these he threw out into the passage-way.

'Well.' Carlos was almost smiling. 'That wasn't very clever of me, was it? I mean, if you had wished to dispose of all of them you'd have thrown Cola in here, too. I missed that.' He sniffed the air professionally. 'Nitrous oxide, I'd say. You know, laughing gas.'

'Not bad for a doctor,' Petersen said. 'I thought that gas was confined only to dentists' surgeries. Nitrous oxide, a refined form of. With this, you don't come out of the anaesthetic with tears in your eyes, laughing, singing and generally making a fool of yourself. Normally, you don't come out of it at all, by which I mean you'd just keep on sleeping until you woke up at your usual time, quite unaware that anything untoward had happened to you. But I'm told that if you've recently undergone some sort of traumatic experience immediately before you've been gassed, the tendency is to wake up directly the effects of the gas have worn off. They also say that if you had something weighing on your mind, such as a nagging conscience, the same thing happens.'

Carlos said: 'That's a strange sort of thing for a soldier to know about.'

'I'm a strange sort of soldier. Alex, take up your gun while I have a look around.'

'Look around?' Carlos did just that. The cabin, if one could call it such, held five canvas cots and that was all: there wasn't as much as even a cupboard for clothes. 'There's nothing to look around for.'

Petersen didn't bother to reply. He ripped blankets from the cots and flung them on the deck. Nothing had lain beneath the blankets. He picked up a rucksack — there were five of them in the cabin — and unceremoniously dumped the contents on a cot. They were innocuous. Among some clothes and a rudimentary toilet kit there was a considerable amount of ammunition, some loose, some in magazines, but those, too, Petersen considered innocuous: he would have expected nothing else. The second rucksack yielded the same results. The third was padlocked. Petersen looked at Alessandro, who was sitting on the deck, his ravaged face expressionless: the effect was chilling, even a hint of balefulness would have been preferable to this emptiness but Petersen was not the man to be moved by expressions or lack of them.

'Well, now, Alessandro, that wasn't very clever, was it? If you want to hide a thing you do it inconspicuously: a padlock is conspicuous. The key.'

Alessandro spat on the deck and remained silent.

'Spitting.' Petersen shook his head. 'Unpleasant, for second-rate villains. Alex.'

'Search him?'

'Don't bother. Your knife.'

Alex's knife, as one would have expected of Alex, was razor sharp. It sliced through the tough canvas of the rucksack as if through paper. Petersen peered at the contents.

'Yes, indeed, twinges of conscience.' He extracted a very small butane burner and an equally small kettle. The kettle had no top — the spout had a screwed top. Petersen shook the kettle: the glugging of water inside was unmistakable. Petersen turned to Carlos.

'Doesn't say much for the hospitality of the *Colombo*, does it, when a man has to bring along his own equipment for making tea or coffee or whatever.'

Carlos looked slightly puzzled. 'Any passenger aboard this ship can have as much tea or coffee or any other drink that he wants.' Then his face cleared. 'For shore use, of course.'

'Of course.' Petersen tipped the remainder of the contents of the rucksack on to another cot, rummaged briefly around, then straightened. 'Although, mind you, it's difficult to see how we can make any of those refreshing beverages without any tea or coffee to make them. I've found out all I want to know even although I knew in advance anyway.' He turned his attention to the fourth rucksack.

Carlos said: 'If you've already found out what you want to know why keep on?'

'Natural curiosity together with the fact that Alessandro, I'm afraid, is not a very trustworthy man. Who knows, this bag might contain a nest of vipers.'

There were no vipers but there were two more gas-grenades and a Walther with a screwed-on silencer.

'And a stealthy killer to boot,' Petersen said. 'I've always wanted one of those.' He put it in his pocket and opened up the last rucksack: this yielded only a small metal case about half the size of a shoe-box. Petersen turned to the nearest of his prisoners who happened to be Franco.

'You know what's inside this?'

Franco didn't say whether he did not not.

Petersen sighed, placed the muzzle of his Luger against Franco's knee-cap and said: 'Captain Tremino, if I pull the trigger, will he walk again?'

'Good God!' Carlos was used to war but not this kind of war. 'He might. He'll be a cripple for life.'

Petersen took two steps back. Franco looked at Alessandro but Alessandro wasn't looking at him. Franco looked at Petersen and the levelled Luger.

Franco said: 'I know.'

'Open it.'

Franco released two brass clips and swung back the lid. There was no explosion, no release of gas.

Carlos said: 'Why didn't *you* open it?'

'Because the world is full of untrustworthy people. Lots of these boxes of tricks around. If an unauthorized opener doesn't know where a secret switch or button is he's going to inhale a very nasty gas. Most of the latest safes incorporate some such device.' He took the box from Franco. The interior was shaped and lined with velvet and contained glass ampoules, two round boxes and two small hypodermic syringes. Petersen took out one of the round boxes and shook it: it rattled. Petersen handed the box to Carlos.

'Should interest a medical man. At a guess, a variety of liquids and tablets to render the victim temporarily or permanently uncon-scious, by which I mean dead. Seven ampoules, you observe. One green, three blue, three pink. At a guess, the green is scopolamine, an aid to flagging memories. As for the difference in colour in the other six ampoules, there can be only one reason. Three are lethal, three non-lethal. Wouldn't you agree, Captain?'

'It's possible.' It was Carlos' night for being unhappy and Petersen was no longer as surprised by his unhappiness as he had been earlier, nor at the obvious apprehension in which he held Alessandro. 'There's no means of telling one from the other, of course.'

'I wouldn't bet on that,' Petersen said. He turned round as George came through the doorway. 'All is well?'

'A little trouble with the young lady,' George said. 'She put up a surprisingly spirited resistance to the confiscation of her radio.'

'Nothing surprising about that. Fortu-nately, you're bigger than she is.'

'I'm hardly proud of that. The radios are in the captain's cabin.' George looked around the cabin which looked as if a small tornado had lately passed by. 'Untidy lot, aren't they?'

'I helped a little.' Petersen took the box from Carlos and handed it to George. 'What do you make of that?'

It is difficult to conceive of a beaming, plump and cherubic face changing in an instant to one of graven stone but that was what happened to George's.

'Those are death capsules.'

'I know.'

'Alessandro's?'

'Yes.'

George looked at Alessandro for some seconds, nodded, and turned back to Petersen. 'I think perhaps we should have a talk with our friend.'

'You're making a mistake.' Carlos' voice was not quite as steady as it could have been. 'I'm a doctor. You don't know human nature. Alessandro will never talk.'

George faced him. His expression hadn't changed and Carlos visibly recoiled.

'Be quiet, little man. Five minutes alone with me, ten at the most, and any man in the world will talk. Alessandro is a five minute man.'

'It may come to that,' Petersen said. 'It probably will. But first things first. Apart from the capsules, we picked up one or two other interesting objects. This silenced gun, for instance.' He showed George the Walther. 'Two gas-grenades and a spirit burner and kettle and about two hundred rounds of ammunition. What do you think the kettle was for?'

'One thing only. He was going to gas us, steal some real or imagined document, steam open the envelope — odd, that he should be convinced that there was an envelope around — study the contents, reseal the envelope, return it to our cabin, gas us again, wait a few seconds, replace the envelope, remove the gas-canister and leave. When we woke up in the morning we almost certainly wouldn't be aware that anything had happened.'

'That's the only way it could have happened or was intended to happen. There are three questions. Why was Alessandro so interested in us? What were his future plans? And who sent him?'

'We'll find all that out easily enough,' George said.

'Of course we will.'

'Not aboard this ship,' Carlos said.

George studied him with mild interest. 'Why not?'

'There will be no torture aboard any vessel I command.' The words sounded more resolute than the tone of the voice.

'Carlos,' Petersen said. 'Don't make things any more difficult for yourself — or us — than you can help. Nothing easier than to lock you up with this bunch of villains: you're not the only person who can find his way to Ploče. We don't want to nor do we intend to. We realize you find yourself in an invidious situation through no fault of your own. No torture. We promise.'

'You've just said you'll find out.'

'Psychology.'

'Drugs?' Carlos was immediately suspicious. 'Injections?'

'Neither. Subject closed. I had another question but the answer is obvious — why did Alessandro choose to surround himself with such a bunch of incompetents? Camouflage. A dangerous man might well be tempted to surround himself with other dangerous men. Alessandro's too smart.' Petersen looked around. 'No heavy metal objects and only a cat could get out of that porthole. Carlos, would you have one of your men bring us a sledge-hammer or as near to it as you have aboard.'

The suspicion returned. 'What do you want a sledge-hammer for?'

'To beat out Alessandro's brains,' George said patiently. 'Before we start asking questions.'

'To close this door from the outside,' Petersen said. 'The clips, you understand.'

'Ah!' Carlos stepped into the passage-way, gave an order and returned. 'I'll go and have a look at the fallen hero. Not much I can do for him, I'm afraid.'

'A favour, Carlos. When we leave, may we go up to your cabin or whatever you call the place we met you first?'

'Certainly. May one ask why?'

'If you'd been standing frozen in that damned passage-way for an hour and a half you'd understand why.'

'Of course. Restoratives. Help yourselves, gentlemen. I'll step by and let you know how Cola is.' He paused then added drily: 'That should give you plenty of time to prepare your intensive interrogation of me.'

He left almost immediately to be replaced by Pietro, bearing a small sledge-hammer. They closed the door and secured one of the eight water-tight clips. One was enough. George struck it with one blow of the hammer. That, too, was enough — not even a gorilla could now have opened that clip from the inside. They left the sledge-hammer in the passage-way and went directly to the engine-room, which was unmanned, as they had known it would be: all controls were operated from the wheel-house. It took them less than a minute to find what they were looking for. They made a brief excursion to the upper deck then repaired to Carlos' cabin.

★ ★ ★

'A thirsty night's work,' George said. He was on his second, or it could have been third, glass of grappa. He looked at the von Karajans' radios on the deck beside him. 'These would have been safer in our cabins. Why have them here?'

'They'd have been too safe in our cabins. Young Michael would never have dared to try to get at them there.'

'Don't try to tell me that he might try to get at them here.'

'Unlikely, I admit. Michael, it is clear, is not cast in the heroic mould. He might, of course, be a consummate actor, but I don't see him as an actor any more than a hero. However, if he's desperate enough — and he must have been desperate to try to get off a message at the time and place he did — he might try.'

'But the radios will be in the safe as soon as Carlos returns. And Carlos has the only key.'

'Carlos might give him that key.'

'Oh! So that's the way our devious mind

works. So we keep an eye on our Michael for the remainder of the night? Not that there's all that much left of it. And if he does try to recover the radios, what does that prove except that there is a connection between him and Carlos?'

'That's all I want to prove. I don't expect either would say or admit to anything. They don't have to. At least, Michael doesn't have to. I can have him detained in Ploče for disobedience of orders and suspicion of trying to communicate with the enemy.'

'You really suspect him of that?'

'Good Lord, no. But, no question, he's been trying to communicate with someone and that someone might as well be a spy. It'll look better on a charge sheet. All I want to see is if there's any connection between him and Carlos.'

'And if there is you're prepared to clap him into durance vile?'

'Sure.'

'And his sister?'

'She's done nothing. She can come along with us, hang around Ploče or join him in, as you say, durance vile. Up to her.'

'The very flower of chivalry.' George shook his head and reached for the grappa. 'So we may or may not suspect a connection between Carlos and Michael but we do suspect one between Carlos and Alessandro.'

'I don't. I do think that Carlos knows a great deal more about Alessandro than we do but I don't think he knows what Alessandro is up to on this passage. A very simple point. If Carlos were privy to Alessandro's plans then he, Alessandro, wouldn't have bothered to bring along a kettle and burner: he'd just have gone to the galley and steamed the envelope open.' He turned round as Carlos entered. 'How's Cola?'

'He'll be all right. Well, no danger. His shoulder is a mess. Even if it were a flat calm I wouldn't touch it. It needs a surgeon or an osteologist and I'm neither.' He unlocked a safe, put the radio gear inside then relocked the door. 'Well, no hurry for you, gentlemen, but I must return to the wheelhouse.'

'A moment, please.'

'Yes, Peter?' Carlos smiled. 'The interrogation?'

'No. A few questions. You could save us a lot of time and trouble.'

'What? In interrogating Alessandro? You promised me no torture.'

'I still promise. Alessandro tried to assault us and steal some papers tonight. Did you, do you know about this?'

'No.'

'I believe you.' Carlos raised his eyebrows a

103

little but said nothing. 'You don't seem unduly concerned that your fellow-Italian has been made a prisoner by a bunch of uncivilized Yugoslavs, do you?'

'If you mean does he mean anything personally to me, no.'

'But his reputation does.'

Carlos said nothing.

'You know something about his background, his associations, the nature of his business that we don't. Is that not so?'

'That could be. You can't expect me to divulge anything of that nature.'

'Not expect. Hope.'

'No hope. You wouldn't break the Geneva Conventions to extract that information from me.'

Petersen rose. 'Certainly not. Thank you for your hospitality.'

★　★　★

Petersen was carrying a canvas chair and the metal box of capsules when he entered the cabin in which Alessandro and his three men were imprisoned. George was carrying two lengths of heaving line and the sledge-hammer with which he had just released the outside clip. Alex was carrying only his machine-pistol. Petersen unfolded the chair, sat on it and watched with apparent interest as George hammered home a clip.

'We'd rather not have any interruptions, you see,' Petersen said. He looked at Franco, Sepp and Guido. 'Get into that corner there. If anyone moves Alex will kill him. Take your jacket off, Alessandro.'

Alessandro spat on the floor.

'Take your jacket off,' George said pleasantly, 'or I'll knock you out of it.'

Alessandro, not a man of a very original turn of mind, spat again. George hit him somewhere in the region of the solar plexus, not a very hard blow, it seemed, but enough to make Alessandro double up, whooshing in agony. George removed the jacket.

'Tie him up.'

George set about tying him up. When Alessandro had recovered a little from his initial bout of gasping, he tried to offer some resistance, but an absent-minded cuff from George to the side of the jaw convinced him of the unwisdom of this. George tied him in such a fashion that both arms were lashed immovably to his sides. His knees and ankles were bound together and then, for good measure, George used the second heaving line to lash Alessandro to the cot. No chicken was ever so securely trussed, so immobile, as Alessandro was then.

George surveyed his handiwork with some satisfaction then turned to Petersen: 'Isn't there something in the Geneva Conventions about this?'

'Could be, could be. Truth is, I've never read them.' He opened the metal box and looked at Alessandro. 'In the interests of science, you understand. This shouldn't take any time at all.' The words were light enough but Alessandro wasn't listening to the words, he was looking at the implacable face above and not liking at all what he saw. 'Here we have three blue ampoules and three pink. We think, and Captain Tremino who is also a doctor agrees with us, that three of these are lethal and three non-lethal. Unfortunately, we don't know which is which and there's only one simple, logical way to find out. I'm going to inject you with one of these. If you survive it, then we'll know it's a nonlethal ampoule. If you don't, we'll know it's the other ones that are non-lethal.' Petersen held up two ampoules, one blue, one pink. 'Which would you suggest, George?'

George rubbed his chin thoughtfully. 'A big responsibility. A man's life could hang on my decision. Well, it's not all that big a responsibility. No loss to mankind, anyway. The blue one.'

'Blue it shall be.' Petersen broke the

ampoule into a test tube, inserted the needle of the hypodermic and began to withdraw the plunger. Alessandro stared in terrified fascination as the blue liquid seeped up into the hypodermic.

'I'm afraid I'm not very good at this job.' Petersen's conversational calm was more terrifying than any sibilant threats could ever have hoped to be. 'If you're careless an air bubble can get in and an air bubble in the blood stream can be very unpleasant. I mean, it can kill you. However, in your case, I don't think it's going to make very much difference one way or another.'

Alessandro's eyes were staring, his whitened lips drawn back in a rictus of terror. Petersen touched the inside of Alessandro's right elbow. 'Seems a suitable vein to me.' He pinched the vein and advanced the syringe.

'No! No! No!' Alessandro's voice was an inhuman scream torn from his throat. 'God, no! No!'

'You've nothing to worry about,' Petersen said soothingly. 'If it's a non-lethal dose you'll just slip away from us and come back in a few minutes. If it's a lethal dose, you'll just slip away.' He paused. 'Just a minute, though. He just might die in screaming agony.' He brought out a pad of white linen cloth and handed it to George. 'Just in case. But watch your hand, though. When a dying man's teeth clench they stay clenched. Worse, if he draws blood you'll get infected too.'

Petersen pinched the vein between fingers and thumb. Alessandro screamed. George applied the pad to his mouth. After a few seconds, at a nod from Petersen, he withdrew the pad. Alessandro had stopped screaming now and a weird moaning noise came from deep in his throat. He was struggling insanely against his bonds, his face was a mask of madness and a seizure, a heart attack, seemed imminent. Petersen looked at George: the big man's face was masked in sweat.

Petersen said in a quiet voice: 'This is the killer dose, isn't it?' Alessandro didn't hear him. Petersen had to repeat the question twice before the question penetrated the fear crazed mind.

'It's the killer dose! It's the killer dose.' He repeated the words several times, the words a babble of near-incoherent terror.

'And you die in agony?'

'Yes, yes! Yes, yes!' He was gasping for breath like a man in the final stages of suffocation. 'Agony! Agony!'

'Which means you have administered this yourself. There can be no pity, Alessandro, no mercy. Besides, you could still be telling a lie.' He touched the tip of the needle against the skin. Alessandro screamed again and again. George applied the clamp.

'Who sent you?' Twice Petersen repeated the question before Alessandro rolled his eyes. George removed the pad.

'Cipriano.' The voice was a barely distinguishable croak. 'Major Cipriano.'

'That's a lie. No major could authorize this.' Careful not to touch the plunger Petersen inserted the tip of the needle just outside the vein. Alessandro opened his mouth to scream again but George cut him off before he could make a sound. 'Who authorized this? The needle's inside the vein now, Alessandro. All I have to do is press the plunger. Who authorized this?'

George removed the pad. For a moment it seemed that Alessandro had lost consciousness. Then his eyes rolled again.

'Granelli.' The voice was a faint whisper. 'General Granelli.' Granelli was the much-feared, much-hated Chief of Italian Intelligence.

'The needle is still inside the vein, my hand is still on the plunger. Does Colonel Lunz know of this?'

'No. I swear it. No!'

'General von Löhr?'

'No.'

'Then how did Granelli know I was on board?'

'Colonel Lunz told him.'

'Well, well. The usual trusting faith between the loyal allies. What did you want from my cabin tonight?'

'A paper. A message.'

'Perhaps you'd better withdraw that syringe,' George said. 'I think he's going to faint. Or die. Or something.'

'What were you going to do with it, Alessandro?' The tip of the needle had remained where it was.

'Compare it with a message.' Alessandro really did look very ill indeed. 'My jacket.'

Petersen found the message in the inside pocket of the jacket. It was the duplicate of the one he had in his cabin. He refolded the paper and put it in his own inside pocket.

'Odd,' George said. 'I do believe he's fainted.'

'I'll bet his victims never had a chance to faint. I wish,' Petersen said with genuine regret, 'that I had pressed that plunger. No question our friend here is — was — a one-man extermination squad.' Petersen sniffed at the test-tube, dropped it and the ampoule to the deck, crushed them both beneath his heel and then squirted the contents of the hypodermic on the deck.

'Spirit-based,' Petersen said. 'It will evaporate quickly enough. Well, that's it.'

In the passage-way, George mopped his

forehead. 'I wouldn't care to go through that again. Neither, I'm sure, would Alessandro.'

'Me neither,' Petersen said. 'How do you feel about it, Alex?'

'I wish,' Alex said morosely, 'that you had pushed that plunger. I could have shot him as easy as a wink.'

'That would have been an idea. At least he'd have gone without the agony. In any event, he's all washed up as an operative of any kind or will be as soon as he gets back to Termoli. Or even to Ploče. Let's fix this door.'

All eight water-tight clips were engaged and with each clip in turn, to muffle sound, Alex held in position the pad that had been so lately used for another purpose, while George hammered home the clip. When the eighth had been so dealt with, George said: 'That should hold it for a while. Especially if we throw this hammer overboard.'

'Let's make sure,' Petersen said. He left and returned within a minute with a gas cylinder, a welder's rod and a face-mask. Petersen was, at best, but an amateur welder but what he lacked in expertise he made up in enthusiasm. The completed result would have won him no prizes for finesse but that was unimportant. What was important was that for all practical purposes that door was sealed for life.

'What I'd like to do now,' Petersen said, 'is to have a word with Carlos and Michael. But first, I think, a pause for reflection.'

★　★　★

'How does this sound,' Petersen said. He was seated at Carlos' desk, a scotch in front of him and, beside it, a message he had just drafted. 'We'll have Michael send it off by and by. Plain language, of course. COLONEL LUNZ. Then his code number. YOUR WOULD-BE ASSASSINS AND/OR EXTERMINATORS A BUNCH OF INCOMPETENTS STOP ALESSANDRO AND OTHER BUNGLERS NOW CONFINED FORE CABIN *COLOMBO* BEHIND WELDED STEEL DOOR STOP SORRY CANNOT CONGRATULATE YOU GENERAL VON LOHR GENERAL GRANELLI MAJOR CIPRIANO ON CHOICE OF OPERATIVES REGARDS ZEPPO. 'Zeppo', you may recall, is my code name.'

George steepled his fingers. 'Fair,' he said judicially, 'fair. Not entirely accurate, though. We don't *know* that they are assassins and/or etc.'

'How are they to know that we don't know? Should cause quite a stirring in the dovecote. Not too much billing and cooing, wouldn't you think?'

George smiled broadly. 'Colonel Lunz and General von Löhr are going to be fearfully upset. Alessandro said they knew nothing of this set-up.'

'How are they to know that we didn't know,' Petersen said reasonably. 'They'll be fit to be tied and ready to assume anything. I'd love to be listening in to the heated telephone calls among the named parties later on today. Nothing like spreading confusion, dissension, suspicion and mistrust among the loyal allies. Not a bad night's work, gentlemen. I think we're entitled to a small nightcap before going to have a word with Carlos.'

★   ★   ★

The wheelhouse was lit only by the dim light from the binnacle and it had taken Petersen and his two companions some time to adjust their eyes to the gloom. Carlos himself was at the wheel — at a discreet word from Petersen the helmsman had taken temporary leave of absence.

Petersen coughed, again discreetly, and said: 'I am surprised, Carlos — I would almost say acutely distressed — to find a simple honest sailorman like yourself associating with such notorious and unscrupulous characters as General Granelli and Major Cipriano.'

Carlos, hands on the wheel, continued to gaze straight ahead and when he spoke his voice was surprisingly calm. 'I have never met either. After tonight, I shall take care that I never shall. Orders are orders but I will never again carry one of Granelli's murderous poisoners. They may threaten court-martial but threats are as far as they will go. I take it that Alessandro has talked?'

'Yes.'

'He is alive?' From the tone of his voice Carlos didn't particularly care whether he were or not.

'Alive and well. No torture, as promised. Simple psychology.'

'You wouldn't and couldn't say so unless it were true. I'll talk to him. By and by.' There was no hint of urgency in his voice.

'Yes. Well. I'm afraid that to talk to him you'll have to have yourself lowered in a bo'sun's chair to his cabin porthole. Door's locked, you see.'

'What's locked can be unlocked.'

'Not in this case. We apologize for having taken liberties with an Italian naval vessel but we thought it prudent to weld the door to the bulkhead.'

'Ah, so.' For the first time Carlos looked at Petersen his expression registering, if anything, no more than a polite interest.

'Welded? Unusual.'

'I doubt whether you'll find an oxyacety-lene lance in Ploče.'

'I doubt it.'

'You might have to go all the way back to Ancona to have them freed. One would hope you are not sunk before you get there. It would be a terrible thing if Alessandro and his friends were to go to a watery grave.'

'Terrible.'

'We've taken another liberty. You did have an oxyacetylene flame. It's at the bottom of the Adriatic.'

Although he could see no gleam of white teeth, Petersen could have sworn that he was smiling.

4

As the seas had remained rough throughout the crossing and had hardly moderated when they reached what should have been the comparative shelter of the Neretva Channel between the island of Pelješac and the Yugoslav mainland, the seven passengers who were in a position to sit down to have breakfast did not in fact do so until they had actually tied up to the quay in Ploče. True to Carlos' prediction, because they had arrived after dawn and were flying a ludicrously large Italian flag, the harbour garrison had refrained from firing at them as they made their approach towards the port that not even the most uninhibited of travel brochure writers would have described as the gem of the Adriatic.

Breakfast was unquestionably the handi-work of Giovanni, the engineer: the indescribable mush of eggs and cheese seemed to have been cooked in diesel oil, and the coffee made of it, but the bread was palatable and the sea air lent an edge to the appetite, more especially for those who had suffered during the passage.

Giacomo pushed his half-finished plate to one side. He was freshly shaven and, despite the ghastly meal, as cheerful as ever. 'Where are Alessandro and his cut-throats? They don't know what they're missing.'

'Maybe they've had breakfast aboard the *Colombo* before,' Petersen said. 'Or already gone ashore.'

'Nobody's gone ashore. I've been on deck.'

'Prefer their own company, then. A secretive lot.'

Giacomo smiled. 'You have no secrets?'

'Having secrets and being secretive are two different things. But no, no secrets. Too much trouble trying to remember who you are supposed to be and what you are supposed to be saying. Especially, if like me, you have difficulty in remembering. Start a life of deception and you end up by being trapped in it. I believe in the simple, direct lfe.'

'I could believe that,' Giacomo said. 'Especially if last night's performance was anything to go by.'

'Last night's performance?' Sarina, her face still pale from what had obviously been an unpleasant night, looked at him in puzzlement. 'What does that mean?'

'Didn't you hear the shot last night?'

Sarina nodded towards the other girl. 'Lorraine and I both heard a shot.' She

117

smiled faintly. 'When two people think they are dying they don't pay much attention to a trifle like a shot. What happened?'

'Petersen shot one of Alessandro's men. An unfortunate lad by the name of Cola.'

Sarina looked at Petersen in astonishment. 'Why on earth did you do that?'

'Credit where credit is due. Alex shot him — with, of course, my full approval. Why? He was being secretive, that's why.'

She didn't seem to have heard. 'Is he — is he dead?'

'Goodness me no. Alex doesn't kill people.' Quite a number of ghosts would have testified to the contrary. 'A damaged shoulder.'

'Damaged!' Lorraine's dark eyes were cold, the lips compressed. 'Do you mean shattered?'

'Could be.' Petersen lifted his shoulders in a very small shrug indeed. 'I'm not a doctor.'

'Has Carlos seen him?' It was less a question than a demand.

Petersen looked at her thoughtfully. 'What good would that do?'

'Carlos, well — ' She broke off as if in confusion.

'Well, what? Why? What could he do?'

'What could he — he's the Captain, isn't he?'

'Both a stupid answer and a stupid

118

question. Why should he see him? I've seen him and I'm certain I've seen many more gunshot wounds than Carlos has.'

'You're not a doctor?'

'Is Carlos?'

'Carlos? How should I know?'

'Because you do,' Petersen said pleasantly. 'Every time you speak you tread deeper water. You are not a born liar, Lorraine, but you are a lousy one. When first we practise to deceive — you know. Deception again — and it's not your forte, I'm afraid. Sure he's a doctor. He told me. He didn't tell you. How did you know?'

She clenched her fists and her eyes were stormy. 'How dare you cross-examine me like this.'

'Odd,' Petersen said contemplatively. 'You look even more beautiful when you're angry. Well, some women are like that. And why are you angry? Because you've been caught out, that's why.'

'You're smug! You're infuriating! So calm, so reasonable, so sure, so self-satisfied, Mr Clever know-all!'

'My, my. Am I all those things? This must be another Lorraine talking. Why have you taken such offence?'

'But you're not so clever. I *do* know he is a doctor.' She smiled thinly. 'If you were clever you'd remember the conversation in the café last night. You'd remember that it came up that I, too, was born in Pescara. Why should I *not* know him?'

'Lorraine, Lorraine. You're not only treading deep water, you're in over your head. You were not born in Pescara. You weren't born in Italy. You're not even Italian.'

There was silence. Petersen's quiet statement carried complete conviction. Then Sarina, as angry as Lorraine had been a few moments earlier, said: 'Lorraine! Don't listen to him. Don't even talk to him. Can't you see what he's trying to do? To needle you? To trap you? To make you say things you don't mean to say, just to satisfy his great big ego.'

'I *am* making friends this morning,' Petersen said sadly. 'My great big ego notices that Lorraine hasn't contradicted me. That's because she knows that I know. She also knows that I know she's a friend of Carlos. But not from Pescara. Tell me if I'm wrong, Lorraine.'

Lorraine didn't tell him anything. She just caught her lower lip and looked down at the table.

Sarina said: 'I think you're *horrible*.'

'If you equate honesty with horror then, sure, I'm horrible.'

Giacomo was smiling. 'You certainly do

know a lot, don't you, Peter?'

'Not really. I've just learned to learn enough to stay alive.'

Giacomo was still smiling. 'You'll be telling me next that *I'm* not Italian.'

'Not if you don't want me to.'

'You mean I'm not Italian?'

'How can you be if you were born in Yugoslavia? Montenegro, to be precise.'

'Jesus!' Giacomo was no longer smiling, but there was neither rancour nor offence in face or tone. Then he started smiling again.

Sarina looked bleakly at Petersen then turned to Giacomo. 'And what else did this — this — '

'Monster?' Petersen said helpfully.

'This monster. Oh, do be quiet. What other outrage did this man commit last night?'

'Well, now.' Giacomo linked his fingers behind his head and seemed prepared to enjoy himself. 'It all depends upon what you call an outrage. To start with, after he had Cola shot he gassed Alessandro and three other men.'

'Gassed them?' She stared at Giacomo in disbelief.

'*Gassed.* It was their own gas he used. They deserved it.'

'You mean he killed them? *Murdered* them?'

'No, no. They recovered. I know. I was there. Simply,' he added hastily, 'you understand, as an observer. Then he took away their guns, and ammunition, and grenades and a few. other nasty things. Then he locked them up. That's all.'

'That's all.' Sarina breathed deeply, twice. 'When you say it quickly it sounds like nothing, doesn't it? Why did he lock them up?'

'Maybe he didn't want them to have breakfast. How should I know. Ask him.' He looked at Petersen. 'A pretty fair old job of locking up, if I may say so. I just happened along that way as we were coming into port.'

'Ah!'

'Ah, indeed.' Giacomo looked at Sarina. 'You didn't smell any smoke during the night, did you?'

'Smoke? Yes, we did.' She shuddered, remembering. 'We were sick enough already when we smelled it. That was really the end. Why?'

'That was your friend Peter and *his* friends at work. They were welding up the door of Alessandro's cabin.'

'Welding up the door?' A faint note of hysteria had crept into her voice. 'With Alessandro and his men inside! Why on earth — ' She was suddenly at a loss for words.

'I guess he didn't want them to get out.'

The two girls looked at each other in silence. There was nothing more to say. Petersen cleared his throat in a brisk fashion.

'Well, now that's everything satisfactorily explained.' The two girls turned their heads in slow unison and looked at him in total incredulity. 'The past, as they say, is prologue. We'll be leaving in about half an hour or whatever time it takes to obtain some transport. Time to brush your teeth and pack your gear.' He looked at Giacomo. 'You and your friend coming with us?'

'Lorraine, you mean?'

'Got any other friends aboard? Don't stall.'

'All depends where you're going.'

'Same place as you. Don't be cagey.'

'Where are you going?'

'Up the Neretva.'

'We'll come.'

Petersen made to rise when Carlos entered, a piece of paper in his hand. Like Giacomo, he was shaven, brisk and apparently cheerful. He didn't look like a man who hadn't slept all night but then, in his business, he probably slept enough during the day.

'Good morning. You've had breakfast?'

'Our compliments to the chef. That paper for me?'

'It is. Radio signal just come in. Code, so it

doesn't make any sense to me.'

Petersen glanced at it. 'Doesn't make any sense to me either. Not until I get the code book.' He folded the paper and put it in an inside pocket.

'Might it not be urgent?' Carlos said.

'It's from Rome. I've invariably found that whenever Rome thinks something is urgent it's never urgent to me.'

Lorraine said: 'We've just heard that a man has been shot. Is he badly hurt?'

'Cola?' Carlos didn't sound very concerned about Cola's health. 'He thinks he is. I don't. Anyway, I've sent for an ambulance. Should have been here by now.' He looked out of the small window. 'No ambulance. But a couple of soldiers approaching the gangway. If, that is, you could call them soldiers. One's about ninety, the other ten. Probably for you.'

'We'll see.'

Carlos had exaggerated the age disparity between the two soldiers but not by much: the younger was indeed a beardless youth, the older well stricken in years. The latter saluted as smartly as his arthritic bones would permit.

'Captain Tremino. You have a Yugoslav army officer among your passengers?'

Carlos waved a hand. 'Major Petersen.'

'That's the name.' The ancient saluted again. 'Commandant's compliments, sir, and would you be so kind as to see him in his office. You and your two men.'

'Do you know why?'

'The Commandant does not confide in me, sir.'

'How far is it?'

'A few hundred metres. Five minutes.'

'Right away.' Petersen stood and picked up his machine-pistol. George and Alex did the same. The older soldier coughed politely.

'The commandant doesn't like guns in his office.'

'No guns? There is a war in progress, this is a military post, and the commandant doesn't like guns.' He looked at George and Alex, then slipped off his machine-pistol. 'He's probably in his dotage. Let's humour him.'

They left. Carlos watched through the window as they descended the gangway to the quayside. He sighed.

'I can't bear it. I can't. As an Italian, I can't bear it. It's like sending a toothless old hound and a frisky puppy to round up three timber wolves. Sabre-toothed tigers, more like.' He raised his voice. 'Giovanni!'

Sarina said hesitatingly: 'Are they really like that? I mean, I heard a man in Rome yesterday call them that.'

'Ah! My old friend Colonel Lunz, no doubt.'

'You know the Colonel?' There was

surprise in her voice. 'I thought — well, everybody seems to know everything around here. Except me.'

'Of course I know him.' He turned as the lean, dyspeptic looking engineer-chef appeared in the doorway. 'Breakfast, Giovanni, if you would.'

Giacomo said wonderingly: 'You can really eat that stuff?'

'Atrophied taste-buds, a zinc-lined stomach, a little imagination and you could be in Maxim's. Sarina, one does not approach me at the quayside at Termoli, jerk a thumb towards the east and ask for a lift to Yugoslavia. Do you think you'd be aboard the *Colombo* if I didn't know the Colonel? Do you have to be suspicious about everyone?'

'I'm suspicious about our Major Petersen. I don't trust him an inch.'

'That's a fine thing to say about a fellow-countryman.' Carlos sat and buttered bread. 'Honest and straightforward sort of fellow, one would have thought.'

'One would have — look, we've got to go up into the mountains with that man!'

'He seems to know his way around. In fact, I know he does. You should reach your destination all right.'

'Oh, I'm sure. Whose destination — his or ours?'

126

Carlos looked at her in mild exasperation. 'Do you have any option?'

'No.'

'Then why don't you stop wasting your breath?'

'Carlos! How can you talk to her like that?' Lorraine's voice was sharp enough to bring a slightly thoughtful look to Giacomo's face. 'She's worried. Of course she's worried. I'm worried, too. We're both going up into the mountains with that man. You're not.' She was either nervous or had a low temper flash-point. 'It's all very well for you sitting safe and sound here aboard the *Colombo*.'

'Oh, come now,' Giacomo said easily. 'I don't think that's being too fair. I'm quite sure, Carlos, that she didn't mean what she implied.' He looked at Lorraine in mock-reproval. 'I'm sure Carlos would willingly leave his safe and sound ship and accompany you into the mountains. But there are two inhibiting factors. Duty and a tin leg.'

'I *am* sorry.' She was genuinely contrite and put her hand on Carlos' shoulder to show it: Carlos, who was addressing himself to the confection that Giovanni had just brought, looked up at her and smiled amiably. 'Giacomo's right' she said. 'Of course I didn't mean it. It's just that — well, Sarina and I feel so helpless.'

'Giacomo is in the same position. He doesn't look in the slightest bit helpless to me.'

She shook his shoulder in exasperation. 'Please. You don't understand. We don't know what's going on. We don't know *anything*. He seems to know everything.'

'He? Peter?'

'Who else would I be talking about?' For so patrician-looking a lady she could be very snappish. 'Perhaps I can shake you out of your complacency. Do you know that he knows where Giacomo and I are going? Do you know that he seems to know about my background? Do you know that he knows I'm not Italian? That he knows that you and I knew each other in the past, but not in Pescara?'

If Carlos was shaken he concealed it masterfully. 'Peter knows a great number of things that you wouldn't expect him to. Or so Colonel Lunz tells me. For all I know Colonel Lunz told him about you and Giacomo, although that wouldn't be like the Colonel. He may have expected you aboard. He didn't seem annoyed by your presence.'

'He was annoyed enough by Alessandro's presence.'

'He wouldn't know about Alessandro. Alessandro is controlled by another agency.'

She said quickly: 'How do you know that?'

'He — Peter — told me.'

She removed her hand and straightened. 'So. You and Peter have your little secrets too.' She turned to Sarina. 'We can trust everybody, can't we?'

Giacomo said: 'Carlos, you're beginning to look like a hen-pecked husband.'

'I'm beginning to feel like one, too. My dear girl, I only learnt this during the night. What did you expect me to do? Come hammering on your cabin door at four in the morning to announce this earth-shaking news to you and Sarina?' He looked up as the dyspeptic engineer-chef appeared again in the doorway.

'Breakfast has been served, Carlos.'

'Thank you, Giovanni.' He looked at Lorraine. 'And before you start getting suspicious of Giovanni he only means that he's given food to our friends in the fore cabin.'

'I thought the door was locked.'

'Oh dear, oh dear.' Carlos laid down knife and fork. 'Suspicious again. The door *is* locked. Breakfast was lowered in a bucket to their cabin porthole.'

'When are you going to see them?'

'When I'm ready. When I've had breakfast.' Carlos picked up his knife and fork again. 'If I get peace to eat it, that is.'

George said: 'Took a bit of a risk back there, didn't you? Chanced your arm, as they say, pretending you knew all about their plans and backgrounds when you knew nothing.'

'Credit's all yours, George. Just based on a couple of remarks of yours about ethnic background. Couldn't very well tell them that, though. Besides, Lorraine gave away more than I extracted. I don't think she'd make a very good espionage agent.'

They were threading their way through cranes, trucks, both army and civilian, and scattered dock buildings, a few yards behind the two Italian soldiers. The snow had stopped now, the Rilić hills were sheltering them from the north-east wind but the temperature was still below freezing point. There were few enough people around, the early hour and the cold were not such as to encourage outdoor activity. The soldiers, as Carlos had said, were either reservists or youths. The few civilians around were in the same age categories. There didn't seem to be a young or middle-aged man in the port.

'At least,' George said, 'you've established a kind of moral ascendancy over them. Well, over the young ladies, anyway. Giacomo doesn't lend himself to that sort of thing.

That paper Carlos gave you — a message from our Roman allies?'

'Yes. We are requested to remain in Ploče and await further orders.'

'Ridiculous.'

'Isn't it?'

'You think sending that cablegram was wise? We might have expected this.'

'I did. I hoped to precipitate exactly this. We know what to expect and we've got the initiative. If we'd got clear of the port without trouble and then were stopped by a couple of tanks up the valley road we'd have lost the initiative. Our two guards in front there — they're not very bright, are they?'

'You mean they didn't search us for handguns? One's too old to care, the other's too inexperienced to know. Besides, look at our honest faces.'

The two guards led the way to a low wooden hut, obviously a temporary affair, up some steps and, after knocking, into a small room about as spartan and primitive as the exterior of the hut — cracked linoleum on the floor, two metal filing cabinets, a radio transceiver, a telephone, a table and some chairs. The officer behind the table rose at their entrance. He was a tall thin man, middle-aged, with pebble glasses which explained clearly enough why he wasn't at the front. He peered at them myopically over the tops of his glasses.

'Major Petersen?'

'Yes. Glad to meet you, Commandant.'

'Oh. I see. I wonder.' He cleared his throat. 'I have just received a detention order — '

'Ssh!' Petersen had a finger to his lips. He lowered his voice: 'Are we alone?'

'We are.'

'Quite sure?'

'Quite sure.'

'In that case put your hands up.'

★   ★   ★

Carlos pushed his chair back and rose. 'Excuse me. I must have a look at that cabin door.'

Lorraine said: 'You mean you haven't seen it yet?'

'No. If Peter says it's welded, then it is. I should imagine one welded door looks very much like another. Curiosity, really.'

He was back in just over a minute.

'A welded door is a welded door and the only way to open it is with an oxyacetylene flame-cutter. I've sent Pietro ashore to try and find one. I don't have much hope. We had one but Peter and his friends dropped it over the side.'

Lorraine said: 'You don't seem worried about it.'

'I don't get worried about trifles.'

'And if you can't get them out?'

'They'll have to stay there till we get back to Termoli. Plenty of facilities there.'

'You could be sunk before you get there. Have you thought of that?'

'Yes. That would upset me.'

'Well, that's better. A little compassion, at least.'

'It would upset me because I've really grown quite fond of this old boat. I would hate to think it would be Alessandro's tomb.' Carlos' face and voice were cold. 'Compassion? Compassion for that monster? Compassion for a murderer, a hired assassin, a poisoner who travels with hypodermics and ampoules of lethal liquids? Compassion for a psychopath who would just love to inject you or Sarina there and giggle his evil head off as you screamed your way to death? Peter spared him: I wish he'd killed him. Compassion!' He turned and walked out.

'And now you've upset him,' Giacomo said. 'Nag, nag, nag. It's bloody marvellous. People — well, Peter and Carlos — tried, judged and condemned when you don't have the faintest idea what you're talking about.'

'I didn't mean anything.' She seemed bewildered.

'It's not what you mean. It's what you say. You could always try watching your tongue.' He rose and left.

Lorraine stared at the empty doorway, her face woebegone. Two large tears trickled slowly down her cheeks. Sarina put her arm around her shoulders.

'It's all right,' she said. 'It really is. They don't understand. I do.'

★   ★   ★

Ten minutes later Petersen and his two companions arrived. Petersen was driving an elderly truck, civilian not army, with a hooped canvas roof and canvas flaps at the rear. Petersen jumped down from the driving seat and looked at the five on the deck of the *Colombo* — Carlos, Giacomo, Lorraine, Michael and Sarina, the last four with their rucksacks and radios beside them.

'Well, we're ready when you are,' Petersen said. He seemed in excellent spirits. 'We'll just come aboard for our gear.'

'No need,' Carlos said. 'The two Pietros are bringing that.'

'And our guns?'

'I wouldn't want you to feel undressed.' Carlos led the way down the gangway. 'How did things go?'

'Couldn't have been better. Very friendly, cooperative and helpful.' He produced two papers. 'A military pass and a permit for me to drive this vehicle. Only as far as Metković but it will at least get us on the way. Both signed by Major Massamo. Would you two young ladies come up front with me? It's much more comfortable and the cab is heated. The back is not.'

'Thank you,' Lorraine said. 'I'd rather sit in the back.'

'Oh, no, she wouldn't,' Sarina said. 'I'm not putting up with this walking inquisition all by myself.' She took Lorraine's arm and whispered in her ear while Petersen lifted patient eyes to heaven. At first Lorraine shook her head vigorously, then reluctantly nodded.

They shook hands with Carlos, thanked him and said goodbye. All except Lorraine — she just stood there, her eyes on the dockside. Carlos looked at her in exasperation then said: 'All right. You upset me and I, forgetting that I'm supposed to be an officer and a gentleman, upset you.' He put his arm round her shoulders, gave her a brief hug and kissed her none too lightly on the cheek. 'That's by way of apology and goodbye.'

Petersen started up the rather asthmatic engine and drove off. The elderly guard at the gate ignored Petersen's proffered papers and lackadaisically waved them on: he probably didn't want to leave the brazier in his sentry-box. As he drove on, Petersen glanced to his right. Lorraine, at the far end of the seat was staring straight ahead: her face was masked in tears. Petersen, frowning, leaned forward and sideways but was brought up short by a far from gentle elbow in the ribs. Sarina, too, was frowning and giving an almost imperceptible shake of the head. Petersen looked at her questioningly, got a stony glance in return and sat back to concentrate on his driving.

★　★　★

In the back of the truck, already heavily polluted by George's cigars, Giacomo kept glancing towards the tarpaulin-covered heap in the front. Eventually, he tapped George on the arm.

'George?'

'Yes.'

'Have you ever seen a tarpaulin moving of its own accord?'

'Can't say that I have.'

'Well, I can see one now.'

George followed the direction of the pointing finger. 'I see what you mean. My goodness, I hope they're not suffocating under that lot.' He pulled back the tarpaulin to reveal three figures lying on their sides, securely bound at wrists and ankles and very effectively gagged. 'They're not suffocating at all. Just getting restless.'

The light inside the back of the truck was dim but sufficient to let Giacomo recognize the elderly soldier and his very junior partner who had come aboard earlier in the morning to collect Petersen and the other two. 'And who's the other person?'

'Major Massamo. Commandant — Deputy Commandant, I believe — of the port.'

Michael, seated with Alex on the opposite side of the truck, said: 'Who are those people? What are they doing here? Why are they tied up?' The questions didn't betray any real interest: the voice was dull as befitted one still in a state of dazed incomprehension. They were the first words he had spoken that day: sea-sickness and the traumatic experience he had undergone during the night had wrought their toll to the extent that he had not even been able to face breakfast.

'The Port Commandant and two of his soldiers,' George said. 'They are here because we couldn't very well leave them behind to raise the alarm the moment we were gone, and we couldn't very well shoot them, could we? And they're bound and gagged because we couldn't very well have them raising a song and dance on the way out of the harbour. You do ask stupid questions, Michael.'

'This is the Major Massamo that Major Petersen mentioned? How did you manage to get him to sign those permits you have?'

'You, Michael, have a suspicious mind. It doesn't become you. He didn't sign them. I did. There were lots of notices in his room all signed by him. You don't have to be a skilled forger to copy a signature.'

'What's going to happen to them?'

'We will dispose of them at a convenient time and place.'

'Dispose of them?'

'They'll be back in Ploče, safe and unharmed, this evening. Good heavens, Michael, you don't go around shooting your allies.'

Michael looked at three bound and gagged men. 'Yes. I see. Allies.'

★   ★   ★

They were stopped at roadblocks at the next two villages but the questioning was very perfunctory and routine. At the third village, Bagalović, Petersen pulled up by a temporary army filling station, descended, gave some papers to the corporal in attendance, waited until the truck had been fuelled, gave the corporal some money for which he was rewarded by a surprised salute, then drove off again.

Sarina said: 'They don't look like soldiers to me. They don't behave like soldiers. They seem so — so — what is the word? — apathetic.'

'A marked lack of enthusiasm, agreed. Their behaviour doesn't show them up in the best of light, does it? The Italians can, in fact, be very very good soldiers, but not in this war. They have no heart for it, in spite of Mussolini's stirring, martial speeches. The people didn't want this war in the first place and they want it less and less as time goes by. Their front-line troops fight well enough, but not from patriotism, just professional pride. But it's convenient for us.'

'What were those papers you gave to that soldier?'

'Diesel coupons. Major Massamo gave them to me.'

'Major Massamo gave them to you. Free fuel, of course. That tip you handed to the soldier. I suppose Major Massamo gave you the money as well?'

'Of course not. We don't steal.'

'Just trucks and fuel coupons. Or have you

just borrowed those?'

'Temporarily. The truck, anyway.'

'Which, of course, you will return to Major Massamo?'

Petersen spared her a glance. 'You're supposed to be apprehensive, nervous, not full of nosey questions. I don't much care to be cross-examined. We're supposed to be on the same side, remember? As for the truck, I'm afraid the Major won't be seeing it again.'

They drove on in silence and after another fifteen minutes ran into the town of Metković. Petersen parked the truck in the main street and stepped down to the roadway. Sarina said: 'Forgotten something, haven't you?'

'What?'

'Your keys. You've left them in the ignition.'

'Please don't be silly.' Petersen crossed the street and disappeared into a store.

Lorraine spoke for the first time since leaving Ploče. 'What did he mean by that?'

'What he says. He knows so much that he probably knows I can't drive anyway. Certainly not this rackety old monster. Even if I could, what place would I have to drive to?' She touched the back of the cab. 'Wood. I couldn't get five yards — that fearful Alex could shoot through that.' She looked and sounded doleful in the extreme.

140

Lorraine said: 'Wouldn't it be nice to see him, just once, make a mistake, do something wrong?'

'I'd love it. But I don't think we should want it. I have the feeling that what is good for Major Petersen is good for us. And vice versa.'

★ ★ ★

Twenty minutes elapsed before Petersen returned. For a man who might have been regarded as being on the run, he was in no hurry. He was carrying a large wicker basket, its contents covered with brown paper. This he took round to the back of the truck. Moments later he was back in the driving seat. He seemed in good humour.

'Well, go on,' he said. 'Ask away.'

Sarina made a moue, but curiosity won. 'The basket.'

'An army marches on its stomach. Stretch a point and you might regard us as part of an army. Provisions. What else would I have been buying in a food store? Bread, cheese, hams, various meats, goulash, fruits, vegetables, tea, coffee, sugar, a spirit stove, kettle and stewpan. I promised Colonel Lunz to deliver you in fairly good condition.'

In spite of herself, she smiled faintly. 'You

141

sound as if you wanted to deliver us in prime condition at a slave market. Overlooked your fat friend, didn't you?'

'My first purchase. George had the top off a litre flask of beer within five seconds. Wine, too.'

They cleared the outskirts of the town. Sarina said: 'I thought the permit took you only as far as Metković?'

'I have two permits. I showed only one to Carlos.'

Half an hour later Petersen recrossed the Neretva and pulled up at a fairly large garage on the outskirts of Čapljina. Petersen went inside and returned in a few minutes.

'Just saying 'hallo' to an old friend.'

They passed through the village of Trebižat and not long afterwards Petersen pulled off the highway and turned up a secondary road, climbing fairly steeply as they went. From this they turned on to yet another road which was no more than a grass track, still climbing, until they finally rounded and came to a halt about fifty yards from a low stone building. They could approach no further because the road ended where they were.

They dismounted from the cab and went round to the back of the truck. Petersen tweaked back one of the canvas flaps. 'Lunch,' he said.

Perhaps a minute passed without any signs of activity. Sarina and Lorraine looked at each other in a puzzled apprehension which was in no way lessened by Petersen's air of relaxed calm.

'When George ties a knot,' Petersen said cryptically, 'it takes a fair deal of untying.'

Suddenly the flaps were parted and Major Massamo and his two soldiers, untied and ungagged, were lowered from the tailboard. Massamo and the older soldier collapsed dramatically immediately on touching the ground.

''Who have we here and what have the wicked Petersen and his evil friends done to those poor men',' Petersen said. The young soldier had now joined the two others in a sitting position on the ground. 'Well, the officer is Major Massamo, the Port Commandant, and the other two you have already seen. We have not broken their legs or anything like that. They're just suffering from a temporary loss of circulation.' The other four men in the back of the truck had now jumped to the ground. 'Walk them around a bit, will you?' Petersen said.

George lifted the Major, Giacomo the young soldier, and Michael the elderly soldier. But the last was not only old but fat and didn't seem at all keen to get to his feet.

Sarina gave Petersen what was probably intended to be a withering glance and moved to help her brother. Petersen looked at Lorraine and then at George.

'What shall we do?' His voice was low. 'Stab her or club her?'

Not a muscle flickered in George's face. He appeared to ponder. 'Either. Plenty of ravines hereabouts.'

Lorraine looked at them in perplexity: Serbo-Croat, evidently, was not her language.

Petersen said: 'I can understand now why the boyfriend is along. Bodyguard *and* interpeter. I know who she is.'

'So do I.'

Lorraine could be irritated and imperious at the same time and she was good at being both.

'What are you two talking about? It *is* bad manners, you know.' In another day and age she would have stamped her foot.

'It is our native language. No offence. My dear Lorraine, you would make life so much easier for yourself if you stopped being suspicious of everyone. And yes, we were talking about you.'

'I thought as much.' But her voice was a shade less assertive.

'Just try to trust people occasionally.' Petersen smiled to rob his words of any offence. 'We're as much looker-afterers as your Giacomo is. Will you please understand that we want to take care of you. If anything were to happen to you, Jamie Harrison would never forgive us.'

'Jamie Harrison! You know Jamie Harrison.' Her eyes had widened and a half-smile touched her lips. 'I don't believe it. You know Captain Harrison!'

''Jamie' to you.'

'Jamie.' She looked at George. 'Do you know him?'

'Tush, tush! Suspicions again. If Peter says he knows him then I must know him. Isn't that so?' He smiled as colour touched her cheeks. 'My dear, I don't blame you. Of course I know him. Tall, very tall. Lean. Brown beard.'

'He didn't have a brown beard when I knew him.'

'He has now. And a moustache. Brown hair, anyway. And, as they say in English, he's terribly terribly English. Wears a monocle. Sports it, I should say. Claims he needs it, but he doesn't. Just English.'

She smiled. 'It couldn't be anyone else.'

Major Massamo and his two men, their grimaces bespeaking their still returning circulation, were now at least partially mobile. Petersen retrieved the heavy wicker basket from the back of the truck and led the way up grass-cut steps to the stone hut and produced a key. Sarina looked at the key, then at Petersen but said nothing.

Petersen caught her glance. 'I told you. Friends.' The combination of the creaking hinges as the door swung open and the musty smell from within was indication enough that the place hadn't been used for months. The single room, which made up the entire hut, was icy, bleak and sparsely furnished: a deal table, two benches, a few rickety wooden chairs, a stove and a pile of cordwood.

'Be it ever so humble,' Petersen said briskly. 'First things first.' He looked at George who had just extracted a bottle of beer from the basket. 'You have your priorities right?'

'I have a savage thirst,' George said with dignity. 'I can slake that and light a stove at the same time.'

'You'll look after our guests? I have a call to make.'

'Half an hour. I hope.'

*　*　*

It was an hour later when Petersen returned. George was no believer in doing things by half and by that time the hut was a great deal

146

more than pleasantly warm. The top of the stove glowed a bright cherry red and the room was stiflingly hot. Petersen pointedly left the door open and set on the table a second wicker basket he had brought with him.

'More provisions. Sorry I'm late.'

'We weren't worried,' George said. 'Food's ready when you are. We've eaten.' He peered inside the basket Petersen had brought. 'Took you all that time to get that?'

'I met some friends.'

Sarina said from the doorway. 'Where's the truck?'

'Round the corner. Among trees. Can't be seen from the air.'

'You think they're carrying out an air search for us?'

'No. One doesn't take chances.' He sat at the table and made himself a cheese and salami sandwich. 'Anyone who needs some sleep had better have it now. I'm going to have some myself. We didn't have any last night. Two or three hours. Besides, I prefer to travel at night.'

'And I prefer to sleep at night,' George said. He reached out for another bottle. 'Let me be your trusty guard. Enjoy yourself. We did.'

'After Giovanni's cooking anyone would be ravenous.'

Petersen set about proving that he was no exception. After a few minutes he looked up, looked around and said to George: 'Where have those pesky girls gone to?'

'Just left. For a walk, I suppose.'

Petersen shook his head. 'My fault. I didn't tell you.' He rose and went outside. The two girls were about forty yards away.

'Come back!' he called. They stopped and turned around. He waved a peremptory arm. 'Come back.' They looked at each other and slowly began to retrace their steps.

George was puzzled. 'What's wrong with a harmless walk?'

Petersen lowered his voice so that he couldn't be heard inside the hut. 'I'll tell you what's wrong with a harmless walk.' He told him briefly and George nodded. He stopped talking as the girls approached.

Sarina said: 'What is it? What's wrong?'

Petersen nodded to a small outhouse some yards from the cabin. 'If that's what you're looking for — '

'No. Just a walk. What's the harm?'

'Get inside.'

'If you say so.' Sarina smiled at him sweetly. 'Would it kill you to tell us why?'

'Other ranks don't talk to officers in that tone. The fact that you're females doesn't alter a thing.' Sarina had stopped smiling, Petersen's own tone was not such as to encourage levity. 'I'll tell you why. Because I say so. Because you can't do anything without my permission. Because you're babes in the woods. And because I'll trust you when you trust me.' The two girls looked at each other in incomprehension then went inside without a word.

'A bit harsh, I would have thought,' George said.

'You and your middle-aged susceptibility. Sure, it was a bit harsh. I just wanted them to get the message that they don't wander without permission. They could have made it damned awkward for us.'

'I suppose so. Of course I know they could. But they don't know they could have. For them, you're just a big, bad, bullying wolf and a nasty one to boot. Irrational, they think you are. Orders for orders' sake. Never mind, Peter, when they come to appreciate your sterling qualities, they may yet come to love you.'

Inside the hut, Petersen said: 'Nobody is to go outside, please. George and Alex of course. And, yes, Giacomo.'

Giacomo, seated on a bench by the table, lifted a drowsy head from his folded arms. 'Giacomo's not going anywhere.'

149

Michael said: 'Not me?'

'No.'

'Then why Giacomo?

Petersen was curt. 'You're not Giacomo.'

★ ★ ★

Petersen woke two hours later and shook his head to clear it. As far as he could tell only the indefatigable George, a beaker of beer to hand, and the three captives were awake. Petersen got up and shook the others.

'We're going shortly. Time for tea, coffee, wine or what you will and then we're off.' He started to feed cordwood into the stove.

Major Massamo, who had kept remarkably quiet since his gag had been taken off, said: 'We're going with you?'

'You're staying here. Bound, but not gagged — you can shout your heads off but no-one will hear you.' He raised a hand to forestall a protest. 'No, you won't perish of cold during the long watches of the night. You'll be more than warm enough until help comes. About an hour after we leave I'll phone the nearest army post — it's only about five kilometres from here — and tell them where you are. They should be here within fifteen minutes of getting the call.'

'You're very kind, I'm sure.' Massamo

smiled wanly. 'It's better than being shot out of hand.'

'The Royal Yugoslav Army takes orders from no-one, and that includes Germans and Italians. When our allies prove to be obstructive we're forced to take some action to protect ourselves. But we don't shoot them. We're not barbarians.'

A short time later Petersen looked at the three freshly-bound captives. 'The stove is stoked, there's no possibility of sparks, so you won't burn to death. You'll certainly be freed inside an hour and a half. Goodbye.'

None of the three prisoners said 'goodbye' to him.

Petersen led the way down the grassy steps and round the first corner. The truck was standing in a small clearing without a tree near it. Sarina said: 'Ooh! A *new* truck.'

'"Ooh! A *new* truck",' Petersen mimicked. 'Which is exactly what you would have said when you'd come back to the hut after finding it. It's as I say, you can't trust babes in the woods. Major Massamo would just have loved to hear you say that. He would then have known that we had ditched the old truck and would have called off the hunt for the old truck — there must be a search under way by now — and, when freed, ask for a search for another missing truck and broadcast its details. It's most unlikely, but it could have happened and then I'd have been forced to lumber myself with Massamo again.'

Giacomo said: 'Someone might stumble across the old one?'

'Not unless someone takes it into his head to go diving into the freezing Neretva River. And why on earth should anyone be daft enough to do that? I drove it off only a very small cliff but the water is deep there. A local fisherman told me.'

'Can it be seen underwater?'

'No. At this time of year the waters of the Neretva are brown and turgid. In a few months' time, when the snow in the mountains melts, then the river runs green and clear. Who worries about what happens in a few months' time?'

George said: 'What kindly soul gave you this nice new model? Not, I take it, the Italian army?'

'Hardly. My fisherman friend, who also happens to be the proprietor of the garage I stopped at on the way up here. The army has no local repair facilities here and he does the occasional repair job for them. He had a few civilian trucks he could have offered me but we both thought this was much more suitable and official.'

'Won't your friend be held answerable for this?'

'Not at all. We've already wrenched off the padlock at the rear of the garage just in case some soldier happens by tomorrow, which is most unlikely, as it is Sunday. Come Monday morning, as a good collaborator should, he'll go to the Italian army authorities and report a case of breaking, entering and theft of one army motor vehicle. No blame will attach to him. The culprits are obvious. Who else could it be but us?'

Sarina said, 'And come Monday morning? When the search starts?'

'Come Monday morning this truck will probably have joined the old one. Whatever happens, we'll be a long way away from it by then.'

'You *are* devious.'

'You're being silly again. This is what you call forward planning. Get inside.'

The new truck was rather more comfortable and much quieter than the old one. As they drove off, Sarina said: 'I'm not carping or criticizing but — well, you do have rather a cavalier attitude towards the property of your allies.'

Petersen glanced at her then returned his attention to the road. '*Our* allies.'

'What? Oh! Yes, of course. Our allies.'

Petersen kept looking ahead. He could have become suddenly thoughtful but it was impossible to tell. Petersen's expression did what he told it to do. He said: 'That mountain inn yesterday. Lunchtime. Remember what George said?'

'Remember — how could I? He says so much — all the time. Said about what?'

'Our allies.'

'Vaguely.'

'Vaguely.' He clucked his tongue in disapproval. 'This augurs ill. A radio operator — any operative — should remember everything that is said. Our alliance is simply a temporary measure of convenience and expediency. We are fighting *with* the Italians — George said 'Germans' but it's the same thing — not *for* them. We are fighting for ourselves. When they have served their purpose it will be time for them to be gone. In the meantime, a conflict of interests has arisen between the Italians and the Germans on the one hand and us on the other. Our interests come first. Pity about the trucks but the loss of one or two isn't going to win or lose the war.'

There was a short silence then Lorraine said: 'Who *is* going to win this dreadful war, Major Petersen?'

'We are. I'd rather you'd just call me Peter.

As long as you're otherwise civil, that is.'

The two girls exchanged glances. If Petersen saw the exchange he gave no signs.

* * *

In Čapljina, in the deepening dusk, they were halted at an army roadblock. A young officer approached, shone his torch at a piece of paper in his hand, switched it to the truck's plates, then played it across the windscreen. Petersen leaned out of the window.

'Don't shine that damned light in our eyes!' he shouted angrily.

The light beam dipped immediately.

'Sorry, sir. Routine check. Wrong truck.' He stepped back, saluted and waved them on. Petersen drove off.

'I didn't like that,' Sarina said. 'What happens when your luck runs out? And why did he let us through so easily?'

'A young man with taste, sensibility and discretion,' Petersen said. 'Who is he, he said to himself, to interfere with an army officer carrying on a torrid affair with two beautiful young ladies. The hunt, however, is on. The paper he held had the number of the old truck. Then he checked driver and passengers, a most unusual thing. He had been warned to look out for three desperadoes.

Anyone can see that I'm perfectly respectable and neither of you could be confused with a fat and thin desperado.'

'But they must know we're with you.'

'No 'must' about it. They will, soon enough, but not yet. The only two people who knew that you were aboard the ship were the two who are still tied up in the hut back there.'

'Somebody may have asked questions at the *Colombo*.'

'Possibly. I doubt it. Even if they had, no member of the crew would divulge anything without Carlos' okay. He has that kind of relationship with them.'

Sarina said doubtfully: 'Carlos might tell them.'

'Carlos wouldn't volunteer anything. He might have a struggle with his conscience but it would be a brief one and duty would lose out: he's not going to sell his old girlfriend down the river, especially, as is like enough, there would be shooting.'

Lorraine leaned forward and looked at him. 'Who's supposed to be the girlfriend? Me?'

'A flight of fancy. You know how I ramble on.'

★   ★   ★

Twice more they were stopped at roadblocks, both times without incident. Some minutes after the last check, Petersen pulled into a lay-by.

'I'd like you to get in the back, now, please. It's colder there but my fisherman friend did give me some blankets.'

Sarina said: 'Why?'

'Because from now on you might be recognized. I don't think it likely but let's cater for the unlikely. Your descriptions will be out any minute now.'

'How can they be out until Major Massamo — ' She broke off and looked at her watch. 'You said you'd phone the army post at Čapljina in an hour. That was an hour and twenty minutes ago. Those men will freeze. Why did you lie — '

'If you can't think, and you obviously can't, at least shut up. Just a little, white, necessary lie. What would have happened if I phoned now or had done in the past twenty minutes?'

'They'd have sent out a rescue party.'

'That all?'

'What else?'

'Heaven help Yugoslavia. They'd have traced the call and know roughly where I am. The call *was* sent on the hour by my friend. From Gruda, on the Čapljina-Imotski road away to the northwest of here. What more natural than we should be making for Imotski — an Italian division is headquartered there. So they'll concentrate their search on the Imotski area. There's an awful lot of places — buildings, store-houses, trucks — where a person can hide in a divisional headquarters, and as the Italians like the Germans about as much as they like the Yugoslavs — and the order for my detention comes from the German HQ in Rome — I don't suppose they'll conduct the search with any great enthusiasm. They *may* have double-guessed — I don't think they'd even bother trying — but go in the back anyway.'

Petersen descended, saw them safely hoisted aboard the rear of the track, returned to the cab and drove off.

He passed two more roadblocks — in both cases he was waved on without stopping — before arriving at the town of Mostar. He drove into the middle of the town, crossed the river, turned right by the Hotel Bristol and two minutes later pulled up and stopped the engine. He went round to the back of the track.

'Please remain inside,' he said. 'I should be back in fifteen minutes.'

Giacomo said: 'Are we permitted to know where we are?'

'Certainly. In a public car park in Mostar.'

'Isn't that rather a public place?' It was, inevitably, Sarina.

'The more public the better. If you really want to hide, there's no place like hiding in the open.'

George said: 'You won't forget to tell Josip that I've had nothing to eat or drink for days?'

'I don't have to tell him. He's always known that.'

★　★　★

When Petersen returned it was in a small fourteen-seater Fiat bus which had seen its heyday in the middle twenties. The driver was a small, lean man with a swarthy complexion, a ferocious black moustache, glittering eyes and a seemingly boundless source of energy.

'This is Josip,' Petersen said. Josip greeted George and Alex with great enthusiasm, they were obviously acquaintances of old standing. Petersen didn't bother to introduce him to the others. 'Get your stuff into the bus. We're using the bus because Josip doesn't care too much to have an Italian army lorry parked outside the front door of his hotel.'

'Hotel?' Sarina said. 'We're going to stay in a *hotel?*'

'When you travel with us,' George said

159

expansively, 'you may expect nothing but the best.'

The hotel, when they arrived there, didn't look like the best. The approach to it could not have been more uninviting. Josip parked the bus in a garage and led the way along a narrow winding lane that was not even wide enough to accommodate a car, fetching up at a heavy wooden door.

'Back entrance,' Petersen said. 'Josip runs a perfectly respectable hotel but he doesn't care to attract too much attention by bringing so many people in at once.'

They passed through a short passage into the reception area, small but bright and clean.

'Now then.' Josip rubbed his hands briskly, he was that kind of man. 'If you'll just bring your luggage, I'll show you to your rooms. Wash and brush up, then dinner.' He spread his hands. 'No Ritz, but at least you won't go to bed hungry.'

'I can't face the stairs, yet,' George said. He nodded towards an archway. 'I think I'll just go and rest quietly in there.'

'Barman's off tonight, Professor. You'll have to help yourself.'

'I can take the rough with the smooth.'

'This way, ladies.'

In the corridor upstairs Sarina turned to

Petersen and said in a low voice: 'Why did your friend call George 'Professor'?'

'Lots of people call him that. A nickname. You can see why. He's always pontificating.'

★　★　★

Dinner was rather more than Josip had promised it would be but, then, Bosnian innkeepers are renowned for their inventiveness and resourcefulness, not to mention acquisitiveness. Considering the ravaged and war-stricken state of the country, the meal was a near miracle: Dalmatian ham, grey mullet with an excellent Pošip white wine and, astonishingly, venison accompanied by one of the renowned Neretva red wines. George, after remarking, darkly, that one never knew what the uncertain future held for them, thereafter remained silent for an unprecedented fifteen minutes: no mean trencherman at the best of times, his current exercise in gastronomy bordered on the awesome.

Apart from George, his two companions and their host, Marija, Josip's wife, was also at the table. Small, dark and energetic like her husband, she was in other ways in marked contrast to him: he was intense, she was vivacious: he was taciturn, she was talkative to the point of garrulity. She looked at Michael and Sarina, seated some distance away at one small table, and at Giacomo and Lorraine, seated about the same distance away, at another, and lowered her voice.

'Your friends are very quiet.'

George swallowed some venison. 'It's the food.'

'They're talking, all right,' Petersen said. 'You just can't hear them over the champing noise George is making. But you're right, they are talking very softly.'

Josip said: 'Why? Why do they have to murmur or whisper? There's nothing to be afraid of here. Nobody can hear them except us.'

'You heard what George said. They don't know what the future holds for them. This is a whole new experience for them — not, of course, for Giacomo, but for the other three. They're apprehensive and from their point of view they have every right to be. For all they know, tomorrow may be their last day on earth.'

'It could be yours, too,' Josip said. 'The word in the market-place — we hoteliers spend a lot of time in the market-place — is that groups of Partisans have by-passed the Italian garrison at Prozor, moved down the Rama valley and are in the hills overlooking the road between here and Jablanica. They may even be astride the road: they're crazy enough for anything. What are your plans for tomorrow? If, I may add hastily, one may ask.'

'Why ever not? We'll have to take to the mountains by and by of course, but those three young people don't look much like mountain goats to me so we'll stick as long as possible to the truck and the road. The road to Jablanica, that is.'

'And if you run into the Partisans?'

'Tomorrow can look after itself.'

At the end of the meal, Giacomo and Lorraine rose and crossed to the main table. Lorraine said: 'I tried to have a walk, stretch my legs, this afternoon, but you stopped me. I'd like to have one now. Do you mind?'

'Yes. I mean, I do mind. At the moment, this is very much a frontier town. You're young, beautiful and the streets, as the saying goes, are full of licentious soldiery. Even if a patrol stops you, you don't speak a word of the language. Besides, it's bitterly cold.'

'Since when did you begin to worry about my health?' She was back to being her imperious self again. 'Giacomo will look after me. What you mean is, you still don't trust me.'

'Well, yes, there's that to it also.'

'What do you expect me to do? Run away? Report you to — to the authorities? What authorities? There *is* nothing I can do.'

'I know that. I'm concerned solely with your own welfare.'

Beautiful girls are not much given to snorting in disbelief but she came close. 'Thank you.'

'I'll come along with you.'

'No, thank you. I don't want you.'

'You see,' George said, 'she doesn't even like you.' He pushed back his chair. 'But everyone likes George. Big, cheerful, likeable George. I'll come along with you.'

'I don't want you either.'

Petersen coughed. Josip said: 'The Major is right, you know, young lady. This *is* a dangerous town after dark. Your Giacomo looks perfectly capable of protecting anyone, but there are streets in this town where even the army police patrols won't venture. I know where it's safe to go and where it isn't.'

She smiled. 'You are very kind.'

Sarina said: 'Mind if we come, too?'

'Of course not.'

All five, Michael included, buttoned up in their heavy coats and went out, leaving Petersen and his two companions behind. George shrugged his shoulders and sighed.

'To think I used to be the most popular

person in Yugoslavia. That was before I met you, of course. Shall we retire?'

'So soon?'

'Through the archway, I meant.' George led the way and ensconced himself behind the bar counter. 'Strange young lady. Lorraine, that is. I muse aloud. Why did she sally forth into the dark and dangerous night. She hardly strikes one as a fresh-air fiend or fitness fanatic.'

'Neither does Sarina. Two strange young ladies.'

George reached for a bottle of red wine. 'Let us concede that the vagaries of womankind, especially young womankind, are beyond us and concentrate more profitably on this vintage '38.'

Alex said suddenly: 'I don't think they're all that strange.'

Petersen and George gave him their attention. Alex spoke so seldom, far less ventured an opinion, that he was invariably listened to when he did speak.

George said: 'Can it be, Alex, that you have observed something that has escaped our attention?'

'Yes. You see, I don't talk as much as you do.' The words sounded offensive but weren't meant to be, they were simply by way of explanation. 'When you're talking I look and listen and learn, while you're listening to yourselves talking. The two young ladies seem to have become very friendly. I think they've become too friendly too quickly. Maybe they really like each other, I don't know. What I do know is that they don't trust each other. I am sure that Lorraine went out to learn something. I don't know what. I think Sarina thought the same thing and wanted to find out, so she's gone to watch.'

George nodded a judicious head. 'A closely reasoned argument. What do you think they both went out to learn?'

'How should I know?' Alex sounded mildly irritable. 'I just watch. You're the ones who are supposed to think.'

★ ★ ★

The two girls and their escorts were back even before the three men had finished their bottle of wine, which meant that they had returned in very short order indeed. The two girls and Michael were already slightly bluish with cold and Lorraine's teeth were positively chattering.

'Pleasant stroll?' Petersen said politely.

'Very pleasant,' Lorraine said. Clearly, she hadn't forgiven him for whatever sin he was supposed to have committed. 'I've just come

166

to say goodnight. What time do we leave in the morning?'

'Six o'clock.'

'Six o'clock!'

'If that's too late — '

She ignored him and turned to Sarina. 'Coming?'

'In a moment.'

Lorraine left and George said, 'For a nightcap, Sarina, I can recommend this Maraschino from Zadar. After a lifetime — '

She ignored him as Lorraine had ignored Petersen, to whom she now turned and said: 'You lied to me.'

'Dear me. What a thing to say.'

'George here. His 'nickname'. The Professor. Because, you said, he was loquacious — '

'I did not. 'Pontificated' was the word I used.'

'Don't quibble! Nickname! Dean of the Faculty of Languages and Professor of Occidental Languages at Belgrade University!'

'My word!' Petersen said admiringly. 'You are clever. How did you find out?'

She smiled. 'I just asked Josip.'

'Well done for you. Must have come as a shock. I mean, you had him down as the janitor, didn't you?'

She stopped smiling and a faint colour

touched her cheeks. 'I did not. And why did you lie?'

'No lie, really. It's quite unimportant. It's just that George doesn't like to boast of his modest academic qualifications. He's never reached the dizzying heights of a degree in economics and politics in Cairo University.'

She coloured again, more deeply, then smiled, a faint smile, but a smile. 'I didn't even qualify. I didn't deserve that.'

'That's true. Sorry.'

She turned to George. 'But what are you doing — I mean, a common soldier — '

Behind the bar, George drew himself up with dignity. 'I'm a very uncommon soldier.'

'Yes. But I mean — a dean, a professor — '

George shook his head sadly. 'Hurling pluperfect subjunctives at the enemy trenches never won a battle yet.'

Sarina stared at him then turned to Petersen. 'What on earth does he mean?'

'He's back in the groves of academe.'

'Wherever we're going,' she said with conviction, 'I don't think we're going to get there. You're mad. Both of you. Quite mad.'

5

It was three-thirty in the morning when Petersen woke. His watch said so. He should not have been able to see his watch because he had switched the light off before going to sleep. It was no longer off but it wasn't the light that had wakened him, it was something cold and hard pressed against his right cheek-bone. Careful not to move his head. Petersen swivelled his eyes to take in the man who held the gun and was sitting on a chair beside the bed. Dressed in a well-cut grey suit, he was in his early thirties, had a neatly trimmed black moustache of the type made famous by Ronald Colman before the war, a smooth clear complexion, an engaging smile and very pale blue, very cold eyes. Petersen reached across a slow hand and gently deflected the barrel of the pistol.

'You need to point that thing at my head? With three of your fellow-thugs armed to the teeth?'

There were indeed three other men in the bedroom. Unlike their leader they were a scruffy and villainous looking lot, dressed in vaguely paramilitary uniforms but their appearance counted little against the fact that each carried a machine-pistol.

'Fellow thugs?' The man on the chair looked pained. 'That makes me a thug too?'

'Only thugs hold pistols against the heads of sleeping men.'

'Oh, come now, Major Petersen. You have the reputation of being a highly dangerous and very violent man. How are we to know that you are not holding a loaded pistol in your hand under that blanket?'

Petersen slowly withdrew his right hand from under the blanket and turned up his empty palm. 'It's under my pillow.'

'Ah, so.' The man withdrew the gun. 'One respects a professional.'

'How did you get in? My door was locked.'

'Signor Pijade was most cooperative.' 'Pijade' was Josip's surname.

'Was he now?'

'You can't trust anyone these days.'

'I've found that out, too.'

'I begin to believe what people say of you. You're not worried, are you? You're not even concerned about who I might be.'

'Why should I be. You're no friend. That's all that matters to me.'

'I may be no friend. Or I may. I don't honestly know yet. I'm Major Cipriano. You may have heard of me.'

'I have. Yesterday, for the first time. I feel sorry for you, Major, I really do, but I wish I were elsewhere. I'm one of those sensitive souls who feel uncomfortable in hospital wards. In the presence of the sick, I mean.'

'Sick?' Cipriano looked mildly astonished but the smile remained. 'Me? I'm as fit as a fiddle.'

'Physically, no doubt. Otherwise a cracked fiddle and one sadly out of tune. Anyone who works as a hatchet-man for that evil and sadistic bastard, General Granelli, has to be sick in the mind: and anyone who employs as *his* hatchet-man the psychopathic poisoner, Alessandro, has to be himself a sadist, a candidate for a maximum-security lunatic asylum.'

'Ah, so! Alessandro.' Cipriano was either not a man easily to take offence or, if he did, too clever to show it. 'He gave a message for you.'

'You surprise me. I thought your poisoner — and poisonous — friend was in no position to give messages. You have seen him, then?'

'Unfortunately, no. He's still welded up in the fore cabin of the *Colombo*. One has to admit, Major Petersen, that you are not a man to do things by half-measures. But I spoke to him. He says that when he meets you again you'll take a long time to die.'

'He won't. I'll gun him down as I would a mad dog with rabies. I don't want to talk any more about your psycho friend. What do you want of me?'

'I'm not quite sure yet. Tell me, why do you keep referring to Alessandro as a poisoner?'

'You don't know?'

'I might. If I knew what you were talking about.'

'You know that he carried knockout gas-grenades with him?'

'Yes.'

'You knew that he carried a nice little surgical kit with him along with hypodermics and liquids in capsules that caused unconsciousness — some form of scopolamine, I believe?'

'Yes.'

'Do you know that he also carried capsules which, when injected, led to the victims dying in screaming agony?'

Cipriano had stopped smiling. 'That's a lie.'

'May I get out of bed?' Cipriano nodded. Petersen crossed to his rucksack, extracted the metal box he had taken from Alessandro, handed it to Cipriano and said: 'Take that back to Rome or wherever and have the contents of those capsules analyzed. I would not drink or self-inject any of them if I were you. I threatened to inject your friend with the contents of the missing capsule and he fainted in terror.'

'I know nothing about this.'

'That I believe. Where would Alessandro get hold of such lethal poison?'

'I don't know that either.'

'That I don't believe. Well, what do you want of me?'

'Just come along with us.' Cipriano led the way to the dining-room where Petersen's six companions were already assembled under the watchful eye of a young Italian officer and four armed soldiers. Cipriano said: 'Remain here. I know you're too professional to try anything foolish. We won't be long.'

George, inevitably, was relaxed in a carver chair, a tankard of beer in his hand. Alex was looking quietly murderous. Giacomo just looked thoughtful. Sarina was tight-lipped and pale while the mercurial Lorraine, oddly enough, was expressionless.

Petersen shook his head. 'Well, well, we're a fine lot. Major Cipriano has just said I was a professional. If — '

'That was Major Cipriano?' George said.

'That's what he says.'

'A fast mover. He doesn't *look* like a Major Cipriano.'

'He doesn't talk like one either. As I was

about to say, George, if I were a professional, I'd have posted a guard, a patrolling sentry. Mea culpa. I thought we were safe here.'

'Safe!' Sarina spoke with a wealth of contempt.

'Well, no harm done, let's hope.'

'No harm done!'

Petersen spread his hands. 'There are always compensations. You — and Lorraine — wanted to see me in, what shall we say, a disadvantaged position. Well, you see it now. How do you like it?' There was no reply. 'Two things. I'm surprised they got you, Alex. You can hear a leaf fall.'

'They had a gun at Sarina's head.'

'Ah! And where is our good friend Josip?'

'*Your* good friend,' Sarina said acidly, 'will be helping Cipriano and his men to find whatever they're looking for.'

'My goodness! What a low opinion — what an immediate low opinion — of my friend.'

'Who tipped them off that we were here? Who let them in? Who gave them the keys — or the master key — to the bedrooms?'

'One of these days,' Petersen said mildly, 'someone's going to clobber you, young lady. You've a waspish tongue and you're far too ready to judge and condemn. If that soldier with the gun at your head had taken the second necessary to pull the trigger he'd be dead now. So, of course, would you. But Alex didn't want you to die. Nobody let them in — Josip never locks his front door. Once in, getting the keys would be no trouble. I don't know who tipped them off. I'll find out. It could even have been you.'

'Me!' She stared at him, at first stunned and then furious.

'No-one's above suspicion. You've said more than once that I don't trust you. If you said that, you must have had reasons to think that I have reservations about you. What reasons?'

'You must be out of your mind.' She wasn't mad any more, just bewildered.

'You've turned pale very suddenly. Why have you turned pale?'

'Leave my sister alone!' Michael's voice was an angry shout. 'She's done nothing! Leave her alone. Sarina? A criminal? A traitor? She's right, you must be out of your mind. Stop tormenting her. Who the hell do you think you are?'

'An army officer who wouldn't hesitate to instruct a very raw enlisted man — boy, I should say — in the elements of discipline. Mind you, a show of spirit at last, but I'm afraid it's mistimed and misplaced. Meantime, you should rest content with the knowledge that *you* are not under suspicion.'

'I'm supposed to be pleased with that while Sarina is under suspicion?'

'I don't care whether you're pleased or not.'

'Look here, Petersen — '

'Petersen? Who's Petersen? 'Major Petersen' to a ranker. Or 'Sir'.' Michael made no reply. 'You're not under suspicion because after you'd transmitted this message to Rome yesterday morning I rendered your radio inoperable. You could have used your sister's tonight, but you wouldn't have had the guts, not after being caught out the previous night. I know you're not very bright but the inference is obvious. Alex, a word with you.'

As brother and sister looked at each other in mingled apprehension, incomprehension and dismay, Alex crossed the room and listened as Petersen began talking to him.

'Stop!' The young Italian officer's voice was sharp.

Petersen looked at him patiently. 'Stop what?'

'Stop talking.'

'Why ever should I? You just let me talk to that young man and girl.'

'I understood that. I don't understand Serbo-Croat.'

'Your lack of education doesn't concern me. To compound your ignorance, we're not

176

talking Serbo-Croat but a Slavonic dialect understood only by this soldier here, the fat gentleman with the beer glass and myself. You think, perhaps, that we are planning a suicidal attack on you, three unarmed men against four machine-guns and a pistol? You can't possibly be so crazy as to think we're so crazy. What rank are you?'

'Lieutenant.' He was a very stiff, very correct and very young, lieutenant.

'Lieutenants don't give orders to majors.'

'You're my prisoner.'

'I have yet to be informed of that. Even if I were, which legally I'm not, I'd be Major Cipriano's prisoner and he would regard me as a very important one and one not to be molested or harmed in any way, so don't bother looking at your men. If any of them comes over to try to stop or separate us I'll take his gun from him and break it over his head and then you might shoot me. You'd be court-martialled, cashiered and then, by the stipulations of the Geneva Conventions, face a firing squad. But you know that, of course.' Petersen hoped the lieutenant didn't, for he himself had no idea, but apparently the young man didn't either for he made no further attempt to pursue the matter.

Petersen talked to Alex for no more than a minute, went behind the bar, picked up a wine bottle and glass — this without even a raised eyebrow from the young lieutenant who might have been wondering how many men it took to constitute a firing squad and sat down at the table with George. They talked in low and seemingly earnest tones and were still talking when Cipriano returned with his three soldiers, Josip and his wife, Marija. Cipriano not only looked less buoyant and confident than he had done when he had left the dining-room: he was still smiling, because he was an habitual smiler, but the smile was of such a diminished quality that he looked positively morose.

'I am glad to see that you are enjoying yourselves.'

'We might be just a little justifiably annoyed at having our sleep disturbed.' Petersen replenished his glass. 'But we are of a forgiving nature, happy and relaxed in our carefree conscience. You will join us in a nightcap? I'm sure it would help you to frame a more graceful apology.'

'No nightcap, thank you, but you are correct in saying that an apology is in order. I have just made a telephone call.'

'To the wise men of your intelligence HQ, of course.'

'Yes. How did you know?'

'Where else does all the misinformation

come from? We, as you know, are in the same line of business and it happens to us all the time.'

'I am genuinely sorry to have inconvenienced you all over a stupid false alarm.'

'What false alarm?'

'Papers missing from our Rome HQ. Some misguided genius on General Granelli's staff — I don't know, yet, who it was but I'll find out before the day is over — decided that they had fallen, if that's the word, into the hands of either yourself or one of your group. Very important papers, very top-secret.'

'All missing papers are top-secret. I have some papers with me myself, but I assure you they're not stolen and how top-secret or important they may be I don't know.'

'I know about those papers.' Cipriano waved a dismissive hand and smiled. 'As you're probably well aware. Those other, and much more important papers have never left their safe in Rome. A top-secret filing clerk careless about filing top-secret documents.'

'May one ask what they are about?'

'You may and that's all the answer you'd get. I don't know and even if I did I couldn't tell you. I wish you an undisturbed night — or what's left of it. Again, my apologies. Goodbye, Major Petersen.'

'Goodbye.' Petersen took the extended

hand. 'My regards to Colonel Lunz.'

'I will.' Cipriano frowned. 'I hardly know the man.'

'In that case, my regards to Alessandro.'

'I'll give him more than that.' He turned to Josip and took his hand. 'Many thanks, Signor Pijade. You have been most helpful. We will not forget.'

It was Sarina, nothing if not resilient, who broke the conversational hiatus that followed the departure of Cipriano and his men. '"Thank you, Signor Pijade. Most helpful, Signor Pijade. We won't forget, Signor Pijade."'

Josip looked at her in puzzlement then turned to Petersen. 'Is the young lady talking to me?'

'I think she's addressing the company.'

'I don't understand.'

'I don't think she does either. The young lady, as you call her, is under the ridiculous impression that you notified Major Cipriano — one assumes she thinks it was by telephone — of our presence and then took him and his men on a guided tour of the premises, distributing keys where necessary. She may, of course, be trying to divert from herself the suspicion that she is the guilty party.'

Sarina made to speak but an outraged Marija gave her no chance. Three quick steps and she was before the suddenly apprehensive Sarina. The ivory-knuckled fists and arms held rigidly by her sides spoke eloquently of her outrage: her eyes were stormy and her clenched teeth remained that way even when she spoke.

'Such a beautiful face, my dear.' It is difficult not to hiss when one's teeth are clenched. 'Such a delicate complexion. And I have long nails. Should I tear your face because you insult the honour of my husband? Or would a few slaps — hard slaps — be enough for a creature like you?' In the technique of expressing contempt, Marija Pijade had nothing to learn from anyone.

Sarina said nothing. The apprehensive expression on her face had given way to one of near shock.

'A soldier — not the Major, he's a civilized man and was not there — pointed a gun at me. Like this.' Dramatically, she swung up her right arm and pressed her forefinger against her neck. 'Not pointed. Pushed. Pushed hard. Three seconds, he said, for my husband to hand over the master key. I am sure he would not have fired but Josip handed over the key at once. Do you blame him for that?'

Slowly, dumbly, Sarina shook her head.

'But do you still think Josip betrayed you?'

'No. I don't know what to think, but I don't think that any more. I just don't know what to think. I'm sorry, Marija, I'm truly sorry.' She smiled wanly. 'A soldier threatened me with a gun, too. He pressed it in my ear. Maybe that doesn't make for very clear thinking.'

The cold fury in Marija's face gave way to speculation then softened into concern. She took an impulsive step forward, put her arms round the girl and began to stroke her hair.

'I don't think any of us is thinking very clearly. George!' This over Sarina's shoulder. 'What are you thinking of?'

'Šljivovica,' George said decisively. 'The universal specific. If you read the label on a Pellegrino bottle — '

'George!'

'Right away.'

Josip rubbed a blue and unshaven chin. 'If Sarina and I are not the culprits, then we're no nearer to an answer. Who did talk? Have you no suspicions, Peter?'

'None. I don't need any. I know who it is.'

'You know — ' Josip turned to the bar, picked up a bottle of Šljivovica from a tray George was preparing, filled a small glass, drained it in two gulps and when he'd finished coughing and spluttering said: 'Who?'

'I'm not prepared to say at the moment. That's not because I'm intending to prolong anxiety, increase tension, give the villain enough rope to hang him — or herself — or anything stupid like that. It's because I can't prove it — yet. I'm not even sure I want to prove it. Perhaps the person I have in mind was misguided, or the action may have been unintentional, accidental, inadvertent or even done from the best motives — from, of course, the viewpoint of the person concerned. Unlike Sarina here, I don't go in much for premature judgments and condemnation.'

'Peter!' Marija's voice held a warning, almost peremptory, note. She still had an arm around Sarina's shoulders.

'Sorry, Marija. Sorry, Sarina. Just my natural nastiness surfacing. By the way, if you people want to go to bed, well of course, go. But no hurry now. Change of plan. We won't be leaving until the late forenoon tomorrow. Certainly not before. Giacomo, could I have a quiet word with you?'

'Have I any option?'

'Certainly. You can always say 'no'.'

Giacomo smiled his broad smile, stood up and put his hand in his pocket. 'Josip, if I could buy a bottle of that excellent red wine — '

Josip was mildly affronted. 'Peter Petersen's friends pay for nothing in my hotel.'

'Maybe I'm not his friend. I mean, maybe he's not my friend.' Giacomo seemed to find the thought highly amusing. 'Thanks all the same.' He picked up a bottle and two glasses from the bar, led the way to a distant table, poured wine and said admiringly: 'That Marija. Quite a girl. Not quite a tartar but no shrinking violet. Changes her mind a bit quick, doesn't she?'

'Mercurial, you'd say?'

'That's the word. Seems to know you pretty well. Has she known you long?'

'She does and she has.' Petersen spoke with some feeling. 'Twenty-six years, three months and some days. The day she was born. My cousin. Why do you ask?'

'Curiosity. I was beginning to wonder if you knew everyone in the valley. Well, on with the inquisition. Incidentally, I would like to say that I'm honoured to be the prime suspect and/or the chosen villain.'

'You're neither a suspect nor villain. Wrong casting. If you wanted, say, to dispose of George or Alex or myself, or get your hands on something you thought we had, you'd use a heavy instrument. Surreptitious phone calls or secret tip-offs are not in your nature. Deviousness is not

184

part of your stock-in-trade.'

'Well, thank you. It's a disappointment, though. I take it you want to ask some questions?

'If I may.'

'About myself, of course. Fire away. No, don't fire away. Let *me* give you my curriculum vitae. Behind me lies a blameless existence. My life is an open book.

'You're right, I'm Montenegrin. Vladimir was my given name. I prefer Giacomo. In England they called me 'Johnny'. I still prefer Giacomo.'

'You lived in England?'

'I am English. Sounds confusing, but not really. Before the war I was a second officer in the Merchant Navy — the Yugoslav one, I mean. I met a beautiful Canadian girl in Southampton so I left the ship.' He said it as if if had been the most natural thing in the world to do and Petersen could readily understand that for him it had been. 'There was a little difficulty at first at staying on in England but I'd found an excellent and very understanding boss who was working on a diving contract for the Government and who was one experienced diver short. I'd qualified as a diver before joining the merchant marine. By and by I got married — '

'Same girl?'

'Same girl. I became naturalized in August 1939 and joined the services on the outbreak of war the following month. Because I had a master's ocean-going ticket and was a qualified diver who could have been handy at things like sticking limpet mines on to warships in enemy harbours and was a natural for the Navy, it was inevitable, I suppose, that they put me into the infantry. I went to Europe, came back by Dunkirk, then went out to the Middle East.'

'And you've been in those parts ever since. No home leave?'

'No home leave.'

'So you haven't seen your wife in two years. Family?'

'Twin girls. One still-born. The other died at six months. Polio.' Giacomo's tone was matter-of-fact, almost casual. 'In the early summer of '41, my wife was killed in a Luftwaffe attack on Portsmouth.'

Petersen nodded and said nothing. There was nothing to say. One wondered why a man like Giacomo smiled so much but one did not wonder long.

'I was with the Eighth Army. Long-Range Desert Group. Then some genius finally discovered that I was really a sailor and not a soldier and I joined Jellicoe's Special Boat Service in the Aegean.' Both those hazardous

186

services called for volunteers, Petersen knew: it was pointless to ask Giacomo why he had volunteered. 'Then the same genius found out some more about me, that I was a Yugoslav, and I was called back to Cairo to escort Lorraine to her destination.'

'And what happens when you've delivered her to her destination?'

'When *you've* delivered her, you mean. Responsibility over, from here on I just sit back and relax and go along for the ride. They thought I was the best man for the job but they weren't to know I was going to have the good luck to meet up with you.' Giacomo poured some more wine, leaned back in his chair and smiled broadly. 'I haven't a single cousin in the whole of Bosnia.'

'If it's luck, I hope it holds. My question, Giacomo.'

'Of course. Afterwards. I'd happily turn back now, conscience clear, but I've got to get a receipt or something from this fellow Mihajlović. I think they want me to take up diving again. Not hard to guess why — must have been the same genius who found out that I was an ex-sailor. As Michael said in that mountain inn, it's a funny old world. I spent over three years fighting the Germans and in a couple of weeks I'll be doing the same thing. This interlude, where I'm more or less fighting with the Germans — although I don't expect I'll ever see a German in Yugoslavia — I don't like one little bit.'

'You heard what George said to Michael. No point in rehashing it. A very brief interlude, Giacomo. You bid your charge a tearful farewell, trying not to smile, then heigh-ho for the Aegean.'

'Trying not to smile?' He considered the contents of his glass. 'Well, perhaps. Yes and no. If this is a funny old world, she's a funny young girl in a funny old war. Mercurial — like your cousin. Temperamental. Patrician-looking young lady but sadly deficient in patrician sang-froid. Cool, aloof, even remote at one moment, she can be friendly, even affectionate, the next.'

'The affectionate bit has escaped me so far.'

'A certain lack of rapport between you two has not escaped me either. She can be sweet and bad-tempered at the same time which is no small achievement. Most un-English. I suppose you know she's English. You seem to know quite a bit about her.'

'I know she's English because George told me so. He also told me you were from Montenegro.'

'Ah! Our professor of languages.'

'Remarkable linguist with a remarkable ear.

He could probably give you your home address.'

'She tells me you know this Captain Harrison she's going to work for?'

'I know him well.'

'So does she. Used to work for him before. Peacetime. Rome. He was the manager of the Italian branch of an English ball-bearing company. She was his secretary. That's where she learned to speak Italian. She seems to like him a lot.'

'She seems to like men a lot. Period. You haven't fallen into her clutches yet, Giacomo?'

'No.' Again the broad smile. 'But I'm working on it.'

'Well, thanks.' Petersen stood. 'If you'll excuse me.' He crossed to where Sarina was sitting. 'I'd like to talk to you. Alone. I know that sounds ominous, but it isn't, really.'

'What about?'

'That's a silly question. If I want to talk to you privately I don't talk publicly.'

She rose and Michael did the same. He said: 'You're not going to talk to her without me.'

George sighed, rose wearily to his feet, crossed to where Michael was standing, put his two hamlike hands on the young man's shoulders and sat him in his chair as easily as he would have done a little child.

'Michael, you're only a private soldier. If you were in the American army you'd be a private soldier, second class. I'm a Regimental Sergeant-Major. Temporary, mind you, but effective. I don't see why the Major should have to be bothered with you. I don't see why *I* should have to be bothered with you. Why should you bother us? You're not a boy any more.' He reached behind him, picked up a glass of Maraschino from the table and handed it to Michael, who took it sulkily but did not drink. 'If Sarina's kidnapped, we'll all know who did it.'

Petersen took the girl up to her room. He left the door ajar, looked around but not with the air of one expecting to find anything and sniffed the air. Sarina looked at him coldly and spoke the same way.

'What are you looking for? What are you sniffing for? Everything you do, everything you say is unpleasant, nasty, overbearing, superior, humiliating — '

'Oh, come on. I'm your guardian angel. You don't talk to your guardian angel that way.'

'Guardian angel! You also tell lies. You were telling lies in the dining-room. You still think I sent a radio message.'

'I don't and didn't. You're far too nice for anything underhand like that.' She looked at him warily then almost in startlement as he put his hands lightly on her shoulders, but did not try to flinch away. 'You're quick, you're intelligent — unlike your brother but that's not his fault — and I've no doubt you can or could be devious because your face doesn't show much. Except for the one thing that would disqualify you from espionage. You're too transparently honest.'

'That's a kind of left-handed compliment,' she said doubtfully.

'Left or right, it's true.' He dropped to his knees, felt under the foot of the rather ill-fitting door, stood, extracted the key from the inside of the lock and examined it. 'You locked your door last night?'

'Of course.'

'What did you do with the key?'

'I left it in the lock. Half-turned. That way a person with a duplicate key or a master can't push your key through or on to a paper that's been pushed under the door. They taught us that in Cairo.'

'Spare me. Your instructor was probably a ten-year-old schoolboy. See those two tiny bright indentations on either side of the stem of the key?' She nodded. 'Made by an instrument much prized by the better-class burglar who's too sophisticated to batter doors open with a sledge-hammer. A pair of very slender pincers with tips of either carborundum or titanium stainless steel. Turn any key in a lock. You had a visitor during the night.'

'Somebody took my radio?'

'Somebody sure enough used it. Could have been here.'

'That's impossible. Certainly, I was tired last night but I'm not a heavy sleeper.'

'Maybe you were last night. How did you feel when you woke up this morning — when you were woken, I mean?'

'Well.' She hesitated. 'I felt a bit sick, really. But I thought I was perhaps over-tired and hadn't had enough sleep or I was scared — I'm not a great big coward but I'm not all that brave either and it was the first time anyone had ever pointed a gun at me — or perhaps I just wasn't used to the strange food.'

'You felt dopey, in other words.'

'Yes.'

'You probably were doped. I don't suggest flannel-foot crept stealthily in and applied a chloroform pad or anything of the kind, for the smell of that lingers for hours. Some gas that was injected through the keyhole from a nozzled canister that may well have come from the chemist's joker shop where Alessandro buys his toys. In any event, I can promise you that you won't be disturbed again tonight. And you rest easy in the knowledge that you're not on anyone's black list. Not judged, not condemned, not even suspected. You might at least have the grace to say that I'm not such an awful monster as you thought.'

She smiled faintly. 'Maybe you're not even a monster at all.'

'You're going to sleep, now?' She nodded so he said goodnight and closed the door behind him.

★ ★ ★

Almost an hour elapsed before Petersen, George and Josip were left together in the dining-room. The others had been in no hurry to depart. The night's events had not been conducive to an immediately renewed slumber and, besides, they were secure in the knowledge that there would be no early morning start.

George, who had returned to his red wine, was making steady inroads on his current uncounted bottle, looked and spoke as if he had been on mineral water all the time. There was, unfortunately, not the same lack of evidence about his cigar-smoking: an evil-smelling blue haze filled the upper half of the room.

'Your friend, Major Cipriano, didn't over-stay his welcome,' Josip said.

'He's no friend of mine,' Petersen said. 'Never seen him before. Appearances mean nothing but he seems a reasonable enough character. For an intelligence agent, that is. Have you known him long?'

'He has been here twice. As a bona-fide traveller. He's no friend. Thanking me for my help was just an attempt to divert suspicion from whoever tipped him off. A feeble attempt, he must have known it would fail but probably the best he could think up at the time. What was his object in coming here?'

'No mystery about that. Both the Germans and Italians are suspicious of me. I have a message to deliver to the leader of the Četniks. On the boat coming across from Italy one of his agents, an unpleasant character called Alessandro, tried to get this message from me. He wanted to see if it was the same as a copy he was carrying. He failed, so Cipriano got worried and came across to Ploče. He was tipped off as to our whereabouts, came up here — almost certainly by light plane — and, when we were herded down here, went through our possessions, steamed open the envelope containing my message, found that it was unchanged and resealed it. Exit Cipriano, baffled but satisfied — for the moment anyway.'

George said: 'Sarina?'

'Someone got into her room in the early hours of this morning. That was after she had been doped. Her radio was used to call up Cipriano. Sarina says she trusts me now. I don't believe her.'

'It is as always,' George said mournfully. 'Every man's — and woman's — hands are against us.'

'Doped?' Josip was incredulous. 'In my hotel? How can anyone be doped in my hotel?'

'How can anyone be doped anywhere?'

'Who was this villain?'

'Villainess. Lorraine.'

'Lorraine! That beautiful girl?'

'Maybe her mind is not as beautiful as the rest of her.'

'Sarina. Now Lorraine.' George shook his head sadly. 'The monstrous regiment of women.'

Josip said: 'But how do you know?'

'Simple arithmetic. Elimination. Lorraine went for a walk tonight and returned very hurriedly. She didn't go for the walk's sake. She went for something else. Information. You went with her, Josip. Do you recall her doing or saying anything odd?'

'She didn't do anything. Just walked. And

195

she said very little.'

'That should make it easy to remember.'

'Well, she said it was odd that I didn't have the name of the hotel outside. I told her I hadn't yet got around to putting it up and that it was the Hotel Eden. She also said it was funny that there were no streets signs up, so I gave her the name of the street. Ah! So she got the name and address, no?'

'Yes.' Petersen rose. 'Bed. I trust you're not going to stay here for the remainder of the night, George.'

'Certainly not.' George fetched a fresh bottle from behind the bar. 'But we academics must have our moments for meditation.'

★　★　★

At noon that day, Petersen and his six companions had still not left the Hotel Eden. Instead, they were just sitting down to a lunch which Josip had insisted they have, a meal that was to prove to be on a par with the dinner they had had the previous evening. But there was one vacant seat.

Josip said: 'Where is the Professor?'

'George,' Petersen said, 'is indisposed. In bed. Acute stomach pains. He thinks it must have been something he had to eat last night.'

'Something he had to eat!' Josip was indignant. 'He had exactly the same to eat as anyone else last night — except, of course, a great deal more of it — and nobody else is stricken. My food, indeed! *I* know what ails the Professor. When I came down early this morning, just about two hours after you went to bed, the Professor was still here, still, as he said, meditating.'

'That might help to account for it.'

That might have accounted for it but it didn't account for George's appearance some ten minutes after the meal had commenced. He tried to smile wanly but he didn't look wan.

'Sorry to be late. The Major will have told you I was unwell. However, the cramps have eased a little and I thought I might try a little something. To settle the stomach, you understand.'

By one o'clock George's stomach seemed to have settled in a most remarkable fashion. In the fifty minutes that had intervened since his joining the company he had consumed twice as much as anyone else and effortlessly disposed of two large bottles of wine.

'Congratulations are in order, George,' Giacomo said. 'One moment at death's door and now — well, an incredible performance.'

'It was nothing,' George said modestly. 'In many ways, I am an incredible man.'

197

Petersen sat on the bed in George's room. 'Well?'

'Satisfactory. In one way, not well. There were two items that one would not have looked for in such an aristocratic young lady's luggage. One was a very small leather case with a few highly professional burglarious tools. The other was a small metal box with some sachets inside, the sachets containing a liquid. When squeezed, the liquid turned into a gas. I sniffed only a very tiny amount. An anaesthetic of some kind, that's certain. The interesting thing is that this little box, though smaller than Alessandro's, was made of and lined with the same materials. What do we do with this young charmer?'

'Leave her be. She's not dangerous. If she were, she wouldn't have made so amateurish a mistake.'

'You said you knew the identity of the miscreant. She's going to wonder why you haven't disclosed it.'

'Let her wonder. What's she going to do about it?'

'There's that,' George said. 'There's that.'

6

It was snowing heavily and the temperature was below freezing when Petersen drove the stolen Italian truck out of Mostar shortly after two o'clock that afternoon. The two girls beside him were silent and withdrawn, a circumstance that affected Petersen not at all. Relaxed and untroubled, he drove as unhurriedly as a man with all the time in the world and, after passing unhindered through a check-point at Potoci, slowed down even more, an action dictated not by any change of mood but by the nature of the road. It was narrow, twisting and broken-surfaced and urgently in need of the attentions of road repair gangs who had not passed that way for a long time: more importantly, they had begun to climb, and climb quite steeply, as the Neretva valley narrowed precipitously on either side of the river which sank further and further below the tortuous road until there was an almost sheer drop of several hundred feet to the foaming river that lay beneath them. Given the unstable nature of the road, the fact that there were no crash-barriers or restraining walls to prevent their sliding off the slippery road and the fact that the river itself increasingly disappeared in the thickening snowsqualls, it was not a route to lighten the hearts of those of an imaginative or nervous disposition. Judging by the hand-clenching and highly apprehensive expression of Petersen's two front-seat companions, they clearly came well within that category. Petersen had neither comfort nor cheer to offer them, not through any callous indifference but because on the evidence of their own eyes they wouldn't have believed a word he said anyway.

Their relief was almost palpable when Petersen abruptly turned off the road into a narrow gully which suddenly — and to the two girls, miraculously — appeared in the vertical cliff-side to their right. The road was no road at all, just a convoluted, rutted track that offered only minimal traction for the almost constantly spinning rear wheels, but at least there was no way they could fall off it: high walls of rock pressed in closely on both sides. Perhaps five minutes after leaving the main road, Petersen stopped, cut the engine and dropped down.

'This is as far as we go,' he said. 'As far as we can go in this truck, anyway. Stay here.' He walked round to the back of the truck, parted the curtains, repeated his words and disappeared into the swirling snow.

He was back within a few minutes, sitting beside the driver of a peculiar open vehicle which looked as if it might once have been a small truck that had had both its top and rear sliced off. The driver, clad in British warm — a thick, khaki, woollen overcoat — could have been of any nationality: with a fur cap pulled down to eyebrow level, a luxuriant black beard and moustache and a pair of horn-rimmed sunglasses, there wasn't a single distinguishable feature of his face to be seen except for a nose that could have belonged to anyone. Petersen stepped down as the vehicle came to a halt.

'This is Dominic,' he said. 'He's come to help us along a bit. That's a four-wheel-drive vehicle he's got there. It can go places where this truck can't, but even then it can't go very far, perhaps a couple of kilometres. Dominic will take the two young ladies, all our gear and all our blankets — I can assure you we're going to need those tonight — as far as he can, then come back for the rest of us. We'll start walking.'

Sarina said: 'You mean to tell us you expected this friend of yours to meet us here? And at just this time?'

'Give or take a few minutes. I wouldn't be much of a tour guide, would I, if I got all my connections wrong?'

'This truck,' Giacomo said. 'You're surely not going to leave it here?'

'Why ever not?'

'I thought it was your custom to park unwanted Italian trucks in the Neretva. I saw some lovely parking spots in the god-awful ravine we just came through.'

'A sinful waste. Besides, we might even want it again. What matters, of course, is that our friend Major Cipriano already knows we have it.'

'How would he know that?'

'How would he not know it, you mean. Has it not occurred to you that the informer who tipped him off to our presence in the Hotel Eden would also have given him all the details of our trip from the torpedo boat, including those of this vehicle? Either by radio or before being apparently dragged from an hotel bedroom, it doesn't matter. We passed through a check-point at Potoci about an hour ago and the guard didn't even bother to slow us down. Odd, one might think, except that he had already been given details of our vehicle, recognized it at once and obeyed orders to let us through. Let's get that stuff out quickly. It's turned even colder than I thought it would be.'

It had indeed. A south-east wind had

sprung up, a wind from which they would have been sheltered in the Neretva valley, and was steadily strengthening. This would not normally have been a cold wind but this was a wind that paid no attention to meteorological norms: it could have been blowing straight from Siberia. The four-wheel-drive vehicle was loaded with passengers and gear and drove off in a remarkably short time: there could be no doubt that Dominic's sunglasses were, in effect, snow-glasses.

The five men set out on foot and were picked up some fifteen minutes later by the returning Dominic. The ride along an even more bumpy and deteriorating track was, because of the increase in snowdepth and incline, uncomfortable and haphazard to a degree, and only marginally better and faster than walking. None of the passengers was sorry when the truck pulled up at the track's end outside a ramshackle wooden hut which proved to be its garage. Inside, the two girls were sheltering from the snow. They were not alone. There were three men — boys, rather — in vaguely paramilitary uniforms and five ponies.

Sarina said: 'Where on earth are we?'

'Home, sweet home,' Petersen said. 'Well, an hour and a half's gentle ride and we'll be there. This is the mountain of Prenj, more of a massif, really. The Neretva river makes a big U-turn here and runs around three sides of it, which makes Prenj, in defensive terms, an ideal place to be. Only two bridges cross the river, one to the northwest at Jablanica, the other to the north-east at Konjik, and both of those are easily guarded and defended. It's open to the south-east but no danger threatens from that direction.'

'Gentle ride, you said. Do those horses canter or gallop? I don't like horses.'

'They're ponies, not horses, and, no, they don't canter or gallop. Not on this occasion anyway. They wouldn't be stupid enough to try. It's all uphill and pretty steeply uphill.'

'I don't think I'm going to enjoy this climb.'

'You'll enjoy the view.'

★   ★   ★

It was half an hour later and she was enjoying neither the climb nor the view. The climb, though not impossibly steep, was a difficult enough one and the view, remarkable though it was, engendered in her only a feeling that lay halfway between fascinated horror and paralysed terror. The path, barely two metres in width and sometimes noticeably less, had been gouged out of the side of a slope so steep as to be virtually a cliff-side, and ascended it by a series, a seemingly endless series, of hairpin twists and turns. With every step the pony took, the floor of the narrow valley, when it could be seen at all through the driving snow, seemed more remotely and vertically distant. Only she and Lorraine had been mounted: the other three ponies carried all their securely strapped gear and blankets. Lorraine was on foot now, clutching Giacomo's arm as if he was her last faint hope on earth.

Petersen, walking beside Sarina's pony, said: 'I'm afraid you're not enjoying this as much as I would like you to.'

'Enjoying it!' She shuddered uncontrollably, not with cold. 'Back in the hotel I told you I wasn't a great big coward. Well, I am, I am! I'm terrified. I keep on telling myself it's silly, it's stupid, but I can't help it.'

Petersen said matter-of-factly: 'You're not a coward. It's been like this since you were a child.'

'Like what? What do you mean?'

'Vertigo is what I mean. Anyone can suffer from it. Some of the bravest men I know, some of the most fearsome fighters I've ever met, won't climb a step-ladder or set foot in a plane.'

'Yes, yes. Always. Do you know about it?'

'I don't get it, but I've seen it too often not to know about it. Dizziness, loss of equilibrium, an almost uncontrollable desire to throw yourself over the edge and, in the present case, a conviction on your part that your pony is about to jump out into space at any moment. That's about it, isn't it?'

She nodded, dumbly. Petersen refrained from saying that if she'd known about her condition and the Yugoslav mountains, she should have stayed in Cairo. Instead he moved round the head of the horse and took her stirrup-leather in his hand.

'These ponies are more sure-footed than we are and by a long way. Even if it should suffer from a bout of vertigo now, and ponies never do, I would be the first over the edge. And even if you felt like throwing yourself over, you can't because I'm between you and the cliff edge and I'd stop you and catch you. And I'll change sides at every corner. That way we'll be sure to make it to the top. I won't be so silly as to tell you to sit back and relax: all I can say is that you'll be feeling a lot better in fifteen minutes or so.'

'We'll be away from this cliff by that time?' The tremor was still in her voice.

'We will, we will.' They wouldn't be, but by that time it would be so dark that she would be unable to see the valley below.

It was quite some time after dark when they passed through the perimeter of what seemed to be a permanent camp of sorts. There were a large number of huts and tents, all close together and nearly all illuminated: not brightly illuminated, for at that remote altitude there was no central power grid and the only small generator available was reserved for the headquarters area: for the rest, the great majority of the guerrilla soldiers and the inevitable camp-followers, there was only the light to be had from oil, tallow or coke braziers. Then there came a quite uninhabited and gently rising slope of perhaps three hundred metres before their small cavalcade fetched up at a large hut with a metal roof and two windows which gave out a surprising amount of light.

'Well, here we are,' Petersen said. 'Home or what you'd better call home until you find a better word for it.' He reached up his hands and swung the shivering girl to the ground. She clung to him as if she were trying to prevent herself from falling to the ground which was what she was indeed trying to do.

'My legs feel all funny.' Her voice was low and husky but at least the tremor had gone.

'Sure they do. I'll bet you've never been on a horse before.'

'You'd win your bet but it's not that. The way I hung on to that horse, clung to it — ' She tried to laugh but it was a poor enough attempt. 'I'll be surprised if that poor pony doesn't have bruised ribs for days to come.'

'You did very well.'

'Very well! I'm ashamed of myself. I hope you won't go around telling everyone that you've met up with the most cowardly radio operator in the Balkans.'

'I won't. I won't because I don't go around telling lies. I think you may be the bravest girl I ever met.'

'After that performance!'

'Especially after that performance.'

She was still clinging to him, clearly still not trusting her balance, was silent for a few moments, then said: 'I think you may be the kindest man I've ever met.'

'Good God!' He was genuinely astonished. 'The strain has been too much. After all you've said about me!'

'Especially after everything I said about you.'

She was still holding him, although now only tentatively, when they heard the sound of a heavy fist banging on a wooden door and George's booming voice saying: 'Open up, in the name of the law or common humanity or whatever. We have crossed the burning sands and are dying of thirst.'

The door opened almost immediately and a tall, thin figure appeared, framed in the rectangle of light. He came down the two steps and thrust out a hand.

'It cannot be . . . ' He had an excruciatingly languid Oxbridge accent.

'It is.' George took his hand. 'Enough of the formalities. At stake there is nothing less than the sacred name of British hospitality.'

'Goodness gracious!' The man screwed a monocle, an oddly-shaped oval one, into his right eye, advanced towards Lorraine, took her hand, swept it up in a gesture of exquisite gallantry and kissed it. 'Goodness gracious me. Lorraine Chamberlain!' He seemed about to embark upon a speech of some length, caught sight of Petersen and went to meet him. 'Peter, my boy. Once again all those dreadful trials and tribulations lie behind you. My word, I can't tell you how dull and depressing it's been here during the two weeks you've been gone. Dreadful, I tell you. Utterly dreadful.'

Petersen smiled. 'Hello, Jamie. Good to see you again. Things should improve now. George, quite illicitly, of course, has brought you some presents — quite a lot of presents, they almost broke the back of one of the ponies coming up here. Presents that go clink.' He turned to Sarina. 'May I introduce Captain Harrison. Captain Harrison,' he added with a straight face, 'is English. Jamie, this is Sarina von Karajan.'

Harrison shook her hand enthusiastically. 'Delighted, delighted. If only you knew how we miss even the commonest amenities of civilization in these benighted parts. Not, of course,' he added hastily, 'that there's anything common about you. My goodness, I should say not.' He looked at Petersen. 'The Harrisons' ill luck runs true to form again. We were born under an evil and accursed star. Do you mean to tell me that you have had the great fortune, the honour, the pleasure of escorting those two lovely ladies all the way from Italy?'

'Neither of them think there was any fortune, honour or pleasure about it. I didn't know you had the pleasure of knowing Lorraine before.' Giacomo had a sudden but very brief paroxysm of coughing which Petersen ignored.

'Oh, my goodness, yes, indeed. Old friends, very old. Worked together once, don't you know? Tell you some time. Your other new friends?' Petersen introduced Giacomo and Michael whom Harrison welcomed in what was his clearly customary effusive fashion, then said: 'Well, inside, inside. Can't have you all freezing to death in this abominable weather. I'll have your goods and chattels taken in. Inside, inside.'

'Inside' was surprisingly roomy, warm, well-lit and, by guerrilla standards, almost comfortable. There were three bunks running the length of each side of the room, some tall articles of furniture that could have been either cupboards or wardrobes, a deal table, half a dozen pine chairs, the unheard luxury of a couple of rather scruffy arm-chairs and even two strips of worn and faded carpet. At either end of the room were two doors that led, presumably, to further accommodation. Harrison closed the outside door behind him.

'Have a seat, have a seat.' The Captain was much given to repeating himself. 'George, if I may suggest — ah, foolish of me, I might have known that any such suggestion was superfluous.' George had, indeed, lost no time in doubling in his sparetime role of barman. Harrison looked around him with an air of proprietorial pride. 'Not bad, although I say it myself, not bad at all. You won't find many such havens in this strife-torn land. I regret to say that we live in accommodation such as this all too infrequently, but when we do we make the best of it. Electric light, if you please — you can't hear it but we have the only generator in the base apart from the commander. Need it for our big radios.' He pointed to two six-inch diameter pipes angling diagonally upwards along either wall to disappear through the roof. 'Central heating, of course. Actually, they're only the stove-pipes from our coke and wood stove outside. Would have it inside but we'd all be asphyxiated in minutes. And what do we have here, George?' He inspected the contents of a glass George had just handed him.

George shrugged and said diffidently: 'Nothing really. Highland malt whisky.'

'Highland malt whisky.' Harrison reverently surveyed the amber liquid, sipped it delicately and smiled in rapture. 'Where on earth did you get this, George?'

'Friend of mine in Rome.'

'God bless your Roman friends.' This time assuming his beatific expression in advance, Harrison sipped again. 'Well, that's about all the mod cons. That door to the left leads to my radio room. Some nice stuff in there but unfortunately we can't take most of it with us when we travel which, again unfortunately, is most of the time. The other door leads to what I rather splendidly call my sleeping quarters. It's about the size of a couple of telephone boxes but it does have two cots.'

Harrison took another sip from his glass and went on gallantly: 'Those quarters, naturally, I will gladly vacate for the night for the two young ladies.'

'You are very kind,' Sarina said doubtfully. 'But I — we — were supposed to report to the Colonel.'

'Nonsense. Not to be thought of. You are exhausted by your travels, your sufferings, your privations. One has only to look at you. I am sure the Colonel will gladly wait until the morning. Is that not so, Peter?'

'Tomorrow will be time enough.'

'Of course. Well, we castaways marooned on a mountain top are always eager for news of the outside world. What of the past fortnight, my friend?'

Petersen put down his untouched glass and rose. 'George will tell you. He's a much better raconteur than I am.'

'Well, yes, you do rather lack his gift for dramatic embellishment. Duty calls?' Petersen nodded.

'Ah! The Colonel?'

'Who else. I won't be long.'

*　*　*

When Petersen returned, he was not alone. The two men accompanying him were, like

213

himself, covered in a heavy coating of snow. While they were brushing this off, Harrison rose courteously and introduced them.

'Good evening, gentlemen. We are honoured.' He turned to the newcomers. 'Let me introduce Major Ranković, Major Metrović, two of the Colonel's senior commanders. You venture forth on a wild night, gentlemen.'

'You mean, of course, why have we come?' The speaker, Major Metrović, was a man of medium height, dark, thickset and cheerful. 'Curiosity, of course. Peter's movements are always shrouded in mystery and heaven knows we see little enough of new faces from the outer world.'

'Peter didn't also mention that two of those new faces were young, female and — I speak as a detached observer, of course — rather extraordinarily good-looking?'

'He may have done, he may have done.' Metrović smiled again. 'You know how it is with my colleague and myself. Our minds are invariably preoccupied with military matters. Isn't that so, Marino?'

Marino — Major Ranković — a tall, thin, dark-bearded and rather gloomy character, who looked as if he let Metrović do all the smiling for both of them, didn't say whether it was so or not. He seemed preoccupied and

214

the source of his preoccupation was unquestionably Giacomo.

'I asked them along,' Petersen said. 'I felt it was the least I could do to bring some relief into their cheerless lives.'

'Well, welcome, welcome.' Harrison looked at his watch. 'Won't be long, you said. What do you call short?'

'I wanted to give George a chance to finish his story. Besides, I was detained. Much questioning. And I stopped by at my radio hut to see if you'd made off with anything during my absence. It seems not. Perhaps you mislaid the key.'

'The radio hut?' Sarina glanced at the door at the end of the room. 'But we heard nothing. I mean — '

'My radio hut is fifty metres away. No mystery. There are three radios in the camp. One for the Colonel. One for Captain Harrison. One for me. You will be assigned to the Colonel. Lorraine comes here.'

'You arranged that?'

'I arranged nothing. I take orders, just like anyone else. The Colonel arranged it, Lorraine's assignation here was arranged weeks ago. There's no secret about it. The Colonel, for reasons that may seem obscure to you but which I understand very well, prefers that Captain Harrison's radio operator, like Captain Harrison himself, should not speak or understand Serbo-Croat. The basis of the Colonel's security beliefs is that one should trust nobody.'

'You must have a lot in common with the Colonel.'

'I think that's rather unfair, young lady.' It was Metrović again and he was still smiling. 'I can confirm what the Major has said. I'm the go-between, the translator, if you like, for the Colonel and Captain Harrison. Like the major, I was partly educated in England.'

'Enough,' Harrison said. 'Let us put unworthy thoughts to one side and concentrate on more important things.'

'Such as hospitality?' George said.

'Such as hospitality, as you say. Be seated, please. What is your choice, gentlemen — and ladies, of course?'

They all told him what they wanted, all, that is, except Major Ranković. He crossed to where Giacomo was seated and said: 'May I ask what your name is?'

Giacomo lifted his eyebrows in slight puzzlement, smiled and said: 'Giacomo.'

'That's an Italian name, isn't it?'

'Yes.'

'Giacomo what?'

'Just Giacomo.'

216

'Just Giacomo.' Ranković's voice was deep and gravelly. 'It suits you to be mysterious?'

'It suits me to mind my own business.'

'What's your rank?'

'That's my business, too.'

'I've seen you before. Not in the army, though. Rijeka, Split, Kotor, some place like that.'

'It's possible.' Giacomo was still smiling but the smile no longer extended to his eyes. 'It's a small enough world. I used to be a sailor.'

'You're a Yugoslav.'

Giacomo, Petersen was aware, could easily have conceded the fact but he knew he wouldn't. Ranković was an able soldier but no psychologist.

'I'm English.'

'You're a liar.'

Petersen stepped forward and tapped Ranković on the shoulder. 'If I were you, Marino, I'd quit while I was ahead. Not, mind you, that I think you are ahead.'

Ranković turned. 'What do you mean?'

'I mean that you're still intact and in one piece. Keep on like this and you'll wake up in hospital wondering if you fell under a train. I can vouch for Giacomo. He is English. He's got so long and so distinguished a war record that he puts any man in this room to shame. While you've been pottering around the mountains he's been fighting in France and Belgium and North Africa and the Aegean and usually on assignments so dangerous that you couldn't even begin to wonder what they were like. Look at his face, Marino. Look at it and you'll look into the face of war.'

Ranković studied Giacomo closely. 'I'm not a fool. I never questioned his qualities as a soldier. I was curious, that is all, and maybe, like the Colonel and yourself, I am not much given to trusting anyone. I did not intend to give offence.'

'And I didn't intend to take any,' Giacomo said. His good humour had returned. 'You're suspicious, I'm touchy. A bad mix. Let me suggest a good mix or rather no mix at all. You never mix malt whisky with anything, do you, George? Not even water?'

'Sacrilege.'

'You were right on one count, Major. I am English but I was born in Yugoslavia. Let us drink to Yugoslavia.'

'A toast no man could quarrel with,' Ranković said. There were no handshakes, no protestations of eternal friendship. It was, at best, a truce. Ranković, no actor, still had his reservations about Giacomo.

Petersen, for his part, had none.

Considerably later in the evening an understandably much more relaxed and mellowed atmosphere had descended upon the company. Some of them had paid a brief visit to a mess four hundred metres distant for an evening meal. Sarina and Lorraine had point-blank — and as it turned out, wisely — refused to brave the near blizzard that was now sweeping by outside. Michael, inevitably, had elected to remain with them and Giacomo, after a quick exchange of glances with Petersen, had announced that he was not hungry. Giacomo did not have to have it spelt out to him that, even among his own people, Petersen was suspicious of practically everybody in sight.

Compared to Josip Pijade's midday offerings, the meal was a gastronomic disaster. It was no fault of the Četnik cooks — as elsewhere through that ravaged country, food was at a premium and fine food almost wholly unobtainable. Still, it was a sad come-down from the flesh-pots of Italy and Mostar and even George could manage no more than two platefuls of the fatty mutton and beans which constituted the main and only course of the evening. They had left as soon as decency permitted.

Back in Harrison's radio hut their relative sufferings were soon forgotten.

'There's no place like home,' Harrison announced to nobody in particular. Although it would have been unfair to call him inebriated, it would have been fair to pass the opinion that he wasn't stone cold sober either.

He bent an appreciative gaze on the glass in his hand. 'Nectar emboldens me. George has given me a very comprehensive account of your activities over the past two weeks. He has not, however, told me *why* you went to Rome in the first place. Nor did you seek to enlighten me on your return.'

'That's because I didn't know myself.'

Harrison nodded sagely. 'That makes sense. You go all the way to Rome and back and you don't know why.'

'I was just carrying a message. I didn't know the contents.'

'Is one permitted to ask if you know the contents now?'

'One is permitted. I do.'

'Ah! Is one further permitted to know the contents?'

'In your own language, Jamie, I don't know whether I'm permitted or not. All I can say is that this is purely a military matter. Strictly, I am not a military man, a commander of troops. I'm an espionage agent. Espionage agents don't wage battles. We're far too clever for that. Or cowardly.'

Harrison looked at Metrović and Ranković in turn. 'You're military men. If I'm to believe half you tell me, you wage battles.'

Metrović smiled. 'We're not as clever as Peter.'

'You know the contents of the message?'

'Of course. Peter's discretion does him credit but it's not really necessary. Within a couple of days the news will be common knowledge throughout the camp. We — the Germans, Italians, ourselves and the Ustaša — are to launch an all-out offensive against the Partisans. We shall annihilate Titoland. The Germans have given the name of the attack 'Operation Weiss': the Partisans will doubtless call it the Fourth Offensive.'

Harrison seemed unimpressed. He said, doubtfully: 'That means, of course, that you've made three other offensives already. Those didn't get you very far, did they?'

Metrović was unruffled. 'I know it's easy to say, but this time really will be different. They're cornered. They're trapped. They've no way out, no place left to go. They haven't a single plane, fighter or bomber. We have squadrons upon squadrons. They haven't a tank, not even a single effective anti-aircraft

221

gun. At the most, they have fifteen thousand men, most of them starving, weak, sick and untrained. We have almost a hundred thousand men, well-trained and fit. And Tito's final weakness, his Achilles' heel, you might say, is his lack of mobility: he is known to have at least three thousand wounded men on his hands. It will be no contest. I don't say I look forward to it, but it will be a massacre. Are you a betting man, James?'

'Not against odds like that, I'm not. Like Peter here, I lay no claim to being a military man — I never even *saw* a uniform until three years ago — but if the action is so imminent why are you drinking wine at your leisured ease instead of being hunched over your war maps, sticking flags in here, flags in there, drawing up your battle plans or whatever you're supposed to be doing in cases like this?'

Metrović laughed. 'Three excellent reasons. First, the offensive is not imminent — it's two weeks away yet. Second, all the plans have already been drawn up and all the troops are already in position or will be in a few days. Third, the main assault takes place at Bihać, where the Partisan forces are at present centred, and that's over two hundred kilometres north-west of here. We're not taking part in that: we're staying just where we are in case the Partisans are so foolish, or optimistic or suicidal to try to break out to the south-east: stopping them from crossing the Neretva, in the remote possibility of a few stragglers getting as far as here, would be only a formality.' He paused and gazed at a darkened window. 'There may well be a fourth possibility. If the weather worsens, or even continues like this, the best laid plans of the High Command could well go wrong. A postponement would be inevitable. Nobody's going to be moving around the mountains in those impossible weather conditions for days to come, that's for sure. Days might well become weeks.'

'Well, yes,' Harrison said. 'One sees why you face the future with a certain resigned fortitude. On the basis of what you say the chances are good that you won't even become involved at all. For myself, I hope your prognosis is correct — as I've said I'm no man of war and I've become quite attached to these rather comfortable quarters. And do you, Peter, expect to hibernate along with us?'

'No. If the Colonel has nothing for me in the morning — and he gave no indication tonight that he would have — then I shall be on my way the following morning. Provided, of course, that we're not up to our ears in snowdrifts.'

'Whither away, if one is — '

'Permitted to ask? Yes. A certain Italian intelligence officer is taking an undue amount of interest in me. He's trying either to discredit me or hamper me in my operations. Has tried, I should say. I would like to find out why.'

Metrović said: 'In what way has he tried, Peter?'

'He and a gang of his thugs held us up in a Mostar hotel in the early hours of this morning. Looking for something, I suppose. Whether they found it or not I don't know. Shortly before that, on the boat coming from Italy, some of his minions tried to carry out a night attack on us. They failed, but not for the want of trying, for they were carrying syringes and lethal drugs which they were more than prepared to use.'

'Goodness me.' Harrison looked suitably appalled. 'What happened?'

'It was all quite painless, really,' George said with satisfaction. 'We welded them up in a cabin on the boat. Last heard of they were still there.'

Harrison looked reproachfully at George. 'Missed this out in your stirring account of your activities, didn't you?'

'Discretion, discretion.'

'This Italian intelligence officer,' Metrović said, 'is, of course an ally. With some allies, as we know, you don't need enemies. When you meet up with this ally what are you going to do? Question him or kill him?' The Major seemed to regard that as a very natural query.

'Kill him?' Sarina looked and was shocked. 'That nice man. Kill him! I thought you rather liked him.'

'Liked him? He's reasonable, personable, smiling, open-faced, has a firm handshake and looks you straight in the eye — anyone can tell at once that he's a member of the criminal classes. He was prepared to kill me, by proxy, mind you, through his hatchet-man Alessandro — which, if anything, makes it an even more heinous intention on his part — so why shouldn't I be prepared to pre-empt him? But I won't, at least not right away. I just want to ask him a few questions.'

'But — but you might not even be able to find him.'

'I'll find him.'

'And if he refuses to answer?'

'He'll answer.' There was the same chilling certainty in the voice.

She touched her lips with the back of her hand and fell silent. Metrović, his face thoughtful, said: 'You're not the man to ask questions unless you're pretty certain of the answers in advance. You're after confirmation of something. Could you not have obtained this confirmation at the hotel you mentioned?'

'Certainly. But I didn't want the place littered with corpses, not all of which might have been theirs. I'd promised to deliver this lot intact first. Everything in its due turn. Confirmation? I want confirmation of why Italy is planning to pull out of this war. That they want out I don't for a moment doubt. Their people never wanted this war. Their army, navy and air force never wanted it. Remember when Wavell's army in North Africa overwhelmed the Italians? There was a picture taken just after the last battle, a picture that was to become world-famous. It showed about a thousand Italian prisoners being marched off to their barbed wire cages escorted by three British soldiers. The sun was so hot that the soldiers had given their rifles to three of the prisoners to carry. That about sums up the Italian attitude to the war.

'Given a cause that is close to their hearts, the Italians can fight as gallantly as any people on earth. This cause is not close to their hearts — it couldn't be further away from it. This is Germany's war and they don't like fighting Germany's war because, basically, they don't like the Germans. It has been repeatedly claimed, both by the Italians and the British that the Italians are, at bottom, pro-British. The truth is, of course, that they're just pro-Italian.

'No-one is more acutely aware of this than the Italian high command. But there's more to it of course than just patriotism. There's no lack of first-class minds in the Italian high command and it's my belief that they are convinced, even at this early stage, that the Germans are going to lose the war.' Petersen looked round the room. 'It may not be your belief, it may not be my belief, but that's irrelevant. What matters is that I'm convinced it is their belief and that they are even now figuring out a way to arrive at an accommodation — for want of a better word — with the British and Americans. This accommodation, of course, would take the form of a full-scale surrender but, of course, it would be nothing of the sort. It would involve full-scale cooperation upon the part of the Italians with every aspect of the British and American forces just short of the front-line engagement of their troops in the front line.'

'You seem very sure about this, Peter,' Metrović said. 'How can you be so sure?'

'Because I have access to sources and

information that none of you has. I am in constant touch with both Italian and German forces in this country and, as you know, I'm a frequent visitor to Italy and have talked to literally hundreds of Italians there, both military men and civilians. I am neither literally deaf nor figuratively dumb. I know, for instance, that Italian Intelligence and German Intelligence are barely on civil speaking terms with each other and most certainly do not trust each other round the nearest corner in the street.

'General Granelli, Head of Italian Intelligence and Cipriano's boss — Cipriano is this Intelligence Major I was talking about — is an evil and warped character but out-and-out brilliant. He knows the situation and the options as well as anyone and is in no doubt that the Germans are going to go down in dust and flames and has no intention of joining them there. He's also pretty certain that I know quite well what the true situation is and that if I start voicing my doubts — my convictions, rather — out loud I could be a positive danger to him. I think he's been twice on the point of having me eliminated and has twice changed his mind at the last minute. I know there's going to be a third time which is one reason why I want to get out of here — before Cipriano or some other comes, in the guise of a loyal ally, naturally, and arranges for an accident to happen to me. But the main reason, of course, for my departure is to get to their link-man before he gets to me.'

'Link-man? Link-man?' Harrison shook his head in bafflement. 'You speak in riddles, Peter.'

'A riddle with a childishly easy answer. If the Germans go down who else is going to go down with them?'

'Ah-ha!'

'As you've just said, ah-ha. All those who have fought with them, that's who. Including us. If you were General Granelli and with Granelli's keen eye to the future, which of the opposing forces in Yugoslavia would you back?'

'Good Lord!' Harrison sounded slightly stunned. He looked around the room. The others, if not quite stunned, looked for the most part deeply pensive, not least Ranković and Metrović. 'What you are saying is that Granelli and this Major Cipriano are working hand-in-hand with the Partisans and that Cipriano is the master double-agent?'

Petersen rubbed his chin with his hand, glanced briefly at Harrison, sighed, poured himself some more red wine and did not deign to answer.

Petersen's radio shack did not begin to compare in magnificence with Harrison's, which they had left only a few moments previously, a premature departure arising directly from the conversational hiatus that had ensued immediately after Harrison's last words, a lacuna that went on and on and on. Harrison and the two Četnik officers were sunk in profound reverie, Sarina and Lorraine, by their expressions not by words, had made it clear that their aversion to Petersen had not only returned but was in fuller flood than ever and Alex and Michael, as ever, had nothing to say. Those two master conversationalists, George and Giacomo, had battled bravely but only briefly on. It was a lost cause.

The hut would have been big enough to serve as a one-car garage, if the car were small enough. Three beds, a table, three chairs, a cooking stove and that was all: the radio room was a tiny office next door.

'I am sad and disturbed,' George said. 'Profoundly disturbed.' He poured himself a large glass of wine and drank half of it in one apparently endless gulp just to show how profoundly disturbed he was. 'Sad, perhaps, is a better word. The realization that one's life and one's lifework has been a failure is a bitter pill to swallow. The damage to one's pride and self-esteem is irreparable. The effect, overall, is crushing.'

'I know what you mean,' Petersen said sympathetically. 'I've felt that myself.'

George might not have heard him. 'You will not have forgotten the days when you were my student in Belgrade?'

'Who could, ever? As you said yourself, not more than a hundred times, a walk with you through the rose-arboured groves of academe was an experience to remain with one always.'

'Remember the precepts I preached, the eternal verities I cherished? Honour, honesty, straightforwardness, the pure in mind, the open heart, the outright contempt for deceit, deception, dishonesty: we were, remember, to go through the darkness of this world guided solely by the light of the everlasting flame of truth?'

'Yes, George.'

'I am a broken man.'

'I'm sorry, George.'

7

There were six of them in all, and six tougher looking and more villainous characters it would have been almost impossible to imagine, far less find. There was a curious likeness about them. They were all just over medium height, all lean and broad-shouldered, all clad exactly alike: khaki trousers tucked into high boots, belted khaki canvas jacket over a khaki tunic, and khaki forage caps. They carried no badges, no identification marks. All were armed in precisely the same fashion: machine-pistols in hands, a revolver at waist level and hunting knives stuck into a sheath on the right boot. Their faces were dark and still, their eyes quiet and watchful. They were dangerous men.

Surprise had been complete, resistance — even the thought of a token resistance — unthinkable. The same company as had been in Harrison's hut the previous evening, had been there just a few minutes before eight that evening when the outside door had burst open and three men had been inside the door with levelled guns before anyone could even react. Now there were six inside, and the door was closed. One of the intruders, a little shorter and a little broader than the others, took a pace forward.

'My name is Crni.' It was the Serbo-Croat word for black. 'You will take off your weapons, one by one, and place them on the floor.' He nodded at Metrović. 'You begin.'

Within a minute every gun in the room — at least every visible gun — was lying on the floor. Crni beckoned Lorraine. 'Pick up those guns and put them on that table there. You will not, of course, be so stupid as to even think of firing any of them.'

Lorraine had no thought of firing any of them, her hands were shaking so much that she had some difficulty in picking them up. When they were on the table Crni said: 'Are either of you two young ladies armed?'

'They're not,' Petersen said. 'I guarantee it. If you find a weapon on their persons or in their bags you can shoot me.'

Crni looked at him almost quizzically, reached under his canvas jacket and produced a piece of paper from his tunic. 'What's your name?'

'Petersen.'

'Ah! Major Peter Petersen. At the very top of the list. One can see they're not carrying a weapon on their persons. But their bags?'

'I've searched them.'

The two girls momentarily stopped being apprehenisve and exchanged indignant glances. Crni smiled slightly.

'You should have told them. I believe you. If any man here is carrying a gun on his person and conceals the fact, then if I find it I'll shoot him. Through the heart.' Crni's matter-of-fact tone carried an unpleasant degree of conviction.

'There's no need to go around making all those ludicrous threats,' George said complainingly. 'If it's cooperation you want, I'm your man.' He produced an automatic from the depths of his clothing and nudged Alex in the ribs. 'Don't be foolish. I don't think this fellow Crni has any sense of humour.' Alex scowled and threw a similar automatic on the table.

'Thank you.' Crni consulted his list. 'You, of course, have to be the learned Professor, number two on our list.' He looked up at Alex. 'And you must be number three. It says here 'Alex brackets assassin'. Not much of a character reference. We'll bear that in mind.' He turned to one of his men. 'Edvard. Those coats hanging there. Search them.'

'No need,' Petersen said. 'Just the one on the left. That's mine. Right-hand pocket.'

'You are cooperative,' Crni said.

'I'm a professional, too.'

'I know that. I know quite a lot about you. Rather, I've been told quite a lot.' He looked at the gun Edvard had brought him. 'I didn't know they issued silenced Lugers to the Royal Yugoslav Army.'

'They don't. A friend gave it to me.'

'Of course. I have five other names on this list.' He looked at Harrison. 'You must be Captain James Harrison.'

'Why must I?'

'There are two officers in Yugoslavia who wear monocles? And you must be Giacomo. Just the one name. Giacomo.'

'Same question.'

'Description.'

Giacomo smiled. 'Flattering?'

'No. Just accurate.' He looked at Michael. 'And you, by elimination, must be Michael von Karajan. Two ladies.' He looked at Lorraine. 'You're Lorraine Chamberlain.'

'Yes.' She smiled wanly. 'You have my description, too?'

'Sarina von Karajan bears a remarkable resemblance to her twin brother,' Crni said patiently. 'You eight are coming with me.'

George said: 'May I ask a question?'

'No.'

'I think that's downright uncivil,' George said plaintively. 'And unfair. What if I wanted to go to the toilet?'

'I take it you are the resident comedian,' Crni said coldly. 'I hope your sense of humour bears with you in the days to come. Major, I'm going to hold you personally responsible for the conduct of your group.'

Petersen smiled. 'If anyone tries to run away, you'll shoot me?'

'I wouldn't have put it as crudely as that, Major.'

'Major this, Major that. Major Crni? Captain Crni?'

'Captain,' he said briefly. 'I prefer Crni. Do I have to be an officer?'

'They don't send a mess-boy to bring in apparently notorious criminals.'

'Nobody's said you're a criminal. Not yet.' He looked at the two Četnick officers. 'Your names?'

Metrović said: 'I'm Major Metrović. This is Major Ranković.'

'I've heard of you.' He turned to Petersen. 'You eight will be taking your baggage with you.'

'That's nice,' George said.

'What is?'

'Well,' George said reasonably, 'if we're taking our baggage with us it's hardly likely that you're going to shoot us out of hand.'

'To be a comedian is bad enough. To be a buffoon, insufferable.' He turned back to

Petersen. 'How many of the eight have their baggage here? Men and women, I mean?'

'Five. Three of us have our baggage in a hut about fifty yards away — myself and those two gentlemen here.'

'Slavko. Sava.' This to two of his men. 'This man Alex will show you where the hut is. Bring the baggage back. Search it very carefully first. And be just as careful in watching this man. He has an appalling record.' For a fleeting moment the expression on Alex's face made Crni's statement more than credible. 'Hurry nothing, watch everything.' He looked at his watch. 'We have forty minutes left.'

*   *   *

In less than half that time all the luggage had been packed and collected. George said: 'I know I'm not allowed to ask a question so may I make a statement? Oh, that's a question, too. I want to make a statement.'

'What?'

'I'm thirsty.'

'I see no harm.'

'Thank you.' George had opened a bottle and downed a glass of wine in what appeared near-impossible time.

'Try that other bottle,' Crni suggested.

George blinked, frowned, but willingly did what he was told. 'Seems satisfactory. My men could do with a specific against the cold.'

'Seems satisfactory?' George stared at him. 'You suggest that I could have doctored some bottles, poisoned bottles, against just such an impossible eventuality? Me? A faculty dean? A learned academic? A — a — '

'Some academics are more learned than others. You'd have done the same.' Three of his men took a glass: the other two held their unwavering guns. There was a discouraging certainty about everything Crni said and did: he seemed to take the minutest precautions against anything untoward, including, as George had said, the impossible eventuality.

Metrović said: 'What happens to Major Ranković and myself?'

'You remain behind.'

'Dead?'

'Alive. Bound and gagged but alive. We are not Četniks. We do not murder helpless soldiers, far less helpless civilians.'

'Nor do we.'

'Of course not. Those thousands of Muslims who perished in south Serbia died by their own hands. Cowards, were they not?'

Metrović made no reply.

'And how many more thousand Serbians

238

— men, women and children — were massacred in Croatia, with the most bestial atrocities ever recorded in the Balkans, just because of their religion?'

'We had no hand in that. The Ustaša are no soldiers, just undisciplined terrorists.'

'The Ustaša are your allies. Just as the Germans are your allies. Remember Kraguje-vac, Major, where the Partisans killed ten Germans and the Germans rounded up and shot five thousand Yugoslav citizens? Marched the children out of schools and shot them in droves until even the execution squads were sickened and mutinied? Your allies. Remem-ber the retreat from Užice where the German tanks rolled backwards and forwards over the fields until all the wounded Partisans lying there had been crushed to death? Your allies. The guilt of your murderous friends is your guilt too. Much as we would like to treat you in the same fashion we will not. I have my orders and, besides, you are at least technically our allies.' Crni's voice was heavy with contempt.

Metrović said: 'You are Partisans.'

'God forbid!' The revulsion in Crni's face was momentary but unmistakable. 'Do we look like guerrilla rabble? We are paratroopers of the Murge division.' The Murge was the best Italian division then operating in

239

south-east Europe. 'Your allies, as I said.' Crni gestured towards the eight prisoners. 'You harbour a nest of vipers. You can't recognize them as such, far less know what to do with them. We can do both.'

Metrović looked at Petersen. 'I think I owe you an apology, Peter. Last night I didn't know whether to believe your assessment or not. It seemed so fantastic. Not any more. You were right.'

'Much good that's done me. My forecast, I mean. I was twenty-four hours out.'

'Tie them up,' Crni said.

★ ★ ★

Immediately after leaving the hut, to nobody's surprise, they were joined by two other soldiers: Crni was not the man to spend almost an hour inside any place without having a guard posted outside. That those were elite troops was beyond question. It was a bitter night, with driving snow, a biting wind and zero visibility but Crni and his men not only put up with the extreme conditions but seemed positively to revel in them.

Metrović had been wrong more than once the previous night. He had said that nobody was going to be moving around the mountains in those impossible weather conditions for days to come: Crni and his men were there to prove him wrong.

Once they were well clear of the camp Crni and his men produced torches. The prisoners were arranged so that they trudged on in single file through the deepening snow — it was already almost knee-high — while four of the guards walked on either side of them. By and by, at a command from Crni, they halted.

Crni said: 'Here, I'm afraid, we have to tie you up. Your wrists. Behind your backs.'

'I'm surprised you haven't done it before,' Petersen said. 'I'm even more surprised that you want to do it now. You have in mind to kill us all, perhaps?'

'Explain yourself.'

'We are at the head of that track leading down the mountain-side to the valley floor?'

'How do you know?'

'Because the wind hasn't changed since yesterday. You have ponies?'

'Two only. For the ladies. That was all you required yesterday.'

'You are very well informed. And the rest of us are to have our hands bound behind our backs just in case we feel tempted to give you or one of your men a brisk shove over the precipice. Mistake, Captain Crni, mistake. Out of character.'

'Indeed?'

'Two reasons. The surface of that rock is broken and slippery with either ice or hard-packed snow. If a man slips on that surface how is he, with his hands tied behind his back, going to grab at the ground to stop himself sliding over the edge — and how's he going to be able to maintain his balance in the first place with his hands tied? To keep your balance you have to be able to stretch both arms wide. You should know that. It's as good as sending people to their deaths. Second reason is that your men don't have to be anywhere near the prisoners. Four of them well in advance, four well behind, the prisoners, maybe with a couple of torches, in the middle. What positive action could the prisoners take then except commit suicide by jumping off the precipice? I can assure you that none of them is in the least suicidally inclined.'

'I am not a mountaineer, Major Petersen. I take your point.'

'Another request, if I may. Let Giacomo and myself walk alongside the young ladies' ponies. I'm afraid the young ladies don't care too much for heights.'

'I don't want you!' Even the prospect of the descent had brought a note of hysteria into Sarina's voice. 'I don't want you!'

'She doesn't want you,' Crni said drily.

242

'She doesn't know what she's saying. It's just a personal opinion of mine. She suffers severely from vertigo. What have I to gain by saying so?'

'Nothing that I can see.'

As they lined up by the cliff-top, Giacomo, leading a pony, brushed by Petersen and said, sotto voce: 'That, Major, was quite a performance.' He vanished into the snow with Petersen looking thoughtfully after him.

A steep descent, in treacherous conditions, is always more difficult and dangerous than a steep ascent and so it was to prove in this case. It is also slower and it took them all of forty minutes to reach the valley floor but reach it they did without incident. Sarina spoke for the first time since they had left the plateau.

'We are down?'

'Safe and sound as ever was.'

She gave a long quavering sigh. 'Thank you. You don't need to hold my horse any more.'

'Pony. Whatever you say. I was getting quite attached to the old lady.'

'I'm sorry,' she said quickly. 'I didn't mean it that way. It's just that you're so — so awful and so kind. No, *I'm* the person who is awful. *You're* the person they're after.'

'As is only fitting. My rank.'

243

'They're going to kill you, aren't they?'

'Kill me? What a thought. Why should they? A little discreet questioning perhaps.'

'You said yourself that General Granelli is an evil man.'

'General Granelli is in Rome. Haven't you given any thought as to what is going to happen to you?'

'No, I haven't.' Her voice was dull. 'I don't think I care what's going to happen to me.'

'That,' said Petersen, 'is what is known as a conversation stopper.'

They moved on in silence, the still heavily falling snow now at their backs, until Crni called a halt. He had the beam of his torch directed at the Italian army truck Petersen had stolen two days previously.

'It was thoughtful of you, Major, to leave transport so conveniently at hand.'

'If we can help our allies — you didn't arrive by this.'

'It was thoughtful, but not necessary.' Crni moved the beam of the torch. Another, even larger Italian truck, was parked close by. 'All of you, into that truck. Edvard, come with me.'

The eight prisoners were ushered into the larger truck and made to sit on the floor crowded up against the cab. Five soldiers followed them and sat on side benches towards the rear. Five torch beams were directed forwards and in the light of the beams it was possible to see that an equal number of machine-pistol barrels were pointed in the same direction. The engine started up and the truck jolted off. Five minutes later they turned right on to the main Neretva road.

'Ah!' Harrison said. 'Bound for the bright lights of Jablanica, I see.'

'On this road, where else?' Petersen said. 'After that the road divides. We could be going anywhere. I would guess that Jablanica is as far as we go. It's getting late. Even Crni and his men have to sleep.'

Shortly afterwards the driver stopped both the truck and the engine.

'I don't see any bright lights around here,' Harrison said. 'What are those devils up to now?'

'Nothing that concerns us,' Petersen said. 'Our driver is just waiting for Crni and his friend Edvard to join him up front.'

'Why? They have their own transport.'

'Had. It's in the Neretva now. That lad who met us yesterday — you remember, Dominic, the driver with the sunglasses — would not have failed to note the make and number of the truck. When and if Ranković and Metrović are discovered and freed — which may not be for hours yet — the proverbial hue and cry may be raised. 'May', I say. I doubt it. The Colonel is not a man to publicize the security gaps in his forces. But Crni doesn't strike me as a man to take the slightest chance.'

'Objection,' Giacomo said. 'If your friend Cipriano is the man behind this, he already knows the description of the truck. So what's the point in destroying the truck?'

'Giacomo, you sadden me. We don't *know* that Cipriano is the man behind this but if he is he wouldn't want to leave any clue that would point a finger at him in connection with the abduction. Remember that, officially, he and the Colonel are sworn allies, faithful unto death.'

Voices came from up front, a door banged, the engine started again and the truck moved off. 'That must be the way of it,' Giacomo said to no-one in particular. 'Pity about the truck, though.'

They jolted on through the snow-filled night, torch beams and barrels still pointed at them, until suddenly Harrison said: 'At last. Civilization. It's a long time since I've seen city lights.'

Harrison, as was his custom, was exaggerating to a considerable extent. A few dim lights appeared occasionally through the opened back of the truck but hardly enough to lend the impression that they were driving through a metropolis. By and by the truck pulled off on to a side road, climbed briefly, then stopped. The guards apparently knew where they were and did not wait for orders. They jumped down, lined up torches and guns as before and were joined by Crni.

'Down,' he said. 'This is as far as we go tonight.'

They lowered themselves to the ground and looked around them. As far as could be judged from the light of the beams, the building before them appeared to be standing alone and seemed, vaguely, to be shaped like a chalet. But, in the darkness and the snow it could have been just any building.

Crni led the way inside. The hallway presented a pleasant contrast to the swirling cold of the wintry night outside. The furnishings were sparse enough, just a table, a few chairs and a dresser, but it was warm — a small log fire burned in a low hearth — and warmly if not brightly lit: electric power had not yet reached this part of Jablanica and suspended oil lamps were the norm.

'Door to the left is a bathroom,' Crni said. 'Can be used anytime. There will, of course,' he added unnecessarily, 'be a guard in the hall all the time. The other door to the left leads to the main quarters of the house and does not concern you. Neither do those stairs.' He led the way to an opened door on the far right and ushered them inside. 'Your quarters for the night.'

The room was unmistakably such as one would only find in a chalet. It was long, wide and low, with beamed ceiling, knotted pine walls and an oak parquet floor. Cushioned benches ran both sides of the room, there was a table, several armchairs, a very commodious dresser, some cupboards and shelves and, best of all, a rather splendid log fire several times the size of the one in the hallway. The only immediately incongruous note was struck by some canvas cots, blankets and pillows stacked neatly in one corner. It was George, inevitably, who discovered the second and not so immediately incongruous note. He pulled back the curtains covering one of the two windows and examined with interest the massive bars on the outside.

'It is part of the general malaise of our times,' he said sadly. 'With the onset of war, the deterioration of standards is as immediate as it is inevitable. The rules of honour, decency and common law go by default and moral degeneracy rears its ugly head.' He let fall the curtains. 'A wise precaution, very wise. One feels sure that the streets of Jablanica are infested by burglars, house-breakers, footpads and other criminals of that ilk.'

Crni ignored him and looked at Petersen who was inspecting the bedding. 'Yes, Major, I can count, too. Only six cots. We have a room upstairs for the two young ladies.'

'Considerate. You were very sure of yourself, weren't you, Captain Crni?'

'Oh, no, he wasn't,' George said disgustedly. 'A blind man could drive a coach and four with bells on through Mihajlović's perimeter.'

For a second time Crni ignored him. He had probably come to the conclusion that this was the only way to treat him.

'We may or may not move on tomorrow. It certainly won't be early. Depends entirely on the weather. From now on our travel will be mainly on foot. Should you be hungry, there's food in that cupboard there. The contents of that high dresser will be of more interest to the professor.'

'Ah!' George opened the doors and looked appreciatively at what was, in effect, a comprehensively stocked miniature bar. 'The window bars are superfluous, Captain Crni. I shall not be moving on tonight.'

'Even if you could, where would you go?

When you ladies want to sleep, let the guard know and I'll show you your room. I may or may not wish to interrogate you later, it depends on a call I have to make.'

'You surprise me,' Petersen said. 'I thought the phone system had ceased to work.'

'Radio, of course. We do have one. In fact, we have four, the other three being yours and those two very modern sets belonging to the von Karajans. I expect the code books will also prove to be useful.'

He left behind him a profound and fairly lengthy silence interrupted only by the sound of a cork being extracted from a bottle. Michael was the first to speak.

'Radios,' he said bitterly. 'Code books.' He looked accusingly at Petersen. 'You know what this means, don't you?'

'Yes. Nothing. Crni was amusing himself. All it means is that we will be put to the trouble of getting ourselves a new code. What else do you think they'll do after they discover the books are missing? They will do this, of course, not to protect themselves against their enemies but against their friends. The Germans have twice broken the code that we use among ourselves.' He looked at Harrison, who had seated himself, cross-legged, in an arm-chair before the fire and was contemplating a glass of wine that George had just handed him. 'For a man who has just been driven from house and home, Jamie, or snatched from it, which comes to the same thing, you don't look all that downcast to me.'

'I'm not,' Harrison said comfortably. 'No reason to be. I never thought I'd find quarters better than my last one but I was wrong, I mean, look, a real log fire. Carpe diem, as the man says. What, Peter, do you think the future holds for us?'

'I wouldn't know how to use a crystal ball.'

'Pity. It would have been nice to think that I might see the white cliffs of Dover again.'

'I don't see why not. No one's after your blood. I mean, you haven't been up to anything, have you, Jamie? Such as sending clandestine radio messages, in codes unknown to us, to parties also unknown to us?'

'Certainly not.' Harrison was unruffled. 'I'm not that kind of person, I don't have any secrets and I'm useless with a radio anyway. So you think I might see the white cliffs again. Do you think I'll be seeing the old homestead on Mount Prenj again?'

'I should think it highly unlikely.'

'Well now. A fairly confident prediction and without a crystal ball.'

'For that, I don't need a crystal ball. A person who has occupied the — ah

— delicate position you have done will never again be employed in that capacity after he's been captured by the enemy. Torturing, brain-washing, reconversion to a double-agent, that sort of thing. Standard practice. You'd never be trusted again.'

'I say, that's a bit thick, isn't it? A blameless, stainless reputation. It's hardly my fault that I've been captured. It wouldn't have happened if you people had looked after me a bit better. Thank you, George, I will have a little more. Now that I'm happily out of that place, I've no intention of ever returning to it, not unless I'm dragged forcibly back to it, kicking and screaming in the accepted fashion.' He raised his glass. 'Your health, Peter.'

'You have taken an aversion to the people, the Četniks, the Colonel, myself?'

'A profound aversion. Well, not to you, although I must admit I don't care overmuch for what might be called your military politics. You're a total enigma to me, Peter, but I'd rather have you on my side than against me. As for the rest, I despise them. An extraordinary position for an ally to find himself in, is it not?'

'I think I'll have some wine, too, George, if I may. Well, yes, Jamie, it's true, you have made your discontent — I might even say displeasure — rather guardedly evident from time to time but I thought you were doing no more than exercising every soldier's inalienable right to complain loudly and at length about every conceivable aspect of army life.' He sipped his wine thoughtfully. 'One gathers there was something a little more to it than that?'

'A little more? There was a great deal more.' Harrison sipped his wine and gazed at the burning logs, a man relaxed, at peace with himself. 'In spite of the fact that the future looks somewhat uncertain, in some ways I owe our Captain Crni a favour. He's done no more than to pre-empt my decision, my intention, to leave Mount Prenj and its miserable inhabitants at the first convenient opportunity. Had it not been for the unexpected happening of the past couple of hours, you'd have discovered that I'd already made an official request for an official recall. But, of course, as matters stood before the appearance of Captain Crni, I wouldn't have made any such disclosures anyway.'

'I could have misjudged you, Jamie.'

'Indeed you could.' He looked around the room to see if there was anyone else misjudging him, but there was no-one thinking along those lines: a magnet to the iron filings, he had the undivided attention of every person in the room.

'So you didn't — don't — like us?'

'I should have thought that I had made that abundantly clear. I may be no soldier, and the good Lord knows that I'm not, but I'm no clown either, all appearances to the contrary. I'm educated after a fashion: in practically any intellectual field that matters the average soldier is a virtual illiterate. I'm not educated in the way George is, I don't float around in cloud-cuckoo-land or wander among the groves of academe.' George looked profoundly hurt and reached for the wine bottle. 'I have been educated in a more practical fashion. Wouldn't you agree, Lorraine?'

'I would.' She smiled and said as if by rote: 'B.Sc., M.Sc., A.M.I.E.E., A.M.I.Mech.E. Oh, he's educated, all right. I used to be James's secretary.'

'Well, well, well,' Petersen said. 'The world grows even smaller.' Giacomo covered his face with his hand.

'Bachelor of Science, Master of Science we understand,' George said. 'As for the rest, it sounds as if he was coming down with a terminal illness.'

'Associate Member of the Institute of Electrical Engineers,' Lorraine said. 'Associate Member of the Institute of Mechanical Engineers.'

'It's unimportant.' Harrison was impatient. 'Point is I've been trained to observe, evaluate and analyze. I've been out here less than two months but I can tell you it took only a fraction of that time and a minimum of observation, evaluation and analysis to realize that Britain was backing the wrong horse in the Yugoslav stakes.

'I speak as a British officer. I don't want to sound overly dramatic, but Britain is locked, literally, in mortal combat with Germany. How do we defeat the Germans — by fighting them and killing them. How should we judge our allies or potential allies, what yardstick should we use? One. Only one. Are *they* fighting and killing Germans? Is Mihajlović? Is he hell. He's fighting with the Germans, alongside the Germans. Tito? Every German soldier caught in the sights of a Partisan rifle is a dead man. Yet those fools and dolts and idiots in London keep sending supplies to Mihajlović, a man who is in effect their sworn enemy. I am ashamed for my own people. The only possible reason for this — God knows it's no excuse — is that Britain's war, as far as the Balkans is concerned, is being run by politicians and soldiers, and politicians are almost as naïve and illiterate as soldiers.'

George said: 'You speak harsh words about your own people, James.'

'Shut up! No, sorry, George, I didn't mean that, but in spite or maybe because of your vast education you're just as naïve and illiterate as any of them. Harsh but true. How does this extraordinary situation come about? Mihajlović is a near Machiavellian genius in international diplomacy: Tito is too busy killing Germans to have any time for any such thing.

'As far back as September 1941 Mihajlović and his Četniks, instead of fighting the Germans, were busy establishing contacts with your precious Royalist government in London. Yes, Peter Petersen, precious I said and precious I did not mean. They don't give a damn about the unimaginable sufferings of the Yugoslav people, all they want to do is to regain royal power and if it's over the bodies of one or two millions of their countrymen, so much the worse for their countrymen. And, of course, Mihajlović, when contacting King Peter and his so-called advisers could hardly help contacting the British government as well. What a bonus! And naturally, at the same time, he contacted the British forces in the Middle East. For all I know the dunderheaded brasshats in Cairo may still regard the Colonel as the great white hope for

Yugoslavia.' He gestured towards Sarina and Michael. 'In fact, the dunderheads unquestionably still do. Look at this gullible young couple here, specially trained by the British to come to the aid and comfort of the gallant Četniks.'

'We're not gullible!' Sarina's voice was strained, her hands twisted together and she could have been close to either anger or tears. 'We weren't trained by the British, we were trained by the Americans. And we *didn't* come to give aid and comfort to the Četniks.'

'There are no American radio operator schools in Cairo. Only British. If you received American training it was because the British wanted it that way.' Harrison's tone was as cool and discouraging as his face. 'I think you're gullible, I think you tell lies and I believe you came to help the Četniks. I also think you're a fine actress.'

'Good for you, Jamie,' Petersen said approvingly. 'You got one thing right there. She *is* a fine actress. But she's not gullible, she doesn't tell lies — well, maybe one or two little white ones — and she didn't come to help us.'

Both Harrison and Sarina stared at him in astonishment. Harrison said: 'How on earth can you say that?'

'Intuition.'

'Intuition!' Harrison, was, for Harrison, being heavily sardonic. 'If your intuition is on a par with your judgment you can mothball the two of them together. And don't try to side-track me. Hasn't it struck you as ironic that when you and your precious Četniks' — Harrison was very fond of the word 'precious' and used it, always in its most derogatory sense, with telling effect — 'were receiving arms and payments from the Germans, Italians and Nedić's quisling Serb régime, that you were simultaneously receiving arms and payments from the western allies — this, mark you, at a time when you were fighting along with the Germans, Italians and Ustaša in an attempt to destroy the Partisans, Britain's only real allies in Yugoslavia?'

'Have some more wine, Jamie.'

'Thank you, George.' Harrison shook his head. 'I confess myself to being totally baffled and, when I say that, I mean baffled all round. By you Četniks and by my own people. Can it really be that there are none so blind as will not see? Are you so gagged and blinkered by your all-consuming and wholly misguided sense of patriotism, by your blind allegiance to a discredited royalty that your myopic eyes are so reduced to a ten-degree field of tunnel vision that you have no concept of the three hundred and fifty degree of peripheral vision that lies beyond? Are my people in London similarly affected? They have to be, they have to be, for what else could explain the inexplicable, the incomprehensible idiocy of keeping on sending supplies to Mihajlović when they have before them incontrovertible evidence that he is actively collaborating with the Germans.'

'I'll bet you couldn't say that again,' Petersen said admiringly. 'All the big words, I mean. As you say, Jamie, it's all probably reduced to a factor of vision, what lies in the eye of the beholder.' He rose, crossed over to the fireplace and sat down beside Sarina. 'This is not really a switch, we're talking about the same thing. How did you enjoy your tête-à-tête with the Colonel this morning?'

'Tête-à-tête? I didn't have any tête-à-tête with him. Michael and I just reported to him. You told us to. Or have you forgotten?'

'I've forgotten nothing. But I think you have. Walls have ears. Not original, but still true.'

She glanced quickly at Michael then back again. 'I don't know what you're talking about.'

'Walls also have eyes.'

'Stop brow-beating my sister!' Michael shouted.

'Brow-beating? Asking a simple question is brow-beating? If that's what you call brow-beating maybe I should start beating you about the brow. You were there, too, of course. You got anything to tell me? You have, you know. I already know what your answer should be. Your truthful answer.'

'I've got nothing to tell you! Nothing! Nothing at all!'

'You're a lousy actor. Also, you're too vehement by half.'

'I've had enough of you, Petersen!' Michael was breathing quickly and shallowly. 'Enough of your bullying my sister and me.' He jumped to his feet. 'If you think I'm going to stand — '

'You're not going to stand, Michael.' George had come up behind Michael and laid his hands on his shoulders. 'You're going to sit.' Michael sat. 'If you can't keep quiet I'll have to tie and gag you. Major Petersen is asking questions.'

'Good Lord!' Harrison was or seemed outraged. 'This *is* a bit thick, George. A bit high-handed, I must say. Peter, I don't think you're any longer in a position to — '

'And if *you* don't keep quiet,' George said with a trace of weariness in his voice, 'I'll do the same thing to you.'

'To me!' No question, this time the outrage was genuine. 'Me? An officer? A Captain in the British Army! By God! Giacomo, you're an Englishman. I appeal to you — '

'Appeal is denied. I wouldn't hurt an officer's feelings by telling him to shut up, but I think the Major is trying to establish something. You may not like his military philosophy but at least you should keep an open mind. And I think Sarina should too. I think you're both being foolish.'

Harrison muttered 'My God' twice and subsided.

Petersen said: 'Thanks, Giacomo. Sarina, if you think I'm trying to hurt you or harm you then you are, as Giacomo says, being foolish. I couldn't and wouldn't. I want to help. Did you and the Colonel have or not have a private conversation?'

'We talked, if that's what you mean.'

'Of *course* you talked. If I sound a bit exasperated, it's pardonable. What did you talk about? Me?'

'No. Yes. I mean, among other things.'

'Among other things,' he mimicked. 'What other things?'

'Just other things. Just generally.'

'That's a lie. You talked just about me and, maybe, a bit about Colonel Lunz. Remember, walls can have both ears and eyes. And you can't remember what you said when you sold me down the river which is where I am now. How many pieces of silver did the good Colonel give you?'

'I never did!' She was breathing quickly now and there were patches of red high up on her cheeks. 'I didn't betray you. I didn't! I didn't!'

'And all for a little piece of paper. I hope you got your due. You earned your thirty pieces. You didn't know that I'd picked up the paper later, did you?' He brought a piece of paper out from his tunic and unfolded it. 'This one.'

She stared at it dully, looked at him equally dully, put her elbows on her knees, her face in her hands. 'I don't know what's going on.' Her voice was muffled. 'I don't know any more. I know you're a bad man, a wicked man, but I didn't betray you.'

'I know you didn't.' He reached out a gentle hand and touched her shoulder. 'But I know what's going on. I have done all along. I'm sorry if I hurt you but I had to get you to say it. Why couldn't you have admitted it in the first place? Or have you forgotten what I said only yesterday morning?'

'Forgotten what?' She took her hands from her face and looked at him. It was difficult to say if the hazel eyes were still dull for there were tears in them.

'That you're far too nice and too transparently honest to do anything underhand. There were three pieces of paper. The one I gave to the Colonel, this one I'd made out before leaving Rome — I never picked anything up after your talk with him — and the one Colonel Lunz had given to you.'

'You *are* clever, aren't you?' She'd wiped the tears from her eyes and they weren't dull any more, just mad.

'Cleverer than you are, anyway,' Petersen said cheerfully. 'For some inexplicable reason Lunz thought that I might be some kind of spy or double agent and change the message, forge a different set of orders. But I didn't, did I? The message I gave the Colonel was the one I received and it checked with the copy Lunz had given you. Paradoxically, of course — you being a woman — this annoyed you. If I had been a spy, a sort of reconverted renegade who had gone over to the other side, you would have been no end pleased, wouldn't you? You might have respected me, even liked me a little. Well, I remained an unreconstructed Četnik. You were aware, of course, that if I *had* changed the orders that Mihajlović would have had me executed?'

A little colour drained from her face and

she touched her hand to her lips.

'Of course you were unaware. Not only are you incapable of double-dealing, not only are you incapable of thinking along double-dealing lines, you're not even capable of thinking of the consequences to the double-dealer who has overplayed his hand. How an otherwise intelligent girl — well, never mind. As I've said before, in this nasty espionage world, leave the thinking to those who are capable of it. Why did you do it, Sarina?'

'Why did I do what?' All of a sudden she seemed quite defenceless. She said, almost in a monotone: 'What am I going to be accused of now?'

'Nothing, my dear. I promise you. Nothing. I was just wondering, although I'm sure I know why, how it came about that you went along with this underground deal with Colonel Lunz, something so completely alien to your nature. It was because it was your only way into Yugoslavia. If you had refused, he'd have refused you entrance. So I've answered my own question.' Petersen rose. 'Wine, George, wine. All this talk is thirsty work.'

'What is not common knowledge,' George said, 'is that listening is even thirstier work.'

Petersen lifted his replenished glass and turned towards Harrison. 'To your health,

Jamie. As a British officer, of course.'

'Yes, yes, of course.' Clutching his glass Harrison struggled to his feet. 'Of course. Your health. Ah. Well. Extenuating circumstances, old boy. How was I — '

'And a gentleman.'

'Of course, of course.' He was still confused. 'A gentleman.'

'Were you being a gentleman, Jamie, when you called her a gullible liar, and an aider and comforter to us miserable lot? This lovely and charming lady is not only not that, she's something you've been looking for, something to gladden your patriotic heart, a true blue loyalist and not a true blue Royalist, a patriot in your best sense of the word, what you would call a Yugoslav. As dedicated a Partisan as one can be who has never seen a Partisan in her life. That's why she and her brother came back to this country the hard way, to give — as you would put it in your customary stirring language, Jamie — their services to their country, i.e., the Partisans.'

Harrison put down his glass, crossed to where Sarina was sitting, stooped low, lifted the back of her hand and kissed it. 'Your servant, ma'am.'

'That's an apology?' George said.

'For an English officer,' Petersen said, 'that is — as an English officer would say — a jolly handsome apology.'

'He's not the only one who's due to make an apology.' Michael wasn't actually shuffling his feet but he looked as if he would have liked to. 'Major Petersen, I have — '

'No apology, Michael,' Petersen said hastily. 'No apology. If I'd a sister like that, I wouldn't even talk to her tormentor, in this case, me. I'd clobber him over the head with a two by four. So if I don't apologise to your sister for what I've done to her, don't you apologize to me.'

'Thank you very much, sir.' He hesitated. 'May I ask how long you've known that Sarina and I were — well, what you say we are.'

'From the first time I saw you. Rather, let me say I suspected something was far wrong when I met you in that Rome apartment. You were both stiff, awkward, ill at ease, reserved, even truculent. No smile on the lips, no song in the heart, none of the eagerness, the youthful enthusiasm of those marching off into a glorious future. Ultra-cautious, ultra-suspicious. Wrong attitude altogether. If you'd been flying red flags you couldn't have indicated more clearly that something was weighing heavily on your minds. Your pasts were so blameless, so your concern was obviously with future problems such — as became evident quite soon — how you were going to transfer yourselves to the Partisan camp after you had arrived at our HQ. Your sister lost little time in giving you away — it was in the mountain inn when she tried to convince me of her Royalist sympathies. Told me she was a pal of King Peter's — prince, as he was then.'

'I never did!' Her indignation was unconvincing. 'I just met him a few times.'

'Sarina.' The tone was mildly reproving.

She said nothing.

'How often must I tell you — '

'Oh, all right,' she said.

'She's never met him in her life. She sympathized with me about his club foot. Young lad's as fit as a fiddle. Wouldn't know a club foot if he saw one. Well, all this is of interest but I'm afraid only academic interest.'

'Oh, I don't know,' Giacomo said. 'It's of more than academic interest to me.' He was, as always, smiling, but in the circumstances, it was difficult to say what he was smiling about. 'However, as a matter of academic interest, I'm totally in agreement with those kids — sorry, I mean Sarina and Michael. I don't want to fight — I mean I don't want to fight in those damned mountains; the Aegean and the Royal Navy will do me very nicely, thank you — but if I have to it'll be with the Partisans.'

'You're like Jamie,' Petersen said. 'If you're going to fight anybody it's going to be the Germans?'

'I think I made that pretty clear to you back in the Hotel Eden.'

'You did. It's still only a matter of academic interest. What are you going to do about it? How do you intend going about joining your guerrilla friends?'

Giacomo smiled. 'I'll wait for a break.'

'You could wait for ever.'

'Peter.' There was a note of appeal, almost desperation, in Harrison's voice. 'I know you owe us nothing, that you have no responsibility for us any more. But there must be a way. However different our philosophies, we're all in this together. Come on, Peter. We could settle our differences afterwards. Meantime — well, a man of your infinite resources and — '

'Jamie,' Petersen said gently. 'Can't you see the fence down the middle of this room. George, Alex and I are on one side. You five are on the other. Well, you, the von Karajans and Giacomo are. I don't know about Lorraine. It's a mile high, that fence, Jamie, and not for climbing.'

'I see his point, Captain Harrison,' Giacomo said. 'The fence is not for climbing.

Besides, my pride wouldn't let me try it. I must say, Major, it's not like you to leave loose ends lying around. Lorraine, here. Doesn't she fit into a category? For our edification, I mean.'

'Category? I don't know. And not to give you offence, Lorraine, but I don't really care now. It doesn't matter. Not any more.' He sat down, glass in hand, and said no more. As far as anyone could tell, Major Petersen had, for the first time in their experience, lapsed into a brooding silence.

It was a silence, punctuated only by the occasional glug-glug as George topped empty wineglasses, that stretched on and uncomfortably on, until Lorraine said suddenly and sharply: 'What's wrong? Please, what's wrong?'

'Speaking to me?' Petersen said.

'Yes. You're staring at me. You keep on staring at me.'

'Being on the wrong side of a fence doesn't stop a man from having good taste,' Giacomo said.

'I wasn't aware of it,' Petersen said. He smiled. 'Besides, as Giacomo said, it's no hardship. I'm sorry. I was a long long way away, that's all.'

'And speaking of staring,' Giacomo said cheerfully, 'Sarina's no slouch at it either. Her eyes haven't left your face since you started your Rodin the thinker bit. There are deep currents, hereabouts. Do you know what I think? I think she's thinking.'

'Oh, do be quiet, Giacomo.' She sounded positively cross.

'Well, I suppose we're all thinking one way or another,' Petersen said. 'Heaven knows we've plenty to think about. You, Jamie, you're sunk in a pretty profound gloom. The bright lights? No. The white cliffs? No. Ah! The lights of home.'

Harrison smiled and said nothing.

'What's she like, Jamie?'

'What's she like?' Harrison smiled again, shrugged and looked at Lorraine.

'Jenny's wonderful,' Lorraine said quietly. 'I think she's the most wonderful person in the world. She's my best friend and James doesn't deserve her. She's worth ten of him.'

Harrison smiled like a man who was well-pleased with himself and reached for his wineglass; if he was wounded, he hid it well.

Petersen looked away until his eyes lighted casually on Giacomo, who nodded almost imperceptibly: Petersen smiled slightly and looked away.

★ ★ ★

Twenty more minutes passed, partly in desultory conversation but mainly in silence, before the door opened and Edvard entered. 'Major Petersen?'

Petersen rose. Giacomo made to speak but Petersen forestalled him. 'Don't say it. Thumb-screws.'

He was back inside five minutes. Giacomo looked disappointed. 'No thumb-screws?'

'No thumb-screws. I would like to say that they're bringing out a rack and that you're next. No rack. But you're next.'

Giacomo left. Harrison said: 'What was it like. What did they want?'

'Very humane. Very civilized. What you would expect of Crni. Lots of questions, some very personal, but I just gave them name, rank and regiment, which is all you're legally required to give. They didn't press the matter.'

Giacomo was back in even less time than Petersen. 'Disappointing,' he said. 'Very disappointing. They'd never have made the Spanish Inquisition. The courtesy of your presence, Captain Harrison.'

Harrison was away a little longer than either but not much. He returned looking very thoughtful. 'You're next, Lorraine.'

'Me?' She stood and hesitated. 'Well, if I don't go I suppose they'll come for me.'

'It would be most unseemly,' Petersen said. 'We've survived. What's a lion's den to an English girl like you?'

She nodded and left, but left reluctantly. Petersen said: 'How was it, Jamie?'

'An urbane lot, as you say. Seemed to know a surprising amount about me. No questions that had any military bearing that I could see.'

Lorraine was absent for at least fifteen minutes. When she returned she was rather pale and although there were no tears on her cheeks it seemed clear that she had been crying. Sarina looked at Petersen, Harrison and Giacomo, shook her head and put her arm round Lorraine's shoulders.

'They're a gallant lot, aren't they, Lorraine? Chivalrous. Concerned.' She gave them a withering glance. 'Maybe they're just shy. Who's next?'

'They didn't ask to see anyone.'

'What did they do to you, Lorraine?'

'Nothing. Do you mean — no, no, they didn't touch me. It was just some of the questions they asked . . . ' Her voice trailed off. 'Please, Sarina, I'd rather not talk about it.'

'Maraschino,' George said authoritatively. He took her by the arm, seated her and proffered a small glass. She took it, smiled gratefully and said nothing.

Crni came in accompanied by Edvard. He was, for the first time anyone had seen, relaxed and smiling.

'I have some news for you. I hope you will find it good news.'

'You're not even armed,' George said. 'How do you know we won't break every bone in your bodies? Better still, use you as hostage to escape? We are desperate men.'

'Would you do that, Professor?'

'No. Some wine?'

'Thank you, Professor. Good news, at least I think it's good news, for the von Karajans, Captain Harrison and Giacomo. I am sorry that we have been guilty of a small deception but it was necessary in the circumstances. We are not members of the Murge Division. We are, thank heavens, not even Italians. We are just common-or-garden members of a Partisan reconnaissance group.'

'Partisans.' There was no excitement in Sarina's voice, just incomprehension tinged with disbelief.

Crni smiled. 'It's true.'

'Partisans.' Harrison shook his head. 'Pon my soul. Partisans. Well, now. I mean. Yes.' He shook his head then his voice rose an octave. 'Partisans!'

'Is it true?' Sarina had Crni by the arms and was actually shaking him. 'Is it true?'

'Of course it's true.'

She searched his eyes as if searching for the truth, then suddenly put her arm around him and hugged him. She was very still for a moment then released him and stepped back. 'I'm sorry,' she said. 'I shouldn't have done that.'

He smiled. 'There's no regulation that says that a young recruit, female, may not hug an officer. Not, of course, to make a practice of it.'

'There's that, too, of course.' She smiled uncertainly.

'There's something else?'

'No, not really. We're terribly glad to see you.'

'Glad?' Harrison said. 'Glad!' The initial shock absorbed, he was in a state bordering on euphoria. 'Nothing less than a merciful providence has sent you our way!'

'It wasn't a merciful providence, Captain Harrison. It was a radio message. When my commanding officer says 'move', I move. That's the 'something else' you wouldn't talk about, Miss von Karajan. Your fears are groundless. Military regulations don't allow me to shoot my boss.'

'Your boss?' She looked at him, then

Petersen, then back at Crni. 'I don't understand.'

Crni sighed. 'You're quite right, Peter. You, too Giacomo. No espionage material among this lot. If there were they wouldn't have to be hit over the head with the obvious. We're both Partisans. We're both in intelligence. I am the ranking subordinate officer. He is the deputy chief. I'm sure that makes everything clear.'

'Perfectly,' George said. He handed Crni a glass. 'Your wine, Ivan.' He turned to Sarina. 'He doesn't really like being called Crni. And don't clench your fists. All right, all right, this is life in a nutshell. Decisions, decisions. Do you kiss him or do you hit him?' The bantering note left George's voice. 'If you're mad because you've been fooled, then you're a fool. There was no other way. You and your hurt pride. You've got your Partisans and he hasn't to face a firing squad. Don't you know how to be glad, girl? Or is there no room for emotions like relief and gratitude in the minds of you spoilt young aristocrats?'

'George!' She was shocked, less because of the words than the tone she had never heard before. 'George! I am so selfish?'

'Never.' His good humour instantly restored, he squeezed her shoulders. 'It's just that I thought it would rather spoil the flavour of the moment if you were to give Peter a black eye.' He glanced sideways. Harrison, his forehead on his forearms on the table, was softly pounding the table with his fist and muttering to himself. 'You are not well, Captain Harrison?'

'My God, my God, my God!' The pounding with the fist continued.

'A Šljivovica?' George said.

Harrison lifted his head. 'And the awful thing is that I am cursed with total recall. That,' he added irrelevantly, 'was why I was so good at passing exams. I can remember every word I said in that stirring speech about patriotism and duty and loyalty and myopic idiocy and — I can't go on, I can't.'

'You mustn't reproach yourself, Jamie,' Petersen said 'Think what it did for our morale.'

'If there was any justice, any compassion in this world,' Harrison said, 'this floor would open up beneath me at this very moment. A British officer, I called myself, thereby meaning there was no other. A highly skilled observer, evaluator, analyzer. Good God! Total recall, I tell you, total recall. It's hell!'

'I'm sorry I missed that speech,' Crni said.

'Pity,' Petersen said. 'Still, you've heard about Jamie's total recall. He can repeat it to you verbatim any time you want.'

'Spare the vanquished,' Harrison said. 'I

heard what you said to Sarina, George, but I remain bitter. Fooled, fooled, fooled. And doubly bitter because Peter didn't trust me. But you trusted Giacomo, didn't you? He knew.'

'I told Giacomo nothing,' Petersen said. 'He guessed — he's a soldier.'

'And I'm not? Well, that's for sure. How did you guess Giacomo?'

'I heard what you heard. I heard the Major telling — suggesting rather, to Captain Crni that his intention to rope us up before descending that cliff path was dangerous. Captain Crni is not the man to take an order or suggestion from anyone. So then I knew.'

'Of course. I missed it. So you didn't trust any of us, did you Peter?'

'I didn't. I had to know where I stood with you all. Lots of odd things have been happening in Rome and ever since we left Rome. I had to know. You'd have done the same.'

'Me? I wouldn't have noticed anything odd in the first place. When did you come to the decision that you were free to talk? And why did you decide to talk? My God, when I come to think of it, when have you ever been free to talk? My word, I can't imagine it, I just can't. Can you, Sarina? Living the life of a lie, surrounded by enemies, one false move, one unconsidered slip, one careless word and pouf! And he spent almost half his time with us!'

'Ah! But I spent the other half with our own people. Holiday, you might say.'

'Oh, God, holiday. I knew — and I haven't known you long — that you were something different, but this — but this — it passes my comprehension. And you, a man like you, you're only the deputy chief. I'd love to meet the man you call chief.'

'I don't call him 'chief.' I call him lots of other things but not that. As for loving to meet him, you don't have to bother. You've already met him. In fact, you've described him. Big fat clown, naïve and illiterate, who spends his time floating around in cloud-cuckoo-land. Or was it the groves of academe? I don't remember.'

Harrison spilled the contents of his glass on the table. He looked dazed. 'I don't believe it.'

'Nobody does. I'm his right arm, only, in charge of field operations. As you know, he seldom accompanies me. This mission was different but, then, this was an unusually important mission. Couldn't be trusted to bunglers like me.'

Michael approached George, a certain awed incredulity in his face. 'But in Mostar you told me you were a Sergeant Major.'

'A tiny prevarication.' George waved his hand in airy dismissal. 'Inevitable in this line of business. Tiny prevarications, I mean. But I did say it was a temporary not substantive rank. Generalmajor.'

'Good God!' Michael was overcome. 'I mean 'Sir'.'

'It's too much.' Harrison didn't even notice when George courteously refilled his glass. 'It's really too much. Too much for the reeling mind to encompass. Maybe I haven't such a mind after all. Tell me next that I'm Adolph Hitler and I'd seriously consider the possibility.' He looked at George, shook his head and drained half his glass. 'You see before you a man trying to find his way back to reality. Now, where was I? Ah, yes. I was asking you when you came to the decision you were free to talk.'

'When you told me — or Lorraine did — about your Jenny.'

'Ah, yes, of course. Jenny. I see.' It was plain that Harrison was quite baffled. He suddenly, physically, shook himself. 'What the hell has Jenny got to do with this?'

'Nothing, directly.'

'Ah Jenny. Lorraine. The question that Captain Crni asked me through there.'

Lorraine said in a quiet voice: 'What question, James?'

279

'He asked me if I knew Giancarlo Tremino — you know, Carlos. Of course I said yes, I knew him very well.' He looked down at his glass. 'Perhaps I shouldn't have answered. I mean, they weren't torturing me or anything. Maybe I don't have such a mind after all.'

'It wasn't your fault, James,' Lorraine said. 'You weren't to know. Besides, there's been no harm done.'

'How do you know there's been no harm done, Lorraine?' Sarina sounded bitter. 'I know it wasn't Captain Harrison's fault. And I know it wasn't really Captain Crni who asked the question. Don't you know that Major Petersen *always* finds out what he wants? Are we still to regard ourselves as prisoners in this room, Captain Crni?'

'Good God, no! As far as I'm concerned the house is yours. Anyway, you don't ask me. Major Petersen is in charge.'

'Or you, George?' She smiled faintly. 'Sorry. I'm not used to the Generalmajor yet.'

'Quite frankly, neither am I. George is fine.' He smiled and wagged a finger at her. 'Don't try to spread dissension in the ranks. Outside my head office, which at the moment is a disused shepherd's hut up near Bihać, Peter is in sole charge. I just point in the general direction and then get out of the way. If you know you're not in his class, as I'm wise enough to know, you don't interfere with the best field operative there is.'

'Could I speak to you, Major? In the hall?'

'Ominous,' he said and picked up his glass. 'Very ominous.' He followed her out and closed the door behind them. 'Well?'

She hesitated. 'I don't know quite how to say this. I think — '

'If you don't know what to say and you're still at the thinking stage, why waste my time in this really melodramatic fashion?'

'It's not silly. It's not dramatic! And you're not going to make me mad. What you've just said sums you up. Superior, cutting, con-temptuous, never making allowances for people's faults and weaknesses: and at the same time you can be the most thoughtful and kind person I know. It's not just that you're unbearable. You're unknowable. Jekyll and Hyde. The Dr Jekyll bit I like and admire. You're brave, George thinks you're brilliant, you take incredible risks that would destroy a person like me and, best of all, you're very good at looking after people. Anyway, I knew last night that you couldn't belong to those people.'

Petersen smiled. 'I won't give you the chance of telling me again how nasty I am, so I won't say you're being wise after the event.'

'You're wrong,' she said quietly. 'It was

something that Major Metrović said last night about Tito's Achilles' heel, his lack of mobility, his three thousand wounded men. In any civilized war — if there is such a thing — those men would be left to the enemy who would treat them in hospital. This is no civilized war. They would be massacred. You could never be a party to that.'

'I have my points. But you did not bring me out here to point those out.'

'I did not. It's the Mr Hyde side — oh, I *don't* want to lecture but I dislike that side, it hurts me and it baffles me. That a man so physically kind can in other ways be so cold, detached, uncaring to the point of not being quite human.'

'Oh, dear. Or, as Jamie would put it, I say, I say.'

'It's true. In order to gain your own ends, you can be — you are — indifferent to people's feelings to the point of cruelty.'

'Lorraine?'

'Yes. Lorraine.'

'Well, well. I thought it was axiomatic that two lovely ladies automatically disliked each other.'

She seized his upper arms. *'Don't* change the subject.'

'I must tell Alex about this.'

'Tell him what?' she said warily.

'He thinks you detest one another.'

'Tell Alex he's a fool. She's a lovely person. And *you* are tearing her to pieces.'

Petersen nodded. 'She's being torn to pieces all right. But I'm not the person who's doing the tearing.'

She looked closely at him, her eyes moving from one of his to the other, as if hoping that would help her find the truth. 'Then who is?'

'If I told you, you'd just go and tell her.' She said nothing, just kept up her intense scrutiny of his face. 'She knows who is. But I don't want her to think that it's public knowledge.

She looked away. 'Two things. Maybe, deep down, you do have some finer feelings after all.' She looked at his eyes again and half-smiled. 'And you don't trust me.'

'I'd like to.'

'Try.'

'She's a good, honest, patriotic British citizen and she's working for the Italian secret service, specifically for Major Cipriano and she may well be responsible, however indirectly, for the deaths of an untold number of my fellow countrymen.'

'I don't believe it! I don't believe it!' Her eyes were wide and full of horror and her voice shook. 'I don't! I don't! I don't!'

'I know you don't,' he said gently. 'That's

because you don't want to believe it. I didn't want to believe it myself. I do now. I can prove it. Do you think I'm so stupid as to say I can prove a thing when I can't. Or don't you believe me either?'

'I don't know what to believe,' she said wildly. 'Yes, I do. I do. I do know what to believe. I don't believe Lorraine could be like that.'

'Too lovely a person, too honest, too good, too true?'

'Yes! Yes! That's what I believe.'

'That's what I believed, too. That's what I still believe.'

Her grip on his arms tightened and she looked at him almost beseechingly. 'Please. Please don't make fun of me.'

'She's being blackmailed.'

'Blackmailed! Blackmailed! How could anyone blackmail Lorraine?' She looked away, was silent for some seconds, then looked back again. 'It's something to do with Carlos, isn't it?'

'Yes. Indirectly.' He looked at her curiously. 'How did you know that?'

'Because she's in love with him,' Sarina said impatiently.

'How do you know *that?*' This time he was openly surprised.

'Because I'm a woman.'

'Ah, well, yes. I suppose that explains it.'

'*And* because you had Captain Crni ask her about Carlos. But I knew before that. Anyone could see it.'

'Here's one who didn't.' He thought. 'Well, hindsight, retrospect, yes. But I said only indirectly. Nobody would be stupid enough to use Carlos as a blackmail weapon. They'd find themselves with a double-edged sword in their hands. But, sure, he's part of it.'

'Well?' She'd actually arrived at the stage where she had started shaking him, no mean feat with a person of Petersen's bulk. 'What's the other part of it?'

'I know, or I think I know, the other part of it. But I haven't any proof.'

'Tell me what you think.'

'You think because she's honest and good and true that she has led a blameless life, that she can't possibly have any guilty secrets?'

'Go on.'

'I don't think she's got any guilty secrets either. Unless you call having an illegitimate child a guilty secret, which I don't.'

She took her right hand away from his arm and touched her lips. She was shocked not by what he had said but because of its implications.

'Carlos is a doctor.' He sounded tired and, for the first time since she had met him, he looked tired. 'He qualified in Rome. Lorraine lived with him during the time she was Jamie Harrison's secretary. They have a son, aged two and a half. It's my belief that he's been kidnapped. I'll find out for sure when I have a knife at Cipriano's throat.'

She stared at him in silence. Two tears trickled slowly down her cheeks.

8

At nine o'clock the next morning Jablanica looked so much like an idealized Christmas postcard that it was almost unreal, untrue in its breathtaking beauty. The snow had stopped, the clouds were gone, the sun shone from a clear pale blue sky and the air on the windless slopes, where the trees hung heavy with snow, was crisp and pellucid and very cold. It required only the sound of sleigh-bells to complete the illusion. But peace on earth and goodwill to all men were the last considerations in the thoughts of those gathered around the breakfast table that morning.

Petersen, his chin on his hand and his coffee growing cold before him, was obviously lost in contemplation. Harrison, who showed remarkably little after-effects from the considerable amount of wine he had found necessary to drown his chagrin and bring himself once more face to face with reality, said: 'A penny for them, Peter, my boy.'

'My thoughts? They'd be worth a lot more than that to the people I'm thinking about.

Not, may I add hastily, that they include any of those sitting around the table.'

'And not only do you look pensive,' Harrison went on, 'but I detect a slight diminution in the usual early morning ebullience, the sparkling cheer. You found sleep hard to come by? The change of beds, perhaps?'

'As I sleep in a different bed practically every night in life that would hardly be a factor, otherwise I'd be dead by this time. Fact is, I was up nearly all night, with either George or Ivan, in the radio room. You couldn't possibly have heard it, but there was a long and violent thunderstorm during the night — that's why we have cloudless skies this morning — and both transmission and reception were close on impossible.'

'Ah! That explains it. Would it be in order to ask who you were talking to during the long watches of the night?'

'Certainly. No secrets, no secrets.' Harrison's expression of disbelief was only fleeting and he made no comment. 'We had, of course, to contact our HQ in Bihać and warn them of the impending attack. That, alone, took almost two hours.'

'You should have used my radio,' Michael said. 'It's got a remarkable range.'

'We did. It was no better than the other.'

'Oh. Then perhaps you should have used me. After all, I do know that equipment.'

'Of course you do. But, then, our people in Bihać don't know Navajo which is the only code you are familiar with.'

Michael looked at him, his mouth fallen slightly open. 'How on earth did you know that? I mean, I've got no code books.' He tapped his head. 'It's all up here.'

'You sent a message just after Colonel Lunz and I had been talking to you. You may be a good radio operator, Michael, but otherwise you shouldn't be allowed out without a minder.'

Sarina said: 'Don't forget I was there also.'

'Two minders. I'll bet you never even checked to see if the room was bugged.'

'Good God!' Michael looked at his sister. 'Bugged! Did you — how could you have known we were going to stay — '

'It could have been bugged. It wasn't. George was listening on the balcony.'

'George!'

'You talked in plain language. George said it wasn't any European language he'd ever heard. You had an American instructor. The Americans labour under the happy delusion that Navajo is unbreakable.'

'Now you tell me,' George said. He seemed in no way upset.

289

'Sorry. Busy. I forgot.'

'Peter's expertise in espionage is matched only by his expertise in codes. The two go hand-in-glove. Makes up codes all the time. Breaks them, too. Remember he said the Germans had twice broken the Četnik code. *They* didn't. Peter gave them the information. Not that they know that. Nothing like spreading dissension among allies.'

Harrison said: 'How do you know the Germans didn't monitor and break your transmission last night?'

'Impossible. Only two people know my codes — me and the receiver. Never use the same code twice. You can't break a code on a single transmission.'

'That's fine. But — not trying to be awkward, old boy — will this information be of any use to your Partisans? Won't the Germans know that you've been kidnapped or disappeared or whatever and might pass this message on. If they did, surely they would change their plan of attack.'

'Don't you think I have considered this, Jamie? You simply don't even begin to know the Balkans. How could you, after less than a couple of months? What do you know of the deviousness, the plotting and counter-plotting, the rivalries, the jealousies, the self-seeking, the total regard for one's own power base, the distrusts, the obsession for personal gain, the vast gulf between the Occidental and Byzantine minds? I don't think there's even a remote chance of the Germans finding out.

'Consider. Who knows I've got the plans? As far as the Colonel is concerned, there are only two plans, he's got both and I've never seen a copy. Why should he think so? Metrović will have given him the name of Cipriano but I'll bet the Colonel has never heard of him and even if he has what's he going to tell him? Even if he did tell him Cipriano would be too smart to believe it was the Murge division — a commando unit like Ivan's never discloses their true identity. Again, apart from the fact that the Colonel's pride would probably stop him anyway from letting anyone know that his defences have been breached, he could be Machiavellian enough to want the Germans to be taken by surprise, not, of course in order that they should be defeated but that they should suffer severe casualties. Sure, he wants the Partisans destroyed but, when and if it happens, he wants the Germans out of the country. Basically, they're both his natural enemies.

'And even if the Germans did eventually find out, so what? It's too late to change plans and, anyway, there *are* no other plans they could make. There *is* no alternative.'

'I have to agree,' Harrison said. 'They'll go ahead as planned. Forewarned, one takes it, is forearmed. A satisfactory night's work, no?'

'It was unimportant. They would almost certainly have found out in any case. We have a considerable number of reliable contacts throughout the country. In the areas held by the Germans, Italians, Četniks and Ustaša — and that's most of the country — there are reliable solid citizens, or are so regarded by the Germans, Italians, Četniks and Ustaša, who, while cheerfully collaborating with the enemy, send us regular and up-to-date reports of the latest enemy troop movements. In other words, they are Partisan spies. Their reports are far from complete but enough to give Tito and his staff a fair indication of the enemy's intentions.'

'I suppose that happens in every war,' Harrison said, 'But I didn't know the Partisans had spies in the enemy's camp.'

'We have had from the very beginning. We couldn't have survived otherwise. What took up most of our time last night was the distressing discovery — well, we first suspected it about ten weeks ago — that the enemy have spies in *our* camp. Even more distressing was the discovery that they had spies in the Partisan HQ. In retrospect, it was naïve of us, we should have suspected the possibility and taken precautions long ago. In fairness to us, we weren't complacent — we were just under the fond misapprehension that every Partisan was a burning patriot. Some, alas, burn less brightly than others. This, and not acting as message boys for General von Löhr, is what has been occupying George, Alex and myself in Italy in the past two weeks. It was a matter of such vital importance that George was actually sufficiently motivated to drag himself away from his snug retreats in Bihać and Mount Prenj. Those spies in our camp had become a major threat to our security: we were trying to uncover the Italian connection.

'That there was, and is, an Italian connection, is beyond dispute. Not German, not Četnik, not Ustaša — specifically Italian, for it has been the Italian Murge division, first-class mountain troops, that have been causing us all the trouble. Our Partisans are as good, probably even better mountain troops, but hundreds of them have been killed by the Murge division in the past few months. Never in pitched battle. Invariably in isolated, one-off, incidents. A patrol, a localized troop movement, a transfer of wounded to a supposedly safer area, a reconnaissance group behind enemy lines

— it came to the stage where none of those was immune to a lightning strike by specialized Murge units who apparently knew, always, exactly where to strike, when to strike, how to strike — they even seemed to know the number and composition of the Partisan groups they would be attacking, even the approximate number of the groups themselves. Our small-scale guerrilla movements were becoming very hampered, almost paralysed: and a partisan's army's survival depends almost exclusively on mobility, flexibility and long-range reconnaissance.

'The Murge, of course, were receiving precise advance information of our movements. The information had to be coming from a person or persons in the neighbourhood of our HQ. Those secret messages, messages which led hundreds of men to their deaths, were not of course written down, addressed to the enemy and dropped in the nearest letterbox: they were sent by radio.' Petersen broke off as if to collect his thoughts, his eyes wandering, unseeingly, as it seemed, round the table. Lorraine, he could see, was unnaturally pale: Sarina had her hands clasped tightly together. Petersen appeared to notice nothing.

'I'll carry on for a moment,' George said. 'At this time, you must understand that Peter has been overcome by his habitual modesty. Peter couldn't believe that the traitors could be any long-serving Partisans. Neither could I. Peter suggested that we check the approximate dates of the first transmissions — the times of the first unexpected swoops by the Murge units — with the time of the arrival of the latest recruits to the Partisans. We did and found that this checked with the arrival of an unusually high number of ex-Četniks — Četniks regularly desert to us and it's quite impossible to check out the credentials and good faith of all of them or even a fraction of them.

'Peter and some of his men checked on a small number of those and found two who had access to long-range transmitters hidden in a forest on a hillside. They wouldn't talk and we don't torture. They were executed. Thereafter the number of unexpected attacks by the Murge fell off rapidly: but they still continued at sporadic intervals. Which, of course, could only mean that there were still some traitors around.'

George helped himself liberally to some beer. It was but breakfast time, but George claimed to be allergic to both tea and coffee.

'So we went to Italy, the three of us. Why? Because we — are or were — Četnik intelligence officers and naturally associated with our Italian counterparts. Why? Because we were convinced that the messages were being relayed through Italian Intelligence. Why? Because a fighting division has neither the facilities, the ability, the organization nor the cash to mount such an operation. But Italian Intelligence has all of these in abundance.'

'Amidst the welter of 'whys', George,' Harrison said, 'why the cash?'

'It's as Peter said,' George said sadly. 'You haven't got the Balkan mentality. Come to that, I doubt whether you have the universal mentality. The Četnik agents, like agents and double-agents the world over, are not motivated simply by altrusim, patriotism or political conviction. The little gears in their minds only mesh efficiently under the influence of the universal lubricant. Money. They are rather highly paid and, considered dispassionately, deserve to be: look what happened to those two unfortunates unmasked by Peter.'

Petersen rose, walked to the window and stood there, gazing down the gentle valley that sloped away from their chalet. He seemed to have lost interest in the conversation.

'All in all,' Harrison said, 'a fair night's work.'

'That wasn't quite all of it,' George said.

'We have located Cipriano.'

'Cipriano!'

'None other. Lorraine, my dear! You look so pale. Are you not well?'

'I feel — I feel a little faint.'

'Maraschino,' George said unhesitatingly. 'Sava!' This to one of Crni's soldiers who rose at once and crossed to the liquor cupboard. 'Yes, indeed. The worthy Major himself.'

'But how on earth — '

'We have our little methods,' George said complacently. 'We have, as Peter told you, our reliable, solid citizens everywhere. Incidentally, you can now forget all that Peter told you — thank you, my boy, just give it to the lady — all he told you about Cipriano working hand-in-glove with the Partisans. I'm afraid he grossly maligned the poor man but at the moment he deemed it prudent to divert any suspicions that Majors Metrović and Ranković might have been harbouring from himself to an absent person. Cipriano was conveniently absent. Our Peter is a very convincing actor, no?'

'He's a very convincing liar,' Sarina said.

'Oh, tush! Hurt pride again. We're just mad because he fooled you, too. Anyway, Cipriano's in Imotski, doubtless closeted with the Murge brigade commander there and hatching fresh devilish schemes against our poor

Partisans. I shouldn't have to explain any of this. You will remember that Peter said in Mount Prenj that he wanted to get to the link-man — Cipriano — because he was aiding and abetting the Partisans. What he meant to say was he wanted to get at the link-man because he was a deadly enemy of the Partisans but he couldn't very well say that, could he, in front of Metrović and Ranković? Come, come, my children, you disappoint me: you had all night long to work out something as simple and obvious as that.'

George yawned behind a massive hand. 'Excuse me. Now that I'm breakfasted and am once more at peace with myself, I intend to retire and rest lightly for two or three hours. We will not be moving out until the afternoon at the earliest. We await an urgent communication from Bihać but it will take some time to collect and collate the information we want. Meantime, how do you people propose to spend the morning?' He raised his voice. 'Peter. Those people are free to come and go as they want, inside and out, aren't they?'

'Of course.'

Captain Crni smiled and said: 'May I suggest that you put on your coats and I'll show you around our little town. There's not much to show so it would be a short walk and hardly exhausting. Apart from the fact that it's a lovely morning I know where we can get the best coffee in Bosnia. Far better than that awful swill we've just had.'

Sarina said, 'That way we can still be watched, can't we?'

Captain Crni bowed gallantly. 'It would always be a pleasure to watch you and Miss Chamberlain. If however, you wish to go alone and report to the nearest Italian command post that we are Partisans and have designs on a certain Italian intelligence major, then you are by all means free to do so. That, Miss von Karajan, is the extent to which we trust you.'

'I *am* sorry.' She reached out an impulsive hand and caught his forearm. 'That was a terrible thing to say. Two or three days in this country and I find I can't trust anyone, not even myself.' She smiled. 'Besides, you're the only one who knows where the coffee shop is.'

They left — without Giacomo who had elected to remain behind — shortly afterwards. Petersen said wearily: 'She doesn't trust anyone. God knows I don't blame her. George, I am a hypocritical liar. Even when I say nothing, I'm a hypocritical liar.'

'I know what you mean, Peter. Sometimes a tiny voice reaches down to my conscience

— God knows how it ever finds it — and says exactly the same thing. The clarion call to duty strikes a pretty cracked note at times. Sava?'

'General?'

'Go to the window in the front room and watch the road. If they return unexpectedly, call me. I'll be upstairs. I'll let you know when you can stop the watch. Shouldn't be more than a few minutes.'

★   ★   ★

After lunch a very refreshed-looking Petersen — he'd had four hours' sleep — crossed to where Lorraine sat with Sarina on a bench seat by a window and said: 'Lorraine, please don't start getting worried because there is no need to. George and I would like to talk to you.'

She bit her lip. 'I knew you would. Can — can Sarina come?'

'Certainly.' He looked at Sarina. 'Provided, of course, that you don't say 'Oh!' and 'Ah!' and 'monster' and clench your fists. Promise?'

'Promise.'

Petersen ushered them to an upstairs room where George was already seated, a large tankard on the table before him and a crate, presumably for emergency, on the floor beside him. Petersen said: 'George?'

George shook his head positively. 'Would you come between a man and his thirst.'

'I would have thought you slaked that pretty thoroughly at lunch.'

'This is a post-prandial beer,' George said with dignity. 'Pray proceed.'

'This will be short and painless,' Petersen said to Lorraine. 'I'm not a dentist and you don't have to tell lies. As you must have guessed, we know everything. I can promise you, and George will confirm, that neither retribution nor punishment waits for you. You're a victim and not a villain and acted under extreme duress. Besides, you didn't even know what you were doing. All transmissions were not only in code but in Yugoslav code and you don't understand a word of Serbo-Croat. George's word, of course, carries immense weight in the war councils, almost totally so in cases such as this, and they listen to me a bit, too. No harm will come to you or Carlos or Mario.'

She nodded, almost composedly. 'You know about our son, of course?'

'Yes. When was he kidnapped?'

'Six months ago.'

'You have no idea where he is being held?'

'No. Well, vaguely.' She was no longer composed. 'In this country, I know. Major

Cipriano wanted him out of Italy. I don't know why.'

'I can understand. There are certain things that even Cipriano can't do in Italy. How do you know he's in this country?'

'They let Carlos see him twice. That was twice when I said I wasn't going to work for them any more because I was sure he was dead. But I don't know where he is.'

'Yes. I see. It doesn't matter.'

'It doesn't matter!' She was no longer composed and her eyes were masked in tears.

George took his evil-smelling cigar from his mouth. 'What Peter means is that Cipriano will tell him.'

'Cipriano will tell — ' She broke off, nodded and shivered involuntarily.

'We have your code books, Lorraine. We searched your room when you were out this morning.'

'You searched her room!' Sarina said indignantly. 'What right — '

Petersen rose and opened the door. 'Out.'

'I'm sorry. I forgot. I — '

'You promised.'

'Don't you ever give anyone a second chance?'

Petersen didn't answer. He closed the door, sat down and said: 'False bottoms to kitbags are really dreadfully passé these days. But, then, I don't suppose either you or Cipriano ever dreamed that you would come under suspicion. No names in your book but we don't need them. There are code numbers, call-up signs and call-up times. It will take us little enough time to trap them.'

'And then?'

George removed his cigar again. 'Don't ask silly questions.'

'Tell me, Lorraine. You had no idea why you had been sent to Mount Prenj? Oh, you knew what you were to do, but not why. Well, Cipriano knew that you knew Jamie Harrison and that he trusted you completely — after all, you *were* his confidential secretary — so that he would never suspect you of double-dealing: transferring messages from our diehard Četnik friends in Bihać to him in Rome or wherever, messages which he could re-transmit to the Murge regiment. But the real reason, of course, is that we had destroyed the only two long-range transmitters they had. With short-range transmitters their contacts with Rome could only be sporadic at best. But Mount Prenj is only two hundred kilometres from Bihać. It would be an awfully short range transmitter that couldn't reach there.' Petersen paused and considered. 'Well, that's all. No, one more thing.' He smiled. 'Yes. One more thing.

Purely personal. Where did you first meet Carlos?'

'Isle of Wight, where I was born. He was sailing at Cowes.'

'Of course, of course. He told me that he often went sailing there before the war. Well, I hope you'll both go sailing there again after the war.'

'Will — will Carlos be all right, Major Petersen?'

'If you can refer to a Generalmajor as George you can refer to a Major as Peter. Why shouldn't he be? He's in the clear. Under both Italian military and civilian law he has committed no criminal offence, aided and abetted no-one. With any luck we might see him later on tomorrow.'

'What! Carlos?' Her face was transformed.

Petersen looked at Sarina. 'Yes, you were right, no question.' He didn't say what she had been right about. 'Certainly. Carlos. He hasn't been up to any aiding or abetting yet, but tomorrow he will.'

She didn't seem to hear him or, if she did, her mind was elsewhere.

'He's still in Ploče?'

'Yes.'

'He hasn't gone back to Italy?'

'Alas, no. Some disaffected citizen has put sugar in his diesel oil.'

She looked at him for a long moment then smiled slowly. 'It wouldn't have been one of those solid, reliable citizens you talk about, would it?'

He smiled back at her. 'I am not responsible for the actions of solid, reliable citizens.'

★　★　★

At the foot of the stairs Sarina took Petersen's arm and held him back. 'Thank you,' she said. 'Thank you very much. That was very kind.'

He looked at her in amazement. 'What else did you expect me to do?'

'Nothing, I suppose. But it was wonderful. Especially about Carlos.'

'Today I'm not an ogre? Not a monster?'

She smiled and shook her head.

'And tomorrow? When I have to find out where the little boy is? Do you understand what I mean?'

She stopped smiling.

Petersen shook his head sadly. '*Souvent femme varie, bien fol est qui s'y fie'.*'

'What is that meant to mean?'

'Picked it up from George. Something King Francis I scratched with a diamond on a pane of glass at Chambord. 'Often does woman change, and very foolish is he who trusts her'.'

'Pfui!' she said. But she was smiling again.

Towards the middle of the afternoon Petersen and Crni walked into the lounge, carrying several machine-pistols and hand-guns.

'Replacement equipment. Ivan here took ours away so it's only fair that he should replace them. We'll be leaving shortly. Ivan, Edvard and Sava are coming with us.' He glanced at his watch. 'Twenty minutes, shall we say? I want to get through the nasty bit of the Neretva gorge in daylight but not to arrive at our destination until it's dark, for the usual reasons.'

'I'm not looking forward to that,' Sarina said.

'Have no fear. I'm not driving. Sava is. He's a truck driver in civilian life.'

'What destination?' Harrison said.

'Ah! I forgot. A new acquaintance for you, Jamie, but an old friend of ours. The proprietor of the Hotel Eden in Mostar, one Josip Pijade.'

'A solid and reliable citizen,' Lorraine said.

'A very solid, very reliable citizen. You have a faraway look on your face, George. What are you thinking of?'

'Venison.'

9

And venison it was. Josip and Marija had excelled themselves and achieved the seemingly impossible — the venison tasted even marginally better than the last time. George excelled himself in a corresponding fashion, but failed to achieve the impossible: halfway through his third massive helping of venison he had to admit defeat. Sleep that night, unlike the last occasion, was undisturbed by unwelcome visitors. Breakfast was a late and leisurely meal.

'I wish we'd had you up in the damned Mount Prenj for the past two months,' Harrison said to Josip after the meal. 'But it's been worth the wait. I wish someone would station me here for the duration. He directed his attention towards Petersen. 'Are we permitted to know our plans — well, your plans — for the day?'

'Of course. They're concerned primarily, though not entirely, with one person — Cipriano, his apprehension and interrogation. The Bihać affair we can consider as being virtually a closed matter. As you know, we failed to make contact yesterday, but Ivan and I had better luck during the small hours — reception, as you know, is always better at night. They've come up with no fewer than sixteen Četnik-turned-Partisan suspects, there can't be more than two, at the most three. We send out a coded message at a certain hour on a certain wavelength and note will be taken as to which of the sixteen is absent at the time. He will not of course be apprehended until the other one or two have been similarly trapped. Routine. Forget it.' That the words were tantamount to a death sentence was evident to everyone, except, apparently, Petersen.

'Cipriano,' Giacomo said. 'Still at Imotski?'

'He is. We have two men up there on a twenty-four hour watch. We're in radio contact. Spoke to them last an hour ago. Cipriano's up and around but shows no sign yet of moving on. He's got quite an entourage with him.' He looked at Alex. 'You might be interested in hearing the description of one of them.'

'Alessandro?' Alex said hopefully.

'No other.'

'Ah.' Just for once Alex registered a trace of expression: it was as near to a happy smile as Alex would ever come.

'Plus, I'm almost certain from the description, Alessandro's three henchmen. Seems that Carlos must have found a flame-cutter somewhere. We don't, of course, know which way the fox is going to jump — there are several different exit routes he can take from Imotski — but we'll be told immediately that is known. He could, of course, be taking a back road to Ploče and hitch-hiking a lift home with Carlos — if the *Colombo*'s diesel lines have been cleared out — but I think that unlikely. I think he'll be heading for the military airfield just outside the town here and the fast way back to Rome. Ivan and I are just going out to the airport to check.'

'Check what?' Harrison asked.

'Whether there's air transport standing by for him.'

'Won't the airfield be guarded?'

'We are two Italian officers. I've just promoted myself to Colonel and will probably outrank anyone there. We'll just walk in and ask them.'

'That won't be necessary, Peter,' Josip Pijade said. 'My cousin, who owns a garage just outside the airport, works there as a part-time repair and maintenance engineer. Not, unfortunately, on the planes, but on the plant, otherwise the Italian air force would be experiencing mysterious crashes. I have but to lift the phone.'

'Thank you, Josip.'

Josip left. Lorraine said: 'Another solid and reliable citizen?'

'Yugoslavia is full of them.'

Josip was back in two minutes. 'There is an Italian plane on standby. *And* it's reserved for Major Cipriano.'

'Thank you.' He nodded to the small transceiver on the table. 'I'll take this with me. Call up if you hear from Imotski. We're almost certain of the route Cipriano will take into town so Ivan and I will go and select an ambush spot. We may take your car, Josip?'

'Take me, too. I know the perfect spot.'

Sarina said: 'We can go into town?'

'I think so. I won't be needing you until nightfall. The only attention you're liable to attract is wolf-whistles from the licentious Italian soldiery.' He looked at Giacomo. 'I'd feel happier if you went along.'

'No sacrifice too great,' Giacomo said.

Sarina smiled. 'We need protection?'

'Only from the licentious soldiery.'

★ ★ ★

The call came, inevitably enough, when they were halfway through lunch. Marija came in and said: 'They've just left They're heading for Posušje.'

'The Mostar road. Excuse us,' Petersen

310

said. He rose as did Alex, Crni and Edvard.

George said: 'I wish I were coming with you. But everyone knows I'm not a man of action.'

'What he means,' Petersen said coldly, 'is that his jaws haven't even got out of second gear yet and he's barely touched his first litre of beer.'

Sarina said: 'You will be careful, won't you?'

Petersen smiled and said: 'Coming, Giacomo?'

'Certainly not. That's a public bar through there. The licentious soldiery might come in any moment.'

'There's your answer about being careful, Sarina. If Giacomo thought there was the slightest chance of shooting an Italian full of holes he'd be the first aboard the truck. He knows there's no hope. But thanks all the same.'

★ ★ ★

Alex, white handkerchief in hand, stood on a low knoll in the rough grazing field opposite the tree-lined lane which led off the main Lištica-Mostar road. In the lane itself, with engine running, Petersen sat in the cab of the Italian army truck which was parked only feet

311

from the entrance to the road.

Alex raised the handkerchief high above his head. Petersen engaged first gear and waited, clutch depressed, accelerator at half-throttle. Alex brought the handkerchief sharply down and, clutch released, the truck moved forward under full throttle. Three seconds later Petersen jammed on the brakes, bringing the truck to an abrupt halt, fair and square across the width of the main highway.

The Italian army command car which, fortunately for its occupants, was travelling at only a moderate speed, had no chance: even as the driver stamped on the foot-brake he must have realized that his options were limited indeed: he could either keep to the road and hit the side of the truck head-on or swerve to his right into the field where Alex was — a swerve to the left would have fetched him up against the trees lining the lane. Prudently, he chose the latter course. Locked tyres screeching on the tarmac, the car bust through a low wooden fence, broke into the field while balanced on only two wheels, teetered for a couple of seconds then came to rest as it fell over on its left side, wheels still spinning slowly in the air.

Within seconds, rifle butts had smashed in the right-hand windows of the car but the need for haste was not there: the five occupants, unhurt except for cuts about their faces, were too dazed to recognize the presence of their assailants, far less offer resistance: when they did recover some sense of awareness, the sight of the four machine-pistol muzzles only inches from their heads made the thought of offering any resistance too ludicrous for contemplation.

★ ★ ★

When Petersen and Crni returned to the hotel they found George and his companions — inevitably, in George's case — in the bar. Equally inevitably, George was presiding behind the counter.

'Good afternoon, gentlemen.' George was at his affable best.

'You've finished lunch, then?' Petersen said.

'And it wasn't bad. Not bad at all. What shall it be? Beer?'

'Beer is fine.'

'Aren't you going to ask him what happened?' Sarina said indignantly.

'Ah. Alex and Edvard have been cut off in their prime?'

'They're in the truck and the truck is in the car park.'

'That's what I like. Solicitude. Making sure

that the prisoners are not doing themselves an injury. When do you propose to bring them inside?'

'When it's dark. I can't very well march them through the streets, bound and gagged, in broad daylight, can I?'

'True.' George yawned and slid off his stool. 'Siesta.'

'I know,' Petersen said sympathetically. 'Go, go, go all the time. Wears a man down.'

George left in dignified silence. Sarina said: 'Doesn't go in much for congratulations, does he?'

'He postponed his siesta. That shows he's deeply moved.'

'So you got Major Cipriano. What do you think of that, Lorraine?'

'I suppose I should be weeping for joy. I am glad, I'm terribly glad. But I *knew* he would. I never for a moment doubted it. Did you?'

'No. It's very irritating.'

''*Souvent femme varie*',' Petersen said sadly. 'Josip, would you send someone with your hotel wagon to pick up the prisoners' luggage and take it upstairs. No, not upstairs: I can examine it just as well down here.' He turned to Sarina. 'And you keep quiet.'

'I didn't say anything!'

'You were about to tell me that that was

314

something else I was very good at. Examining other people's luggage, I mean.'

★   ★   ★

The five prisoners were brought in by the back entrance as soon as it was reasonably dark. The hotel doors were locked. Cipriano, Alessandro and the three others were settled in chairs and their gags removed. Their wrists remained bound behind their backs. The normally tranquil and civilized Major Cipriano had undergone a radical transformation. His eyes glared and his face was suffused in anger.

'What is the meaning of this — this abominable outrage, Petersen? Have you gone mad? Stark raving mad? Untie me at once! I'm an officer, an Italian officer, an *allied* officer!'

'You're a murderer. Your rank and nationality is of no importance. Not when you're a mass murderer.'

'Untie me! You're crazy! By God, Petersen, if it's the last thing I do — '

'Has it occurred to you that you may already have done your last thing on earth?'

Cipriano stared at Petersen. His lack of understanding was total. Suddenly, he noticed Josip for the first time.

'Pijade! Pijade! You — *you* are a party to this monstrous outrage!' Cipriano was so clearly nearly bereft of reason that he struggled futilely with his bonds. 'By God, Pijade, you shall pay for this treachery!'

'Treachery.' Petersen laughed without mirth. 'Speak of treachery while you may, Cipriano, because you're going to die for it. Pijade will pay, will he? How will he do that, Cipriano?' Petersen's voice was very soft. 'Your eternal curses from the bottom of hell where you'll surely be before midnight tonight?'

'You're all mad,' Cipriano whispered. The anger had drained from his face: he had suddenly become aware that he was in mortal danger.

Petersen went on in the same gentle tone: 'Hundreds of my comrades lie dead because of you.'

'You are mad!' His voice was almost a scream. 'You must be mad. I've never touched a Četnik in my life.'

'I am not a Četnik. I'm a Partisan.'

'A Partisan!' Cipriano was back to his husky whispering again. 'A Partisan! Colonel Lunz suspected — I should have listened — ' He broke off and then his voice strengthened. 'I have never harmed a Partisan in my life.'

'Come in,' Petersen called.

Lorraine entered.

'Do you still deny, Cipriano, that you have masterminded the deaths of hundreds of my fellow-Partisans? Lorraine has told me everything, Cipriano. Everything.' He produced a small black book from his tunic. 'Lorraine's code book. In your own handwriting. Or perhaps you don't recognize your handwriting, Cipriano, I'm sure you never thought that you would be signing your own death warrant with your own handwriting. I find it ironic, Cipriano. I hope you do too. But irony isn't going to bring all those hundreds back to life, is it? Even although the last of your spies will have been trapped and executed by the end of the week, those men will still be dead, won't they, Cipriano. Where's the little boy, Lorraine's little boy? Where's Mario, Cipriano?'

Cipriano made a noise in his throat, a harsh and guttural and meaningless sound and struggled to his feet. Giacomo glanced at Petersen, correctly interpreted the nod and, with evident satisfaction, hit Cipriano none too gently in the solar plexus. Cipriano collapsed into his chair, harsh retching noises coming deep from his throat.

Petersen said: 'George?'

George emerged from behind the bar, carrying two pieces of rope in his hand. He ambled across the saloon, dropped one piece to the floor and secured Cipriano firmly to his chair with the other. Then he picked up the second rope, already noosed, and dropped it over Alessandro's chest before the man realized what was happening. Seconds later and he was trussed like the proverbial turkey.

'Cipriano isn't going to tell me because Cipriano knows that he's going to die, whatever happens. But you'll tell me where the little boy is, won't you, Alessandro?'

Alessandro spat on the floor.

'Oh dear.' Petersen sighed. 'Those disgusting habits are difficult to eradicate, aren't they?' He reached behind the bar and produced the metal box of syringes and drugs he had taken from Alessandro aboard the *Colombo*. 'Alex.'

Alex produced his razor-sharp knife and slit Alessandro's left sleeve from the shoulder to where the ropes bound him at the elbow level.

'No!' Alessandro's voice was a scream of pure terror. 'No! No! No!'

Cipriano leaned forward and struggled against his bonds, his face suffused dark red as he tried to force words through his still constricted throat. Giacomo tapped him again to ensure his continued silence.

318

'I'm afraid I cut him a little,' Alex said apologetically. He was hardly exaggerating: Alessendro's arm was, indeed, quite badly gashed.

'No matter.' Petersen picked up the syringe and selected a phial at apparent random. 'Save the trouble of searching for a vein.'

'Ploče!' Alessandro whispered. His voice was strangled with fear. His breath coming and going faster than once every second. 'Ploče. I can take you there! 18 Fra Spalato! I swear it! I can take you there!'

Petersen replaced the syringe and phials and closed the lid. He said to the girls: 'Alessandro, I'm afraid, was psychologically disadvantaged. But I never laid a finger on him, did I?'

Both girls stared at him, then looked at each other. As if by some telepathic signal, they shuddered in unison.

★　★　★

When Alessandro's arm had been bandaged and Cipriano recovered, they made ready to leave. As Alex approached him with a gag, Cipriano looked at Petersen with empty eyes and said: 'Why don't you kill me here? Difficult to dispose of the body? But no trouble in the Adriatic, is it? A few lengths of chain.'

'Nobody's going to dispose of you, Cipriano. Not permanently. We never had any intention of killing you. I knew Alessandro would crack but I didn't want to waste time over it. A bit of a pragmatist, is our Alessandro, and he had no intention of sacrificing his life for a man he believed to be already as good as dead. We have every moral justification for killing you but no legal justification. Spies are shot all the time: spy-masters never. Geneva Conventions say so. It does seem unfair. No, Cipriano, you are going into durance vile. A prisoner of war, for however long the war lasts. British Intelligence are just going to love to have a chat with you.'

Cipriano had nothing to say, which was perhaps understandable. When the reprieve comes along just as the guillotine is about to be tripped, suitable comment is hard to come by.

Petersen turned to his cousin as Cipriano's gag was being fastened. 'Marija, I would like you to do me a favour. Would you look after a little boy for a day or two?'

'Mario!' Lorraine said. 'You mean Mario?'

'What other little boy would I be talking about. Well, Marija?'

'Peter!' Her voice was full of reproach.

'Well, I had to ask.' He kissed her on the

cheek. 'The bane of my life, but I love you.'

'So we part once more,' Josip said sadly. 'When do we meet again?'

'Dinner-time. George is coming back for the rest of that venison he couldn't finish last night. So am I.'

★ ★ ★

Edvard stopped the truck several hundred yards short of the entrance to the docks. Alex and Sava dropped down from the back of the truck followed by a now unbound and ungagged Alessandro — they were in the main street and there were a number of people around. The three men turned, without any undue haste, down an unlit side-street.

Crni, seated up front with Petersen, said: 'Do you anticipate any trouble at the control gate?'

'No more than usual. The guards are old, inefficient, not really interested and very susceptible to arrogant and ill-tempered authority. That's us.'

'Cipriano's wrecked command car is bound to have been found some time ago. And the people in charge at the airport must be wondering where he's got to.'

'If a Yugoslav found it, it will have made his

321

day and he would have driven by without stopping. Whether the airport was expecting him I don't know — Cipriano seems an unpredictable fellow who does very much what he wants. Even if it's accepted by now that he's genuinely missing, where are they going to start looking? Ploče's about as unlikely a place as any.'

And so it proved. The sentry didn't even bother to leave his box. Beyond the gate, the docks were deserted — the day's work was over and the freezing temperatures were hardly calculated to encourage night-time strollers. Even so, Petersen told Edvard to stop two hundred metres short of where the *Colombo* was berthed, left the cab, went round to the back, called Lorraine's name and helped her down.

'See that light there? That's the *Colombo*. Go and tell Carlos to switch off his two gangway lights.'

'Yes,' she said. 'Oh, yes.' She ran a few steps then halted abruptly as Petersen called her.

'Walk you clown. No one in Ploče ever runs.'

Three minutes later the gangway lights went out. Two minutes after that the prisoners had made their unobserved way up the unlighted gangway and the truck had disappeared. The gangway lights came on again.

Carlos sat in his usual chair in his cabin, his good left hand tightly held in both of Lorraine's, the expression on his face not so much uncomprehending and stunned but comprehending and still stunned.

'Let me see whether I've got this right or whether I'm just imagining it,' Carlos said. 'You're going to lock up my crew and myself, abscond with Lorraine and Mario, imprison Cipriano and his men aboard and steal my ship?'

'I couldn't have put it more succinctly myself. Except, of course, that I wouldn't have used the word 'abscond'. Only, of course, if you consent. The decision is entirely up to you. And Lorraine, too. But I think Lorraine has already made up her mind.'

'Yes, I have.' There was no hesitation in her voice.

'I'll be dismissed from the Navy,' Carlos said gloomily. 'No, I won't, I'll be court-martialled and shot.'

'Nothing will happen to you. There is not a chance in the world. George and I have gone over it time and again.'

'My crew will talk and — '

'Talk? Talk what about? They're sitting in the mess-room with machine-pistols at their heads. If you had a machine-pistol at your head would you have any doubt whatsoever that your ship had been taken over by force?'

'Cipriano — '

'What of Cipriano. Even if he survives his captivity, which he unfortunately probably will as the British don't shoot prisoners, there's nothing he can do. There is no way your version and that of the crew — and this will become the official version — can be disproved. And he would never dare lay a personal charge against you — by the time peace comes you can call for the testimony of several solid and respected citizens of Yugoslavia who will testify to the fact that Cipriano kidnapped your son. The penalty in Italy for kidnapping is life imprisonment.'

'Oh, do come on, Carlos,' Lorraine said impatiently. 'It's not like you to dilly-dally. There *is* no other way.' She gently touched his chin so that his eyes came round to hers. 'We've got Mario back.'

'True, true.' He smiled at her. 'That's all that matters to you, isn't it?'

'Not all.' She smiled in return. 'You're back too. That matters a little. What's the alternative, Carlos? Peter doesn't want to kill Cipriano, and if Cipriano is free our life is finished. He *has* to be imprisoned in a safe place and that means in British hands, and the only way to get him there is in this boat. Peter doesn't make mistakes.'

'Correction,' Sarina said sweetly. 'Peter *never* makes mistakes.'

''*Souvent femme varie*'' Petersen said.

'Oh, do be quiet.'

'If I'm locked up,' Carlos said, 'When will I — and my crew — be released?'

'Tomorrow. An anonymous phone message.'

'And Lorraine and Mario will stay with your friends?'

'Only a few days. Until we provide them with new identity papers. George is a close friend of *the* master forger in the Balkans. Lorraine Tremino, we had thought. In these troublous times you should have no difficulty in establishing a long-established family unit. A marriage certificate, George?'

George lowered his tankard. 'For my friend, a trifle. Venue? Rome? Pescara? Cowes? Wherever. We shall see what forms he has available.'

The door opened and Alex entered, Sava close behind him. Alex had a curly-haired little boy by the hand. The boy looked around him, wonderingly, caught a sight of Carlos and ran to him, arms outstretched. Carlos picked him up and set him on his knees. Mario wound his arms round his neck and gazed wonderingly at Lorraine.

'He's only a little boy,' George said comfortingly. 'For a little boy, Lorraine, six months is a long time. He will remember.'

Harrison coughed. 'And I am to go with Giacomo on this perilous voyage, this rendezvous with eternity?'

'Your choice, Jamie, but Giacomo has to have somebody. Besides, you know as well as I do that the Illyrian Alps are not your homeland and that there's no useful function you can perform here any more. More important, as a serving British officer you will lend credulity — total credibility — to Giacomo's story — apart from convincing the British of the true state of affairs out here, about which you feel so strongly.'

'I will go,' Harrison said. 'A twisted smile on my face, but I will go.'

'You'll untwist your smile when the fast Royal Navy patrol boat comes out to meet you. We will radio Cairo. I don't have their call-up sign but you do, don't you, Sarina?'

'Yes.'

'As a final back-up we will give you a letter explaining the situation fully. Do you have a typewriter, Carlos?'

'Next door.' Carlos had handed Mario over

to Lorraine. The little boy, while not objecting, still had a suspicious frown on his face.

'This letter will be signed by the Generalmajor and myself. Can you type, Sarina?'

'Of course.'

'Of course. As if it were the most natural thing in the world. Well, I can't. You should, at least, be pleased. A chink in my armour. Come on.'

Carlos said, 'I don't like to say this, Peter, but I think you've missed something. It's a long long way to the south of Italy where I assume this rendezvous will be made.'

'Your diesel lines are cleared? Your tanks are full?'

'Yes. That's not my point. Oh, I'm sure that Giacomo can steer by the sun and the compass but a rendezvous has to be precise. Latitude this, longitude that.'

'Indeed. But there are some things you don't know about Giacomo.'

Carlos smiled. 'I'm sure there are. What?'

'Do *you* have a foreign-going master's ticket?

'No.' Carlos smiled again. 'Don't tell me. Giacomo has.'

★　★　★

In the tiny cabin next door Petersen said: 'You liked Cairo, didn't you?'

'Yes.' Sarina looked puzzled. 'Yes, I did.' Her puzzlement changed to suspicion. 'Why?'

'Aristocratic young ladies like you are not cut out for this life. All the cold and ice and snow and mountains. Besides, you suffer from vertigo.'

'I'm coming with you.' The tone in her voice was final.

Petersen looked at her for a long moment then smiled. 'A Partisan.'

'I'm coming with you.'

'So is Michael.'

'I'm coming with you in a different way.'

Petersen pondered. 'If things like that have to be said I think that I should really — '

'You talk so much I'd have to wait for ever.'

He smiled and touched the auburn hair. 'About this letter.'

'Romance,' she said. 'Life is going to be full of it.'

'One little thing you've overlooked, Peter,' Harrison said.

'Peter never overlooks anything.'

Petersen looked at Sarina and raised his eyes. '*Souvent* — '

'Please.'

'Giacomo and I are going to be alone,' Harrison said. 'We have to sleep. Five dangerous men to be watched. How are we — '

'Alex?'

'Yes, Major?'

'The engine-room.'

'Ah!' A rare, a very rare smile touched Alex's lips. 'The oxyacetylene welder.'

We do hope that you have enjoyed reading this large print book.

Did you know that all of our titles are available for purchase?

We publish a wide range of high quality large print books including:
Romances, Mysteries, Classics
General Fiction
Non Fiction and Westerns

Special interest titles available in large print are:
The Little Oxford Dictionary
Music Book
Song Book
Hymn Book
Service Book

Also available from us courtesy of Oxford University Press:
Young Readers' Dictionary
(large print edition)
Young Readers' Thesaurus
(large print edition)

For further information or a free brochure, please contact us at:
Ulverscroft Large Print Books Ltd.,
The Green, Bradgate Road, Anstey,
Leicester, LE7 7FU, England.
Tel: (00 44) 0116 236 4325
Fax: (00 44) 0116 234 0205

Other titles published by
The House of Ulverscroft:

THE CRIMSON CHALICE

Victor Canning

When a party of marauding Saxons destroy her father's villa, young Roman girl Gratia, 'Tia' escapes. She comes upon the body of the heir to the chieftanship of a British tribe in the west. Baradoc, a prisoner of Phoenician traders, was sold as a slave and is also escaping the Saxons. However, after being attacked he was left for dead by his cousin, the next heir. Tia nurses him back to health, and they continue together to the safety of her uncle's villa in Aquae Sulis . . . Their son, Arturo, inherits his father's desire for uniting Britain against the Saxons.

THE CIRCLE OF THE GODS

Victor Canning

Arturo's dream, like that of his father, Baradoc, is to unite Britain against the marauding Saxons. Always a wild and arrogant youth, he grows up and leads a rebellion against Count Ambrosius. He raises a small force of men which attacks Saxon settlements. Then, with Durstan and Lancelo to lead the troops, Arturo's great campaign begins . . .

BIRDS OF A FEATHER

Victor Canning

A fortunate man, Sir Anthony Swale is married to a loyal wife; he lives in a grand house in Somerset and leads a very privileged life. He devotes most of his time to collecting rare art treasures, particularly from behind the Iron Curtain. And he will pay any price for the right piece — including treason. But then his treachery is discovered — and agents working for the Government decide it is time to take discreet action . . .

THE BOY ON PLATFORM ONE

Victor Canning

Cheerful Peter Courtney, a fourteen-year-old, is an unusual boy. Exceptionally gifted, he's able to repeat, fully, any text which is read to him once — even in French. When his widowed father's business fails, he takes Peter around London's social clubs to perform professionally. Because of his skills he finds himself involved with the Secret Service. He is required to use his gift to receive important information regarding traitors to the British and French Governments — but this places Peter and his father in danger. Now they must escape and leave everything behind . . . in hiding from an assassin who is thorough and systematic.

TALES OF MYSTERY AND HORROR: VOL.III

Edgar Allan Poe

These *Tales of Mystery and Horror* include the story of Bedloe, a wealthy young invalid, who has a strange tale to tell his physician, after he experiences a form of time travel, in *A Tale of the Ragged Mountains* . . . And *The Conversation of Eiros and Charmion* is a very strange tale of a comet approaching earth, causing it to contain pure oxygen. The result of this has a devastating effect on people . . .

THE HAPPY PRINCE AND OTHER TALES

Oscar Wilde

The Happy Prince and Other Tales is a collection of fables — *The Happy Prince* had been, in life, a joyful personality. However, now, immortalised by a gold and jewel encrusted statue, he's saddened by the poverty of his citizens. Unable to move, he enlists the help of a swallow to help his people . . . In *The Nightingale and the Rose*, a nightingale overhears a student complaining that his professor's daughter will not dance with him, as he is unable to give her a red rose. But will the nightingale's sacrifice be enough?

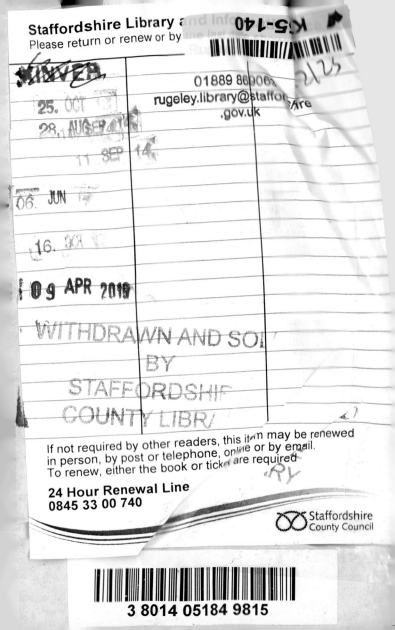

THE CHRISTMAS BABY SURPRISE

BY
SHIRLEY JUMP

MILLS & BOON

First published in Great Britain 2013
by Mills & Boon, an imprint of Harlequin (UK) Limited,
Eton House, 18-24 Paradise Road, Richmond, Surrey TW9 1SR

© Shirley Kawa-Jump, LLC 2013

ISBN: 978 0 263 90147 4
ebook ISBN: 978 1 472 00535 9

23-1013

Harlequin (UK) policy is to use papers that are natural, renewable and recyclable products and made from wood grown in sustainable forests. The logging and manufacturing processes conform to the legal environmental regulations of the country of origin.

Printed and bound in Spain
by Blackprint CPI, Barcelona

New York Times bestselling author **Shirley Jump** didn't have the will-power to diet, nor the talent to master under-eye concealer, so she bowed out of a career in television and opted instead for a career where she could be paid to eat at her desk—writing. At first, seeking revenge on her children for their grocery store tantrums, she sold embarrassing essays about them to anthologies. However, it wasn't enough to feed her growing addiction to writing funny. So she turned to the world of romance novels, where messes are (usually) cleaned up before The End. In the worlds Shirley gets to create and control, the children listen to their parents, the husbands always remember holidays, and the housework is magically done by elves. Though she's thrilled to see her books in stores around the world, Shirley mostly writes because it gives her an excuse to avoid cleaning the toilets and helps feed her shoe habit.

To learn more, visit her website at www.shirleyjump.com.

To my husband,
who makes everything better with his smile.

CHAPTER ONE

WHEN EMILY WATSON ran away from her life, she did it in style. A pair of dark brown skinny jeans, four-inch heels, a shimmery cream shell, all topped with an over-size green cardigan belted at the waist. The clothes were designer, the shoes custom-made, but Emily didn't care. The labels had never mattered to her, and a part of her missed the days when she bought jeans at the Goodwill and topped them with a ratty T that had been washed until the cotton became soft as silk.

She threw a couple suitcases into the trunk of the Volvo she'd bought, even though Cole had hated the big boxy car, then drove away from the house that no longer felt like home. Four hours later, she wound through the hilly roads of Brownsville, Massachusetts, then past glimmering Barrow Lake, until the big leafy trees parted, exposing the long gravel road that led up to the Gingerbread Inn. A small hand-painted sign with a wooden arrow pointing up the hill announced the inn, the familiar marker faded by time.

She rolled down the window and took in a deep breath of fresh, sweet fall air, along with the sense of being home. At peace. Finally.

The tires of Emily's Volvo crunched over the gravel,

sending pebbles scattering to the side. Anticipation filled her as she made her way up the road. Finally, she was back here. In the one place where life made sense, the one place where she had found peace, and most of all, the one place where she hoped to find herself again.

She put a hand over her belly. Too soon to feel anything more than an almost-imperceptible curve beneath her pants but Emily had taken to talking to Sweet Pea, as she'd dubbed the baby inside her. "Almost there, Sweet Pea."

And there, Emily vowed, she would start a new life. She'd left almost all remnants of her old life behind, to come here and get some time to think, plan, strategize her next move. Because no matter what, Emily Watson refused to return to the status quo. Or return to Cole, the man she had once loved. The man she had married— and now was ready to divorce.

Once upon a time was a long, long time ago. The years spent in a lonely, unfulfilling marriage had taught Emily that fairy tales should be reserved for the foolish.

The two-story Georgian-style inn came into view. Shaded at first by the late-fall sun above, it looked sad, lonely, dark. As she drew closer, Emily slowed the car. The anticipation built, then as her eyes adjusted and she saw the full view of the inn, her anticipation imploded into disappointment. What had happened?

The once white gingerbread trim had faded to a dingy gray. Paint peeled off the wooden clapboards, and the wraparound front porch sagged in the center, as if the inn was frowning. Weeds sprang up among the stones of the walkway, and the landscaping that had once been so beautiful it had been featured in a local gardening magazine had become overgrown and tired.

But that wasn't what hit Emily the hardest. It was the red-and-white For Sale sign tacked to the building, hanging a little askew, as if even the Realtor had lost hope.

She parked, got out, but didn't take a step. What was she supposed to do now? She'd counted on staying at the Gingerbread Inn, not just for an escape, but as a way to find closure and connection. A long time ago, she had formed her best memories here, with Andrea and Casey and Melissa—

Oh, Melissa.

Just the thought of her late friend made Emily's heart ache. But Melissa had made it clear she wouldn't want that. *Get on with your life and your dreams,* she'd written in her final letter. *Don't let anything hold you back.*

Don't let anything—even a For Sale sign?

Emily's hand went to her belly again. She had to do this. Not just for herself, but for Pea, too. Sure, she could afford to stay at a hotel, even jet to Italy and spend a week in a villa, but that wasn't where Emily's heart lay. It wasn't the place she needed so desperately to be right now.

Emily glanced down at her hand, at the ornate diamond ring in its platinum setting. She slid it off and tucked it in her pocket. It was time to accept that she was moving on.

Away from Cole.

The front door of the inn opened, and a petite gray-haired woman came out onto the porch. She had on a deep orange apron with yellow edging, a pale pink T-shirt, a pair of denim shorts and sneakers that had seen better days. Emily's face broke into a grin, and she crossed the drive in fast strides. "Carol!"

The inn owner's face lit with recognition and she came hurrying down the steps. "Emily Watson? Oh my goodness, I can't believe it's you!"

The two women embraced, a long hearty hug, the kind that came from years of friendship. Emily had spent so much time at the inn in the summers of her childhood that Carol seemed more like an aunt or an extra grandmother than the owner. She still carried the scent of home-baked bread, as if everything good about the world surrounded Carol Parsons.

A wet nose nudged at Emily's jeans. She grinned and looked down at a golden shaggy dog that had a little Golden in her, a little something else. "Is this Wesley's daughter?"

Carol nodded. "Meet Harper. She's a bit of a mutt, but she's lovable and goofy and all the things you want in a dog."

Emily bent down and ruffled Harper's ears. "You've got a heck of a reputation to live up to, missy."

The dog wagged her tail, lolled her tongue and looked about as unworried as a retriever mix could look. Then she turned and bounded off into the woods, barking an invitation to play at a squirrel.

Emily rose. "I'm so glad you're still here, Carol. When I saw the For Sale sign, I was afraid…"

"Don't you worry. I'm still here. Hanging on by a thread, but here. Anyway, that's a sad story for another day." Carol gestured toward the inn. "Do you want to come in? Stay a while?"

"Actually…" Emily pointed toward the bag in the back of her car. "I was hoping to stay a long while."

Carol's green eyes searched Emily's, and then her face filled with compassion, understanding. "You stay as long as you want, dear. There's always a room for you here."

That was what Emily loved about Carol. She'd never asked questions, never pried. Merely offered a helping hand and a shoulder to cry on, whenever one was needed. Emily hadn't had that kind of bond with her own mother, or heck, any of the female relatives in her family. But she had with Carol, and had looked forward to her summers here as much as she looked forward to sunshine after a cloudy day. She'd spent more time in the kitchen of the inn, helping Carol knead bread and peel potatoes, than probably anywhere else in the world.

The two of them headed inside the inn. The porch creaked a warning as Emily crossed the rotting floorboards. The swing needed a coat of paint, and several of the balustrades had fallen to the ground below. The front door still had the large beveled glass panel that defined its elegance, but inside, everything else looked old, tired, worn. The hardwood floor of the foyer had darkened with age, and one of the parlor's windows rattled against the breeze trying to make its way under the sill. A water stain on the ceiling spoke of plumbing trouble above, while the steam radiators hissed and sputtered a weak wave of heat to break fall's chill.

Emily stowed her bag by the door, then followed Carol into the kitchen. This room, too, had been hit hard by time. The once-bright and happy sunflower wallpaper was peeling, and the white vinyl floor was scuffed and torn in some places. The same long maple table dominated the center of the kitchen, flanked by eight chairs, enough for the help to have dinner, or a few up-too-late teenage girls to grab a midnight snack.

Carol crossed to the coffeepot. "Do you want a cup?

I've also got some bread that just came out of the oven. It's warm, if you want a slice."

"No coffee, but I'd love some bread. Who can turn down that bit of heaven? Do you have honey for it?"

"I do indeed. If there's one thing that's still producing here, it's the bees." Carol grinned, but Emily could see the pain behind the facade. Carol retrieved two mugs of coffee, a plate of bread slices and some honey before returning to the table. She held her cup between her hands and let out a long sigh. "I bet you're wondering why this place looks like this and why I have it up for sale."

"Yeah, but I understand if you don't want to talk about it." Emily had plenty going wrong in her own life that she wasn't keen to discuss, either.

"It's okay. It's been hardest for me to tell the regular guests. Those people are like my family, and to think that the Gingerbread Inn will one day no longer exist… it just breaks my heart. But there's only so much I can do." Carol dropped her gaze to her coffee. "After my husband died, this place got to be too much for one person. Revenue dropped off when the economy struggled, and I just couldn't afford to hire people to keep up with the maintenance. I love it here, I really do, but it's got to the point now where the whole thing is too much. I don't even know where to begin to repair and rebuild. So I put it on the market. Maybe I'll get enough money to pay for a little cottage near the beach."

Harper wriggled through the dog door in the kitchen, took one look at the two women and ducked under the kitchen table, her tail beating a comforting patter against the tile floor. Carol gave the dog a loving pat.

"I hate to see you sell it. I like knowing the inn is here, if…" Emily sighed. "If I ever need it."

Carol's green eyes met Emily's, and her face filled with concern. She reached out, covered one of Emily's hands with her own. "What's the matter, honey?"

"Just a lot going on in my life right now," Emily said. An understatement if there ever was one.

This morning, she'd walked out on her ten-year marriage. They'd already been separated for six months, but separated was a loose term when it came to Cole. He'd stopped by at least once a week, for everything from his favorite golf club to checking to make sure the lawn mower had enough gas for when the landscapers came by.

It was as if he didn't want to accept it was over. Okay, she hadn't made that message any clearer by sleeping with him again. One crazy night, fueled by nostalgia and memories, and she'd forgotten all the reasons they were wrong for each other. The reasons she had asked for a separation. The reasons why she couldn't live with a man who broke her heart almost every day.

Emily finally realized that if she wanted space, she'd have to get it for herself. And with the new life inside her, she needed to have a clear head to make one big decision.

File for divorce or try one more time.

"Well, you take whatever time you need," Carol said. "If there's one thing this place is perfect for, it's thinking."

"I'm counting on that," Emily said, then got to her feet for a second slice of bread. It didn't help her think, but it sure helped her feel like she'd come to the right place. Something about being back at the Gingerbread Inn filled her soul, and right now, Emily Watson needed that more than anything.

* * *

Cole Watson bounded up the stairs of his house—okay, technically it wasn't his right now, even if he was still making the mortgage payments—with a bottle of wine in one hand and a dozen roses in the other. He reached for the front door handle, then paused.

This was Emily's house now. That meant no barging in, something she'd made clear more than once. He lived in a condo across town. A space of his own that was as empty as a cavern, and still echoed loneliness when he walked in at the end of the day. *That* was his home, like it or not, and this place no longer was, which meant he had to stop acting like he could barge in, grab the remote and prop his feet on the coffee table. He rang the bell, even though it felt weirder than hell to ring the bell of a house he still wrote a check for every month. Waited. No answer. Rang it again.

Nothing.

He fished out his key—she'd never changed the locks, something he had taken as a good sign—unlocked the door and went inside, pausing in the vast two-story foyer. Even fully furnished, professionally decorated, the massive house felt empty, sad. Seven thousand square feet of gleaming marble and granite, and it seemed…

Forlorn.

The same copper bowl he remembered them buying on a trip to Mexico sat on the foyer table, waiting for his keys. A neat stack of mail addressed to Cole sat beside the bowl under the Tiffany lamp he had bought for their first anniversary. In the parlor to the right, the same white love seat and armchairs that Emily had hated and he had bought anyway sat, facing the east garden. And down the hall, he could see the wrought-iron kitchen table and chairs, a gift from his mother years ago.

The house was the same, but…different. Off, somehow.

Then Cole spied the slip of paper atop the mail and realized why. He laid the wine and roses on the foyer table and picked up the note.

> Went out of town. Don't know when I'll be back. Don't call me. I need some time to think. To figure out my next step.
> Emily

The cold, stark words hit him hard. They were separated. Did he think she was going to leave him some gushy love note? Still, the reality stung, and reminded him that the marriage he thought he had and the one he did have were two very different things.

Went out of town. Where? Why? With someone?

That thought pained him the most, and drove home the other fact that Cole had yet to face. If he and Emily couldn't repair their marriage, then at some point she would move on, find someone else. Another man would see her smile, make her laugh, hold her in the dark of night.

And rightly so, because they were over and had been for a long time. Didn't matter if Cole was having trouble accepting the fact.

Against his hip, his cell phone buzzed. He flipped it out and answered the call. "Cole here."

"We've got a wrinkle in the product launch," said Doug, his project manager. "There was a bad storm in Japan, and the plant that's supposed to make the screens for us was damaged pretty heavily. They aren't sure when they'll be back online."

"Call someone else."

"I did. There's a backlog on the materials. Seems we wiped out the inventory. It'll be two weeks before they can produce more—"

"I'll take care of it. Get me on the first flight to..." Cole fingered the note in his hands. *I need some time to think. To figure out my next step.*

The next step. There were only two options—get back together or get divorced. It didn't take a rocket scientist to figure out which way Emily was leaning.

Don't call me.

She didn't want him to contact her. The bridge he'd hoped might still be there between them, the connection he'd been counting on when he'd shown up with wine and roses, was gone. She'd underlined the words. Made it clear she didn't want him coming close.

His marriage was over.

"Cole? Did you want a flight to the plant in Japan? Or to the manufacturer in Poland?"

Cole Watson, who had never had an indecisive moment in his life, stood in the empty foyer of the house he no longer lived in and wavered. "Uh..."

He glanced at the note again. *Figure out the next step.*

Then he glanced at his left hand. At the gold band that still sat there, and had for the past ten years. He imagined it gone, imagined this house gone, sold. Neither of those thoughts gave him more than a flicker of loss.

But then he glanced at the five letters at the bottom of the note. *Emily.*

Gone.

That thought ripped a seam in his heart. He crumpled the note in his fist and dropped it into the copper bowl. It circled the bowl, then landed with a soft plunk in the center. "The screens can wait," he said to Doug. "I have another matter to take care of first."

"But, but—"

"Don't worry, Doug. I'll handle it." Cole could hear the panic rising in Doug's voice. The man had a tendency to panic first, think second. "By the time I'm through, we'll look back at this moment as a blip on the radar. A momentary setback."

But as Cole hung up the phone and tried to figure out where in the world his wife might have gone and how he was going to deal with whatever next step was coming his way, he realized he wasn't talking about the screens at all. He was talking about his marriage.

CHAPTER TWO

IN THE SMALL but cozy bedroom where she'd spent many a childhood summer, a blank computer screen and blinking cursor stared back at Emily, waiting for her to fill it with words. Something it had been doing for the past twenty minutes. She'd type a word, backspace, delete. Type another. Backspace, delete. What had happened to her? In college, she had been able to write short stories like a chicken producing eggs. Now when she finally had time and space to write, she couldn't manage to get a word onto the page. This was her dream, and all she could do was stare at it.

Her focus had deserted her. Heck, it had left town months ago. She needed to get her priorities in line again. Somehow.

A light fall breeze whispered through the couple inches of open window, dancing with the white lace curtains and casting sparkles of sunshine on the white-and-blue space. The low sounds of a radio playing downstairs, probably while Carol worked, made for a harmony with the chatter of the birds outside. It was a serene, perfect setting, the kind of place any writer would love to have. Well, any writer without writer's block, that was.

Emily crossed to her bag, and tugged out the envelope she'd tucked into the front pocket. Melissa's last note, mailed to her, and she presumed, also to the other girls.

Dear Gingerbread Girls,

I'm laughing as I write that little nickname for us. Remember those crazy summers we had at the Gingerbread Inn? All those adventures in town and late at night? It's no wonder someone dubbed us the Gingerbread Girls. Heck, we were always together, thick as thieves, Carol used to say.

I miss that. I know we've all got older and have gone on with our lives, but oh how I miss those summers, those connections. That's the one big regret I have now. That we couldn't figure out a time for a reunion and now it's too late. I won't get to see you all one last time.

Promise me you'll get together. Promise me you'll keep the Gingerbread Girls alive. Promise me you'll all follow your dreams, the ones we talked about that day by the lake. I still have my rock. Sometimes I hold it and think back to that day.

You are all the best friends I could ever hope for and I will be forever grateful for the summers we spent together.

Melissa

Tears blurred the letter in Emily's eyes. She drew in a shaky breath, then propped the letter beside the computer, holding it in place with a small oval stone that she had kept with her for the past fifteen years. Somewhere out there, two other matching stones sat in drawers or on desks, or somewhere. Did Andrea and Casey see the stones the same way? Did they remember that day?

The women had fallen out of touch over the years, separated by busy lives and families. Maybe it was time to get the Gingerbread Girls back together. Before Emily could think twice, she shot off a quick email to both Andrea and Casey, including her cell phone number and an invitation to come to the inn. She left off the news about the For Sale sign, because she hoped to find a way to talk Carol out of that choice.

And in the process, she would write this book, damn it. She would follow her dreams. Emily needed this do over. Needed it…a lot.

A knock sounded on the door. Emily got to her feet and opened the bedroom door to Carol. "Good timing," Emily said with a laugh. "I've got writer's block on the first word."

"I've got some coffee and cookies that should help with that," Carol said. "But first, there's someone here to see you."

"Someone here to see me?" How could that be? She'd told no one where she was going, and had only sent the email to the other girls a couple minutes ago. Unless they were in the driveway when they got it, there was no way either Andrea or Casey could show up that fast. No one else would be able to track her down so quickly. No one but—

"Cole."

Carol grinned. "How'd you guess? Yes, he's here. Waiting in the parlor to talk to you." Then her good friend's face fell. "Are you okay, honey? Do you want me to tell him to come back later?"

"No." Emily knew Cole and knew he wouldn't take no for an answer. The qualities that had made him a successful businessman had made him a terrible husband. Win at all costs. That pretty much summed up Cole. When they'd been dating, she'd seen that attitude as one that meant he wanted her and their life together more than anything in the world. But she'd been wrong. What Cole wanted, more than anything or anyone, was success, regardless of the cost to attain it. Then as the years went on, he'd employed that approach to arguments, major decisions, everything. She'd had enough and walked away.

But Cole refused to get the message.

"I'll talk to him," Emily said. "Just give me a minute."

"Sure, hon. Take whatever time you need. I'll talk his ear off. Might as well make him suffer." Carol let out a little laugh, then put an understanding hand on Emily's arm. "If it helps, he looks miserable."

Emily thanked Carol, then shut the door. She faced her reflection in the oval mirror that hung over the antique dresser. She was still clad in a pair of pale blue flannel pajamas, her hair in a messy topknot on her head, and her face bare of makeup. She looked a million miles away from Cole Watson's wife.

Perfect.

Without doing so much as tucking a wayward strand of hair back into place, Emily spun on her sock-clad feet and headed out of the room and down to the parlor. She no longer cared what she looked like when she saw Cole. She was no longer going to be the woman who stressed about every crease, every spot, who worried about her public image as the CEO's wife. She was going to be who she was—before.

Cole stood by the window, his back to her. He wore a tailored dark blue suit that emphasized his broad shoulders, tapered waist, the hours he spent in the gym. His dark hair was getting a little long and now brushed against the back of his collar. Her heart skipped a beat when she saw him, just as it always had. That was one thing that had never changed—her attraction to him. Her hormones had never listened to her brain.

He turned as she approached, even though she'd made almost no sound entering the room. "What are you doing here?" he said, or rather, barked.

So much for some kind of tender moment. What had she expected, really? They were no longer together, and maybe someday her heart would get the message. "How did you find me?"

"There is only one place in the world that you have talked about missing, and it's this place. I took a chance that's where you'd go, and I was right."

Well, he'd listened to her talk about the inn. Too bad he hadn't listened to any of the other problems between them. "Where I am and what I'm doing is no longer your concern, Cole," she said.

"You're my wife, Emily."

"We've been separated for six months. I'm not your anything anymore."

His face took on a pained look, but it disappeared a split second later. "Be that as it may, I should at least know where you are, in case something happens."

"Well, now you know." She turned on her heel and headed out of the room.

He caught up to her, his hand reaching for her, but

not connecting, as if he'd just remembered they were no longer together. She noticed the glint of gold, the ring he still wore. Because he hadn't thought to take it off? Or because he hadn't given up yet?

"Wait," he said. "Don't go. I want to talk to you."

She wheeled around. When she met his blue eyes, a little hitch caught in her throat. A hitch she cursed. "We're done talking, Cole. Nothing's changed in ten years—nothing's changing now. Just—" she let out a long sigh "—let me go. Please."

And this time, he did just as she asked. Emily walked out of the room, and Cole didn't follow. She paused at the top of the stairs, waiting until she heard the click of the door. Then she returned to her room, put a hand on her belly and told herself she'd done the right thing.

Cole stood on the ramshackle porch for a long time. How had it got to this point? What had he missed?

There had been a time when he could smile at Emily, or take her out for a night on the town, and whatever was wrong between them would disappear for a while. But this time, he'd sensed a distance, a wall that had never been there before. Or maybe he'd just never noticed it until now.

Until his wife had crossed two states to get away from him. To this place, this…inn.

He glanced at the run-down house behind him. The overgrown grounds. The peeling paint. Why had Emily come here, of all the places in the world? With what they had in their joint bank account, she could have afforded a five-star hotel in the south of France. Instead, she came to this…

Mess.

Frustration built inside him, but there was nowhere to go with that feeling. Nowhere but back home to New York, and to work. He took a step off the porch, and as he did, a crunch sounded beneath his foot and the top step crumpled beneath his weight, sending his leg crashing through a hole and down onto the soft earth below. He let out a curse, then yanked his leg out.

The door opened. Cole's hopes rose, then sank, when he saw the inn's owner, Carol, not Emily, come onto the porch. "Are you okay? I thought I heard a crash," Carol said.

"The step broke." Cole put up a hand of caution. "That porch isn't safe. You might want to block it off or hire someone to fix it."

"Okay." One word, spoken on a sigh, topped by a frown.

Cole had been in business long enough to read the signs of a beleaguered owner, one who had more bills than cash. "I could call someone for you. Considering I broke the step, I should be the one to fix it." Sympathy filled him. He still remembered those early, cash-strapped days when he'd been building his business, watching every dime and trying to do everything himself. Sacrifice had been at the top of his to-do list for many years.

Carol shook her head. "I couldn't possibly ask you—"

"Consider it done," Cole said. He had his phone half-way to his ear before he reconsidered.

Fixing that board would only take a minute or two. Calling someone to fix that board would take a lot longer. At least an hour, even if he paid a rush fee, to get someone out here, just to nail a board in place. Judging by the looks of the place, the inn's owner had enough problems on her plate without adding in a wait on a contractor.

"If you have some nails and a piece of wood, I could put in a temporary fix," Cole said. Where the heck had that come from? He hadn't done contractor work for years. His hands were so soft from working at a desk they might as well be mittens.

"I have lots of supplies," Carol said, pointing to a building a few yards away. "Help yourself."

"Will do." Maybe it would feel good to work with his hands again. And maybe he was just trying to delay leaving, hoping for a miracle with Emily.

Carol went back inside, so Cole headed for the garage. It took him a little while, but he found a tape measure, some plywood and a hammer and nails. He measured the space, ripped the board on a dusty table saw, then hammered the wood onto the risers. The actions came naturally to him, as if he had never walked away from construction.

The sun beat down on him, brought sweat to his brow and a warmth to his back. He had hung his suit jacket over the porch rail, taken off his tie and rolled up his sleeves. By the time he finished, all four stairs had new treads. And yes, it had probably taken as long as it would have taken had he called someone, but he had the bonus of feeling like he'd done something productive. Something he could look at and see, an almost-instant result, the opposite of how things happened when he made decisions at his desk.

Emily came out onto the porch. Surprise lit her features when she saw him. "What are you doing?"

"Fixing the board I broke. Then I noticed the other

steps were about ready to break, so I replaced those, too."

She moved closer and peered over the railing at his work. "You still remember how to do all that?"

"Like riding a bike." Cole leaned against the handrail, which he'd made more secure with a few nails earlier. "It was just like the old days."

Did she remember those days? That tiny apartment they'd lived in, how they'd rushed home at the end of the day, exhausted but excited to see each other? She'd bandaged his cuts, he'd bring her a glass of cheap wine, and they would sit on the fire escape and watch the city go by. The world would be perfect for a little while.

"I guess you don't forget some things," she said.

"No, you don't." But he wasn't talking about hammers or measurements or anything related to construction. "Do you remember those days, Em?"

"Of course." Her voice was soft, her green eyes tender, then she cleared her throat and drew herself up. "We've moved a long way away from those days, though. In more ways than one."

He pushed off from the rail and stood beneath her. "What if we could get them back? What if we could be the people we used to be? Would we have a chance then?"

She bit her lip and shook her head. "Fixing some steps doesn't bring us back there, Cole. You've changed…I've changed. What we want has changed. You can't turn back the clock." She gave the railing a tap. "Have a safe trip back."

Then she went inside and shut the door, closing the door on him, as well. Cole stood there a long, long time, then picked up the tools, returned them to the garage, got in his car and drove away. He'd done all he could here, he realized. And the sooner he accepted that fact, the better.

But as he left the Gingerbread Inn, and the run-down building got smaller and smaller in his rearview mirror, Cole wondered…if he could turn back the clock with the inn, maybe it would be enough to turn back the clock with his wife, too.

CHAPTER THREE

By BREAKFAST THE next day, Emily had ten pages written and a swelling sense of satisfaction. They might not be good pages, heck, they might not even be publishable pages, but they were closer than she'd got to her dream of publishing a novel in years. All those years in high school and college when she'd written short stories, and made fits and starts at different novels, but never finished any of them. Now with hours of uninterrupted time, her creativity exploded, with pages springing to life as fast as she could write them. She got to her feet, stretching after the long hours in the hard wooden desk chair.

Nausea rolled through her in a wave. She gripped the back of the chair, drew in a deep breath and waited for it to pass. It didn't.

"Hey, kiddo," she said to her belly, "I thought this was supposed to end with the first trimester."

The baby, of course, didn't answer, and the nausea kept on pitching and rolling her stomach, neither caring that the calendar said Emily was just past three months pregnant. Her clothes still fit, if a little snugly, but she knew it wouldn't be long before she would start to show.

And that would mean telling people about the baby. People like Cole.

Emily sighed. She loved her husband—she really did—but she had stopped being *in* love with him a long time ago. She'd tried, Lord knew she'd tried, to make it work, thinking maybe if she kept acting like a wife, she'd feel like one. But the relationship they had had when they'd first got married had drained away, like a hose with a pinhole. The loss had come so gradually that one day she'd woken up and realized it was over, in her heart, in her head, and continuing the facade would only hurt both of them. Six months ago, she'd asked Cole to move out, and he'd gone, without a fight.

Then Cole had come to her one night, telling her he'd do anything to have his wife back. He'd been so sincere, so racked with sorrow, she'd believed him, and found the old passion ignited. One crazy night, a night where she'd believed yes, he finally got it, and maybe they could make it work—

And in the morning he was gone, off on yet another business trip. She was left alone again. She'd had a good cry, called a lawyer and filed for a formal separation.

Two weeks later, she'd realized her period was late and that one night had resulted in the only thing Emily had ever wanted—and Cole never had.

A child.

She'd kept the pregnancy a secret, and kept her distance from Cole, resolving to do this on her own. Now she had a baby on the way into her life and a husband on his way out. Either way, Emily was determined to make her new existence work.

She pulled on some sweatpants and an old T-shirt, then headed out of her room and downstairs toward the kitchen. A little dry toast should take the edge off this nausea, and then she could go back to work on the book.

Emily was just reaching for the loaf of bread on the counter when she heard a *tap-tap-tapping* coming from outside the window. She leaned over the sink, and peeked out into the bright late-fall day.

Cole stood on a ladder, perched against the side of the building, hammering in a new piece of siding. He'd switched from dress clothes to a crisp new pair of jeans and a dark blue T-shirt that hugged the planes of his chest. Sunglasses obscured his blue eyes, and a leather tool belt hung at a sexy angle from his hips. For a second, her heart melted.

"He was here when I woke up this morning," Carol said as she entered the kitchen.

Emily turned around and put her back to the window. What did Cole think he was doing? Did he think that fixing the inn's porch would fix them, too? "Why?"

"I don't know. I'm just glad for the help. Anything he can fix helps me in selling this place."

Emily sighed. "It's going to be so weird not to have this place here anymore. The Gingerbread Inn is such a big part of my childhood."

Carol paused by the coffeepot. "Do you want a cup?"

"Uh, no. I'll have tea instead." Emily grabbed the kettle off the stove, filled it with water, then set it over the flame. Outside, Cole had stopped hammering. Emily resisted the urge to look outside and see what he was doing now. Maybe if she ignored him, he'd leave. Either way, he rarely stayed away from the office for more than a few hours, so whatever "fixing" he was doing would be done soon and Cole would go back to being his usual Type A, nose-to-the-grindstone self. She'd be on her own, just her and the baby, which was exactly what she wanted, she told herself. Her hand strayed to her stomach, a protective barrier.

Emily looked up and noticed Carol watching her. "What?"

"Tea, huh?"

Emily fished an herbal tea bag out of the glass mason jar next to the stove and held it up. "Yup."

"Decaf, too. In the morning." Carol cupped her hands around her mug of coffee and assessed Emily. "Anything you want to share?"

"Nope, nope." She'd said that too fast, Emily realized. But she wasn't ready to tell anyone about the baby yet. She thumbed toward her room. "I should get back to writing. I'm on a roll."

If she stayed in this kitchen one more minute, she was sure Carol would read the truth in her face. The kettle whistled and Emily turned to pour the water. She heard a sound behind her and pivoted back.

Cole stood in the kitchen, watching her. In jeans and a T-shirt, he looked so much like the man she'd fallen in love with that Emily's heart stuttered, and she had to remind herself to breathe. Cole still had the same lean physique as he'd had in college, and her mind flashed images of every muscle, every plane. Her hormones kept overriding her common sense.

Carol murmured some excuse about needing to start laundry and headed out of the room. Emily shifted her gaze away from Cole and down to her teacup. She dipped the bag up and down, up and down, avoiding Cole's blue eyes. "What are you doing here?" she asked him.

"Helping Carol out."

"I can see that." She let out a frustrated gust. "Why?"

"She's obviously in a tight spot right now and—"

"Cole, stop making up excuses for being here. I've been married to you for ten years, and you have never so much as hung a picture in all that time. So don't tell me you got this sudden urge to become Homer Handyman."

"Homer Handyman?" She could hear the smile in his voice, as he crossed the room and poured himself a cup of coffee. "I'm not making up excuses, Emily. I saw Carol needed help, and I wanted to do what I could. I haven't worked with my hands since college, and I have to admit, it feels good."

"Then go home and build a box or something. Don't stay here."

Cole paused in front of her and waited until she lifted her gaze to his. "Home isn't home for me anymore."

She refused to feel bad about that. Refused to let the echoes in his voice affect her. Their marriage had disintegrated, and Cole knew that as well as she did. "Why are you really here, Cole?"

His blue eyes softened, and for a moment, she saw the Cole she used to know. The Cole she had fallen in love with on a bright spring day on the NYU campus. "Because this place means a lot to you," he said quietly.

The cold wall between her heart and his began to defrost, and Emily found herself starting to reach for Cole, for the man she used to know, used to love. Then his cell phone rang, the familiar trill that signaled a call from the company's CFO, and Cole stepped back, unclipping the phone with one hand and putting up a finger asking her to wait a minute with the other.

Emily shook her head, then grabbed her tea and

walked out of the kitchen before she was once again foolish enough to believe that anything had changed.

Chaos had descended on the offices of Watson Technology Development, if the number of calls, texts and emails Cole had received in the past hour were any indication. He'd been gone less than forty-eight hours and people were in a panic.

Rightly so, he supposed, considering he spent more hours at WTD than anywhere else in the world. Ever since the day he'd started it, Cole had dedicated most of his waking hours to the company that bore his name. In the beginning, the hours had been a necessity, as he worked his way up from a one-man office to a global company with offices in three U.S. cities and two foreign locations, building computers, cell phones and custom technology solutions for his customers.

It took him a good hour to calm down his assistant, and to wade through all the crises that needed his attention. The urge to run back to the office and handle everything himself ran strong in Cole, but every time he glanced at the pile of wood and tools, he remembered that he was here for another reason.

Not to fix the Gingerbread Inn—though that was the reason he'd given Emily—but to fix his marriage. Deep in his heart, Cole knew he had run out of chances, and if he let Emily go this time, what they had between them would die like a plant stuck in a dark corner for too long. That was partly his fault, he knew, and the only way to fix it was to stay here. Put in the time, handle the project of his marriage like he did any project at work—lots of man-hours.

When he hung up with the office, he flipped out his

phone and made a quick list of everything that the Gingerbread Inn needed done to make it sellable. By the time he got to number fifty, he knew he needed two things—a couple of professionals, because some of the jobs were out of his realm—and a second set of hands.

Another half hour on the phone and he had a plumber, electrician and a roofer lined up to come out and give him estimates. The last call he made was to the one man he knew who would drop everything at a moment's notice and travel anywhere in the world, just because a friend asked him to.

"Joe," Cole said when the call connected. "How would you like to vacation in Massachusetts for the holidays?"

Joe laughed. "Did I just hear the great and busy Oz say the word *vacation?*"

"It won't be a long one, but yes, I'm taking some time off. I'm working on a project here and could use an extra set of hands." Cole explained about the inn and its owner's financial struggles. "Plus, Em's here."

"She is? How's that going?"

"Not so well. I'm just trying—" he sighed, pressed a finger to his temple "—to give us one more chance. I'm hoping that she sees my being here as being committed to her, to us."

"I always thought you two were going to live a long and happy life together," Joe said.

"Yeah, me too." Cole sighed again.

His friend thought for a second. "Give me a couple days to tie up the loose ends I have here, and then I'll join you. It'll be good to catch up. How long has it been?"

"Too long," Cole said. "Far too long."

He hung up with Joe, then put his phone away and surveyed the work ahead of him. There was plenty to do, for sure. His gaze wandered to the second-floor bedroom where Emily was staying. The room was only twenty feet or so away, but it might as well have been on the moon.

Earlier, in the kitchen, there'd been a moment, a split second, really, where he'd thought maybe he could see a bridge back to them. Somehow, he needed to build more of those moments. One on top of another, and the bridge would connect them again. He hoped.

He headed back into the house and found Emily in the kitchen, opening a package of saltines. She'd changed into a pair of jeans and a fitted T-shirt. The clothes outlined her hourglass shape, the narrow valley of her waist, the tight curve of her rear end, and sent a roar of desire through him. Damn, he'd missed her. In a hundred different ways.

"Hey, Emily," he said.

She turned around, a saltine in her hand. "Cole."

There was no emotion in that syllable, nothing that he could read and pinpoint as a clue to how she felt about him. He cleared his throat, took a step closer.

"I was thinking of taking a break for lunch," he said. "Would you like to go into town with me? I need to get some supplies, too."

"Sorry, no. I'm, uh, working on something."

"Working on something? What?"

"Something personal," she said, and turned toward the cabinet to get a glass.

The door had shut between them, and she had no intentions of opening it—that much was clear. Cole should cut his losses, go back to New York and bury himself in work. Accept the divorce and move on, like she had.

Then why did he stay in the kitchen like a lovelorn teenager? He grabbed a glass of water that he didn't want, hoping Emily would talk to him. Instead, she gathered her crackers and her drink and headed for the hall. "Em?"

She turned back. "Yeah?"

"Is there any chance?"

The question hung in the sunny kitchen for a long moment. Emily's green eyes met his, and for a second, hope leaped in his chest. She shook her head and lowered her gaze. "No, Cole, there isn't."

Then she brushed by him and out of the room, leaving Cole more alone than he could ever remember feeling.

CHAPTER FOUR

TWO FRIENDLY, HAPPY emails greeted Emily when she got back to her room. Andrea and Casey, both thrilled to hear from her and chock-full of their own news. Casey, the more dramatic of the three, was full of boisterous stories about her life, while Andrea talked about working at her family shop during tough economic times. They were both surprised to hear the inn was up for sale, and both said they'd try to make it out there before the holidays. "I'd love to give the place one more goodbye," Casey wrote, "and give you a great big hug, too. It'll be great to see you all and maybe raise a toast to Melissa. We'll stand out on the dock and give her a proper goodbye."

Emily wrote back, telling them that sounded like a fabulous idea, and encouraging her friends to arrive as soon as possible. Her hands hovered over the keyboard while she debated how much to tell them. "Things are going great with me," she said finally, lying through her fingers. "Can't wait to see you!" She left it on a bright, cheery note, even adding a smiley face. Then she hit Send, and tried to work on her book again.

The words wouldn't come. After eating the saltines, her nausea had passed, and her stomach rumbled, reminding her it was lunchtime. A lunch she could have enjoyed with Cole, if she'd taken him up on his offer.

Doing so would only tempt her all over again, and the last thing she needed was to be tempted by Cole. She placed a hand on her belly and splayed her fingers against the tiny life deep inside her. "We'll be okay, Sweet Pea. I promise."

Carol poked her head into Emily's room. "I made a salad for lunch. Want some?" Carol noted Emily's hesitation, and added, "Cole left. Said he had to go to town."

"Lunch sounds good. I was just starting to get hungry." Emily shut the laptop's lid, then followed Carol to the kitchen. Harper lay on the small rug in front of the back door, snarfling and twitching, probably chasing a rabbit in her doggy dreams.

Carol laid two heaping plates of spinach, strawberry and feta salad on the table. Sprinkles of roasted pecans and a raspberry vinaigrette finished off the tasty lunch. "So," Carol said when she sat across from Emily, "when are you due?"

"When…what?" Heat rushed to Emily's cheeks. "What are you talking about?"

"Honey, I may not be able to know how to save this place, but I know when a woman is expecting. The tea, the nausea, the saltines. Plus you just have that look about you."

"What look?"

"That excited-slash-terrified look." Carol grinned. "My sister had three kids, and she looked like that every time."

Emily picked at the salad. "May 17."

Carol's face exploded in a smile, and she jerked out

of the chair to gather Emily in a tight, warm hug. "I'm so happy for you, honey."

"Thank you," Emily said, and for the first time, the joy of what was coming began to infuse her. Sharing the news made it real, somehow, and that allowed her to imagine the future with the child she had always wanted.

A child Cole hadn't wanted.

But that didn't matter. She and Cole were over, even if he had yet to fully get the message. She was going to have this baby alone and be just fine. She'd wanted a baby almost from the day they got married. Cole had kept telling her they should wait. For what, she wasn't even sure now. All she knew was that he found one excuse after another not to have a child.

Finally, Emily was building the family she'd dreamed of. Granted, a family without a father, but Emily had no doubt she'd more than make up for Cole's absence.

"Cole must be over the moon about the baby," Carol said.

Emily shook her head. "He doesn't know. And I'm not telling him," she added before Carol said anything. "We've been separated for some time now, and after I get back to New York, I think…no, I know, I'm going to file for divorce."

"What? But then…why is he here?"

"Because Cole is the kind of man who never loses. Even when the battle isn't his to win." She shrugged, and cursed the tears that rushed to her eyes. "Our marriage has been over for a long time, but he won't accept that."

Carol's hand covered Emily's. "I don't know about over, if you have that little gift growing inside you right now."

"That night was a mistake." Emily shook her head. "One I won't repeat. My marriage is *over*, Carol. I'm just looking ahead to the future with just me and the baby."

The doorbell sounded a happy little trill. "We can talk later," Carol said. "Let me get the door. You stay, finish your salad. And don't worry, I won't say anything to Cole."

Emily smiled up at her old friend. "Thank you."

A minute later, Carol was back with a tall, trim, white-haired man beside her. "I'm not quite sure what all we need done around here," she said as she walked into the room. "My home repair skills are pretty limited."

"Seems to me like you need a little of everything." The man's gaze swept the kitchen, taking in the water stains on the ceiling, the dripping faucet, the worn countertops. "The house has good bones, though, and that's what matters. You've got a great place here, miss."

A shy smile curved across Carol's face. "Oh, I'm far from a miss these days."

The man gave her a grin that crinkled the corners of his pale blue eyes. "I disagree."

Carol let out a little laugh. "Well, thank you, Martin."

They were flirting, Emily realized. Something she had never seen Carol do before. Carol tore her gaze away from the man and waved toward Emily. "This is Emily, an old friend and one of the regular visitors to the Gingerbread Inn," she said. "Emily, this is Martin Johnson. Cole hired him to do some work around here."

Emily stood, shook Martin's hand. Harper sat in the corner of the kitchen, her tail wagging, while she watched the exchange between the humans with curiosity in her brown eyes.

"I'm mainly a plumber, but I know how to do just

about anything. That's what comes from buying my own fixer-upper twenty years ago." He grinned. "I'm still working on it two decades later. The carpenter's always the one who doesn't get time to build his own furniture."

"I bet that drives your wife crazy," Carol said.

"Would if I had one," Martin said. "But my Sarah passed away, going on ten years now."

"I'm so sorry," Carol said. "Listen, we were just having lunch. Could I get you something to eat, and we can talk about the repairs? I've got leftover meat loaf in the fridge if you want a meat loaf sandwich."

Martin's grin widened. "I haven't had one of those for years and years. But I hate to put you out. I'm sure you're busy."

Carol giggled. Actually giggled. "Oh, it's no trouble at all. You sit, and I'll fix the sandwich."

Emily had finished her salad and rose to put her plate in the sink. "Nice to meet you, Martin," she said to the handyman, then turned to Carol. "I'm going to go back to work for a little bit."

"Okay," Carol said. "Be sure to get out and enjoy this bright sunshine, too. It's an absolutely gorgeous fall day."

Emily glanced out the window. "You know, that sounds like a great idea. I think I'll take a notebook and head down to the dock."

"Sounds like a perfect way to spend an afternoon," Carol said.

Martin and Carol started talking about the repairs needed at the inn. Their conversation flowed easily, with a little undercurrent of interest on both sides.

A few minutes later, Emily threw on a thick sweatshirt, then grabbed a notebook and a pen and headed outside. Cole's rental car was nowhere to be seen. A part of her hoped he'd done what he always did—hired someone to do what needed to be done so he could go back to work. Whenever she had something on the honey-do list, Cole would pick up the phone and solve the problem. There were times when she wanted to yell at him that she didn't want hired help. She wanted her husband to be the one to hang the pictures, move the sofa, trim the old maple tree in the backyard. Because that meant he would be home for more than a few minutes, and she'd feel like they were in this life together, not two trains running on parallel tracks that slowly diverged in opposite directions.

The lake's water glistened under the bright sun, as if diamonds had been sprinkled across the smooth, lightly rippled surface. The same wooden bench she remembered sat at the end of the dock, weathered and gray. She sat down, drew her feet up to her chest and leaned against the armrest. The sun warmed her face and shoulders, and soon Emily was immersed in her ideas. She scribbled all over the notepad, plot twists and character details flowing as fast as her pen could put the words on the page.

It was as if a waterfall had been held back too long, she realized. Maybe that's what it was—all those years of trying to be Cole's wife, putting everything she wanted to do to the side so that she could keep the perfect house and the perfect life, then be the perfect wife at banquets and dinners and parties. Her self had disappeared somewhere among the gossip-filled brunches with the other wives, the afternoons spent playing another round of golf while Cole networked. She'd forgotten the ambitions she'd had when she graduated, the dreams she was going to pursue. But now here, finally, she was doing it. Taking Melissa's advice and living her life before it was too late.

"Enjoying the day?"

Cole's voice jerked her to attention. Her pen skittered across the page. "You scared me."

"Sorry. You were so lost in what you were doing there, I guess you didn't hear me clomping down the dock."

"You never clomp, Cole." She chuckled. "You're a little too refined for that."

"Oh, are you saying I've gotten soft in my days behind a desk?"

The word *soft* made her glance over at his trim body, still muscular and strong, thanks to frequent gym workouts. He'd put a thick black leather jacket over the T-shirt and jeans, giving him an almost...dangerous air. The day she'd met him, he'd been wearing a leather jacket much like this one. In an instant, she was back in time, standing on a sidewalk and apologizing for running into Cole because she'd had her nose buried in a book, reading while she'd walked to class. He'd told her she should never apologize for a good story, and as he helped her pick up her schoolbooks, they'd started talking, and it felt like they hadn't stopped talking for a solid month. By the holiday break, she was in love with him and by the end of the school year, Cole had proposed. All because she'd seen the leather jacket and thought he was sexy, and she'd been intrigued by a man who looked like a biker but talked like a scholar.

What was she doing? Getting distracted by the man she no longer wanted?

"Mind if I share the seat?" he asked. "Grab a little break?"

"Sure." She turned, put her feet on the dock and moved to make room on the bench for him. As soon as she did, she regretted the decision. The bench was small, and Cole was so close, it would only take a breath of movement for her thigh to be touching his.

"I got you something when I was in town," he said, and handed her a small brown bag.

"What's this?"

He waved at the bag. "Open it and see."

She peeked inside the bag. A shiny wrapper with a familiar logo winked back at her. "You got me my favorite snack cakes?"

"Thought you might be craving them."

For a second, she thought he knew she was pregnant, and she panicked. Then Cole chuckled. "If I remember right, you were always craving those things. I think we cleaned out the campus cafeteria on a weekly basis. What'd you use to say?" He leaned back, thinking. "There's always a reason—"

"To celebrate with cake." She took the package out of the bag. "Of course, that's what I said when I had the metabolism of a twenty-year-old."

Cole reached up, as if he was going to brush away the bangs on her forehead, but withdrew without touching her. She swallowed the bitter taste of disappointment. "You're still as beautiful now as the day I met you, Emily."

She got to her feet. "Cole—"

He reached for her hand. When Cole touched her, electricity sizzled in Emily's veins, and her heart caught.

"I'm not saying anything other than that you're beautiful, Emily. No reason to run."

It did look ridiculous to hurry off the dock just because Cole had complimented her. She retook her seat. "Let's just keep this friendly, okay?"

"Sure." If he was disappointed, he didn't show it. He propped his feet on the railing in front of him, leaned back on the bench and tilted his face to the sun, eyes closed.

It was as if all the years of stress and long hours melted away. Cole looked younger, happier, more peaceful than she had seen him in a long time. Maybe working on the inn was doing him some good. For years, she'd worried about him having a heart attack at work because he worked too much, ate at odd hours and had more stress on his shoulders than anyone she knew.

"I met Martin," she said, unwrapping the snack cake and taking a bite. It was heaven on her palate. "Did you hire him to do all the work around here?"

"Nope. Just to help on the things I'm not good at. I figure I'll stay a few more days." He opened his eyes and turned to look at her. "If that's okay with you."

How could she say no? He was helping Carol, and Carol desperately needed help if she was going to keep the inn running. Plus, Cole looked so relaxed, so happy, something Emily had rarely seen in him.

When the baby was born, she and Cole would have to be civil. Attend family gatherings together sometimes, or maybe just meet to talk about their child. With the baby, Emily knew Cole would never be totally out of her life. Someday, maybe she'd stop reacting when he smiled at her or touched her. Maybe.

"It's fine, Cole. I'm just surprised you want to do it."

"Working with my hands has made me feel…useful." He chuckled. "I know, I know, they need me at work and that should do the same, but this is different. When I fixed those steps, I saw an immediate response to a problem. One minute they were a hazard, the next they were ready for visitors. It's like every corner of this place is crying out for attention."

She wanted to say that she had done that for years, and he'd never noticed. Or listened. "Maybe we should have bought a fixer-upper instead of built a house. Then you could have had projects all the time."

"You still have that honey-do list, don't you?"

She shook her head. "I gave it to Bob. The contractor you hired to do the renovations on the kitchen? He's taking care of all those things while I'm gone."

"Oh, that's good." He sounded disappointed.

A part of her wanted to believe that if she went back to New York right now, Cole would take up that honey-do list and insist on being home more often, being there, being with her. But the sensible part of her knew this time at the inn was a temporary reprieve. The problems in their marriage ran deeper than a remodeling project. Instead, it would be better, and smarter, to use this time together as a way to forge their future together. Their real future, not a fantasy one.

"Cole…" She paused, laying her hands in her lap, her appetite for the snack cake gone. "I think we should sell the house. I don't need one that big, and you aren't living there anymore and…"

"Let's wait," he said. "Give it some time—"

"We've been separated six months, and really, a divorce is just a formality at this point. The sooner we get these things settled, the faster we can move on."

"What if I don't want to move on?"

The pain in his voice hurt her. She had no doubt he still cared, but she knew how this would end. She'd read this same story a hundred times over the course of their marriage. "Cole, we've tried this. The big fight, the talk of ending it. You come back, try for a few days, then before you know it, you're back at work and I'm in a marriage of one person. Let's just make it official, okay? Instead of pretending that we're ever going to be a family."

She gathered her things and got to her feet. She started to pass by him, when Cole reached out. "Emily."

His voice was harsh, jagged, filled with need and regret. Feelings she knew well because she'd felt them herself. She hesitated, standing on the dock under the bright November sun while the water lapped gently at the pilings, and looked down at the man she had pledged to love forever.

"I'm sorry, Cole. I really am," she said softly, then placed a kiss on his cheek.

At the last second, Cole turned, and his mouth met hers. Heat exploded in that kiss, and Cole jerked to his feet, hauled her to his chest and tangled his hands in her hair. Her mind went blank, and her body turned on, and everything inside her melted. All the perfect little arguments she had against being with Cole disappeared and for a moment, Emily Watson was swept back into the very fairy tale she had thought stopped existing.

CHAPTER FIVE

FOR ONE LONG sweet moment, Cole's life was perfect. Then Emily broke away from him, and stumbled back a step. "We...we can't do that. We're getting divorced, Cole."

He scowled. "I know what's going on between us."

"Then let's stop getting wrapped up in something that's never going to work. We made that mistake a few months ago, and—"

"And what?"

She shook her head and backed up another step. "And it was a mistake."

"So you're giving up, just like that?"

Her gaze softened, and though Cole wished he read love in that look, what he really saw was sympathy. "No, Cole, I never gave up. You did that for both of us a long time ago. And now you're doing what you always do. Fighting to win, because Cole Watson never loses at anything. Too bad you never realized that you lost me a long, long time ago."

He stood on the dock for a long time, listening to the soft patter of her feet as she headed up the dock and toward the inn. The water winked back in the sunlight, bright and cheery. For the hundredth time, Cole wondered what the hell he was doing here and why he was trying so hard to save his marriage when his wife didn't want him to.

The lake blurred in front of him, and his mind drifted back over a decade into the past. To a beach in Florida, a run-down motel and the happiest five days of his life. Things had been simpler then, he realized, before the company and the money and the big house, and all the things he thought would improve their life. Instead, it had cost him all he held dear.

Somehow, he needed to get back to that simple life, to the world that had once seemed to consist of just him and Emily. Then his phone started buzzing against his hip, and he knew doing that was going to be harder than he'd thought.

Emily buried herself in words for two hours that afternoon. She cracked the window, letting some of the crisp, fresh air filter past the lacy curtains and into the room. The sounds of chirping birds and the occasional whine of the table saw broke the quiet of the day. The pages flew by, as she took her characters and had them battle past the challenges in their lives, striving for success, even against impossible odds. The book was going very, very well and each new chapter she started gave Emily a little burst of energy and satisfaction. She was doing it. Finally.

She sat back in the chair and stretched. If only solving her own life problems was as easy as solving those of her fictional characters.

It didn't help that she had complicated things herself by kissing Cole. It was as if there were two parts to her heart—the part that remembered the distance, the fights, the cold war of the past few years, and the part that remembered only the heady beginning of their relationship. The laughter, the happiness and the sex.

Okay, yes, being touched by Cole was the one part of their marriage that had never suffered. Their sex life, when they'd had one, had been phenomenal. He knew her body, knew it well, and had been a wonderful lover.

When he had been there to love her at all.

That was the real problem in their marriage. Cole's absences, fueled by his dogged dedication to the business, meant he was never home. In the early years, she'd supported him, encouraged him to work as much as he needed, but as success began to mount and Emily thought he would finally cut back on his hours, Cole instead worked more, dedicating weekends and vacations to this new project or that customer problem. He'd poured his heart and soul into the company, leaving almost nothing of either one for their marriage.

She got to her feet, gathering her dishes from her afternoon snack and headed down to the kitchen. Carol was peeling potatoes at the table, and had a basket of fresh green beans waiting to be cleaned beside her. Emily put her dishes in the sink, then sat in the opposite chair and started twisting off the stringy ends and breaking the green beans in half, then adding them to a waiting colander. "I remember doing this when I was a little girl," Emily said.

Carol smiled. "You always did like helping me in the kitchen. Half the time I'd have to kick you out and remind you that you were on vacation, not part of the KP crew."

Emily shrugged. "I liked being here."

"Instead of with your own family."

"We weren't much of a family to begin with," Emily said. "My mother was always off doing her thing, my father was always working. And when they were together, they fought like cats and dogs."

An understatement. Emily's parents' marriage had been mostly a marriage of convenience, two high school friends who'd married at the end of senior year, then had a child in quick succession, before realizing they were better friends than lovers. They had lived separate lives and only came together for birthdays and major holidays. The annual "family" summer vacation to the Gingerbread Inn was more of an opportunity to spend time with their friends and play shuffleboard than to bond as a family. The only time all three of them were together was Friday nights, when they all went into town for dinner at their favorite diner.

Carol picked up a fork and pricked holes in the scrubbed potatoes. "So when you grew up you did the opposite, right?"

Emily let out a little laugh and thought about how she had described her parents. She'd done the same thing, though not on purpose. For years, Emily had done her own thing and Cole had worked. The only saving grace—they hadn't caught a child in the middle of that mess. Not until now. Emily covered her belly with her palm. When Sweet Pea arrived, she vowed to give her baby the childhood Emily had never had. "I pretty much carbon copied their life. At least I'm smart enough to get out before bringing kids into that…mess."

"Oh, I don't know if it's the same thing. I saw your parents together. If they were ever in love, it wasn't there by the time they started coming up here in the summers. You and Cole on the other hand…" Carol shrugged.

"Me and Cole what?"

"There's still feelings there. Whether you believe it or not." Carol put the potatoes in the oven beside a chicken roasting on the middle rack.

"That's just because he doesn't want to accept that it's over." Emily took the colander to the sink and ran cool water over the green beans.

"If you ask me, he's not the only one who still cares." Carol put her back to the counter and faced Emily. "I've seen the way you look at him."

Heat rushed to Emily's face. "That's just the hormones." Even as she said the words, though, she knew there was more involved than a rush of hormonal input. She'd kissed him back, with as much desire and depth as he had kissed her. The familiar rush of heat had risen in her, and still simmered in her gut, even now.

She still cared about him, and always would. Love…

She'd avoid that word and combining it with the name Cole. Smarter to do that than to get wrapped up in a fantasy, instead of reality.

Carol just *hmm*ed at that and started the dishes. Emily picked up a dish towel to help dry, but Carol shooed her away. "You're still a guest here, missy. So go do what guests do and relax."

Emily headed outside, forgetting until she heard the tapping of a hammer on nails that Cole was out here, working. Still. She started to turn around and head back into the inn when Cole called out to her.

"Hey, do you mind helping me for a second?" he said. "I could really use a second pair of hands."

He was holding a long board in one hand, a hammer in the other. With the tool belt slung across his hips and sawdust peppering his jeans and work boots, he looked relaxed. Sexy.

A few minutes of helping Cole would be about being nice, not about getting close to him and admiring his body. Or the heat that still rushed through her veins whenever he was near.

"What do you need?" she asked.

"Just hold one end in place. I'm trying to get the rest of the siding repaired on this side of the building, but first I have to fit this fascia board in place."

She stared at him. They'd built the New York house from the ground up, and though Emily had been in charge of the decisions about faucets and paint colors, Cole had handled all the construction details, because he had spent so many years working on houses and knew the lingo. "Fascia board?"

"It goes up there." Cole pointed to the roofline ten feet above them.

She couldn't see any way that Cole could do this job alone, not without risking a broken neck. "Okay. Just don't ask me to hammer. You know how I am with tools."

"Oh, I remember, Emily." He winked at her. "My thumb remembers, too."

"Sorry." She grinned. "Again."

Cole got on one of the ladders and waited for Emily to get on the other one. They stepped up in tandem, until he had the board in place under the gutter and she had aligned her edge with the roofline.

"I'm just teasing you about my thumb," he said with a smile. "It wasn't so bad."

"That's not what you said that day. All we were doing was hanging some pictures, and you made it into a major project. Tape measure, level, laying out the frame placement with masking tape. Our house wasn't the Louvre, you know." She grinned.

"So I'm a little anal about those kinds of things."

"A little?" She arched a brow.

"Okay, a lot. I guess I deserved having you hit my thumb with the hammer."

"Well, as long as we're admitting weaknesses, I guess I was a little impatient. I just wanted the whole thing to be done." She shrugged. "I could have gone slower, and maybe not given you a hammer whack in the process."

"Even if I deserved it?"

She laughed. "Hey, you said it, not me."

He fiddled with the board, aligning it better, then grabbing a nail out of the tool belt and sinking the first one into the plywood. "You know, I think that was the last time we ever worked together on something."

"It was." Emily shifted her weight. A wave of light-headedness hit her, but she shrugged it off. "It's no wonder. That day didn't go very well." It had ended with a fight and Cole sleeping on the couch, too, but Emily didn't mention that. They had an easy détente between them now, and she wanted to preserve that peace a while longer.

"True," he said softly. "Let's hope this goes better."

"It should." She grinned. "We're on opposite ends of the board."

Cole laughed, then dug in his tool belt for a few more nails, hammering them in one at a time. "All append-ages accounted for?" he asked her.

"Yup." The light-headedness hit her again, and she

leaned into the ladder, shifting her grip on the board again. "You almost done?"

"A few more nails. Hold on a second. I have to move my ladder down toward you." He climbed down, shifted the ladder a few feet forward, then climbed back up and started hammering again.

A wave of nausea and dizziness slammed into Emily. She closed her eyes, but it didn't ease the feeling. Her face heated, she swayed again. All she wanted was to get off this ladder. Now.

"Cole, I...I need to get down." She let go of the board, gripped the ladder and climbed down to the ground. The light-headedness persisted so she sat on the edge of the porch, under the cool shadow of the overhang.

In an instant, Cole was there, the board forgotten, his voice filled with concern. "Hey, you okay?"

"Yeah, yeah. Just got a little dizzy being up so high."

"Then you sit. Or, if you want, go inside. I can handle this. The hard part is all done."

"I'm fine. Just give me a minute." She waved him off, part of her wanting him to hold her close and tell her it was all okay, the other part wishing he would go away and leave her be. Heck, wasn't that how she had felt for the past six months? Torn between wanting him close and wanting him gone.

It was as if she couldn't quite give up on the dream. Couldn't let go of the hope that this could all work out. Their marriage was like the Gingerbread Inn, Emily realized. In desperate need of major repairs and a lot of TLC.

The only difference? The inn wasn't past the point of no return yet. Their marriage, on the other hand, was. If anything told her that, it was the conversation the other night about kids where Cole made it clear he wasn't on the same page as she was. Now she was having a baby her husband didn't want, and the sooner she accepted that, the better. Besides, any change in him this week was temporary. She knew that from experience. At the first sign of trouble at the company, Cole would be gone, for weeks on end, and she'd be on her own.

"Are you sure you're okay?" Cole asked. "You look a little pale."

"Yeah, yeah, I'm fine." *Just a little pregnant, is all.*

He looked like he wanted to probe deeper. Instead, Cole cleared his throat and shifted the hammer in his hand. He glanced up at the fascia board they'd installed, then back at Emily. "I, uh, better finish up."

She shifted to the side so he could climb up the ladder and finish hammering in the wood. By the time the last nail was in, Emily had gone inside. Because staying out there watching Cole fix the inn she loved only made her long for the impossible.

Cole's back ached, his shoulders burned and his legs hurt more than after his thrice-weekly run. His hands had calluses and nicks, and a fine shadow of stubble covered his jaw. When he looked in the mirror, he saw a man as far from a billionaire CEO as one could get.

It felt good. Damned good.

Still, he was smart enough to know he couldn't stay here forever. He had a business to get back to, a business that needed his attention. Every day he spent away from WTD was one that impacted the bottom line. People depended on him—*families* depended on him—to keep the profits coming so they could pay their mortgages and put food on their tables. Instead, he was here, working on the Gingerbread Inn, a place that meant something to Emily.

Because he'd thought they stood a chance. After that kiss, hope had filled him. Hope they could find their way back as a couple if they just spent more time together. But it seemed every time they got close, she put up this wall. Or she walked away, shutting the door as effectively with her distance as she had the day she'd asked him to move out of their house.

Did she have a point? Was it all about not wanting to give up? Admit defeat? Was it about the battle, not about love?

His phone vibrated against his hip. Cole flipped it out, shifting from carpenter mode to businessman in an instant. He dropped onto the bottom step, and for the next half hour, worked out the details of a deal with a partner in China, made a decision about firing a lackluster employee and hammered out the contents of the quarterly investor report with Irene, his assistant.

"The place is going nuts without you," Irene said. "You'd think the sun had stopped shining or something."

Cole ran a hand through his hair. This was why he rarely took vacations and worked most weekends. "I'll come back in the morning."

"You will do no such thing." Irene's calm voice came across the line strong and sure. In her sixties, Irene had always been more than an assistant—she'd been a guiding force, a sort of mother not just to Cole but to everyone at WTD. She was plainspoken and filled with common sense, so when she talked, Cole knew he'd do well to listen.

"And why would I stay here when the company is in a panic?"

"Because it'll do all the lemmings around here some good to take on a little leadership. And because it'll do you even more good to do something other than wither away under the fluorescent lighting."

He chuckled. "I am far from withered away, Irene."

"You go entire days without seeing the sunshine. You're here before me, stay long after those with common sense go home. You need to notice the world around you, not just the workload before you."

Wasn't that what Emily had said a hundred times over the years? She'd told him he worked too many hours, was home too few. He'd insisted the company needed him, but maybe it was something more, something deeper inside himself that kept him behind that desk day after day instead of with his wife, enjoying the life he had worked so hard to afford.

Irene had a point. If he took a few days off, then maybe the so-called lemmings he'd hired would step up to the plate and do what he'd hired them to do—lead in his stead. Rather than everyone looking to Cole because he was always there in the driver's seat.

"I'm doing that now."

"Are you? Because I'll bet dollars to doughnuts that you haven't heard those birds chirping in the background or the soft whistle of the breeze through the trees. How about the sun? Is it shining bright, or is it dimmed by cloud cover?"

Cole raised his gaze and squinted. "Bright." His gaze skimmed over the pale blue sky, then down the trees, almost bare now that November was edging toward December. Birds flitted from branch to branch, determined to stay as long as they could before caving to winter's cold. The breeze danced in the last few dangling leaves, waving them like flags. Through the trees, he could see the lake, glistening and inviting while squirrels dashed to and fro, making last-minute preparations for winter. He paused a long moment, letting the day wash over him and ease the tension in his shoulders. "You're right. I never noticed any of that."

"And you need to, Cole. Before it's too late."

"It might already be." He let out a long breath. Irene was the only one who knew about his marital problems. As his right-hand person at WTD, she had seen the end of his marriage coming long before he had. She'd noticed that there'd been fewer and fewer lunches with Emily, more long days when he didn't leave before dark and more weekends spent at the office instead of at home. He'd also given Irene a heads-up about the projects he was working on—both the one with the inn and the one with his marriage.

"Has she kicked you out of that inn yet?" Irene asked. "Told you to leave?"

"Not yet." Though, given her reaction to their kiss, Cole wasn't so sure Emily wanted him around anymore. She hadn't said that out loud yet, but he'd sensed a distance, a wall whenever he got too close. Like when she'd felt ill and he'd asked her if she was okay—Emily had suddenly gone cold and distant.

"If she hasn't kicked you out, then it's not too late. Now get your head out of the office and pay attention to what's around you," Irene said. "I'll handle things here. We'll all be fine."

He chuckled. "Is that an order?"

"You bet your sweet bippy it is. Now let me go so I can get some work done around here. Not all of us can sit around in the sun, listening to the birds chirp, you know." Her words lacked any bite and held only affection and worry.

"Thanks, Irene," Cole said, his voice quiet and warm.

"Anytime, Cole. Anytime." Then she was gone. Cole tucked the phone back into his pocket.

He started to get to his feet, to get back to working on the fascia and soffits. He paused. Looked up at the sky, then sat back down, leaned against the porch post, closed his eyes and drew in the scents and sounds of the world he had missed for too many years.

CHAPTER SIX

EMILY STOOD ON the porch for a good minute, sure she was seeing things. Cole sat on the top step, his back against one of the thick posts, his face upturned to the sun. Asleep. Harper lay on the weathered boards beside Cole, eyes closed, tail tapping a slow, happy rhythm.

Emily smiled. Her workaholic husband, taking a break. Something she hadn't seen in so long, she'd been half-sure he was a robot, not a man. In sleep, he looked younger, boyish almost, with his face relaxed, his shoulders untensed.

Like the man she used to know. The man she had fallen in love with.

Her hand strayed to her abdomen, and for a second, she allowed herself to picture Cole's face when she told him about the baby. To imagine a future where he brought them home from the hospital, and they formed a little family of three.

Then Cole's phone started buzzing, the screen lighting with yet another call. A dose of reality inserting itself before she got wrapped up in a fantasy.

Carol came out on the porch. "He's asleep?" she whispered.

Emily nodded. "Doesn't happen very often."

Carol chuckled. "I've known men like that. Would rather work themselves half to death than admit they need a nap. Or a helping hand. I tell you, men are some of God's most stubborn creatures."

Emily laughed. "I agree with that."

The buzzing at his waist finally roused Cole. He jerked upright, disoriented for a second, reaching for the phone with an instinct well honed over the years. Just before he pressed the button to answer it, he noticed Emily and Carol, and set the phone back in the holster. "Sorry, I, uh, guess I fell asleep."

Cole ignoring a work call? And taking a nap in the middle of the day? That made for two miracles in the space of a few minutes—and two things Emily never thought she'd see.

"You're human…sleep happens." Carol smiled. "Either way, I'm glad you woke up. Dinner's in the kitchen and just waiting for some hungry people to come along."

Cole got to his feet and brushed the sawdust off his jeans. "A home-cooked meal? Can't remember the last time I had one of those."

"That's because you have to be home to have one." The words slipped from Emily's lips before she could stop them. Sometimes it seemed the years of resentment lay in wait behind paper walls, waiting for any small opening.

"You're right." Cole paused beside her on the porch. His blue eyes met hers. "But I also have to have a home to go to."

She shook her head and looked away before the familiar argument about their separation sprang up between them on this pretty fall day. She didn't want to fight anymore. Not one more disagreement. She'd had enough of those to last her a lifetime.

"Let's not do this," Cole said, as if he'd read her mind. "It's too nice of a day to argue about anything other than whether the sky is a cerulean-blue or cornflower-blue."

She smiled. "Cornflower. Definitely."

"I agree," Cole said.

Carol put a hand on each of their shoulders. "There's a home here, and a meal, and both of you are invited to the table if you promise to mind your manners."

Cole grinned. "Yes, ma'am."

Maybe it was the way he said *ma'am,* or maybe it was the way he smiled, but Emily found her anger melting in the light of both, and she paused in the doorway to shoot Cole a conspiratorial smile. "That means no food fights, you know."

"Too bad." He leaned in toward her, smelling of soap and sunshine. "Because sometimes cleaning up afterward can be a hell of a lot of fun."

"I remember." The words whispered into the small space between them, the memory charging the air. They'd come home from their quick three-day honeymoon to the tiny one-bedroom apartment that had been their first home. She'd worked half the day on a dinner for her new husband, poring over a cookbook she'd got out of the library, fixing chicken and peas and baked potatoes, then attempting a chocolate cream pie because he'd once said that was his favorite. "I really messed that meal up, didn't I?"

He chuckled as he followed her into the inn and down the long hall toward the dining room that flanked the western side of the house and looked out over the lake. "It wasn't *that* awful."

"Your memory is faulty. The chicken was burned, the peas shriveled and dried, and the potatoes under-cooked." She shook her head. "But you ate every bite."

"Couldn't disappoint my new wife and tell her that she couldn't cook."

"I *still* can't cook." That had been the one benefit to Cole's sizable income—the convenience of ordering already-made meals. Emily vowed to learn to cook before the baby came. She imagined herself baking cookies and whipping up macaroni and cheese, with Sweet Pea helping measure and stir. Emily would never be Betty Crocker, but if she could at least master the basics, she could create the kind of warm, cozy home she'd always wanted.

"You might not be able to cook," Cole said. "But you can make a pie that sticks to my forehead."

She laughed. The laughter felt good, and she realized it had been far too long since she'd had a damned good laugh. "I didn't mean to throw it at you, but when you ate it like it was the most delicious pie you ever ate, I got so mad."

"It *was* the most delicious pie I ever ate, Emily."

They had stopped outside the dining room, lingering by the doorway while Carol put the finishing touches on the table. Harper sat in the corner, waiting and hoping for a scrap.

Emily stood within inches of Cole. Close enough to touch, to see the gold flecks in his eyes, to get wrapped up in the tempting scent of his cologne, the draw of his warm body. She moved away, headed for the table before she did any of those foolish things.

"How could you say that pie was good?" She reached for the pile of silverware on the corner and placed it beside the place settings. Avoiding the desire washing over her, the need to kiss him again, as strong as when they'd first dated. Damn. When would she stop wanting Cole? The separation and divorce would be much easier if her body got on board with her brain. "I forgot the sugar. That was the worst pie ever."

Cole slipped in beside her, tucking the folded napkins under the knives. "It was the most delicious pie ever, Emily," and he paused a beat until she looked up at him, "because you made it with love."

She held his gaze for a long moment, then shook her head and stepped away. Oh, how she wanted to believe in that look in his eyes, the words he spoke, but she was afraid, so afraid, that if she did, they'd end up traveling the same path as before. They'd done it countless times over the years. Now, with a baby caught in the mix, Emily couldn't afford to hold on to a fairy tale that she knew had an unhappy ending.

"Unfortunately, you need more ingredients than love to hold a recipe together and make it work," she said and turned away before he saw the tears brimming in her eyes.

Cole had to admire Carol, the inn's owner. She could have brokered a Middle East peace treaty with ease. She'd sensed the tension between Cole and Emily the instant she sat down at the table, and managed to shift the conversation to subjects that kept the room feeling light and lively. As they ate, they talked about the weather, the repairs to the inn, the Patriots' chances of making it to the Super Bowl. Fun, easy, small talk.

"Did Emily ever tell you the story about the lake's history?" Carol asked Cole as she laid warm plates of homemade apple pie before them. Melting scoops of vanilla ice cream puddled over the flaky crust. The impressive dessert could have starred on a magazine cover.

Emily let out a little laugh. "Oh, not this one. It's not even true."

"It is, too," Carol said, then grinned. "Or at least partly true."

"Let me guess," Cole said. Even though he was stuffed from the amazing roast chicken, potatoes and green beans, he dived into the pie with gusto. "Barrow's Lake has its own resident Loch Ness monster?"

"No, no, though that might draw in more visitors, and that'd be good for business." Carol put a finger on her lips. "Hmm…if only I could buy a Loch Ness monster in the pet store."

"Two words," Cole said. "Inflatable toy."

"I'll keep that in mind for the summer tourists." Carol laughed. "Well, our lake story is a little more innocuous. Way back, years ago, before the invention of the car—"

"When dinosaurs roamed the earth," Emily added.

"Well, maybe not that far back in time. But close." Carol leaned forward, her eyes bright with excitement as she told the story. "There used to be two families, one on either side of the lake, one with a daughter, one with a son, about the same age. They didn't know each other, and in these years when this area was just beginning to get settled by people in wagons and log homes, there was no Facebook or Skype or high school to bring them together. Then John Barrow, one of the original Barrows to settle here, opened a little store smack-dab in the center of the road between the two families. You can still see the remains of its foundation, past that big pine tree." She pointed out the window. "The shop wasn't much, just a general sundries kind of place. The teenagers ran into each other there one summer day, and fell in love. They'd meet at the store every afternoon after they finished their chores and spend time together. But the families were at war over something no one can remember now, and the teens were forbidden from seeing each other."

"Nevertheless, they sneaked away every afternoon," Emily put in, "because they were deeply in love and couldn't bear to be apart."

"That's right. Sometimes true love is stronger than parental rule." Carol grinned. "And that was how it was for these two. But oh, the ruckus it raised in their families. So one stormy fall night, they made plans to run away and get married. Before they could leave, their parents found out and rushed down to the store to interrupt the rendezvous. The kids panicked, took a boat and rowed out to the middle of the lake, thinking they could make it across and leave from the other side. The storm that night was strong, and the water rough, and the boat capsized. Sadly, both kids drowned."

"That's terrible," Cole said. Even though the event had happened decades ago, he could imagine the heartbreak and loss, particularly on such a small community. "How devastating for those families."

"It was an awful tragedy, and one that haunted this area for years." Carol gestured toward the moon-kissed lake outside the windows. "There are people who say you can still see the ghosts of the doomed lovers in the fog that rises over the lake at night."

"And according to Carol, if you're out in that fog, you're destined to fall in love." Emily grinned. "When us girls were teenagers, we'd run outside if we saw the fog, but none of us fell in love with the boys here for the summer."

"That's because none of them were right for you," Carol said. "You have to be with the right one for the fog to work."

Emily laughed and got to her feet, grabbing the empty plates as she did. "And all the stars and moon have to be aligned just right, too. It's a legend, Carol, and not one I believe in."

Carol wagged a finger at her. "You'll see. Some foggy night, true love will come your way."

Emily didn't answer that. Instead, she brushed open the swinging door with her hip and set the plates in the sink, then filled it with soapy water. By the time she returned, Cole and Carol were talking about the repairs on the Inn, instead of silly age-old legends.

Just as well. The last thing she needed Cole to do was drag her down to the lake in the middle of the night because he believed some legend about dead teenagers would fix their marriage. No kiss on a foggy night was going to repair the damage the years of distance had created.

Maybe if they had gone to counseling when the problems first started, it would have righted the ship's course. She'd asked Cole to go, but time and time again, Cole had put off the appointment. She'd given up after a while and stopped asking him. If their marriage was important to him, she'd reasoned, he would have made the time to save it.

Then again, she hadn't gone on her own, either, or fought very hard to get Cole to the appointments. She'd been just as guilty about finding other things to fill her time. Maybe because deep down she was afraid to confront the issues between them—and find out they were beyond fixing.

"You know, Cole, it doesn't make much sense for you to drive all the way into the city tonight," Carol was saying as Emily picked up the platter of chicken, "when I have rooms right upstairs. Why don't you stay here? It's the least I can do to thank you."

Cole stay here? Emily prayed he'd say no, that he would do what he always did, say he needed to leave in the morning to get back to the office. But no, he grinned and nodded instead. Damn. Having him stay here was a definite complication, especially to her hormones and her heart. She needed to stay firm in her resolve and not be swayed by a smile.

"That'd be great, Carol. I'll have my luggage sent over in the morning." Cole rose, stretched his back and let out a yawn. "Just the thought of driving back to the hotel makes me exhausted."

"Well, I'm exhausted just hearing you talk about it." Carol gave the two of them a smile. "I hate to ask this, but I'm really tired. Lots of early mornings and a little stress over this renovation/sale thing. Would you two mind clearing up the rest of the dishes? I'd like to get to bed early."

Emily shot Carol a curious look, but the innkeeper just muffled a yawn and kept her gaze averted. Emily suspected Carol of a little matchmaking, what with telling the story of the two doomed lovers and asking Cole to stay at the inn. Maybe with Carol out of the room, Emily could make Cole see that his being here wasn't a good idea. "No problem. See you in the morning, Carol."

Carol thanked them, then hurried out of the room. Harper stayed behind, ever hopeful for scraps. Cole and

Emily gathered the rest of the dishes and brought them into the kitchen. "You don't have to help," Emily said to Cole as she slipped on an apron and tied it behind her back. "I know how you hate doing dishes."

He shrugged. "I used to hate it. Now I've kind of gotten used to it."

"You're doing your own dishes?" She shot him a glance. In his jeans and T-shirt, he looked like a guy who did his own dishes, a million miles away from the wealthy, driven CEO. "You're not having a maid do them?"

"It's not like I cook a gourmet meal every night," Cole said. "I usually have one plate, one cup and a fork to wash. No need to pay the maid to do that."

"Yeah, me, too." She'd let the household help go, too, after their separation. She'd seen no sense in paying people to clean up after one person. Plus doing her own housework kept her busy instead of focusing on how Cole's absence made the house echo in ways it never had before.

"Nothing drives home the fact that you're alone like washing your dishes." Cole took the clean dishes from the strainer, swiped them dry with a towel and put them in the cabinets. "I guess that's when it finally hit me."

"What did?" Emily stowed the leftovers in the fridge.

Cole put his back to the sink and crossed his arms over his chest, the pink-and-white-striped towel a strange juxtaposition in his muscular hands. "That this wasn't a fight we'd get over in a couple days. That this separation could be permanent. I'd come home from work and look at that plate and cup and fork in the sink and think…" He let out a gust and shook his head. "I'd think how sad they looked."

"Really?" Over the years, Cole had rarely opened up about his feelings. She'd asked him what he was thinking, but most of the time, he'd withdrawn and in the end, she'd be left feeling cold, alone. This was the most he'd shared in a long, long time.

"All those years we lived together, I don't think I ever noticed if we had five plates or fifty," he went on. "I couldn't tell you what the pattern was on our silverware if you paid me. But I notice the plates now. I notice when there's one." He nodded toward the sink. "Or more than one."

Her heart softened. She put the empty serving dishes in the soapy water, then picked up one of the plates and started washing it, instead of falling into that vulnerable look on Cole's face and in his voice. "I notice now, too," she said quietly. "It's like the plate and cup are lonely."

"Maybe I should buy a whole set." Cole grinned. "Or just bring mine back home so they'd be together again. Happy. Complete."

The thought of him returning, of the two of them being happy and complete, together again, caused her heart to race and her throat to close. Hope warred with caution. She concentrated on getting the plate clean, watching the bubbles circle and circle the rim. "We've tried that before, Cole. It didn't work."

"What's that saying about success? That it's about not giving up?"

She could see the saying now, one of those kitschy posters that she had hung in her college dorm, then again in their run-down first apartment because it was the only wall decor they could afford. By the time they moved to the big house, the poster had been relegated to a landfill. But the saying and the image of a determined competitor in a tough tug-of-war had stuck with Emily. "'Success seems to be largely a matter of hanging on after others have let go.' William Feather said it," she said.

"I'm hanging on, Emily," Cole said softly. "I really am."

She placed the clean plate in the strainer, then picked up the next one. "Why?"

"Because we had something once. And I think we can have it again. And because I'm ready for change."

How she wanted to believe him. Her brain reminded her heart that he had said all this before, and gone back to his workaholic ways as soon as the crisis passed. How could she know this time would be any different?

Another clean plate in the strainer. She tackled the third one. The only sound in the room was the running water and the soft clanging of dishes. "Change how?"

"Working less. More vacations. More time for you and me to get back to where we were."

She'd heard all these words before. Dozens of times over the years, and every time, she had believed them, only to be hurt in the end. Granted, the time he had spent working on the repairs to the inn was the most time he'd ever taken off work before, and maybe that meant something. Maybe it meant he had changed. Hope kept a stubborn hold on her heart, but she refused to give it space and room.

Not until she'd asked the most important question.

She rinsed the last plate, put it in the strainer, then tackled a pan, keeping her gaze away from Cole's. "And what about a family?"

He let out a nervous laugh. "Family? Emily, we're *far* from ready for kids."

It's what he'd said a thousand times over the years. Every time she'd brought up kids, he'd said it wasn't the right time, or that they'd talk about it later. She pulled the plug, let the soapy water drain, and placed her hands on the rim of the sink. All that silly, foolish hope in her chest drained away, too.

"When *do* you think we'll be ready? When we get a bigger house or the company reaches another sales goal or we have another million saved in retirement?" She snorted and turned away from him. "It's never the right time, Cole."

"We're a few pieces of paper away from being divorced, Emily. I'd say that's the worst possible time to have a child."

Emily sighed. "Yeah, Cole, it is." Then she left the kitchen and headed up to her room, where the pillow would muffle her hurt.

CHAPTER SEVEN

COLE SLEPT THROUGH his alarm. Slept through the buzzing of his phone. Slept through the sunrise. He'd slept in the best hotel rooms in the world, owned a mattress that cost more than a small car, and yet he had never slept as soundly or as well as he had in the double bed in the pale blue room on the second floor of the Gingerbread Inn.

He rolled over, blinked a bleary eye at his phone and decided whoever was calling him could wait a little longer. This…decadence filled him with a peace he had never felt before. Whatever was happening at work would be there later, while Cole just…was. Right here, right now, in a cozy bedroom across the hall from Emily, in a quaint inn in Massachusetts. He lay in the bed, watching the sun dance on the floor, while birds chirped a song above the faint sounds of a distant lawn mower.

Then he heard the soft melody of a woman's voice, singing along with the radio. It took him a moment to realize it was Emily's voice. He hadn't heard her singing in…

Hell, ten years. At least.

He pulled on his jeans and padded barefoot out of his room and across the hall. Her door stood ajar, the bed made, the room neat and clean. When had Emily become a neatnik? She'd always been the messier one in their relationship, something that had driven him crazy when they were together. Then, when he was on his own, he'd missed seeing her makeup on the bathroom counter, her coat tossed over the dining room chair, her shoes kicked off on the bedroom carpet. He'd tried leaving his own things out but it wasn't the same. He hesitated only a moment, then took a single step inside the room. "Em?"

The bedroom was empty. Light and steam spilled out of the attached bathroom. The shower was running, and Cole could see the familiar outline of his wife's curves behind the translucent white curtain. Desire rushed through him, hardened against his jeans. How long had it been since he'd been with Emily?

Months. Three, to be exact. A long damned time.

He hesitated. He knew he should leave but couldn't tear his gaze away from her shapely outline, the curve of her breasts, her hips. She was hidden by the curtain, yet he knew every dimple, every valley, every scar. He knew how to make her moan, how to make her smile, how to make her...

His.

Except she wasn't his anymore, and he needed to face that. Accept it. Move on.

Since the separation, he'd told himself he should take off his ring. Date again. But he hadn't. No woman had interested him the way his wife did. And maybe never would. He missed her, damn it, for more than just the warmth of her body against his.

The water stopped with a screech and a shudder of

old pipes. Cole told himself to move. Leave. He didn't do either.

The song ended and a commercial came on the radio. Emily's voice trailed off as she reached up and tugged down the towel draped over the shower curtain. She jerked back the curtain and let out a shriek. "Cole! You scared me. What are you doing in here?"

Shit. He should have left. Now he looked like some overeager hormonal teenager, which was how he felt whenever he was around Emily. Even now, even after everything.

"Your, uh, door was open. And I heard you singing and..." He forced his gaze up from the hourglass shape outlined by the fluffy white towel. "I can't remember the last time I heard you singing."

A flush filled her cheeks and her gaze shifted to the floor. "I'm a terrible singer."

"Didn't sound that way to me. It was nice." He swallowed hard. "I've missed your singing. You used to sing all the time when we were first married."

She laughed. "That's because we couldn't even afford a TV. My singing was our only entertainment."

"I wouldn't say it was our *only* entertainment." His gaze met hers. Heat filled the space between them. Cole had never been so acutely aware of his wife's naked body, and the thin scrap of cotton separating them. She'd put on a few pounds in the past couple months, but they only added to her curves and made her more desirable. He ached to take her in his arms, to let the towel fall to the floor and to taste that sweet, warm, peach skin.

"Those were different days then," she said, her voice low and soft. She fiddled with the edge of the towel. "Better days."

Had she stopped singing because she'd stopped being happy? Started again today because she was happier without him? Or had he stopped paying attention to Emily so long ago that he didn't notice her singing? Her happiness?

"You liked it better when we were poor?" he asked. "Living in that tiny fifth-floor walk-up, freezing in the winter and roasting in the summer?"

"Yeah, I did."

He'd hated those days. Always struggling, feeling like he'd failed, the constant battle to get his business off the ground at night while he sweated on a construction site during the day. Working, working, working, and getting frustrated at how long it took to get from nowhere to somewhere. "Why? We had nothing, Emily."

"Nothing except each other," she said. She raised her gaze to his. Tears shimmered in her green eyes. "That was always enough for me, Cole. But it was never enough for you."

He let out a gust. Why did it always come down to this? Didn't she understand, he'd done all of this for her? For them? For their future together? The hours he'd worked, the effort he'd put in to take the business from their apartment kitchen table to a global power had been a constant source of friction between them. In the early days, Emily had supported him, but as the years wore on, that support had eroded into frustration and a cold, silent war.

"You can't blame me for wanting more, Emily. For wanting success. Look at us now. We have everything we always wanted."

A bittersweet smile crossed her face. "No. You have everything *you* ever wanted." The smile shifted, became something he couldn't read, as if Emily had a secret that only she knew. She nodded toward the door. "I'd appreciate it if you left now."

He did as she asked and left the room, shutting the door behind him, and feeling more lost than he had ever felt before. Cole was a smart man who had built his company from nothing into a global player. Who had taken them from a run-down apartment to a mansion in a tony suburb outside New York City. All along, he'd thought he was on the same path that Emily wanted.

Now it turned out he'd been wrong. For a long, long time.

Sleep eluded Emily. She tossed and turned, then got up, tried to write and couldn't get any further in the book. The whole day had been like that, her creativity stalled. Her mind was still stuck on the moment Cole had walked into the bathroom and looked at her with that hungry, admiring gaze she knew so well. One step forward, and she would have had him in her arms, in her bed, in her.

She craved that, deep down inside, in places that only Cole knew. But she'd held her ground, and after he left the room, she'd told herself she'd done the right thing. Even if it didn't feel that way.

Her stomach rumbled. She pulled on a robe and headed downstairs to the kitchen. The inn was silent, and only a small light burned on the kitchen table. Moonlight streamed in through the windows, providing enough light for her to make her way through the rooms.

Emily pulled open the fridge, and mulled over the choices. She settled on the leftover apple pie. A second later, she was dishing a hearty slice onto a small dessert plate. After all, she was eating for two now. She could afford an extra serving of dessert once in a while. She heard a sound and looked up to find Cole standing in the kitchen.

He wore only a pair of old gray sweatpants that she knew well. He'd had them for as long as she could re-member, the fleece worn and soft as butter. His chest was bare, and the desire that had been burning inside her all day roared to life again. Her hand flexed at her side, itching to touch the hard muscular planes, to draw his warmth to her.

"Great minds think alike," Cole said, taking a step closer and gesturing toward the pie.

"Do you want a piece?" Then she looked down and realized she'd taken the last of the pie. "Sorry. Um, would you like to share?"

"If you don't mind."

"Not at all." She pulled open the drawer and handed a second fork to Cole. He leaned over one side of the kitchen island, she leaned over the other side and they each took a bite of the pie. Their heads were so close, they nearly touched. It was so much like the early days, when they'd been inseparable and in love, that Emily could almost believe she'd gone back in time. She ached to run her fingers through Cole's dark hair, to kiss the crumbs off his lips, to giggle when his shadowy stub-ble tickled her chin.

"Carol's pies are legendary," she said instead.

"I can see why."

Emily forked up another bite. "The other Ginger-bread Girls and I would sneak down here in the middle of the night all the time and eat the leftovers. She'd yell at us in the morning, but half the time she was laughing at the same time. And sometimes she'd bake an extra pie, just so we'd have one to scavenge."

"Those must have been some amazing summers," Cole said.

"They were. Some of my best memories are wrapped up in this place." She sighed. "I'm going to hate to see it sold off and turned into condos or something awful like that."

He scooped up some ice cream. "Why don't I buy it? Let Carol run it…keep things as they are."

Emily let out a gust. She put her fork down and leaned away from the counter. "Not everything can be fixed with money, Cole."

"I'm just trying to help."

She read honesty in his face, and relaxed. He had helped over the past few days, more than he knew. She couldn't fault him for wanting to do more. After all, finding solutions to impossible situations was Cole's specialty. He'd built a business on designing creative answers to customer problems.

For years, he'd been the one she relied on to solve everything from a checking account error to a strange noise coming from her engine. For the past six months, she'd relied only on herself. As scary as it had been, the independence had given her a newfound confidence. It was a feeling she wanted to keep, which meant no more running to Cole to fix the things that went awry. "Listen, I appreciate all the help you're giving Carol with the repairs, I really do."

"But…?"

She forked up some pie, but didn't eat it. Instead, she turned to the fridge. "Do you want some milk?"

"Yes," he said, coming around the counter to face her, "but I also want you to tell me what you aren't saying."

She grabbed the gallon jug, then two glasses, and poured them each an icy glass of milk. She slipped onto one of the bar stools and wrapped her hands around the glass. She debated whether to tell him what she was thinking, then decided she'd done enough of ignoring the issues, and maybe it was time to speak up instead of letting those thoughts simmer. "You have a tendency to throw money at a problem and then leave," she said. "At least when it comes to us."

He dropped into the opposite bar stool. "I don't do that."

"When something needed fixing at the house, you called someone to do it. When I needed to buy a new car, you called a friend at a dealership and had him show me the newest models. When I wanted to go on a vacation, you called a travel agent and told her to send me anywhere I wanted to go."

"What's wrong with that? It's problem solving."

Emily bit her lip, then raised her gaze to his. "The problem wasn't the leaky faucet or the old car or the need for some time in the sun. It was that I wanted to do those things with you, Cole. I wanted *you and me* to install that faucet, even if it was messy and frustrating and time-consuming to do it. I wanted *you* to go with me to pick out a car, and go along on the test drive, and give me your opinion, then laugh when I bought what was prettiest. I wanted *you* to go on vacation with me and—" she exhaled "—just be. You and me for a few days."

He reached up and brushed a tendril of hair off her

head. "I never knew, Emily. Why didn't you say anything?"

She slipped off the stool and away from his touch before she found herself in his arms again. In the darkened, silent room it was so tempting just to curve against Cole's bare chest and to forget the separation, the problems between them, the difficult road yet to come. Instead she crossed to the window and looked out over the darkened lake beyond the trees. "I could say that I never said anything because you were never home to talk to, but really, that's just an excuse. I never said anything because—" and now her throat swelled and tears rushed to her eyes "—I didn't want to hear you say no."

He was behind her in a second, wrapping her in his arms, and despite her resolve a second ago, she allowed herself to lean back into him, just this once, just for this minute. "I wouldn't have said no, Emily."

"Ah, but you did, Cole. A hundred times." She stepped out of his embrace, and turned to face him. "Every time we went our separate ways, you to work, me to my charity work and golf dates and all those meaningless things that filled the hours between breakfast and bed, it added a little distance to the gulf between us. Eventually, that gulf got too wide, Cole, and crossing it was a Herculean task." She shook her head. "I couldn't do it anymore."

He took in her words, then nodded. "And to be honest, I don't think I even realized that gulf existed until you asked for a separation. I had on these blinders that told me everything was just fine. When it was far from that."

"That was my fault, too. I didn't speak up." Emily flicked a crumb off the counter and watched it skitter into the sink. "When I was growing up, my parents fought all the time. If they were getting along, it made me nervous. It was like being around a purring tiger. You never knew when it would lash out again. That made me afraid to rock the boat, so I'd let things go that I should have done something about."

"I wish you had said something. I couldn't read your mind, Em. Though Lord knows I tried."

"Would you have listened?" She shifted closer to him. "You've been so dedicated to the company for so long that I don't think you would have heard me if I'd said the house was on fire."

"Well, I think I would have heard that." He chuckled, then sobered. "You're right. But you don't understand, Em. A company is like a puppy. It needs constant attention or it will wither and die."

"That's why you hire good people. To give you a break once in a while."

He shook his head. "You sound like Irene."

Emily raised a shoulder, dropped it again. "If everyone is saying the same thing, maybe they have a point."

"Or maybe none of them understand the demands on me as the owner. Being at the top is far more difficult than anyone understands." He let out a long sigh, then ran a hand through his hair. "Just when I think everything is under control and I can step back, something goes wrong. Hell, you wouldn't believe the number of calls and emails I've got just in the couple of days I've been here."

Tension had knotted his shoulders, furrowed his brow. The part of Emily that still cared about Cole filled with concern. She knew that look. Knew it well. She'd seen it hundreds of times. Before he had a team of employees under him, Cole would come home to their cramped apartment, a smokestack ready to blow, and she would be his sounding board. When had Cole stopped coming to her? When had she stopped asking him to share his day? "Do you want to talk about it?" she asked.

"You've got enough on your plate."

She could see him distancing himself, doing what he always did and taking all the problems on his shoulders. Putting another brick in the wall between them. Her first instinct was to throw up her hands and walk away, but really, had doing that made anything better?

Emily reached out and put a hand on his arm, a touch of comfort, but one that sent a zing through her. "Remember when we first got married and you were working around the clock, trying to pay the bills and launch the business?"

He nodded. "We'd stay up half the night, eating junk food and talking."

She laughed. "Kind of like we're doing tonight."

His gaze softened, and she let her touch drop away. "Yeah, kind of like tonight."

"Then why don't we sit down and talk it out? I may not know anything about technology, but I can be a good listener." *I'm still here, Cole,* she wanted to say. *I've always been here. Even if you stopped reaching out to me.* "I know you, Cole. If you're up in the middle of the night, it's because something is troubling you."

His features softened. "You still know me better than I know myself."

She didn't reply because a part of her felt like she didn't know him at all. Maybe they'd kept too much of themselves back for too long to ever find that connection again.

"Before I came down here, I was pacing my room, jotting down ideas, trying to figure out a solution to a problem at work." Then he waved it off. "But I don't want to keep you up, too. Go to bed, Em. I'll figure it out."

Maybe he'd stopped coming to her because she'd stopped asking. Stopped being there. Could he be caught in the same feeling of disconnect as she was?

Either way, she hated seeing this stress and tension on his face. She reached out and gave his hand a light touch. "Let's finish that pie and save the world. Or at least the world of Watson Technology Development."

"You sure you want me to bore you with the details?"

"I don't mind. If you want my opinion, that is."

"Of course I do, Em. You've always had great ideas when it came to the business. Maybe I should have hired you to work for me as a consultant."

She laughed. "That would have been a disaster."

"Maybe yes, maybe no." A tease lit his eyes. "Will you work on commission?"

She feigned deep thought. "Depends. Is there pie involved?"

"Always." He grinned. They crossed to the bar and took their seats again. The small kitchen light washed the room in a pale gold glow, while the moonlight added touches of silver. Outside, an owl hooted, but the world was quiet and still, except for this small corner of the Gingerbread Inn.

Cole steepled his fingers, a move Emily knew signaled he was getting serious. "I've got a huge order for the next generation of cell phones from one of my biggest customers. The launch is in place, the customer is ready for the rollout, but the product is delayed. We've had them under development for over a year, and things were on track, but then the plant that is making the screens was damaged in a storm. We found a backup supplier for the screens, but their quality hasn't been the best. So now we're stuck without a screen supplier, and the first order is due to drop in a week."

"All you have left to do is add the screens?"

He nodded. "If we had some to add, yes."

"Then do what you do best, Cole. Build it yourself." She tapped the counter before him. "Remember when you first started out, you had those prototype screens you made? You never used them because you found a supplier who could make them cheaper."

"That's right. They're still in the warehouse some-where." He sat back, and Emily could see the wheels turning in Cole's head. "We could substitute those, at least for the first drop order, and that'll give the Japa-nese supplier time to get back online and ship the order to us." He gave his forehead a smack. "I can't believe I didn't think of it myself."

She shrugged. "Sometimes it's just a matter of hear-ing another opinion."

"A smart and wise opinion at that." He leaned back on the bar stool, his gaze skimming over her fea-tures. "I've missed hearing your opinion, Em. I guess I stopped asking. Or I stopped getting up in the middle of the night for pie."

If he had, would things be different? If he'd included her in the day-to-day of his company? Or asked her to do more than just attend another banquet or golf tournament? "It's been a long time since you asked what I think," she said.

"I'm sorry."

"Yeah, me, too."

The moment extended between them, full of regrets and missed opportunities. Cole was the first to look away, shifting his gaze to the plate before them. "Last bite. It's all yours. Payment for services rendered, as agreed."

"Oh, you can have it, Cole. I don't—"

He speared the last bit of pie, then held it before her lips. "I know you, Emily. And I know you want this."

His voice was low and dark, and sent a wave of temptation through her. Not for the pie—he was right, she always wanted pie—but for him. Damn. She'd always wanted him, too. No matter what.

She opened her lips and took the bite from him, slow, easy, their gazes locked, and the piece of pie became about much more than just some slices of cinnamon-glazed apples and flaky crust. Heat unfurled in her gut, and for a second she wished Cole would just lean her back against that counter and take her right here, right now. That it could be like it used to be, without the muddle of the past ten years.

"Delicious." he said. "Isn't it?"

"Very." She licked her lips and watched Cole watching her tongue. "Too bad it's all gone."

"Definitely too bad." Was she talking about the pie? Or the fact that she had enjoyed Cole feeding her? Enjoyed that one-on-one attention, like a laser?

The clock on the wall ticked by the wee hours. Somewhere outside, an owl hooted. Cole's eyes met Emily's. "Oh, Em, what are we doing here?"

"Having pie."

"And now that the pie is gone?"

He was talking about more than whether they were going to put the dish in the sink or grab another snack. Cole was asking her the one question she couldn't answer. What was going to happen next? With them?

As much as she wanted to believe they could take this moment and use it to rebuild their marriage, she was acutely aware that a new life was growing inside her. A child Cole didn't want.

She'd become a package deal, her and Sweet Pea. The problem was, Cole only wanted half the package.

She drew back. "I don't know, Cole. I really don't."

"Then let's leave it here, on this sweet, pie-flavored note." He quirked a grin in her direction. "Always leave them wanting more, isn't that the old saying?"

"And do you? Want more?" Damn it all, she still wanted him, still couldn't back away.

He cupped her jaw, his thumb tracing over her lips, following the path her tongue had taken. "God, yes," he said. "That's one thing that's never changed, Emily. I always want you. Always have. Always will."

That sent a little thrill through her, but she tamped it down. Desire was never their problem. She'd wanted him from the moment she'd met him, and still did. She drew in a breath, held it, then exhaled again, with a dose of clarity. "A marriage requires more than just sexual attraction."

He sat back on the stool. A whisper of cold air filled the space between them. "Then let's work on the other things a good marriage requires." She started to protest, but he held up a finger, stopping her. "We're here together for a few days at least, right? And yes, I know we're separated and a step away from divorced, but at the very least, let's try to learn how to connect with each other so that going forward, everything is amicable."

It made sense, though she doubted his motives were that simple. Cole had made it abundantly clear that he wanted to get back together and didn't want a divorce. At the same time, he'd made it clear he didn't want children.

Still, the part of her that had got up in the middle of the night, worried, scared and lonely, craved the connection they'd had in their early days. Would it be so bad to rely on him, just for a few days, especially as she got used to the idea of the changes that lay ahead for her? What could it hurt?

Or was she just looking for a reason to be close to the man who was no longer her perfect fit?

"Tell me," he said, draping an elbow over the bar, "what has you up in the middle of the night besides pie?"

"There are other reasons to get up besides sneaking the last piece of pie?" She grinned.

"I don't know. Pie's a pretty compelling reason." He leaned in closer to her, and for a second, she thought—no, hoped—he was going to kiss her. "So what's on your mind? I know you, Emily, and I know that look on your face. The way your brow furrows right there—" he laid a gentle finger on her temple "—tells me you're worried about something."

In that moment she wanted to tell Cole about the baby. Tell him how worried she was that she wouldn't be a good mother or that she would let the baby down somehow. A long time ago, Cole had been her best friend, the one she told everything to. But as they'd drifted apart, their friendship had eroded, and that,

Emily knew, was what she mourned most about the end of her marriage.

Besides, if she told him about the baby, she knew how he'd react. He'd be angry that she had deviated from the careful plan they'd had. He didn't want kids now—and maybe not even later. He'd made that clear several times over the years and had reiterated the point the other day.

"I'm, uh, writing a book," she said. "I got a little writer's block and I was up, trying to figure out the next step in the plot."

He arched a brow in surprise. "You're writing a book?"

"I used to do that back in college, you know. I just put it aside for a while."

"I remember. Why?"

"What do you mean, why?"

"Why did you ever stop writing? You used to love doing it."

"Well, when we first got married, we were both working a crazy amount of hours while you got the business off the ground. Then once you were successful, my days got sucked up with things to support that." She fiddled with the fork, tapping it against the empty plate. "That's an excuse, really. I had the time, if I'd really wanted to find it. I just didn't."

"Why not?"

She raised a shoulder, dropped it. "I guess I was afraid. Once I finish a book, I have to send it out, and that…"

"Means you could get rejected."

She exhaled. "Yeah."

"But you've started now." Cole's hand covered hers. "That's all that matters. And if no publisher wants your book, I'll buy a printing press and—"

Emily jerked to her feet. Damn it. Why did he always return to the same answer? "Cole, I don't want you to solve my problems with money. I wasn't even asking you to solve it. I just wanted to talk, like you did with me, and have you listen, and most of all, let me find my own solution. If I get rejected, I get rejected. Maybe I'm not meant to be a writer. But you have to let me find that out instead of trying to fix everything with money."

"I don't do that."

"Yes, you do. When I was upset because my mother was moving to Florida, you bought her a house near ours. When I struggled to learn golf, you hired the best PGA coach in the business and flew him out to show me how to improve my swing. When I was sick with the flu, you had a doctor move into the guest room to be sure I was taken care of."

"That's what money buys, Emily. There's nothing wrong with that."

"Yeah, there is," she said. She put the dishes in the sink and propped her hands on either side. "It's the whole reason we're not together anymore, Cole. You talk about wanting to fix our relationship, about being a better husband, about being there for me. That was all I ever wanted, Cole, you. And what did I get instead?" She turned away from the sink. "Your checkbook."

"I was just trying to make things easier."

"Because it's easier to throw money at a problem than to actually get your hands—and your heart—into it." She shook her head, and wondered why she kept letting hope rise in her when they always circled back to the same disappointing end. Even if they stayed to-gether and had the baby, she didn't need a crystal ball to predict the future. Cole would buy toys and trips to

Disney World, but never be there for the first steps and
soccer games. She let out a long, sad breath. "All I ever
wanted was you."

Then she left the room, before the tears in her eyes
spilled down her cheeks and told Cole the truth. That
all she wanted now, *and always,* was him.

CHAPTER EIGHT

"A MAN COULD hurt himself doing that."

Cole turned at the familiar voice. Joe Bishop stood in the driveway of the Gingerbread Inn, grinning like a fool. Damn, it was good to see him. Cole notched the ax into the turned-over log beside him, then headed down the hill and over to his friend, one of the few people Cole had known since childhood. The two men exchanged a hearty hug while Harper barked and leaped around them, excited to see another newcomer. "I'm glad you're here, Joe. And not to help chop wood, though if you want to grab an ax, I won't stop you."

Joe laughed. "Count on you to show an old buddy a good time."

"Come on, let's get something to drink." Cole gestured to Joe to follow him. They circled around to the back door of the inn and went into the kitchen, where Cole pulled two icy beers out of the fridge and handed one to Joe. "We had some good times back in the day, more than one, if I remember right."

"If you're talking about your bachelor party," Joe said, "my memory of that night is a little fuzzy. In a good way."

Cole chuckled. "That was one wild night."

"Indeed. So was your wedding." Joe grinned. "That was, what, ten years ago? Every once in a while, I still think about that night. And the cute bartender I met." He winked. "Remember how she did that little shake when she mixed martinis? I think I ordered five of them just to see her shimmy."

Joe, still a ladies' man, the one in their group least likely to settle down. He'd started a landscaping business out of high school, and though he'd been successful enough to be able to expand and conquer the greater Boston area, Joe liked to keep his business small and manageable, so he could take off at a moment's notice for a weekend with a pretty woman.

"To unforgettable women," Cole said, tipping his bottle to connect with Joe's.

Joe took a long gulp. "Speaking of unforgettable women…how's Emily?"

The beer lost its appeal for Cole. He set his bottle on the steps, then sat down. How was Emily? That was the million-dollar question. Last night, he'd thought they were making progress, getting close again. For a second, it had been like the old days when they were united by their struggles to get from nowhere to somewhere. Then somehow, the closeness derailed again.

He was missing something, some detail, but what it was, he couldn't say. Was it just about the money?

He used to think they both wanted success, but Emily seemed to resent the very thing he'd worked so hard to achieve. Admittedly, she had a point about him hiring people instead of doing the work himself. But a man could only spread himself so thin. Didn't she understand he'd done it to ease their lives rather than complicate them?

Cole shrugged. He had no answers last night, and he had fewer now. "She's here. I'm here. But it's like we're on different planets."

Joe sat on the step beside Cole. "Things have gotten that bad between you two?"

"There are times when I think we have a chance, then other times…" He shrugged. "Not so much. Maybe she's right."

"Right about what?"

"That I can't let go because I can't admit I lost. That this is more about winning than about love."

Joe snorted. "That I can see. I have played racquetball with you, remember. I also recall one particularly crazy basketball game in your driveway. You are definitely a win-at-all-costs guy, Cole."

Cole cupped the beer between his palms and watched leaves flutter to the ground. In a couple of weeks, all would be bare here, covered with white, winter making its mark on the land around him. Even the trees caved to Mother Nature's power, giving up their leaves, their greenery, all their finery, to an enforced slumber that would last for the next three months.

"I think this time, that attitude is costing me my marriage. The problem? I honestly don't know if I can change. That's the very thing that's made me successful and what drives me every day. But it could also be the thing driving my wife away." He took a drink. "Maybe I should give her what she wants and leave."

"What does Emily say is the problem?"

"She says I try to solve everything with money rather than with just being there."

"And do you?"

"Well, yeah. But it's easier that way and leaves me

time to—" Cole cut off the words and let out a curse. How could he have missed the obvious answer?

"What?"

"It leaves me time to work. To put into the company. Instead of her."

Joe tapped Cole on the head. "Ding, ding, ding. I think he finally got it."

"What's wrong with being successful, though? Isn't that the American dream?"

"Hell, yes, it is. But what's the good of all that success if you end up a sad old man sitting in a dark room, all alone at the end of your life?"

Cole chuckled. "Gee, thanks for the bright picture of my future." He said the words like a joke, but even he could see it ending up that way. He'd invest all his energy in the company, and then end up alone, because he'd forgotten to save some of that energy for the people in his life.

"So what are you going to do about it?" Joe asked.

"Get back to work," Cole said, getting to his feet and leaving the beer on the stoop. "That's the only answer I know."

He picked up the ax and went back to chopping wood. As the metal blade hit log after log, slivering them into fireplace-sized chunks, Cole told himself he was making progress, when he knew damned well he wasn't doing much more than staying in place.

"You can do this," Emily muttered to herself and faced the daunting task assembled before her on the kitchen counter. Carol had gone into town for the day, off on a hair and manicure day arranged by Emily, who'd figured the stressed inn owner could use a little R & R. Martin

Johnson, who'd been around the inn often to help Cole with some of the repair projects, had asked Carol if she might want to meet for lunch. Carol had fretted for an hour over her outfit for the day, changing three times before she left.

While Carol was gone, Emily promised to make dinner for everyone. She had to learn how to cook sometime. Better to start now and get some kind of kitchen skills under her belt before the baby came, or Emily would be weaning Sweet Pea on General Tso's chicken and fried rice from Mr Chow.

"Can't have you eating takeout every day, can I, Sweet Pea?" she said to the tiny bump under her belly. "Okay, let's figure this out."

She braced her hands on the counter and read over the recipe again. Seemed simple enough. For someone who knew what they were doing. Outside, she heard the sound of two axes hitting logs over and over as Cole and Joe chopped wood for the fireplace at the inn. At the rate they were going, Carol would be well stocked into next winter.

Joe had come into the kitchen earlier for some lunch, and spent some time catching up with Emily, telling her that Cole had asked him to help out with the repairs. She was glad. Not just because Cole needed the help, but because it was nice to see Cole's friend, and to hear about his life for the past few years.

Except every time she looked at Cole and Joe together, it was like her wedding day all over again. She was walking down the aisle toward a nervous Cole flanked by a grinning Turner, then backed up by Joe, who'd been smiling through his hangover. Emily remembered the excitement, the rush of joy, the hopes and dreams she'd had that afternoon, when Cole had lifted her veil and kissed her. It had been a simple, small wedding on a limited budget, but perfect.

Thinking about the wedding made her melancholy and nostalgic. Not a good strategy right now, because it muddied the very waters she had come here to clear. So she'd make a chicken potpie and let the task take her mind in a different direction.

She reached for the onion, celery and carrots and placed them on the cutting board, then picked up the chef's knife. She grabbed the onion first and raised the blade.

"I wouldn't do that if I were you."

She looked up to find Cole standing in the back door. Damn. How did the man always manage to look so handsome? He had on a thick dark green sweatshirt, dark jeans and new work boots. His hair was getting a little long, she noticed, but it only added to his sex appeal. "Do what?"

"Cut the onion first. Leave that for last. That way, you aren't crying over your carrots. Or—" he took a step inside "—you could wait for me to wash up and I can help you."

"You? Help me. Cook." She scoffed. "Right. What have you ever cooked?"

"I'll have you know reheating takeout takes real skill." He grinned, then crossed to the sink, pushed up his sleeves and scrubbed his hands. When he was done, he grabbed a second cutting board and knife and set them up across from Emily. "Two terrible cooks in the kitchen has to be better than one, don't you think?"

She laughed. "It could be double the disaster."

Cole leaned over the bar and lowered his voice. "Then blame it all on me and call for pizza."

The temptation to have him here, in the close quarters of the kitchen, rolled over her. Every nerve in her body was tuned to his presence, even when he was outside working. She'd glanced out the window a hundred times already this morning, catching quick glimpses of him replacing some of the siding. He surely had a long list of outdoor activities to complete, yet he wanted to be here, to help her make a chicken potpie. Nothing else. Right?

"Deal." She turned the cookbook toward him. "We're making chicken potpie."

Cole skimmed the directions. "I'm good with the chicken and vegetables part, but I have to admit, the words roux and piecrust have me terrified. What the hell is a roux?"

She laughed. "I have no idea."

Cole read over the directions again. "Sure you don't want to just call for pizza?"

"Cole Watson, you're not giving up already, are you?"

"Me? Never."

"Me, either." She turned the book back toward herself. "Besides, I need to learn how to do this."

"Why? Why now?"

"Because it's about darn time I learned how to cook," she said, instead of the truth—that she had this dream of baking cookies with her child. Of being in the kitchen with Sweet Pea on a stool, helping to measure and stir. Building a family life of just two. She'd wanted that for so long—

Then why did the thought suddenly sadden her?

Outside, she could hear the sound of Joe chopping

wood. She gestured toward the door. "If you want to help Joe, I can handle this."

Cole arched a brow.

"I can figure it out. And if I don't, I'll blame you and call for pizza." She grinned, half hoping he'd leave, half hoping he'd stay.

"I'd rather stay and help you. I should learn to cook, too, since I'm living on my own now."

She didn't remind him that he could afford a team of chefs to make him food around the clock.

"After all," Cole said, leaning in toward her again, "didn't you say you always wanted me to help you instead of hiring someone to do the work? Let me help you, Emily."

She considered him for a moment. What would it hurt? Maybe together they could puzzle through this whole roux and piecrust thing. He had a point. She couldn't say no when he was offering the very thing she'd asked him for.

"Okay, then, you have onion duty." She plopped the offending vegetable onto Cole's cutting board.

"You just want to see me cry."

"No, but it is definitely a bonus." She took the celery, trimmed off the ends and began to cut it into little green crescent shapes. Across from her, Cole had peeled the onion and sliced it down the middle. He made slow, neat, precise slices in the vegetable, so exact it was as if he'd measured them.

Cole stopped cutting and looked up at her. "What?"

"You're treating that onion like it's a prototype or a stock report. It won't break if you chop it fast, Cole. We only have so long to get dinner on the table."

"I like things neat," he said.

"Neat? That's an understatement. You should have been an accountant, Cole, with all those straight lines. Though, there were a couple times you didn't mind a mess. One in particular I remember." The last few words came out as a whisper. "Remember the closet in our first apartment?"

"That wasn't a closet—it was an overgrown shoe box. It was impossible to keep neat." He stopped slicing and looked up at her, and a knowing smile curved across his face. The kind of smile that came with a shared history, a decade of memories. It was a nice, comfortable place to be.

"The ties," Cole said. "You're talking about the ties."

Oh, how she would miss this when her marriage was dissolved. All the memories they held together would be divided, like the furniture and the dishes and the books on the shelves. She'd be starting over with someone else. A blank slate, with no inside jokes about food fights and messy closets.

Emily craved those memories right now, craved the closeness they inspired. Just a little more, she told herself, and then she'd be ready to let go. "Remember that day you couldn't find the red one with the white stripes?"

He nodded. "The one you gave me for our first Christmas. I said it was my lucky tie and I wanted to wear it on my first sales call."

Their gazes met, the connection knitting tighter. She smiled. "You were so mad, because you like everything all ordered, and this was out of order. So I tore the closet apart looking for it, and because I was frustrated and in a hurry, I just threw all the ties in a pile on the floor. You came in and found me—"

"And at first I was upset at the mess, but then you held up the tie—"

"And I told you that if you made a mess once in a while, maybe you wouldn't be so uptight."

They laughed, the merry sound ringing in the bright and cheery kitchen. "But you forget the best part," Cole said, moving a little closer, his voice darkening with desire. "How we ended up making love on that floor, on top of the ties, and having a hell of a good time."

"In the middle of a mess."

It had been a wild, uninhibited moment. They'd had so few of those. Too few.

Cole caught a strand of her hair in his fingers and let the slippery tress slide away. "Why didn't I do that more often, Emily?"

She ached to lean into his touch, to turn her lips to his palm, to kiss the hand she knew so well. "I don't know, Cole, I really don't."

He held her gaze for a moment, then a mischievous light appeared in his eyes and his hand dropped away. He shifted his attention to the onion again, and this time did a frantic chopping, sending pieces here and there, mincing it into a variety of tiny cubes. "There. Done. And messy as hell."

She laughed. "I think the pie will be all the better for it."

"Oh, yeah? Wait till we make the crust. You might not feel that way with flour in your hair."

"You wouldn't."

He eyed the five-pound bag of all-purpose flour on the counter. "Oh, I would. And I will. I never did get you back for throwing my ties on the floor." Cole came around to the other side of the bar, scooping up a bit of flour in his hand. "Are you sorry about that?" he asked.

There was a charge in the air, fueled by the innuendos and heat between them. It was delicious and sweet and she hoped the feeling stayed. "Not one bit."

Cole held his hand over her head. "You want to re-think your position, Mrs. Watson?"

She hadn't been called that in months, and the name jarred her for a second. She remembered when Cole had first proposed and she had written *Mrs. Cole Watson* a hundred times, until the proposal felt real and she could believe she was really going to marry the man of her dreams. Soon, she wouldn't be Mrs. Watson anymore. Or a missus at all.

"I'm sorry, Cole," she said softly.

He dropped his hand and met her gaze. "They were just ties, Emily. I didn't really care."

"I know," she said. She was trying to hold on to the moment, but knew it was a butterfly, fleeting, impossible to catch. Eventually, Cole would go back to work, and she'd be on her own again. A single mom. Better to end it now than to prolong the inevitable. Emily returned to the vegetables. "Let's, uh, get this pie made before Carol comes home."

If he sensed the change in her, he didn't say anything. He helped her finish chopping the vegetables and cooked chicken, then lifted the heavy food processor onto the counter and helped her assemble the ingredients for the piecrust. "Okay. Here goes nothing," Cole said, pushing the pulse button. Several pulses later, the flour and butter and ice water had coalesced into a crust. "Voilà!" Cole said, lifting off the plastic lid. "Piecrust."

"I am impressed," she said. "What are you doing for your next trick, Superman?"

He grinned. "That you will have to wait to see, Mrs. Watson."

She shook her head and dipped her gaze before he saw the tears that had rushed to her eyes. "Don't call me that, Cole. Please."

"Emily, Emily," he said, tipping her chin until she was looking at him. "We cleaned up the mess with the ties. Why do you have such little faith that we can clean up the mess with our marriage?"

CHAPTER NINE

THE FOUR OF them sat around the long dining room table, helping themselves to big slices of chicken potpie and generous bowls of tossed salad. Carol had brought home a loaf of bread from the bakery in town, which served as the perfect complement to the meal. Cole sat beside Joe, across from Emily and Carol in a warm and cozy room filled with great scents, great food and great people.

This, he thought, *this is what home feels like.*

Was that what he and Emily had missed? Had they been so fixated on getting from A to B that they had missed that critical step of building a home, not just a house?

Or rather, had he? Emily had asked him to be home more often, and he'd promised over and over to do that, only to spend his time at work instead. Then they'd built that house on the hill, and despite the fact that it had a table in the kitchen, a handcrafted one in the dining room and another outdoor eating space, they rarely ate together. Most nights, she had been asleep before he got home, and then he was gone again before she was awake.

"Great job, Emily." Carol gestured toward the chicken potpie. "Maybe I should hire you on as a chef."

Emily laughed. Cole liked it when she laughed, because her face and eyes lit up, and the whole room felt lighter. "I am far from being a chef. Cole's the one who mastered the piecrust. I just read the directions."

"You did more than that, Emily," Cole said. "You taught me how to chop an onion, too."

She dipped her head, a flush shading her cheeks. "I just told you it didn't have to be all perfect."

Joe looked from Cole to Emily and back again. "You got this guy to loosen the reins a little? What'd you do, drug him?"

"Hey, I'm not that bad," Cole said.

"*Right*. You are the only man I know who had a typewritten itinerary for your own bachelor party." Joe chuckled.

Cole scowled. "I like to be organized. So sue me."

Joe leaned toward Emily with a conspiratorial grin. He cupped his hand around his mouth, mocking a whisper. "If you want to drive Cole crazy, just hide his lists and his planners."

"First I'd have to pry his smartphone out of his hands," Emily said, laughter in her voice. "And that's almost impossible."

Cole unclipped the phone and slid it across the table toward Emily. "Hey, I can disconnect the umbilical."

Joe scoffed. "That's not a challenge. It's already after five."

The cell phone sat on the table, one of the things that had built his company to its current position at the top, but also one of the things that had dragged his marriage to the bottom. That was one of the hazards of always being available—it was good for business, but bad for a relationship.

Emily glanced at his phone, then slid it back. "I don't need it. I'm just glad you're getting some time away from the office here."

"Are you glad I'm here?" he asked, his gaze meeting hers.

A small, bittersweet smile crossed her lips. "Of course. You work so hard, I was always worried you'd have a heart attack. You need some time to destress."

That wasn't what Cole had hoped Emily would say. He'd wanted her to say she was glad he was here with her, finally trying to work on their marriage again.

"And in the process," Emily added, "maybe you can get back to what's important."

The last few words had him trying to read Em's face, but her gaze was on her plate, keeping whatever secrets she had hidden behind her wide green eyes.

"That's what this inn was always about. Helping people get in touch with their lives, themselves," Carol said. "And what I'd like to do more of if I end up keeping it. I think it'd make a great retreat for corporate types who want to get out from behind the desk."

"You could make it a win-win," Joe said with a grin. "Give them some hammers and nails or some paint and a paintbrush and put them to work on that project list that Cole drew up. You'll get the stuff done around here, and they'll get to do something other than sit around an office all day. Plus, Cole would get to check things off on one of his lists, and we all know how happy that makes him."

Cole laughed. Damn, it was good to have Joe here. His friend kept him grounded, real. "Joe, only you would make people work on vacation."

Emily dished up some more salad and grabbed another slice of bread. "Says the man who hasn't taken a vacation in years."

"True." Cole gave her a nod, then leaned in with a grin. "Maybe you should have kidnapped me and whisked me away to an undisclosed location. Out of network range, of course."

A mischievous glint shone in her eyes. "That might have been fun."

"Just for the record, if you ever get the urge to do something like that, I'm game." It seemed as if the room had closed to just the two of them. He held her gaze, and his heart skipped a beat. "But you might want to take my phone first."

"If I get that thing in my hands, I'll end up smashing it with a sledgehammer," Emily said with a teasing smile. "It's needier than a three-year-old."

As if on cue, the smartphone began to ring and the caller ID screen lit. Doug, probably calling about another problem with the new product launch. Cole reached forward, pressed the button on the side of the phone, sent the call to voice mail and darkened the screen. The action sent a flicker of anxiety through him, but he pushed it aside. Emily was right. He'd spent far too much time letting work interrupt dinners, and the last thing he wanted was an interruption in this one, when things seemed to be going so well, almost like the old days.

"That's a good start," Emily said, and gave him a smile that he wanted to hold in his heart. "Thank you, Cole."

The dinner ended too soon. Carol began to pick up the dishes and put out a hand to stop Cole and Emily when they rose to help her. "You two go off on a walk or something. Joe and I can get these."

"Are you sure?" Emily asked. "You already do so much."

"That's my job. Your job is to go relax," Carol said. "And that's an order."

"Don't worry about Carol," Joe said. He flexed his biceps. "She's got a whole lotta help."

Cole chuckled. "A whole lotta something, that's for sure." Then he turned to Emily, glad that Carol had made it impossible for Emily to say no. "Want to take a walk? It's not too cold out tonight."

She glanced at Carol, who nodded and waved her off. "Okay. Let me get my coat."

A few minutes later, they were outside, breathing in the crisp fall night air. The scent of a wood-burning stove filled the air, mixing in the fragrance of cedar and oak. "It's a beautiful night," Cole said. "Look at the lake. It's as smooth as glass."

"It's gorgeous. Like a postcard." Her breath frosted in the air, surrounding her face with a soft cloud.

He thought of what she had said before, about how he should learn to make a mess more often, to be less uptight and rigid and planned. Spontaneity had never been Cole's strong suit, yet the happiest times he could remember were when he went off schedule. Maybe that was the key to finding his way back to where they used to be—throwing out the plan and just...

Being.

A rowboat lay on the beach, flanked by a pair of oars. The moon glinted off the wooden boat's hull, making it look like a giant smile in the dark. "Hey, let's take the boat out," he said.

"At night? In the middle of November?"

He leaned in close, catching the sweet scent of her

floral perfume, a fragrance he knew as well as he knew his own name. Her hair drifted across his lips. "Live on the edge, Emily," he whispered. "With me."

She turned to him, her lips an inch away from his. Her eyes widened, she inhaled, and Cole wanted her more in that moment than he could remember. "On the edge? But it's dangerous. It's nighttime, the water is cold and…well, things could go wrong. Remember the story Carol told?"

He brushed the hair off her forehead and let his touch linger there a moment. "Don't worry. I'll be there to catch you." His hand drifted down, along her jaw. "I always will be."

She shook her head, and tears glimmered in her eyes. "Cole—"

"Trust me, Em. Just tonight."

She bit her lip and watched him for a moment, wary, hesitant.

"It'll be fun. Unscripted, spontaneous, fun. I promise."

Then the hesitation disappeared and she smiled. "Okay. As long as you don't rock the boat."

He took her hand and led her down the hill. Her hand felt good in his, right. Long ago, they had stopped holding hands. Why, he couldn't remember. If they ever got back together, he vowed that if Emily was nearby, he would always hold her hand. "Of course. Not rocking the boat is my specialty."

"You're wrong about that, Cole. *I'm* the one who never likes to rock the boat," she said, bending to help him right the boat and slide it into the water. "You're the one who takes chances."

"In business, yes. In my personal life—" he took an

oar, then waited while she climbed into the rowboat before handing her the second oar "—not so much."

Cole gave the boat a push, and it slid into the water with a gentle ripple. He took both of the oars, positioned himself on the bench, then began rowing away from the shore. The oars made a satisfying whoosh sound with each stroke, while his back and shoulder muscles jerked to attention. A fish jumped out of the water behind them, then flopped back in, spattering them. Emily watched him row, a smile playing on her lips. "What?" he asked.

"You look…well, you look sexy and strong doing that."

"Then maybe I should do this more often."

She didn't respond to that, just smiled again and leaned back on the bench. "All the times I've been to the Gingerbread Inn, I've never been out on the lake after dark. It's so peaceful out here."

A perfect setting for a man to propose, Cole thought. When he'd proposed to Emily all those years ago, he'd done what he always did—he'd created a plan for the evening and stuck to his timetable, almost to the minute. Dinner in the city, followed by the ubiquitous and clichéd carriage ride along New York's streets, then pausing by Central Park to slip onto the carriage's carpeted floor and pop the question. He'd known Em was going to say yes before he even asked, because they'd talked about getting married a half dozen times before.

Out here, alone in the dark while fish bobbed in the water around them and geese swam silently along the banks, he had the perfect setting for something unexpected. Something that would show Emily he wasn't here to fix the porch or chop firewood. He was here for them. For a second chance. He gave the oars a final tug, then set them across the center of the boat. Then he leaned forward, dropping to one knee, and reached for his wife's hands.

"What are you doing?" she asked.

"Living on the edge," he said. "Emily, I don't want a divorce. I don't want us to live apart anymore. I want to try again, to give our marriage the chance it needs. Will you try again?"

Her eyes widened, and she backed up a bit. Damn. This was why he planned these things out. So he could have time to write a good proposal, to plan out what he was going to say. That had to rank up there with the top ten least romantic proposals in the history of time. "Cole, there's a lot we need to discuss. Things we haven't settled yet."

"What's to settle? I love you." He held her hands, but noticed she didn't hold his back. Nor did she tell him she loved him. Had her feelings for him changed? Was he reading her all wrong?

"It's about more than love, Cole. It always was. We're…not on the same path anymore."

He grinned. Okay, so she hadn't said she didn't love him, either. He'd take that as a good sign. "We are now. A path that's kind of going in circles in the middle of the lake."

She pulled her hands back and tucked them inside her coat. The air between them dropped a few degrees, and the grin faded from Cole's face.

"I want a family, Cole. I always have. We've put it off forever, and honestly, it's gotten to the point where I don't understand why. You've achieved what you want with the company, I'm writing my book…what more is there to do or get before we have kids?"

Just the word *kids* made him freeze. When he'd first married Em, he'd told her he wanted children, and maybe for a time, he had. But as the years had worn on and he watched his friends have kids and have trouble and turmoil in their families, trouble and turmoil that affected the kids and ruined their childhoods, the more Cole didn't want to change the status quo. But he knew that telling Em would drive her away for good. She had always been set on having children, the one risk Cole didn't want to take. "We always wanted to travel, Em. Have fun, live our lives, before we added kids into the mix."

She let out a gust. "Let's go back to shore. This isn't getting us anywhere."

"Let me ask you this." He leaned toward her, causing the boat to make a gentle rocking motion. "Why do you think having kids will improve our lives?"

"How can you say they won't?" She shook her head. "I don't get you, Cole, I really don't."

"I'm just trying to make sure we have everything in order first." He didn't want to tell her that the thought of being a father was the only thing that truly scared Cole. He knew what he was good at and what he wasn't—and parenting didn't make the list of talents.

"You and your lists and timetables." She let out a gust. "For once, I wish you would just let all that go."

He was losing her. He could hear it in her voice, see it in her face. They had reached a moment of no return, a time when he had to act, instead of just talk. Their relationship stood on a fault line, and only a dramatic shift would keep it from falling apart.

"I can, if you want me to, Em." He tugged his cell out of his pocket and held it over the water. "I can drop this in the water, and not think twice about it. Devote myself entirely to us for the next week or month or year or however long it takes."

"You'd do that? Walk away from the company?"

"If it brings us back together, yes." Then, as if God was testing his resolve, Cole's phone began to ring. Doug, again. The little notification bar under the caller ID showed Doug had called four times with no answer. Definitely an emergency, if he was trying that hard to get hold of Cole.

He glanced at the screen, his stomach churning. The urge to answer the call, to solve the problem, burned inside him. The company had taken so much of his life in the past ten years and even now, even when it mattered, he couldn't let it go. He could feel the need calling to him, like the business held an invisible string to his gut. He wasn't sure which direction the need went— whether it was the company that needed him or him who needed the company. The phone dangled from his fingers, inches from the water. Then his fingers tightened their grip and the decision was made. He realized that at the same time Em did.

Emily gave him a sad little smile. "You might as well answer it."

"What about us?"

"Us?" She took the oars and put them in the water, then began rowing back toward shore. "The only thing I know for sure is that I'm done going in circles."

CHAPTER TEN

COLE CAUGHT UP to her after the boat was back on shore and Emily was already striding up the hill. "Where are you going?" he asked.

"Back inside." Where she belonged. Where she wouldn't have to think about that little rise of hope she'd had a few minutes ago when Cole had offered to throw his phone away—and answered it instead. She should have known better. He was doing what he'd always done—making promises that would dissolve as soon as they got back to real life.

"I thought we were talking."

She spun around. "I am tired of talking, Cole. We've done nothing but that for years. And where did it get us? Nowhere but divorced."

"We're not divorced yet, Emily. There's still—"

"I don't want to hear one more second about how there's still a chance. How many times did I say that to you? How many times did I try to make this work? Try to change our lives? And what did you do?" She cursed under her breath and shook her head, hating the pain in her chest, the tears burning the back of her eyes. God, why did this hurt so much? When would Cole stop having a hold on her heart? She wanted to scream at him, to tell him to stop putting her through this emotional roller coaster. The same one she'd ridden so many times in the past ten years, she could predict the next loop. There'd be a high, a wonderful honeymoon period of flowers and dinners out, followed on its heels by the plummeting lows of Cole's absence, an empty house and an empty bed. "You made a bunch of promises and then went to work. Which is what you're going to do this time, too, Cole. I know you. That is the curse of being married to you for so long. I know what you're going to do, and I keep coming back even though I know it's going to hurt."

"The company—"

"Was always number one. And I was somewhere in distant second place." She refused to cry. To let that hurt any more than it already had. But it did, oh, how it seared against her heart, the truth a branding iron that left a jagged scar.

Silence stretched between them for a long moment. "I never meant for that to happen."

"Yet it did, Cole. Do you know how many times I hoped and prayed and believed, and then you'd break my heart again?" She pressed a hand to her chest and forced herself to take a breath, to be strong, to sever this connection once and for all. "I can't do that anymore. I don't have it in me to go through that pain one more time. *Not one more time.*"

Emily had finally reached her breaking point. Maybe it was the baby, maybe it was being here at the inn, where she had first learned to believe in happy endings. Maybe it was that damned hope that had sprung up inside her when Cole arrived here, and when he stayed, and when he held his phone over the lake.

"The definition of insanity is doing the same thing over and over again and expecting a different result," she said, as much to herself as to him. "I'm *done* with this insanity, Cole."

The statement exited her with a measure of frustration and relief.

Done.

All this time, she'd never used the word *done*. She'd always believed there was a chance, but when he'd answered his phone on the lake, she'd known the truth. He was always going to go back to the way he was, and she was always going to be the one in second place.

"I'm done, Cole," she said again, softer this time.

"What if I'm not? What if I want to keep fighting for us?"

She shook her head, and braced her heart against the hope trying to worm its way back in there. "Where was all that six years ago, Cole? Or hell, six months ago? Now you show up, when it's over, when we're a few pieces of paper away from divorced, and you want me to believe you?"

"I have tried, too, Emily. I have tried to connect with you, tried to make this work. It's not just about the company taking too much of my time. You…" He shook his head. "You stopped giving time."

She opened her mouth to protest, then shut it again. He was right. There'd been dinners she had turned down, lunch dates she had skipped out on, late-night talks she had avoided. Cole would come and go in bursts of trying to fix them, then burying himself in work, and after a while, she learned to maintain her distance rather than trust. "It was too risky."

"Because when it didn't work out, you got hurt. Yeah, well, you weren't the only one."

In those vulnerable words, Emily heard pain, frustration, loss. An echo of what brimmed in her. They'd hurt each other, time and time again. The only thing to do, the only smart course to take, was to end this and stop the hurt, on both sides.

She nodded. "Cole, I can't do this anymore. I mean it. I'm—" she stopped before she said she was pregnant, and trying to conserve her energy, her heart, for the baby "—done."

Maybe if she said it enough, she would stick to that resolve. And Cole would believe her.

He eyed her, then, after a moment, nodded and let out a gust. "Then I guess my being here is a waste of my time."

A waste of his time. That hurt. What did she expect? That he would keep fighting and fighting for their marriage, showing her finally that he was committed? Yeah, maybe she had. And now, after just a few days, Cole was giving up.

"Maybe it is," she said, though the words hurt her throat and cost her something deep inside. She told herself it was better this way, better to let go now than to keep hoping. Sweet Pea needed a dad to depend on, not one who came and went like the wind.

The next day, Emily fiddled with her book for a couple hours but didn't get much accomplished. The words that had flowed so easily earlier now refused to come. Probably because her mind was filled with images of Cole.

She was done, she reminded herself. Done, done, done. He'd surprised her last night, not just with the excursion on the lake, but with the impromptu proposal. How she'd wanted to say yes, to believe that the Cole she'd seen in the past few days, the relaxed, easy man who had fallen asleep in the sun, would be the one she'd wake up next to tomorrow and every day after that.

But he wasn't, nor did he want the same future she did. Ending it now would save her a lot of heartache down the road. Even if it felt the opposite in the light of day.

Emily gave up on writing, tugged on a thick sweatshirt, then headed outside. There was a nip in the air, a definite sign that the pretty fall days were coming to an end.

That meant she also had to start thinking about where she was going to go. She couldn't stay here forever, though a part of her finally felt grounded here in this tiny town in Massachusetts, more familiar than the neighborhood where she'd lived with Cole for all those years. Maybe she'd rent a little house in town, settle down here and build a life with Sweet Pea. It would be a simple, uncomplicated life.

Yet the thought also saddened her. Cole didn't want children, and once they were divorced, she doubted he'd have much to do with their baby. After their cooking fun in the kitchen, she'd hoped that maybe things would be different, but it was clear the same walls stood between them now as always. With Cole, the company came first, and family came in a distant second, if at all. She'd be raising this child on her own, and in the end, Cole would be the loser.

Cole's rental wasn't in the drive, but Martin Johnson's van was, which explained why Carol had been busy fixing her hair when Emily told her she was going for a walk. Emily smiled. The inn owner was a nice woman and deserved a man who would treat her well.

"Hey, Emily," Joe said when she stepped outside. He had a window propped on a sawhorse, removing the old glaze in order to fix a broken pane. "Cole went into town for some supplies. He should be back soon."

"That's okay. I'm not looking for Cole."

Joe leaned the window against the sawhorse and crossed to Emily. "I hate seeing you guys like this. Cole's miserable…you're miserable. Are you sure you can't work it out?"

"I wish we could, I really do. But it's over." She let out a long breath. "I still love him. Heck, I probably always will. But we just want different things out of life."

Joe flashed her a grin. "It seemed like you were on the right track last night at dinner."

"I thought so, too. And in a lot of ways, we are. But not in the most important ways, so I told him last night that I'm done for good." Emily tucked her hair behind her ears. It didn't seem right to feel this sad on such a pretty day. She had something wonderful to look forward to, and she needed to focus on that, not the problems that would soon be in her past. "I'm just tired of waiting for him to be ready to start a family and to put family first."

"Ah, that explains a lot." Joe grabbed a water bottle out of the cooler at his feet and took a long sip. "Did Cole say why he doesn't want to have kids?"

"He keeps saying we haven't done this or that. Traveled enough. Been together long enough." She exhaled. "If you ask me, they're all excuses."

"If you ask me, I think you're right." Joe tipped the bottle in her direction and arched a brow. "The question is why a smart man like Cole would make excuses like that."

Emily threw up her hands. "I don't know."

Joe nodded. His gaze went off to the distance for a moment as if he was trying to decide whether to say the next words. Finally, he returned his attention to Emily. "Did you ever meet Cole's parents?"

"Once. A long time ago, while we were still dating. Then his dad died and his mom moved to Arizona, and… Gosh, I can't believe it's been that long since we've seen his mom." She didn't have the best relationship with her parents, but at least she saw them for holidays and talked to them once a week. Cole, however, didn't call very often and had never wanted to go to Arizona. Yet another aspect of family he kept down the list from his hours at work. That alone should have told her where their child would rank.

"I've known Cole a long, long time," Joe said. "And I knew his parents, too. Let's just say he didn't have the ideal childhood."

"He never talks about it." There were a few conversational topics that Cole steered away from. His childhood was one of them. She'd sensed it hadn't been happy, something she could relate to, and had never pushed him to open up. Had she been avoiding the conversations that would have brought them closer? Had her efforts to keep the peace been part of the problem? "What happened?"

"His father was a tyrant, to put it mildly. Nothing Cole ever did was good enough. Probably why he keeps on trying to be better, even when he's already the best in his industry. And his mother, well, she buried her head in a bottle and ignored everything around her." Joe shook his head. "Cole pretty much raised himself and his little brother. He told me a hundred times that he never wanted to have kids and treat them like that."

"But he's not like either one of them. Why is he still afraid of repeating their mistakes?"

Joe shrugged. "You'd have to ask him."

"Maybe." Emily started to head away. She didn't remind Joe that with the divorce looming, there'd be no conversations with Cole about his past. Done meant done, and she had to move on before she let herself get suckered back into riding that emotional roller coaster.

"Emily?" Joe said. She pivoted back. "Cole might not be the best at showing how he feels, or hell, even saying it, but believe me, that man loves you more than anything in the world. Keep an open heart."

That man loves you more than anything in the world. How she wanted to believe that. But she thought of him answering the phone last night, and knew there were things Cole loved more than her. And always would. "I thought the expression was keep an open mind."

"When it comes to Cole, an open heart's a better idea." Joe gave her a grin, then got back to work on the window.

Emily nodded, not making any promises, then strode down the dock, sat on the end and let her feet dangle above the deep blue water. The breeze skipped across the water, making it look like corrugated denim. Beautiful, serene.

She fingered the rock in her pocket and thought back to the day the four of them had found the rocks, scattered at the edge of the lake. The stones were so similar that the girls had taken it as a sign that they needed to keep them and make them special. So they'd stood by

the water, holding hands and promising to always follow their dreams.

It had taken Emily a while, but she was doing that
now. She wondered if Andrea and Casey were doing the
same thing, or if they were stuck in Neutral like Emily
had been for far too long. Oh, how she missed the other
Gingerbread Girls. Maybe a talk with her friends would
take her mind off Cole, and all that Joe had said.

Emily tugged out her cell, then dialed Andrea. When
her old friend answered, nostalgia filled Emily's heart.
She could think of no one better to share this moment
with than one of the other Gingerbread Girls. "Guess
where I am?"

Andrea paused a moment, thinking. "On the end of
the dock, watching for the Loch Ness monster to show
up."

Emily laughed. "Guilty as charged. I can't believe
we thought Nessie could really be here."

"Didn't keep us from swimming. Heck, our parents
had to drag us out of the water most days."

So many memories, wrapped up in this magical place
and those endless summers they had spent here. Such
a blessing that their parents had loved this place just as
much, bringing the families together summer after summer. The Gingerbread Girls had bonded, and been off all
day, swimming, playing badminton, chasing boys…just
being young and free. "We did have a lot of fun here."

"My best memories are all in that place." Andrea
sighed. "Is Carol still planning on selling?"

Emily hadn't brought up the subject with Carol because she didn't want to hear the answer. She hoped
that once the building was fixed, the innkeeper would

change her mind. "I'm not sure. Cole has been doing a lot of repairs—"

"He's still there?"

Emily tossed a leaf into the water and watched it float away. "He wants a second chance. He keeps telling me things will be different."

"Maybe they will. Maybe the separation really changed him. I mean, he's still there, not at work, right? For a workaholic to take that much time off must mean something. Don't you think?"

Emily wanted to believe that, but she'd had her hopes dashed a thousand times before. And now, with the baby on the way, and Cole's insistence that they not add kids into their marriage, she didn't see a way to make it work, regardless of how many hours he spent here.

Not to mention there were things about himself that he had shared with Joe and not with her. His wife. If anything told Emily that their relationship wasn't on solid ground, that did.

"The fundamental differences between us are still there, Andrea," she said. "Nothing has changed that. I told him I'm moving forward with the divorce."

"I'm sorry. I know that's got to be hard on you."

"I'm okay. One of the things I'm finding by being on my own is that I'm stronger than I thought." She watched a lone bird skim the surface of the water, elegant and clean, then make a sudden dive for a fish. "Plus, I'm finally writing that book I wanted to write, and being responsible for me and only me. So even if Cole wanted to get back together, I'm not the same Emily I was before."

"That's fabulous. And I'll get to see that for myself when I get out there in a couple weeks."

"You're coming? Oh, that's awesome! It'll be so great to see you."

Andrea sighed. "You were right—I do need a break—and what better place to take a break than at the inn with all of you? And maybe the two of us can convince Carol that she needs to hold on to that place."

Emily smiled. "She'd be powerless against the combined strength of the Gingerbread Girls."

"You know it. Together, we were an unstoppable force." Then Andrea's voice lowered almost to a whisper. "Even without Melissa."

"That's why I'm here," Emily said. "Because of her letter. I want to go after my dreams before it's too late."

"That's the right attitude. And I'll be right there with you, soon. Take care, Emily."

"I will. See you soon." She hung up the phone and leaned back to turn her face to the sun. The wind rustled in the trees, creaked with the swaying dock and ruffled her hair. She closed her eyes and just let the day wash over her.

"Maybe I should have built a lake at the house in New York. Added a dock, a little boat." Cole's voice, behind her.

One of these days her stubborn heart would stop leaping every time Cole was around. But that day wasn't today.

She thought about what Joe had said. Maybe there was more to the story, more to Cole than she realized. Maybe she should keep an open heart. For a little while longer.

"And if we had a lake at the house in New York, would we go fishing at the end of the day?" she asked, turning toward him. "I can just see you out there in hip waders with a fly rod."

"What, you don't think I'd look sexy in hip waders?"

She laughed. Picturing Cole in the long boots, with his jeans and mussed longish hair sent a ribbon of heat through her. That resolve to be done, to distance herself from him, fizzled for a moment. "You...you would look sexy in anything. Except maybe hip waders."

"I could rock some hip waders. I'll have to get some just to prove it to you." He cocked a hip and struck a pose.

She laughed more, and realized how long it had been since she'd laughed about something silly with Cole. Those days had got lost in the stress of building a business, then the busyness of the social life expected of someone in the upper orbit of moneymakers. She glanced at Cole and saw the smile lighting his face, his eyes. No matter what happened in the future, she hoped he managed to find more time and room for laughter. "You've looked so relaxed these past few days, Cole. So...happy. I haven't seen you like that in a long time."

He gestured toward the space beside her. Emily nodded, and Cole sat down on the dock's edge. "I didn't realize how much I was working until I wasn't there every day." He glanced over at her. "All those years you told me I needed to take a vacation, and I didn't. I guess I thought the place would fall apart if I wasn't there."

"And is it?"

He chuckled. "Probably. Given how many messages are on my phone, and how often people call me. Like last night. That was a problem with the shipping company that had Doug in a panic. I got it straightened out, then told Doug not to call me unless the building was on fire. I hired good people, and they'll figure those things out. That is, after all, what I pay them to do, as Irene and you have reminded me."

"They're probably all still in shock that you actually took several days off in a row."

He nodded, then picked up a stick from the dock and flung it into the water. "I should have done it years ago. Maybe then we wouldn't be where we are now."

"Maybe." She watched the stick float for a moment, then disappear beneath one of the ripples in the lake. "There was a lot more wrong in our marriage than the fact that we never went on vacations, you know."

"But if we had gone on vacation more often, then maybe we could have talked about those other things." He flung another stick out onto the water and waited until a wave devoured it. "That's why I'm not going back to work anytime soon. I'm staying until this place is fixed or—" he turned to face her "—until we are."

"Cole, I can't—"

He put up a finger, pressing it to her lips. She closed her eyes, inhaled his familiar cologne, and with it, the desire for the man she had married. "Don't say that. I know you want to file. I know you're done. But I started something here that I want to finish, and if we're going to be staying in the same place, all I ask is for a few more days. After ten years, a few days isn't much, Emily. Is it?"

She shivered as the wind kicked up, and tugged the zipper of her sweatshirt higher. "Then tell me the real reason you don't want to have kids, Cole."

He opened his mouth, closed it again. "I never said I didn't want to have kids, Emily. Just not now."

"Why?"

"I don't have a reason why. It's just not the right time."

Why wouldn't he open up to her? Tell her at least what he had told Joe? She wanted to tell him she already knew, but didn't want to betray Joe's confidence, either. The urge to yell at Cole returned, but where had fighting ever got them? All that anger had created a wall, and people didn't communicate through walls. So she took a deep breath instead.

"When will be the right time?" she asked softly. "Because I'm ready now."

More ready than you know.

"I don't know." He waved his hand vaguely. "Down the road someday."

She got to her feet. If he wasn't going to be honest with her, then she was wasting her time hoping for a change. "Just go back to the office, Cole. Staying here and repairing the plumbing or fixing the porch isn't going to change anything between us."

"You don't know that, Emily. If we talk—"

"I came here to get away, Cole. To think, without you around. I don't want to talk anymore. I told you last night that I'm done." She threw up her hands. "Why can't you be done, too? Then we can move on. Both of us."

He scrambled to his feet before she could leave, and reached for her hands. When Cole touched her, the familiar zing of electricity ran through Emily. Would there ever be a day when that didn't happen? And why, oh why didn't her heart and body get the message from her brain?

"Fine. But before we leave this place and move on

to lawyers and court dates and divorce papers, I want to ask you to give us one more chance."

"Cole—" She turned away.

He tipped her chin until she was looking at him again. "Give *me* one more chance at least. Give me the next few days, and let's see what happens. No talk of divorce or separation or anything other than just… getting to know each other again. Having those talks we never had."

She knew she should say no. She even opened her mouth to say the word, but it got stuck in her throat. Maybe Cole realized he needed to open up, too. If he did, then there was a chance they could make this work. A small chance. "And at the end of that time?"

"If we realize we are too far apart to put this back together, that there's really nothing there to keep us together, then I will go back to New York and file myself."

Maybe if she agreed, he'd finally quit fighting a battle he was never going to win. And maybe she would stop looking at him and longing for the man he used to be. She hesitated, her gaze going to the lake, now as serene as a mirror.

"Okay," she said, because that darn bubble of hope refused to die, no matter how much her common sense tried to overrule it, "we'll try it."

A smile winged across Cole's face, and Emily wondered if maybe she shouldn't have given him that hope. Maybe she should have just told him to forget it, that she was having a baby he'd made it clear he didn't want, and it was silly to delay the inevitable.

"Be ready at six," Cole said.

"Why?"

Cole caught her chin, let his thumb trace a light touch

along her bottom lip. Her heart skipped; her breath caught. "I want to take my wife on a date. One that should bring back some memories. Or at the very least, give us some new ones to share."

He turned to walk away, and she thought how much she wanted those. Her hand drifted to her abdomen. Oh, yes, how very, very much.

CHAPTER ELEVEN

COLE HADN'T BEEN this nervous since he was fifteen and asking a girl on a date. The date had been a stumbling, embarrassing event, ending with him spilling popcorn on her at the movies. Back then, he'd thought the stakes could never get higher than asking one of the most popular girls in high school to a movie.

He'd been wrong. Tonight's date would set the tone for whatever came next. He knew that as well as he knew the sun would rise tomorrow. If tonight went badly, it would add another brick to the wall between them. Too many bricks, and he knew the wall would be impossible to tear down.

When he'd proposed the date, he'd started thinking about calling for a limo or a private plane, taking Emily off to an elaborate dinner in Manhattan or a weekend on one of the Virgin Islands. Then he thought about everything she had said and that they had talked about, and realized that in order to solve the problems in the present, he needed to go back to the past.

The problem was that Cole had worked very hard to leave his past in the rearview mirror. As soon as he could shed the things that had held him down, he'd breathe a sigh of relief. Emily had never understood why he didn't want to visit his mother. Why he rarely went back to his hometown.

He'd met her family, and though they were far from perfect, they were a sight better than his parents had been. How could he explain to Emily that he never talked about his childhood because all it did was remind him of the very place he never wanted to be again?

All these years, he'd kept that to himself. Maybe that had been a mistake. Either way, he was here tonight to try to make things better, no matter what that took.

At six on the dot, he strode up the new steps of the porch and pressed the inn's doorbell. He adjusted his tie, shifted from foot to foot on his shiny dress shoes. A second later, Emily opened the door and gave him a curious look. "You rang the doorbell?" she said.

"Yup. I'm here to take my wife on a date. I thought I should do it right."

A small smile curved across her face, and amusement danced in her eyes. Score one for Cole. "Well, then, maybe I should call my dad and have him come over and grill you."

Cole laughed. He put up his right hand. "I promise not to drive too fast, to drink or to take advantage of you tonight. And I will have you home by curfew."

The smile widened. She put out her arm and he slipped it into the crook of his. "Then let's go," she said.

"Your wish is my command, madam." He led her down the porch and over to his rental car, opening the passenger's side door of the Mercedes and waiting for her to sit before coming around to the driver's side.

"What, no limo?" she said when he got behind the wheel.

"I thought we'd do this old school. No limos, no heli-

copters. No red carpets. Just a good old-fashioned date."
He rested his hand on the key fob, then looked over at
her. "Like we used to have. Before…everything."

The smile lit her eyes. "That sounds perfect, Cole."

He put the car in gear. They swung out of the inn's
drive and headed down the tree-lined road. Night was
beginning to fall, and the waning sun dropped a dark
gold hue over the treetops and streets. The pavement
gleamed from an afternoon shower, making wet leaves
cling to the tar in clumps.

"Where are we going?" Emily asked.

He shifted his gaze to her. She'd worn a dress, a simple deep green one that hugged her curves and showed
off her amazing legs. She'd paired the dress with black
heels and a long black trench coat that he'd given her
for Christmas three years ago. Her hair was up, and a
few loose tendrils dusted her neck and jaw. All in all,
the effect was…devastating. Half of him didn't want
to take her anywhere but to bed. Then he remembered
his promise not to take advantage. He redirected his attention to the road before his hormones overruled that
decision. "It's going to be a surprise," he said, "but we
aren't going far."

"No dinner in the city? Hmm…I'm intrigued."

"Good." He took a left, then a right, and after another
mile, he pulled into a parking lot and turned off the car.
A few other cars filled the lot, while a bright white sign
above announced their destination.

Emily turned to him, her eyes bright and excited.
"You brought me to the Barrow's Cove Diner? This was
my favorite place to eat when we were here in the summers. My mom and dad would bring me here on Friday nights. It was the one night we all ate as a family."

Cole grinned. "I know. I remember you telling me about that. But we're not going there quite yet."

He got out of the car, came around, opened her door, then put out his arm. She slipped hers into his again, and when he covered her hand with his own, Cole realized how much he had missed the simple act of touching his wife. When had it become more usual for them not to touch, than to have contact?

"It's still light out. Let's go for a short walk before dinner."

"A pre-feast calorie burn?"

"Something like that." He took her hand with his, and though she tensed, she didn't pull away. Score another point for Cole. He liked to think he was making progress with Emily, but at the same time he sensed she was holding something back. "Remember that game we used to play when we were young and poor?"

"What game?"

"The one where we picked out a house on the street and imagined what we would be doing if we lived inside there." He remembered those days, strolling down the streets of New York at the end of the day, the two of them dreaming and wishing. In those days, it had seemed as if anything was possible, if only they believed hard enough.

"Back when we thought we'd never live in anything bigger than a bread box." She laughed. "We've kind of moved past that, haven't we, Cole?"

"Humor me, Emily." He didn't want to talk about how they weren't living in that giant house together anymore, how they were probably going to sell it and move on to separate residences. For this night, he wanted to pretend it was the old days, when the only thing they could afford was dreams.

She put a finger to her lip and studied the houses on either side of the street. "That one," Emily said, pointing to a small dark blue Cape Cod–style house with white trim. "To me, that house spells traditions. If we lived there, I'd be in the kitchen, cooking dinner and wearing an apron over my dress—"

"And pearls, don't forget the pearls," Cole said.

"Those and high heels, of course. The house would be perfectly organized and clean, and my cooking would be impeccable. Then you would come home from work—"

"Precisely at five."

"And kiss me on the cheek, then sit in the recliner, put your feet up and read the paper while I finish dinner."

"That sounds like a great plan to me."

She gave him a gentle slug. "Yeah, good for the guy. Not so good for the woman. So don't get your hopes up, buddy, because it's never happening. Besides, I still can't cook."

"You made a hell of a chicken potpie the other day."

"With your help." She gave him an appreciative nod.

"Well, if we lived there, I'd help you make chicken potpie, Em. As long as you wore high heels a lot."

She shook her head, dismissing his words with a smile and a laugh. "Your turn. Pick a house."

He gestured toward a boxy white Georgian-style house. "In that house, I live a life of leisure, playing video games all day and eating Cheetos."

"And who is funding this life of leisure?"

"My bestselling novelist wife. Her first novel, *Falling in Love with a Gamer,* hits the top of the bestseller charts and makes us all wealthy beyond our dreams."

"Hey!" She gave him another light jab. "Why is it that all these scenarios have you with the easy life?"

He laughed. "Because I am naturally lazy."

"That is as far from the truth as you can get. You are one of the hardest-working men I have ever met, Cole."

They had reached the end of the street and pivoted to head back toward the diner. "But I thought you hated how many hours I worked."

"I do. I did. But I still admire you for putting in the hours to go after what you wanted. You kept going when other people would have given up. When it comes to business, Cole, you are like a pit bull."

The implication—that he hadn't been that way about their marriage. He saw that now, and prayed for the thousandth time that he wasn't too late. He couldn't read Emily, though, and that concerned him. He'd always thought he knew her better than he knew himself, but lately it was as if she had opened an ever-widening divide between the two of them, one he couldn't get across no matter how hard he tried. Was it because she'd grown so far apart from him that he couldn't reach her? Or was he just that out of tune with the woman he had married?

Too soon, they reached the glass doors of the diner. As soon as they walked inside, Emily was greeted by the diner's hostess, an older woman named Alice, who remembered Emily from years before. The two chatted, then Alice led them over to the last booth in the back corner. "Enjoy your meal, kids," she said to Cole and Emily.

Cole tugged a menu out of the holder behind the napkin dispenser and handed the plastic-coated paper to Emily. "I recommend the chef's special," he said. "Tonight, that's meat loaf and mashed potatoes."

She laughed. "I see you got the best table, too."

"It's the most private one they had. No musicians, but I hear if we stay late enough, Donny Greer will get drunk and start serenading the patrons."

Emily sat back against the red vinyl booth and studied him. "You really know an awful lot about this town for only being here a few days."

He shrugged. "It's a friendly place. You can't leave the hardware store without a new best friend."

"That must drive you crazy," Emily said. "I know how you hate to waste time on small talk."

In a business situation he hated delaying a meeting or a decision with chitchat about sports teams or the weather. In the office, Cole cut to the chase, intent only on getting through this task and on to the next demand on his time.

Since he had arrived in Barrow's Cove, though, he had taken the time to slow down, talk with the locals, enjoy the sunshine and turning leaves. He'd had more conversations with Emily in the past few days than the two of them had had in years. No matter where things went from here, Cole would make time for more of these small, simple conversations. Especially with Emily.

"Actually, I kind of like it," Cole said. "It reminds me of our old neighborhood. Remember Mrs. Timmons?"

Their elderly downstairs neighbor in that first terrible apartment building had possessed a sixth sense that had brought her out of her rooms every time Cole or Emily came home. She'd been an inquisitive woman, but in a grandmotherly way.

The memory lit Emily's eyes. "Oh, my goodness. Mrs. Timmons. A little too friendly sometimes. I think she looked at us as her surrogate kids. Gosh, she was always on our doorstep, making sure we were eating right and getting enough sleep."

"If I remember right," he said, lowering his voice and leaning closer, "we were a little too busy to do much of either. And those were details we never shared with Mrs. Timmons."

Emily's face flushed. She raised the menu, blushed some more when she realized it was upside-down, then hurried to right it. She kept her gaze on the typed pages. "Uh, what are you thinking about ordering?"

"Tonight, I want the biggest burger they make."

"Really? Mr. Healthy Eating is getting a burger?"

"I figure I've burned off a burger and then some, doing all that work on the inn. And there's just something about working in the sun all day that makes a man want some red meat and a beer."

She laughed. "Next you'll be driving a pickup and chewing tobacco."

"I don't think there's a chance of that anytime soon." He grinned.

She studied the menu a while longer, then put it to the side. "You know what? I think I'll have the same. I'm ravenous all of a sudden."

"All that writing working up an appetite?"

"Yeah." She said that too fast, and hoped he wouldn't notice.

The waitress came by, saving Emily from having to answer any other questions about her sudden appetite. They ordered two burgers with fries, with Cole opting for a beer and Emily sticking to ice water.

Cole didn't notice she stayed away from alcohol, nor had he noticed her daily breakfast of crackers, the only thing that helped abate her morning sickness. Maybe he was just being a stereotypical clueless male.

Either way, she couldn't keep this secret forever. Before she knew it, she'd be sporting a baby bump—and that would be something Cole would notice for sure.

When the waitress was gone, Cole reached into his pocket and pulled out a small paper bag. "I have something for you," Cole said, "I meant to wrap it, but…"

"For as long as I've known you, you've never wrapped a present." She shook her head, amusement in her features. "I don't think you even know where we keep the Scotch tape."

He thought a second. "Okay, you've got me there. Where do we keep the Scotch tape?"

"The end drawer in the kitchen. The scissors are in there too, by the way."

He nodded. "I'll remember that for next time. I promise."

She bit her lip, not wanting to spoil the date by reminding him that they were going to sell the house, divvy up their possessions, and then he would have his own place for Scotch tape, and she would have her own. Because a part of her didn't want to be reminded that soon, they'd be living separate lives. She touched the blank spot on her left hand, a reminder she no longer wore her ring. Cole, however, still wore his gold band. As far as she knew, he hadn't taken it off once in ten years.

Instead of the dose of reality, she said, "And the wrapping paper is in the hall closet."

He smiled. "I'll remember that, too, Em. Now, open your gift."

She opened the bag and peeked inside to find a

thick leather-bound journal and a silver pen. She drew them out, admiring the weight and quality of the gifts. "They're...beautiful."

He gestured toward the book. "The journal was hand-made by Beatrice Wickham. She lives on the other side of the lake and has a little corner in the hardware store where she sells her handmade creations. She remembered you and said this would be perfect for, and I quote, 'that little girl who was always writing those stories.'"

Emily ran her hand over the stitched cover. A long crimson ribbon hung from the inside of the book, just waiting to mark her place. Her heart softened at the thoughtfulness of the gift. It was simple and special, not just because it had been handmade by a local artisan, but because it had been crafted in the one place on earth that meant so much to Emily. The same place that had been instrumental in the new direction she was taking with her life. "It's beautiful, Cole." Though the adjective, even repeated a second time, seemed inadequate.

Cole nodded toward the book. "Open it up."

She did as he asked and found an inscription on the first page. Cole's familiar slanted handwriting, all angles and precision, like the man himself, filled the space.

Use this book and pen to write the stories in your heart. Let it take you from once upon a time to happily ever after. And maybe, in the process, you can find your own happily ever after, too.

He hadn't signed his name, or used the word *Love*. She wondered if it was because he didn't want to push her or because he no longer felt that way about her. Either way, the gift touched her.

Because Cole had listened.

For almost ten years, she'd complained that he didn't listen, didn't pay attention, didn't engage. Now he was asking her where they kept the tape and writing words that encouraged her to pursue her dreams. Why now? Why after she had decided the marriage was over, and had steeled herself to say goodbye?

She raised her gaze and cursed the tears brimming in her eyes. "Why didn't you ever do this before?"

He crossed his hands on the table and let out a long breath. "Because I didn't realize that helping me go after my dreams came at the cost of yours. For a long time, I've fooled myself into thinking that you were happy, that you wanted all the same things I did. But now I know you sacrificed your dreams for mine. I'm sorry it took me so long to figure that out."

"It's okay, Cole." She placed her palm on top of the book and imagined the words that would fill it in the weeks ahead. She'd sit on the porch of the inn or on the dock and scribble her ideas and snippets of scenes. It was the perfect vehicle to inspire and encourage her writing. "Thank you very much."

The waitress returned with their drinks. Cole raised his glass toward hers. "To new beginnings."

"To new beginnings," she echoed, and clinked against his. If he only knew the new beginning growing inside her right now.

A part of her felt horrible for keeping the secret from him. He deserved to know about the baby, even if he didn't want it. And maybe if he saw how determined she was to move forward as a single mom, he'd give up this hope that she wanted to go back to the life they'd had before. It was past time to tell Cole about the baby.

"You have that look again," Cole said. "The furrowed brow. The worry in your eyes. What's up?"

That was the problem with being married to a man for ten years. He noticed when she wasn't acting like herself. She tried to work up the courage to tell him, then chickened out at the last second when she saw the waitress approaching with their burgers. "Why don't we talk about it after dinner?"

Cole agreed, and as they dived into the juicy burgers, they talked about everything and nothing. The kind of easygoing conversations they used to have back in their college days, mingled with a lot of laughs. Cole filled her in on some updates about some of the people she knew at the company, and she told him the latest gossip from the wives. They traded golf tips, reminisced about a favorite restaurant that had shut its doors, and in general, acted like an ordinary couple.

All the while, the specter of Emily's secret waited on the sidelines. Once she told him, it would change everything.

When they were done, Cole paid the waitress, adding a generous tip, then took Emily's hand as they left the diner. The move felt so natural, so right. She leaned against his arm as they stepped out into the chilly late-November night. Without a word, Cole released her, and instead drew her close, shielding Emily from the cold. She had missed the simple touches between a couple, the way Cole could read her mind and provide what she needed at the moment she needed it most. Yet another sign he was finally paying attention.

"That was nice," she said.

"Very nice." He pressed a gentle, easy kiss against her forehead, and Emily thought that she couldn't have imagined a more perfect night with her husband. The warm comfort of being with someone who knew her filled Emily, and she began to believe that maybe they could right this sinking ship after all.

The only shadow that lingered at the end of the night was the secret in her belly. She pressed a hand over her abdomen and sent up a silent prayer that maybe Cole would be as excited about their child as she was.

Cole opened the door for her and she slid into the warmth of the rental car. He held her hand the whole way back to the inn, glancing over at her from time to time, as if to make sure she was real. Unspoken tension filled the dark space of the car, the tension that came with knowing they were both going back to a place with beds, a married couple who hadn't been together in a long, long time. Every once in a while, Cole would squeeze her hand, telling her he knew the same thing.

This could end in a sweet, delicious way, with her in his arms, in his bed. Oh, how she wanted that. She'd tell him later, she decided. After just a little more of this, a few more minutes in this perfect bubble.

They pulled into the driveway, and Cole turned off the car, then turned to Emily in the dark. "Let's have more nights like that. From here on out, at least once a week. I think we just forgot how to connect, Emily. If we can start connecting again, then maybe we can get back to where we were."

"Or get to where we are going."

He nodded, then reached up and cupped her jaw. She leaned into the touch, drifted a kiss across his palm.

"Wherever that is, I want to go with you." Cole closed the distance between them and kissed her, softly at first, then shifting to a harder, hungrier embrace. Desire slid through her like hot syrup on pancakes, pooling in her gut, overriding her common sense. She knew Cole's body, and oh, how he knew hers.

Hot need spiked inside her, for the way he could make her body sing, for the touch of his fingers inside her, his kisses running down her body, over her breasts. One kiss, one touch, and she could have that, just one more time. What would it hurt?

Before she could think twice, Emily surged into her husband, driven by a desire too long unmet. She tangled her fingers in Cole's hair, drawing him halfway across the car. He groaned and crushed her to him, one hand sneaking between them in a hot hurry, sliding under her blouse, tugging out of her jeans, and then his hand was on her skin, fingers slipping under the band of her bra, sliding up, over her breast, cupping it while his thumb traced a ravenous circle around her nipple.

She fumbled with the buttons on his shirt, trying to undo them while she arched against his touch, distracted by the magic Cole's fingers created. Then his shirt was undone, untucked, and her hands were on his chest, but it wasn't enough, not nearly enough. She wanted all of him, and wanted him now. "In...inside?"

"Yeah." The word tore from his throat. Cole gave Emily one last heated look of longing, then he drew away, sprinting out of the car and opening her door just as she got her shirt pulled down. They hurried into the inn like two teenagers out past curfew and rushed up the stairs to Emily's room.

As soon as they were inside, Cole spun her around and pressed her against the wall, shutting the door with his foot. His hands slid under her shirt, tugging it over her head and tossing it to the side. "God, Emily, you are beautiful."

She smiled. "Thank you."

He cupped her face with his hands and met her gaze. "I've never stopped wanting you."

The temptation to lose herself in this moment, in Cole's eyes and his touch, washed over her. She wanted him, wanted the magic they'd once had.

Even if it wasn't real.

That realization iced her desire. If she took tonight one step further with Cole, she'd be creating a fictional moment of closeness. That wasn't fair or right for either of them. If they made love, it had to be for all the right reasons—and with all the cards on the table.

This wasn't some one-night stand or a senseless fling with a stranger she'd never see again. No, this was her husband, and she was carrying his baby.

Emily drew in a fortifying breath and put her hands on Cole's chest. "Before we do anything, I have something to tell you."

He covered her hands with his. "If it's how good that burger was, I think it can wait." He started to kiss her again, but she pulled away.

"No, Cole. Please. This is something much more important."

He shifted back. "What do you need to tell me, Em?"

Now that the moment had arrived, Emily hesitated. She knew, for better or worse, that the next two words would change everything between them. Forever.

"I'm pregnant."

It took a solid minute for the words to sink into Cole's brain. They echoed in the quiet space, in his head, and his mind spiraled back through time, to another night, a hot summer evening when he'd gone over to the house on the hill and begged Emily for a second chance. They'd split a bottle of wine, and before he knew it, they were back in the bedroom and she was back in his arms, and he wasn't thinking about pregnancy or anything else but Emily.

"I thought you were on the pill," he said, and even as the words came out of his mouth, he had a feeling that was the wrong first response to such a monumental statement. But he didn't know what else to say or how to react to this.

A child. That was the one thing Cole had never wanted. A chance he'd never wanted to take. He'd told Emily someday they'd have kids because he kept thinking the further he got in life, the better chance there was that he would change his mind, but he hadn't. A little late to realize it, though.

"I was on the pill. But then we broke up and…" She shrugged. "I didn't see the point in taking it if I wasn't having sex."

"Except for that night."

She nodded. "I didn't think one night could…well, I mean, I knew it could, but I wasn't thinking about that then."

"Neither of us were."

He took a step back and ran a hand through his hair. "Pregnant?" Maybe if he repeated the word it would become real, something he could get his head around.

She nodded. "Three months along."

He kept waiting for that rush of joy, of expectation, to come over him, but it was as if Cole's guts had gone cold. No emotions filled him, nothing but shock. He nodded once, then looked at Emily. "What are you going to do about it?"

The light in her eyes dimmed, replaced by a flash of hurt, followed by the flames of anger. "What am I going to *do about it?* Trust me, Cole, you don't need to worry about that. I didn't tell you about the baby because I wanted your money or your support or anything at all from you. I'm having this baby—" as she spoke, her hand covered her belly with a protective touch "—by myself. And I am just fine with that."

"Emily, this is our child—"

"A child you never wanted. We had this conversation just the other day, and you said you didn't want to have kids, not now. Maybe not ever. I *do* want kids. I've wanted kids for a long time, and I'm okay with doing this on my own."

"We're separated. We still might end up divorced. And you think it's wise to bring a child into that?" What was she thinking? How could she do this?

Then his gaze dropped to her belly, and he realized he'd been just as much of a part of the decision. He should have stopped, should have thought. But when it came to Emily, sometimes his reason deserted him.

Now Emily was *pregnant*. The entire thing still seemed surreal, impossible.

"I didn't plan it that way, Cole. It just happened. Babies grow up in single-parent homes all the time and do just fine." She crossed to the door and pulled it open. "Look, I don't want to argue. Why don't we just get some sleep and talk about this tomorrow."

"Is this why you left? So I wouldn't find out?"

She exhaled. "I don't know. I just wanted to go somewhere else. Somewhere to think. The inn seemed like the best place to do that."

"And when were you planning on coming back?"

She knew the answer, because it had always been there, in the back of her head. She'd never admitted it out loud or to herself. Yes, she had run away, to keep from having this very conversation with Cole. To avoid the hurt. "Not until after the baby was born."

"And after you divorced me?"

She nodded. She'd thought it would be so much easier, cleaner, to end her marriage and begin this new life hundreds of mile from Cole. A cowardly move. "I was afraid, Cole, that you would try to talk me out of the divorce."

"Like I have been for the past few days."

"I just didn't want to be standing here, like we are right now, saying the things we're saying." She shook her head. Her eyes burned. Her heart ached.

"Am I that horrible of a man that you would feel like you have to leave the state to divorce me and have my child?" His voice broke, sharpened by hurt.

"No, Cole, you're not horrible at all." She clutched the door. "And that's the problem. I knew if I stayed around you, I'd fall for you all over again. And I can't do that. Not again."

"Then I'll make this easy for you, Emily." He held her gaze for a long, bittersweet moment, then Cole turned on his heel and left the room. A few minutes later, she heard the door of his room shut, followed by the sound of the front door closing, and then his rental car starting, leaving.

Cole was gone.

And even though it was what Emily had wanted

and knew would happen, the sound of him leaving sent a sharp blade through her heart, severing the last strand of hope.

CHAPTER TWELVE

THE MORNING DAWNED, bright and cheery. Emily rolled over and stretched in bed, lazy, warm. Then her head cleared, the sleepiness disappeared, and she realized two things.

It was the day before Thanksgiving. And Cole had left.

What had she expected? Some big teary, emotional moment when she told him about the baby? A Hollywood moment of clarity, where he realized he wanted the baby and her, and they all went off into the sunset, happily ever after?

Nothing had changed. Cole didn't want children, and just because she was having a baby didn't mean he'd changed his mind.

She wanted to pull the covers up, stay in bed and wallow in the hurt and regret, but that would only make it worse. After a while, she rolled out of bed, pulled on a robe, bypassing her laptop and heading downstairs. On the landing, Emily paused and peered out the window at the inn's driveway, half hoping to see Cole's rental car.

But it was gone, just like it had been last night. So was Joe's car. Martin's van was in the drive, and she could hear the sound of pipes clanging in one of the bathrooms. Emily swallowed her disappointment. She'd known this was coming, asked for it to be over and told herself she was ready for the finality of her marriage, but that didn't make it any easier to take or accept.

"Good morning," Carol said when Emily entered the kitchen. Harper got to her feet and wagged her tail. "How are you feeling?"

"Terrible. But not nauseous." Emily let out a little laugh. "I finally have a morning without morning sickness, and it's a day when all I want to do is go back to bed and cry."

"Oh, Emily, I'm sorry. Do you want to talk about it?"

"Yes. No." She spied the overnighted envelope on the table, delivered that morning. "Yes."

Then she dropped into a chair at the kitchen table and poured out her heart to Carol, just like she used to when she was a teenager, and her parents were fighting and all Emily wanted was someone to listen to her and tell her it would all be okay.

She started at the beginning, telling Carol about how her marriage to Cole had started well, then slowly eroded. How she'd still had hope. How the past few days had only increased that hope and made her think maybe Cole would change his mind and want a family like she did.

"Now I'm alone, and he's gone and..." Emily sighed. "I know I'm going to be okay, but right now, it doesn't feel that way at all."

Carol's hand covered Emily's. "It'll be fine, honey. I promise."

Down the road, yes, Emily knew she had become stronger over the past few months and would, indeed, be fine, but the getting from here to there seemed an impossibly long, painful road. "He's gone, Carol. It's what I expected, and what I told him I wanted, but…"

"You also expected him to stay."

Tears rushed to Emily's eyes, spilled onto her cheeks. "Yes."

"You know, it's okay to believe in fairy tales, Emily. You always did, and I hope you always do."

Emily scoffed. "Why? They never come true."

"Maybe not. But believing that the impossible can happen is what gives our days that little bit of magic. And magic is what makes for the best stories. Don't you remember telling me that once?"

Emily smiled. She'd been a little girl when she'd said that to Carol, explaining why she loved to read fairy tales, and how when she grew up, she was going to write her own. "Are you telling me to add a happy ending to my book?"

"And to your life." Carol's fingers squeezed Emily's. "There's still magic left to be found."

The thought warmed Emily. Could there still be magic, for her? For Cole? She wasn't sure if there was any left between them, but for the first time since she'd heard his car leave the drive, she believed there'd be a happy ending for all of them. Somehow.

Her stomach rumbled, prompting Emily to head for the fridge. She reached for the orange juice, then noticed the empty middle shelf. "Carol, you don't have a turkey." She turned back. "Aren't we having Thanksgiving here?"

"To be honest, I've gotten into the habit of not making future plans." Carol sighed. "I just don't know what to do with this place. All these repairs are great, and I truly appreciate them, but…"

"You don't know whether to hold on or let go." Emily's features softened. "I can relate to that."

Carol rose and drew Emily into a hug. The embrace wrapped Emily with the same warmth and acceptance she always found at this inn, and with this woman, who was so much like a mother figure to her. "Then let's hold on together," Carol said. "At least for Thanksgiving. Because we have an awful lot to be grateful for."

Emily thought of the miracle growing inside her. "We do indeed."

Carol ran a hand through her hair, then looked around the kitchen. "Well, if we're going to have a proper Thanksgiving around here, I need to get cracking. There's a million things to do. I need to bring down the holiday dishes and—"

Emily put a hand on Carol's. "Why don't you give me a list and let me go to the store for you?"

"Are you sure?"

Emily nodded. "It'll be nice to get out for a while." And away from the reminders of Cole.

"I sure appreciate it." Carol drew a piece of paper out of the desk drawer, then started making a list. "You buy it…I'll cook it."

Emily laughed. "Deal."

The sound of clanking pipes came from up above them, followed by a muffled thud and a curse. "Uh-oh. I don't think the plumbing is cooperating with Martin. I bet he could use a little help. Maybe you should offer to go up there and help him." Emily winked.

A shy smile spread across Carol's face. "That's a darn good idea."

Emily grabbed a quick breakfast, then got ready

and headed to the store. She parked outside the small grocery that passed for a supermarket in town, then grabbed a cart and started making her way through the aisles, checking off the items on Carol's list. It kept her from thinking about Cole and her future—a future that wouldn't include him.

She paused in the books and magazine aisle and allowed herself a moment to dream, to picture her novel on that shelf. Maybe not today or tomorrow, but someday, she vowed, she'd see that happen.

Her stomach cramped. The first time, she brushed the feeling off. She'd done a lot today, what with the driving and shopping and yanking that heavy turkey out of the refrigerator case. After several days of doing nothing more strenuous than working at a computer, maybe her body was complaining.

Then a second cramp, followed fast on its heels by a third. Emily fumbled in her purse for her cell phone, and dialed Carol's number. No answer. She'd probably left her phone downstairs while she helped Martin. Emily dialed the number for the inn. No answer again.

Panic rushed through Emily. What if something was wrong with the baby? Suddenly, she wanted someone here, someone to hold her hand, keep her calm. Reassure her that it would all be okay. Someone strong and sensible and composed.

She skimmed her thumb over the contacts list and then took a deep breath and called the last person in the world who wanted to deal with her or this baby.

Cole.

Cole sat at his desk and tried like hell to listen to Doug as he talked about the upcoming product launch.

Any other day, he would have been asking questions, analyzing charts of age data, engaged and invested in the process.

Not today. Not one ounce of the usual excitement rose in his chest. In fact, he only heard about every other word Doug said because Cole's mind was on Emily.

His wife. The mother of his unborn child.

A child.

The word sent a combination of anticipation and fear rocketing through him. Even now, hours after Emily had told him, he wanted to both shout the news from the rooftops and run for the hills. He was a walking, talking clichéd contradiction. Him, the man who had always been decisive and driven, derailed by a human the size of a pencil eraser.

"Cole? Did you hear me?"

Cole jerked his attention back to the reports in front of him. "I'm sorry. What did you say?"

"The mid-Atlantic division is predicting a forty percent increase in sales over last year. Customer preorders are through the roof, and media buzz is strong and positive. Your idea for the screen substitution was brilliant and bought us just enough time. The Japanese supplier should be sending their first shipment next week. I think it's going to be a smooth product rollout, all in all."

"Good. Good." Cole's mind went back to Emily. What was she doing right now? Probably cursing his name three ways to the moon. Not that he could blame her. He'd ducked out of there, using the same old excuse about work. He cleared his throat and refocused on Doug's face. "How about the mid-Atlantic? What's the report from there?"

Doug chuckled. "You must be dreaming about turkey and pie or something. Did you hear a word I just said?"

"I heard turkey and pie." Pie made him think of Emily again. Of that first awful pie she'd made him when they were newlyweds, of the late-night apple pie they'd shared and the potpie they'd made. "Uh, why would I be thinking of turkey?"

"Because Thanksgiving is tomorrow." Doug shook his head, then got to his feet. "Why don't I just email you the report? We can talk after the holiday."

"Sorry. Just having trouble getting my mind back on work after being on vacation."

"Totally understandable." Doug grinned. "Must have been a hell of a vacation to get you distracted. Wherever that place is, I want to go."

"The Gingerbread Inn," Cole said softly. "It's like one of those places you read about in a book."

Doug lingered by the door. "You going back?"

The question hit Cole hard. Was he going back? Or staying here? Returning to that empty condo with its single plate and single fork and single glass? Or going back to the big house on the hill, which brimmed with priceless artwork and antiques, yet still felt as empty as a tomb? Or going back to the run-down inn by the lake, where the sunshine warmed his back and good home cooking filled his belly? Where he'd had his best sleep in years. And where the woman he had always loved slept with their baby growing inside her.

"I don't know," Cole said. "I'm not sure there's still a vacancy for me."

Doug laughed. "You're Cole Watson. You built this company from your kitchen table to this." He gave an expansive wave. "When has something that simple stood in your way?"

After Doug was gone, Cole sat in his office and looked around the room. He'd done what Doug had said, built his company from an idea he'd had in that cramped New York apartment, to this. A global leader, an innovator, all those buzzwords people threw out.

He'd worked so hard, spent so many hours here, because he thought those words mattered. Thought all of *this*—the walls, the employees, the profits—mattered. He'd kept reaching for a goal he couldn't see, a goal that moved every time he approached it, because he thought it would fill that driving need deep inside him to succeed. To have it all.

He had the luxury cars. The custom-made mansion on a hill. The fat bank account. What he didn't have was a wife and a marriage.

Everything here was stuff. Inanimate objects. He'd dedicated his life to—

Nothing that mattered, not in the long run.

Damn. How could such a smart man get it so abysmally wrong?

There was a double tap on his door, and Irene poked her head in his office. "Cole? Emily called. She's been trying to reach you."

He yanked his cell out of the holster. "Damn. I had the sound off while I was in the meeting. Let me call her back."

"No, you need to leave." She bustled into the room, grabbed his overcoat off the coat tree and pressed it into his hands. "I already called a car service to take you to the airport. Emily is in the hospital."

"In the hospital?" Cole's heart stopped. He stared at

Irene, absorbing the words. His heart didn't beat. His lungs didn't breathe. His brain didn't function. He heard the words again and—

Then he ran.

Emily shivered in the room, even though the stark white hospital room was kept at a warmer than normal temp. She drew the covers up to her chest and flicked off the television. Only a few channels, and not much to watch on any of them. Her hand went to her abdomen, and she sent up a silent prayer, then closed her eyes and lay back against the firm pillow.

The door opened, but she kept her eyes shut, sure it was the nurse back again to check on her roommate, an older woman given to pushing the nurse button every five minutes. But when she didn't hear any sound from the space next to her, Emily opened her eyes and found Cole standing there, his face ashen, sweat beading on his brow. "Are you okay?" she asked.

"Are you okay?" he said at the same time.

Her heart leaped at the sight of him and the concern on his face. "I'm fine, or I will be. I'm sorry for calling you. I couldn't get ahold of Carol and I didn't have Joe's number and I was scared and…" She shook her head. Calling him had been a mistake. She never should have told Irene she was in the hospital. "It was ridiculous to think you could do anything from all the way in New York. I ended up having the store manager drive me—"

"Is everything okay?"

She nodded. "Just a little preterm labor. The baby's jumping the gun. It's nothing to worry about. Happens all the time. I just have to take it easy for a little while."

Cole exhaled. "Good. I'm glad you're okay."

She noticed he didn't mention the baby. God, why was she such a fool? Calling him, thinking an emergency would change anything? "You can go back to New York. I'm sorry."

He was by her bedside in three fast strides. "Number one, never apologize for calling me when you need me. Regardless of how things go between us, I want you to know that you can always rely on me."

The words *regardless of how things go between us* filled Emily with a bone-deep sadness. For all her talk about divorce, she'd realized in the past few days that a part of her didn't want a divorce at all. She wanted to work things out with Cole, for the two of them to celebrate their baby's arrival and find a new marriage, one where they were there for each other, rather than running along parallel but diverging tracks.

She wanted her husband, damn it.

"Number two," he went on, "if you are sick or in the hospital or anything like that, I want to know about it. I will always watch out for you and care for you, Emily. No matter what."

"Okay. I'll remember that." She shifted against the pillows and sat up. The sheet slipped down, exposing the ugly hospital gown underneath. She was sure her hair was a mess, her makeup smeared and for the first time in a long time, Emily wished she had looked in a mirror before Cole came.

Like a nice hairstyle and neat eyeliner would change anything. She needed to face reality. He hadn't changed his mind and she hadn't changed hers.

"Thanks," she said. "Anyway—"

"I'm not finished." Cole took another step forward.

He stood alongside the bed now, his hip within touching distance of her hand. A part of her wished he would sit on the edge of the bed and just talk to her. Like he had in the past few days.

Then she remembered his reaction to the pregnancy and told herself to stop wishing for things that would never be.

"Number three," Cole said, "I'm staying with you until this baby is born. If there are complications—"

"Nothing I can't handle, Cole. I don't need your help. I can stay with Carol until the baby comes. She could use the extra set of hands, I'm sure." Emily didn't add that she'd been put on modified bed rest for the next several weeks, to stop the early labor contractions. The doctor had told her to reduce stress, not to lift anything heavy and to rest. So far, she wasn't doing well at two out of three of those.

"At least let me hire a nurse to—"

"No. I'll be fine." She didn't want his money or his pity, or anything other than him. Unfortunately, that was the one thing he wasn't offering.

He let out a breath. "Why won't you let me take care of you?"

She leaned forward in the bed and faced Cole. "Because it's not your job anymore." Then she leaned over, tugged out the envelope in her purse and showed him the papers she had had overnighted to her this morning. If she couldn't stick to her resolve to be done with Cole when she was around him, then she had to do something concrete about ending her marriage. "I called my lawyer and he got the papers together for me to file for divorce."

Cole's blue eyes filled with hurt, then the hurt gave way to an icy coldness. "Is that what you really want?"

"Yes." God, she wished he would just leave the room. She wanted to cry, to be alone, to face the fact that her husband didn't want the baby—or the life—that she so desperately did.

"What if something happens to you or…" He waved at her stomach.

That gesture and his avoidance of the word *baby* told her everything she needed to know. "*We* are no longer your concern. Goodbye, Cole." Then she turned over and curled into a ball. She held her tears until she heard the soft click of the door.

Cole didn't answer his phone. He didn't talk to Joe or Carol. He didn't go back to New York.

He had the driver bring him to the inn, then he headed straight out to the gazebo in the back. Cole ripped off his suit jacket, tossing it on the ground, heedless of the price tag of the custom-made suit. Then he started tearing out the old posts from the rotted outbuilding, yanking, kicking, doing whatever it took to wrench the ruined posts out of place. Joe brought down the new wood and laid it on the deck of the gazebo without a word. He returned with a toolbox, laid that beside the wood. Cole kept on working, taking his frustrations out on the decrepit gazebo. After several trips back and forth with supplies, Joe finally went back to the inn, sensing that Cole wanted to be alone.

Except that was the whole problem. He didn't *want* to be alone. He wanted to be with Emily. And she wanted nothing to do with him.

He'd sent a car and driver to the hospital to drive her

back to the inn. Hired a nurse to stay with her. Emily
had dismissed them both, Cole had been told, and opted
to take a taxi instead. When he heard the car's tires on
the gravel drive, he stopped working. But Emily walked
into the inn and never even looked his way.

What the hell was he doing here? Why didn't he just
give up already?

"Here. Take a break." Joe dangled a beer in front
of Cole.

Cole shook his head. "I gotta get this done."

"No, you gotta take a break before you have a heart
attack."

Cole wiped the sweat off his brow. He was breathing heavy and his arms ached. It wasn't the good, job-
well-done ache he'd had over the past few days. No,
this was the pain of a self-induced beating by carpen-
try. Damn, he'd screwed everything up. What was that
about good intentions? His hadn't led him anywhere
he wanted to go.

He let out a sigh, then put down his sledgehammer
and took a seat beside Joe on the floor of the gazebo.
"What am I doing here?"

"Damned if I know." Joe took a sip of his beer. "If
I were you, I'd just leave. She doesn't want you here."

Cole cursed. What did Joe know? Where did he get
off saying that, anyway? "She's just confused."

"Dude, she's not confused. She knows what she
wants. *You're* the one who's confused."

"I'm not goddamn leaving and I'm not goddamned
confused."

"Then leave."

"I told you I'm not—"

Joe leaned in with a grin on his face that said his

reverse psychology had had the desired effect. "If you aren't going to leave," Joe said, "then you better damned well start to fight."

Cole took a long sip of beer and thought about the past few days and the river of contradictory emotions running through him ever since Emily had told him about the pregnancy. "I just don't think I'm ready for kids."

"Hell, who is? They are the most inconvenient creatures in the world, but I hear they're pretty cool to have."

"Yeah, for some people." Cole put the beer aside and got to his feet. He wanted to take Joe's advice and fight for his marriage, but even if he did, where would that leave them? Together, but with a baby on the way. A child, who would look to Cole for love and guidance. For him to be not just a father, but a *good* father.

The one thing he had no idea how to do.

"I gotta get back to work. Sooner I get these projects finished, the sooner I can go back to New York."

"What's stopping you from leaving now? Just hiring this out?"

"I made a commitment to finishing. I keep those commitments." Okay, so that was a lie. He was here because he wanted to make sure Emily was okay.

"Is that why you don't want to get divorced? Because you committed to finishing the marriage?" Joe took a step forward. "Or because you don't want to lose the best woman to ever come along in your life?"

"Will you just let me finish this gazebo? And quit with the questions?" They were the same questions Cole had asked himself and didn't have any answers for then or now.

Joe shook his head. "You are being an idiot, Cole.

You're a smart man, hell, a genius some would say the way you built that business up from nothing. But right now you are being the biggest idiot on the East Coast." Then he grabbed his beer and headed up the hill.

CHAPTER THIRTEEN

PROPPED UP AGAINST the pillows on her bed, Emily sat with her laptop open on her lap and the book file waiting for her input. The packet from her lawyer sat beside her on the floral comforter, also waiting. All it required was a signature, and then the divorce was in process.

Even after everything, she had yet to sign the paper. She still had hope, damn it.

Because she'd seen a little of the old Cole in the past few days. For a long time, she'd given up, thinking the man she remembered from those early days had been sucked into a demanding job and a never-ending drive toward success. But the Cole who had fixed the steps and made the pie and given her the journal was the Cole she had fallen in love with years ago.

And damn it all, the same Cole she still loved.

She went to the window and watched him working on the gazebo like a man possessed. When he'd left the hospital earlier, she had fully expected him to go back to New York. And yet he was here.

Why?

The day had edged into late afternoon, the sun sinking lower and lower in the sky. A cold front was moving in, according to the weather reports. The nice fall days would be over, and soon winter would clamp its snowy grip over the inn. Tomorrow was Thanksgiving, one of her favorite holidays of the year, and the first one in forever that would be filled with homemade food, not a catered turkey. It was the kind of back-to-basics life that she wanted for her child.

A life a thousand miles away from the one Cole wanted.

And that, in the end, was the reality she had yet to accept.

Emily drew on a thick sweater and went downstairs. Carol was sitting by the fireplace, curled up in a chair and reading a book. "How are you feeling?" she asked.

"Much better. I think I just needed some rest."

"Well, you can get plenty of that here." Carol put her book on the side table. "How are you doing emotionally?"

"I don't know." Emily's gaze went to the window. It was getting too dark to see all the way past the trees to the gazebo, but she suspected Cole was still out there, working. "I have a lot of decisions to make."

Carol got to her feet and grabbed an anorak jacket off the hook on the wall. "Why don't you go for a walk before dinner? A little fresh air always makes everything clearer. This is probably one of the last nice nights you'll have around here before the snow starts flying."

"Don't you need help prepping for Thanksgiving tomorrow? I should—"

"You are not supposed to be doing any such thing, missy. You worry about that precious little gift right there—" Carol gestured to Emily's abdomen "—and nothing else. Okay?"

Emily drew Carol into a tight hug. "Thank you."

"No, *thank you*," Carol said, her voice thick with emotion. "You've given me back the one thing I lost."

"What's that?"

Carol drew back and cupped Emily's face with a tender, maternal touch. This was why Emily had always been so drawn to the warm and giving innkeeper. She was more like a mother to Emily than the woman who shared Emily's DNA.

"Hope," Carol said. "I was ready to give up on this place before you came here."

"I couldn't let you do that," Emily said. "This place is home to me."

"No, honey, that's where you're wrong. This place isn't home. Home is where the people you love are. Whether they're in New York or Paris or the Gingerbread Inn." Carol drew the coat closed and pressed a kiss to Emily's forehead. "Now go for that walk."

Emily thanked Carol, then headed outside. She didn't hear any sounds of work and figured Cole had left after all. Just as well, she told herself, if only so she wouldn't give room to the disappointment churning inside her.

Emily walked down the crushed stone path that led from the inn to the lake, her way guided by little landscape lights. It looked almost magical, with the tiny lights against the stark darkness.

"It's so peaceful out here, isn't it?"

She turned at the sound of Cole's voice. Not startled. A part of her knew he hadn't left. Had hoped he had stayed. Because of her and the baby? Or just because he wanted to win the argument of hiring a nursemaid to look after her? "Yes, it is."

"Mind if I walk with you?" he asked.

"Not at all."

They started toward the dock, then detoured to walk the edge of the lake, traversing the path that the teenage lovers had probably taken all those years ago. Except this time, Emily wasn't running away with Cole like the teenagers had.

No, she was finally going to tell him it was over. She had tried, over and over, to make this work. But he had yet to open up to her, nor did he have any interest in raising their child with her. Those two things gave her the answers she needed. Answers she needed to accept once and for all.

"First, I want to apologize," he said. "I reacted badly to you telling me about the baby. You took me by surprise. I never expected—"

"That we'd make love and I could get pregnant?"

"Yeah. Guess I need to repeat high school health class." He walked a while longer, a tall man silhouetted in the dark. "How did we get to this point, Emily? How did we let it go so wrong for so long, and never do anything about it?"

"I don't know, Cole. I really don't." She looked out at the lake, twinkling under the light cast by the crescent moon. She thought of all those dreams she'd had years before, and how far away she'd got from those wishes. "When I was younger, the other girls and I stood here at the edge of the lake and made a promise to each other because of these rocks we'd found. Remember the one I showed you?"

He nodded.

"We thought those rocks were a sign. Of what, I'm not sure, but we decided that day to promise that we would always follow our dreams. I made the promise, and then I didn't keep it. Yeah, I wrote some in high school and college, but once we got married and you started making enough money that I didn't have to work, I didn't go back to writing. I kept finding other things to do, excuses, really, for why I couldn't write. It wasn't just about being afraid of rejection, it was about—" she let out a breath "—failing. If I didn't try, then I couldn't fail, you know what I mean?"

He let out a short, dry laugh. "More than you know."

"Then Melissa died, and we all got these letters from her. I realized that my life was ticking by and I was desperately unhappy, but I hadn't done anything about it. I just kept waiting for things to change, instead of taking the leap and making the change myself."

She had done the same thing with her marriage. Letting it fall apart rather than confronting the issues—and possibly failing. Her inaction had fed into her greatest fear, and now the dreams she'd had when she walked down the aisle with Cole had died.

"And those changes are what brought you here," Cole said.

She nodded. "I thought it was appropriate to go back to the place where the dream began. Plus the inn has served as a nice, quiet retreat, a good place to write my book, to think and to get away."

"From me." The two words were exhaled on a curt note.

"That was the plan." She gave him a crooked smile. "I never imagined you'd follow me."

"I never imagined you'd leave." He took her hand in his. "I guess I thought that this whole separation would blow over, and things would go back to the way they were. I never realized how unhappy you were."

"I should have spoken up more." She'd let fear rule

her choices for too long. If there was one thing she'd learned in the months on her own, it was that she was stronger and able to weather more storms than she thought.

"I should have paid better attention to you and to us," Cole said. "I kept my focus on the wrong things. On the company, instead of on our relationship. I looked around my office this morning and realized all of that was stuff. Things that I had worked to achieve. At the cost of our marriage." He sighed. "That was too high of a price to pay for a better bottom line."

Hearing him say that filled her with a thrill. Her heart had never given up on Cole. Still, her brain raised a caution flag. They had a baby on the way, and that introduced a whole other dynamic. Cole had yet to talk about the baby. It was as if he thought ignoring her pregnancy would keep them from having to deal with it. In a few months, Sweet Pea would be here and there'd be no ignoring him or her then. "I guess we were both looking in the wrong direction. Now I'm just looking ahead, to the baby coming."

He started walking some more, his shoes making impressions in the not-yet-frozen earth. "You asked me why I didn't want kids. I kept telling you, and myself, that it was all about it being the right time, but that's not it."

She waited, afraid to press, afraid of what she might hear next. When he didn't continue, she said, "Then what was it, Cole?"

"I don't talk about my past, Em." He ran a hand through his hair. "With anyone."

"You told Joe."

"Kinda hard not to. We've been friends forever, and

he was at my house a few times when I was younger. He saw what went on." Cole cursed and shook his head. "Let's just say it wasn't pretty."

She swung around in front of him and took his hands. "Tell me, Cole. I'm your wife. I should be your best friend, too. That means knowing the good and the bad about you."

"Do you know why I never told you about my childhood?"

She shook her head.

"Because I'm *ashamed* of it, Emily." His voice sharpened, rose. "I never wanted you to be anything but proud of me. I'm supposed to be the man, the one who leads the family, takes on the challenges—"

She cut off his words with a soft hand against his cheek. "You don't always have to be the strong one, Cole."

His features crumpled, and he turned away. She let him go, sensing that the conversation had brought up something Cole had kept tucked away for a long, long time. A loon called out from the other side of the lake, and a fish flopped its tail against the water. Then Cole turned back, and when he spoke again, his voice had gone hoarse. "I don't know any other way to be, Em."

Her heart broke for her strong, smart, driven husband, who kept all those vulnerable parts of himself behind a tough shell. A facade. "Just be yourself, Cole. That's all I ever wanted."

"I don't even know if I know how to do that. I have no map, no guidebook. I know how to be the best at school or work, but I haven't a clue how to be the best parent."

"Most people don't, Cole. You figure it out as you go along."

"What if I figure it out wrong?" He ran a hand through his hair, then gestured toward a large rock at the edge of the water. They sat down together, facing the lake. Cole took Emily's hand in both of his and rubbed her fingers, providing warmth, protection from the cold.

"Tell me," she repeated, softer this time. "Please."

Maybe then she'd understand him. Maybe then she'd know enough to move forward, in one direction or the other.

Cole paused for so long, his gaze on the soft ripples in the water, that she was afraid he wasn't going to say anything at all. He picked up a handful of rocks and flung one at the lake. It skipped twice, then sank beneath the surface. "My mom started drinking when I was a little boy. She was in a car accident, and I think she drank because of the pain from that. Maybe she drank because it sucked to live with my father. I'm not sure. We never talked about it. But she stopped being any kind of mother to me long before I was in kindergarten."

"Oh, Cole, that's awful."

He shrugged, as if it hadn't bothered him, but she could see the pain in his eyes, in the hunch of his shoulders. To live without a mother at such a young age, no one to kiss his scrapes or tell him bedtime stories, had to have been incredibly tough. Her tough husband, made that way by a childhood as rough as cement.

"My father was a…difficult man," Cole went on. "After my mother started drinking, he got worse. Maybe it was because his world was out of control, so he tried to control it more, through me. I'm not sure. But he had incredibly high standards for me to meet, and there was no choice but to meet them. An A wasn't good enough, it had to be an A+. My room had to pass a military-type inspection. Hell, before I went to school, he would bring me in the kitchen and inspect my clothes, my nails, my hair. If anything was out of place, I'd be punished. I learned not to make mistakes. Ever."

Cole flinched, as if dodging an invisible blow. Emily wasn't sure if he even knew he'd done it. Her heart broke, and she wished she could go back in time and protect the little boy Cole had once been. Stop the bully who had the name Dad and tell Cole it was okay to get dirty, to make messes, to have fun. Take away the bruises and the tears and hug him tight. "Oh, Cole."

"My mother never spoke up or stopped him or did anything but drink more and more and more. So I decided the only way to keep my father happy was to be the best. Never to quit. And always, always to win." He nearly spat the words.

It explained so much about Cole, about his approach to work, to life. To them. "And never to admit a weakness," she added softly.

"Exactly."

"Cole." She shifted on the rock and reached up to trace the features she loved so much, to meet his gaze with her own. Even now, he held himself stoic and strong, as if relating someone else's story. It was a defense, she realized, against more blows. The physical hits may have stopped, but the emotional ones still came at him. "It's not a weakness to need someone."

He jerked away and got to his feet as if the very concept burned him. "It is to me, Emily. I never told you about any of this because I was ashamed of my parents. Of the way I grew up. I didn't want you to pity me or—"

"See you as weak?"

He nodded.

"That's where you're wrong. To me, you are the strongest man in the world because you didn't just survive that past, you *conquered* it."

"I didn't conquer it, Emily. That's the problem. I'm still scared as hell that I'll become my father with my own children." He shook his head and cursed under his breath. The loon called a second time, as if searching for a friend in the cold, dark night. Cole got to his feet and dumped the rest of the rocks onto the ground. "I can't do that to our baby, Emily. Maybe we should do the right thing and just go our separate ways. I'll take care of you financially—"

"Stop, Cole." She wanted to hug him and hit him all at the same time. How could he be so smart and yet so incredibly dumb? "Do you know what the problem is? You're just as afraid of failure as I am."

"I'm not afraid. I'm trying to be sensible."

She let out a gust. "Let me know when you want to stop being sensible and lead with your heart instead of your brain. Do you think I'm not terrified that I'll be a terrible mother? But I love this baby enough already—" her hand went to her abdomen "—to take that chance and to do my best. I'm okay with not being perfect all the time. Life and love are messy, Cole. Like the ties on the closet floor. When you're ready to stop being afraid of a mess, you know where me and your baby will be."

Then she drew her coat closed and headed back into the inn. The light fog had drifted in from the lake, and now swirled around her feet and legs as she walked, as if begging her to give love a second chance.

CHAPTER FOURTEEN

THE PHONE ON the other end rang a half dozen times before it was answered with a flurry of laughter, voices and a barking dog. "Hello?"

"Hey, Pete, it's your big brother." Cole perched on the windowsill of his hotel room in Boston. He should have gone back to New York, but until he was sure Emily was going to be okay, he couldn't bring himself to leave the state. Several stories below, the traffic passed by in a steady stream. People headed out of town to visit friends and family, to share hugs and pie. A holiday he had avoided, finding excuse after excuse to work or be out of town, because he hadn't understood the importance of being grateful for those he loved. Until now. Until he'd lost them.

Now he had a family on the way. And where was he? In a hotel instead of sitting around a Thanksgiving table with Emily.

"Cole!" Pete's voice boomed over the phone. "Long time no hear."

"Too long." Yet another personal relationship that had suffered because of Cole's constant devotion to the company. He vowed to change that from here on out. "Sorry about that. I wanted to call, wish you a happy Thanksgiving."

"Same to you. One of these years, I'll get you to come down to Connecticut for the craziness of our house." Pete shushed the barking dog. "Sorry. Got the wife's entire family here, and our Lab thinks they're all here to visit him. The kids are all excited, probably because they know if we're eating turkey it means Christmas is just around the corner." Pete laughed, an easygoing sound.

Everything about Cole's younger brother was easier and simpler than Cole. The younger Watson had an affable personality, one that rarely stressed about anything. Maybe because Cole had done enough worrying for the both of them when they'd been younger. Cole had done his best to take the brunt of their father's temper, to spare Pete. "How is Diane? The kids?"

"Everyone's great. Our youngest turns two next week, and the oldest is a star in first grade. I think she inherited your genius tendencies."

Cole chuckled. "I am far from a genius."

"Yeah, well, I disagree. You were always smarter than me." Pete's voice softened with love and affection. "So how's Emily?"

Cole didn't want to get into the messy details with his brother. He hadn't called for that, or to talk about how worried Cole was that he was too late to repair the damage in his marriage. "She's great. And, uh, she's expecting."

"A baby? That's fabulous, Cole, really fabulous. I'm thrilled for you. You must be over the moon."

Cole shifted on the sill and put his back to the window. "Can I ask you something?"

"Sure. Anything."

Cole fiddled with the phone cord. "Were you ever

afraid you'd turn out like Dad or Mom when you had your first child?"

The busy noise in the background faded away. There was a soft click, which meant Pete had probably ducked into another room to talk in private. "Hell, yes. Of course I was. With parents like ours, you'd have to be a fool not to worry at least some of that would rub off."

"How did you move past it? Finally take the plunge and have kids?"

Pete chuckled. "It's ironic, you know, you asking me for advice. I've always looked up to you, big brother, to be the leader, the one to tell me what to do."

"I know how to ace a test, launch a business, grow a market share, but when it comes to having a family..." Cole exhaled. "I don't know where to start."

"You start with *love,* Cole," Pete said quietly. "If you love your kids, everything else flows from there."

"Mom and Dad loved us, in their own way, I'm sure. How is that any different?"

"They put other things ahead of that love. Alcohol. Success. Appearances. They led with the least important thing rather than the most important."

Cole thought about that for a minute. It was a concept that applied to business, too. Focus on the most critical areas first, then the other, less-important things would fall into place. "That makes perfect sense."

"Even as the goofball of the family, I can come out with a smart line or two." Pete chuckled. "Hey, the natives are pounding on the door. Turkey's ready and waiting for me to show off my carving skills, and if I don't get in there soon, they're going to riot." Then Pete's voice softened, the little brother worried about the older brother. "You going somewhere for Thanksgiving?"

Cole looked out the window again, but his gaze went farther than the roads he could see. To a cozy, quaint inn deep in Massachusetts. "I'm going home, Pete. Home."

Emily was awake before dawn, the urge to write burning inside her. Her fingers flew across the keyboard, fast and furious, the page count adding up at a rapid pace. A little after eleven, she sat back and let out a sigh. The book needed a lot of revisions yet, but the gist of the story was down. She had written more in these past few days than she had in her entire life. And it felt good, really good.

For an hour, she read, and as she turned the pages in the manuscript, she realized she had told her life story in her characters. The woman struggling to find her place in a marriage that had gone dead, the husband who couldn't give up on the way things used to be. But unlike her own life, her characters had found their way out of the quicksand and back to each other. If only her real life could read as smoothly as the novel did.

The scent of roasted turkey and fresh-baked pies drew Emily's attention, and she put the novel aside. Emily showered, dressed, then headed downstairs. It was Thanksgiving Day. Instead of spending it at the house in New York, eating a catered dinner by herself or with friends while Cole worked and ate at his desk, she was here, at the inn, with Carol, Martin and Joe, her makeshift family.

The only person missing was Cole. Emily told herself that he was the one missing out, the one who would be alone. Still, her heart ached. She paused on the landing, looking for Cole's car. But it wasn't there.

She pressed a hand to her belly. "We'll be okay, Sweet Pea. I promise."

She found Martin and Joe in the living room, watching a football game and talking about things like field goals and Hail Mary passes. Emily ducked into the kitchen and sneaked a fresh-baked biscuit just as Carol turned around. "Hey, no snacking," Carol said.

Emily grinned. "How can I resist fresh-baked bread? Besides, this wasn't for me. It was for the baby."

Carol laughed. "In that case, take a second one."

"Oh, I will. And I'll also have an extra helping of pie. Or two." Emily picked up a whisk and began stirring the gravy. "It all looks awesome, Carol. You are an incredible cook."

"If you want, I can teach you. If you're planning on staying."

Where else was Emily going to go? The house in New York had never been home. This inn came the closest to the warm and loving environment Emily wanted for Sweet Pea. It also offered the perfect refuge for a woman trying to get over a painful divorce. "I'll be here as long as you'll have me," Emily said.

Carol drew her into a one-armed hug. "You're welcome to stay as long as you want."

"Thanks, Carol." The two of them worked together for the next few minutes. Well, Carol worked, and made Emily sit down and do nothing more strenuous than stirring the gravy. Emily tried not to think about Cole's absence, or wonder about whether he was at the office or the big house in New York. All she knew was that he wasn't here. With her.

She cooked and laughed and chatted, but deep inside, disappointment sat like a chunk of concrete. This was what it would be like when the divorce was final. A part of her aware of the empty space at her side, while she forced a smile to her face and feigned happiness. Someday, it would get easier. Someday.

An hour later, they took seats around the dining room table, with the turkey in the center as the star of the meal. Carol sat at the head, Martin to her right and Joe beside him, while Emily sat across from the men and kept her gaze averted from the empty chair beside her.

"Let's all join hands and say thanks," Carol said. The four of them did as she asked, holding hands across their table and bowing their heads. "Thank you, God, for bringing us all together," Carol said, "and thank you for good food and good friends. I am grateful on this day of thanks for the support and help of friends. People like Martin, Joe and Emily."

"I'm grateful for an invitation to a great meal with a beautiful woman," Martin said.

Carol giggled. "Thank you, Martin."

"I'm grateful to be eating a home-cooked meal with some of the best people I know," Joe said. "There's nowhere else I'd want to be today."

Emily opened her mouth to speak, but before she could say anything, she heard a noise behind her.

"I'm grateful for second chances," said a deep baritone voice. "I'm also unbelievably grateful for my wife and for the child she's carrying."

Cole's voice, coming from right beside her. For a second, Emily thought maybe she had wished so hard for him to be here that she had imagined the sound and the words she had wanted to hear. She opened her eyes and looked to her left. Cole stood there, in a pale blue button-down shirt and a pair of jeans, looking relaxed and sexy. He gave her a smile, and her heart flipped over.

Cole.

That man loves you more than anything in the world.

Emily drew her hand out of Joe's, waited for Cole to slide into the seat, then take her hand in his, warm, secure, like coming home. His finger drifted over the ring she'd put back on her finger this morning. He looked up with surprise in his eyes, then gave her a tender, sweet smile. Her heart caught and her throat closed. "I'm grateful for miracles," she said.

"And I'm grateful as hell that it's time to eat now that we're all here. Finally," Joe said with a nod in Cole's direction. Everyone laughed, and they broke apart, sending around the dishes family style while Carol carved the turkey and loaded everyone up with moist, tender slices topped with smooth, steaming gravy. The five of them chatted and laughed during the meal. As Emily looked around at the faces of those who were dear to her, she thought it had to be the best Thanksgiving she'd ever had.

When they were done, Carol shooed Emily and Cole out of the house, insisting the other two could do the cleanup. Emily and Cole grabbed their coats, then ducked out into the chilly evening air. They walked down the same lighted path she had taken the night before, though it felt like a million years ago. Had something changed? Had Cole changed his mind? Did she dare to hope just one more time?

As they neared the lake, Emily bit back a laugh. No

wonder Carol had urged the two of them to go outside. Carol still believed in happily ever after—and in the power of old legends.

A soft gauzy fog came off the lake, a combination of the still-warm water and the cold bite in the air. It drifted over the water like a ghostly blanket, reaching long delicate tendrils across the grassy banks.

"It looks amazing, doesn't it?" Cole said. "Almost magical. As if anything can happen tonight."

"Like a dream," she said. She drew her coat tighter around her. Winter was nipping at their heels, if the bite in the air was any indication.

Cole came around in front of her, opened his own coat and drew her into the warmth of his chest. She was so tempted to stay here, warm and protected, forever. Instead, she stepped back.

"I...I can't, Cole," she said. The words scraped her throat, ached in her heart. "I can't keep getting close then breaking apart. It hurts too much. I mean, I'm glad you came today, but you're just going to leave, and I can't do this anymore." She strode down the dock before the tears in her eyes made it to the surface and undid all her resolve. "I know what you said, but my God, it is so hard for me to trust you. To trust us."

Cole caught up to her and captured her hand. "Don't go, Emily. Please."

She spun toward him. The fog licked at the edges of the dock, as if they were standing in a cauldron. "I can't do this," she said again. "I just can't."

"And I can't live without you. Or our baby."

Those last words stopped her. She swallowed hard, sure she had heard him wrong. That was twice today that he had mentioned the baby. Did that mean he had changed his mind about wanting a family? "You… what?"

Instead of answering, he lifted her left hand to the light. The tiny diamond Cole had given her years ago sparkled in the moonlight. He'd tried to buy her a bigger ring when he made his first million, but she had always preferred the simple small stone. "Why did you put your ring back on?"

She gave a little shrug and a wry smile crossed her face. "No matter how hard I tried, I couldn't give up on us. Or on you. I keep trying, Lord knows I do, but I guess I started believing in happy endings a long time ago, and I just can't stop." Tears brimmed in her eyes, and her fingers closed around his. "You're a good man, Cole Watson, and I always thought I was lucky to marry you."

"Ah, Em, how is it that you always see the best in me?" He brushed away a tendril of hair from her face, his touch so tender, so light.

"Because I'm your wife," she said, "and because… I love you."

His eyes lit, and a smile curved across his face. "Do you? Still?"

"I never stopped." It was the truth and one of the many things she had been afraid to say. Where had that fear got her? Nowhere but filled with regret. If Cole walked away at the end of this, so be it. She would know she had given their marriage every last possible chance. "I've always loved you, Cole. I always will. You stole my heart the day we met, and I've never asked for it back."

"I love you, too, Emily. I love the way you smile, the way your eyes light up when you're excited, the way you curve into me when you're cold. I love your cooking and your messes and your laugh. I just didn't realize how much I loved you, or how deep that love ran inside my heart…until I thought I lost you." His hand reached up again, and his blue eyes locked on hers. "I haven't, have I? Lost you?"

She shook her head, her vision blurring behind the tears. No matter how many times she had said she was done, her heart had never got the message. She still loved her husband, still wanted him. Still wanted to wake up next to him and build a life with their child. "No, Cole. I'm still here."

"Good." He exhaled a long breath of relief. "That's so damned good to hear. The whole way over here, I was so sure I was too late. That you had already signed the papers and moved on in your heart."

She wanted to linger in this moment of connection, in the joy in Cole's eyes, but she couldn't, not until she brought up the one topic they had thus far avoided tonight. "I haven't signed the papers. And I won't, until I'm sure."

"Sure about what?"

She watched the fog undulate across the lake, slow and soft, like a gossamer blanket. On a night many years in the past, two young lovers had stood at the edge of this very lake and taken a giant risk to find their own happy ending.

"I'm still having our baby, and if you don't want to be a real family, I can't stay with you." Emily placed a hand on her abdomen. "Sweet Pea and me are a package deal."

"Sweet Pea?"

She shrugged. "It's what I named the baby until I know whether it's a boy or a girl."

"I like that name. A lot." He took a step forward, his face filled with tentative curiosity. He put out a hand. "Can I?"

She moved her hand away and gave him a nod. "You can't feel anything yet."

Cole's palm was warm, even through her jeans, though when his palm met the tiny bulge of her belly, it seemed as if she and Cole were joined in a deeper way than they ever had been before. Cole lifted his gaze to hers. "When will it start kicking?"

"A couple more months. By then, I'll be fat and ugly."

"You will never ever be ugly, Emily. You are the most beautiful woman in the world."

"And you are the most biased man on the planet."

He chuckled. "Maybe so."

She covered his hand with hers, then drew in a deep breath. "Tell me, Cole, do you want to take the biggest risk of your life and become a father?"

He lifted his gaze to hers, and for the first time ever, she saw trepidation in Cole's eyes. "What if I'm like my own father?"

"You won't be."

"How do you know that?"

She thought a moment, looking for the right words to show him what she saw when she looked at him through her eyes. "Because you ate that terrible chicken and potatoes dinner I made with a smile on your face. Because you made love with me in the messy closet. And most of all, because you are a man who would never hurt anyone you love."

"Ah, but I have hurt you, Emily. Too many times to count." He cupped her jaw and studied her face. "I never meant to. I thought I was building a life for us. I never realized all that time at work was destroying our life at the same time."

She thought of the envelope in her room. The papers that needed only a signature to take that final step to dissolving her marriage. "Where do we go from here, Cole? How do I know that if we get back together, you won't go back to working a thousand hours a week? I want a family, Cole. That means dinners at home and road trips in the summer and picnics in the park."

He reached in his pocket and took out his phone. The screen lit with messages and alerts, as busy as ever, even on a holiday. "This is where we go, Em." He leaned back, then pitched his arm forward. The phone spiraled through the air, then disappeared in the thickening fog before landing in the lake with a heavy plop. A second later, it disappeared under the surface.

She stared at the space where the phone had been, openmouthed. "Why...why would you do that?"

"Because nothing matters more to me than you. Us." His hand went to her belly again. "All of us."

"Really?"

"Really. I've been a fool for too damned long. And I'm not going to be that stupid for one second longer." He cupped her jaw with his hands and brought his mouth within inches. "I love you, Emily. I love our baby. I want to marry you again and do it right this time."

"But how do we fix everything? Where do we begin?"

"We begin with love. Everything else will flow from

that. I promise." Then he drew his wife into his arms and kissed her while the fog wrapped around them, and once again the lake's decades-old legend brought two lovers together, this time in a happy ending.

* * * * *

"He's a real white hat," he heard her brother whisper behind him. "Isn't he?"

Sloan didn't wait to hear Abby's answer as he let himself out through the front door. Whatever the white hats were that the kid was talking about, Sloan knew that he'd never worn one.

Abby might be the first woman he'd felt any interest for in a long while.

But white hats were for the good guys.

They weren't for the guys who'd only ever hurt the ones who least deserved it.

RETURN TO THE DOUBLE C:
Under the big blue Wyoming sky,
this family discovers true love

A WEAVER BEGINNING

BY
ALLISON LEIGH

First published in Great Britain 2013
by Mills & Boon, an imprint of Harlequin (UK) Limited,
Eton House, 18-24 Paradise Road, Richmond, Surrey TW9 1SR

© Allison Lee Johnson 2013

ISBN: 978 0 263 90147 4
ebook ISBN: 978 1 472 00536 6

23-1013

Harlequin (UK) policy is to use papers that are natural, renewable and recyclable products and made from wood grown in sustainable forests. The logging and manufacturing processes conform to the legal environmental regulations of the country of origin.

Printed and bound in Spain
by Blackprint CPI, Barcelona

There is a saying that you can never be too rich or too thin. **Allison Leigh** doesn't believe that, but she does believe that you can *never* have enough books! When her stories find a way into the hearts—and bookshelves—of others, Allison says she feels she's done something right. Making her home in Arizona with her husband, she enjoys hearing from her readers at Allison@allisonleigh.com or PO Box 40772, Mesa, AZ 85274-0772, USA.

For Greg.

Chapter One

The snow covered everything.

Everything except the clear strip down the middle of the street that had been plowed just that morning.

Looking out the front window of the house he'd been renting for the past six months, Sloan McCray studied that strip.

While the middle of the street was whistle clean, the displaced snow formed two-foot walls against the curb on both sides of the street, blocking driveways and parking spaces.

Generally speaking, Sloan didn't worry about the snowplow job as long as it was done. It was his first winter in Weaver—the first snow had fallen in October and hadn't stopped since. He'd had two months to get used to it.

There were five houses on his street. Some of the folks occupying the homes had snowblowers—ancient ones kept running by ingenuity and stubbornness, and new ones that cost as much as Sloan's first motorcycle. He dealt with the annoying snow berm in front of his house the old-fashioned way—with a heavy-duty snow shovel and a lot of muscle.

Not a problem for him.

He'd been well used to being physically active, even before he'd signed on as a deputy sheriff here in Weaver. Pitching heavy snow out of his driveway was a welcome task.

Kept the muscles working.

Kept the mind occupied with the simple and mundane.

Two good things, as far as he was concerned.

He wasn't sold on living in Weaver yet. His job was temporary; he had a one-year lease on the house. He needed to start thinking about what to do after the nine months he'd promised Max Scalise—the sheriff—were up. He should have been spending less time with the snow shovel and more time thinking about what the hell he was going to do with the rest of his life. But tackling that particular question was no more appealing than it ever was.

Standing inside the warmth of his living room, Sloan eyed the snow blocking the driveways. The small blue car had been sitting on the street in front of the house next door for nearly an hour. Footsteps in the snow trailed back and forth from the car to the house.

New neighbors. Moving in on the last day of the year.

He'd been watching them for a while. The woman was young, with shining brown hair that bounced around the shoulders of her red coat with every step. The little kid with her had the same dark hair.

He'd also noticed there wasn't a man in the picture. Not to help them unpack, anyway. Nor to clear away the snow blocking the driveway, much less shovel a path to the door.

He turned away from the window, grabbed his down

vest and headed out the back of his house to the small shed where he stored his bike and tools.

It was the last day of the year and he'd spent too much time thinking already.

Time to start shoveling instead.

"Abby. *Abby.*"

Balancing the heavy box in her hands, Abby Marcum glanced at her little brother. He was clutching the plastic bin containing his collection of video games against his chest, his wary gaze glued to the tall man striding toward them from the house next door. "Who's that *man?*" Dillon was whispering, but his nervousness shouted loud and clear.

"I don't know," she said calmly. "We'll meet lots of new people here in Weaver."

"I don't want new people." His pale face was pinched. "I want our old people."

She hid a sigh behind a smile. Her seven-year-old brother wasn't the only one with misgivings about moving to Weaver. But she wasn't going to show hers to him when he already had more than enough for them both. "We still have our old people," she assured him. "Braden's not so far away that we won't visit." Just not every day. Not anymore.

She hid another sigh at the thought.

Noticing that the man angling across the deep snow had nearly reached them, she looked at Dillon. "Take your box inside. You can think about where to put the television."

He clutched the bin even closer as he retraced his path from the car to the house, not taking his wary attention away from the man for a second.

Abby adjusted her grip on the packing box. She hoped that moving to Weaver hadn't been a huge mistake. Dillon had already endured so much. For two years, she'd tried to follow her grandfather's wishes. He was gone, but she was still trying. She just didn't know if moving Dillon away from the only place of stability he'd ever known had been the right thing to do or not.

The sound of crunching snow ceased when the man stopped a few yards away. "You're the new nurse over at the elementary school." His voice was deep. More matter-of-fact than welcoming.

She tightened her grip on the heavy box, trying not to stare too hard at him. Lines radiated from his dark brown eyes. His overlong brown hair was liberally flecked with grays. What should have been pretty normal features for a man who looked to be in his late thirties, but the sum of the parts made him ruthlessly attractive.

She'd grown up in Braden, which was the closest town of any size to Weaver. She knew how small-town grape-vines worked, so she wasn't particularly surprised that he knew about her before she so much as opened her mouth. "I am. But I'll be splitting my time with the junior high." The schools were next door to each other, sharing their facili-ties. "I'm Abby Marcum." She smiled. "And you are…?"

"From next door." He stabbed the shovel into the snow.

She'd assumed that, given that he'd *come* from the house next door. "So that answers *where*." The muscles in her arms were starting to shake, so she started toward the house, her boots plowing fresh paths through the snow. "What about *who?*"

"That looks too heavy for you."

"Does it?" She kept right on moving, passing him on her way toward the three steps that led up to the front door.

"Would have been easier if you'd cleared the driveway before you started unpacking."

Her fingers dug into the cardboard. "Probably," she agreed blithely and lifted her boot, cautiously feeling for the first porch step. She'd have needed a snow shovel for that, though, and that wasn't something she'd bothered trying to cram into her small car along with everything else. Weaver had hardware stores, after all. And neighbors who had shovels to borrow, too.

The man gave a mighty sigh, his bare hands brushing hers as he lifted the box out of her grasp. "The bottom's about to give way," he said and walked past her into the house.

She hurried after him. "Um, thanks." He was already setting the box on the narrow breakfast bar separating the small living room from the even smaller kitchen. One look at the cardboard told her he was right. The crystal inside could have crashed right through. She flipped open the box and pulled out a few of the glasses she'd wrapped so carefully in newspaper just to make certain they'd safely survived. "My grandmother's crystal."

"Mmm." He didn't sound particularly interested as he looked around the living room. She'd bought the house furnished. And while the furniture that occupied the room was dated, it was clean and in good condition. With the half-dozen boxes that they'd already carried in stacked on the floor against the wall next to the brick fireplace, the small room was almost full. "It's freezing in here."

"I know. Something's wrong with the furnace. I'll get a fire started, though, soon as I get the car emptied. And once the holiday is over, I'll call someone in to get the furnace going."

She smiled across at Dillon, who was perched nervously on the edge of the couch, watching them with big eyes. He still wore his coat. She'd bought it at a clearance sale last year expecting that he would have grown into it by now. But he still looked dwarfed in it. "A fire will have us toasty warm in no time," she told her little brother brightly.

"And then we get popcorn like you promised?"

Dillon loved popcorn like almost nothing else. "Absolutely."

"You've got wood?"

At the deep-voiced question, she focused on the man and felt something jolt inside her. *Lordy.* He really *was* handsome. And vaguely familiar. "Um…no. No wood. But I'll get some." Along with that snow shovel. Having one of her own was better than borrowing.

"Stores are closed today and tomorrow for New Year's." His voice was even. Unemotional. "I've got plenty, though. I'll bring some over." He turned on his boot heel and left the house.

"Who *is* he?" Dillon whispered once he was gone.

"The neighbor. You can put away your games in the television cabinet. Soon as I finish with everything, I'll play a game of 'White Hats 3' with you." She'd gotten the latest version of the video game for him for Christmas and it was already his favorite. "Okay?"

He nodded and she went back outside.

The man had left the snow shovel sticking out of the snow banked against the side of the porch. She looked from it to the house next door. It was two-storied and twice the size of hers.

Definitely large enough to hold a wife and kids if Tall-Dark-and-Nameless had any.

She trudged back to the car and pulled the box containing their new television from the backseat. Her girlfriends from Braden had pooled their money together to buy it as a going-away present. It was mercifully lightweight, and she was heading up the steps with it in her arms when the neighbor appeared again bearing a load of wood in his arms.

She quickly got out of his way as he carried it inside.

He crouched next to the brick hearth and started stacking the wood. As he worked, he looked over at her brother. "What's your name?"

Dillon shot Abby a nervous look. "Dillon."

The man's face finally showed a little warmth. He smiled slightly. Gently. And even though it was directed at her little brother, Abby still felt the effect.

She let out a careful breath and set the television on the floor. Her girlfriends had also given her a box of Godiva chocolates before she'd left, with instructions to indulge herself on New Year's Eve—and share the chocolates with a male other than her little brother.

The chocolates were in her suitcase. She could give the box to her no-name neighbor and technically live up to the promise she'd made. Of course, he'd probably take the chocolates home to his wife. Which wasn't exactly what her girlfriends had in mind.

She shook off the silly thoughts and tried to focus on the television, but her gaze kept slipping back to the man, who was still looking at her little brother.

"You want to bring me some of that newspaper from your mom's crystal?"

"She's not my mom," Dillon said as he slid off the couch and retrieved the crumpled papers that Abby had tossed aside. He sidled over to the man, holding them out at arm's length.

She almost missed the speculative glance the man gave her before he took the paper from Dillon. He wadded it up and stuck it in the fireplace, between a couple of angled logs. "Got a match, bud?"

"Here." Abby quickly pulled a lighter out of her purse and carried it over.

"You smoke?" His tone was smooth, yet she still felt the accusation.

"You sound remarkably like my grandfather used to."

A full beat passed before his lips quirked. "My sister keeps telling me I'm getting old before my time," he said. "Must be true if I strike you as *grand*fatherly." He took the lighter and set the small flame to the newspaper. When he was sure it took, he straightened and left the lighter on the wood mantel.

"Abby's my sister," Dillon said so suddenly that she shot him a surprised look.

The man didn't look surprised. And he wasn't the least bit grandfatherly, though Abby didn't figure it would be appropriate to tell him so. He simply nodded at this additional information, not knowing how unusual it was for Dillon to offer anything where a stranger was concerned. He set the fireplace screen back in place. "What grade are you in?"

But her brother's bravery only went so far. He ducked his chin into his puffy down collar. "Second," he whispered and hurried back to the couch. He sat down on the edge of a cushion again and tucked his bare fingers under his legs.

Abby knew the best thing for Dillon was to keep things as normal as possible. So she ignored the way he was carefully looking away from them and focused on the tall man as he straightened. She was wearing flat-heeled snow boots, and he had at least a foot on her five-one. Probably a good eighty pounds, too, judging by the breadth of his shoulders. "Do you have kids?" Maybe a second-grader who'd become friends with Dillon.

"Nope." Which didn't really tell her whether there was a *wife* or not. "How much more do you need to unload?"

She followed him onto the porch. "A few boxes and our suitcases."

He grabbed the shovel as he went down the steps and

shoved it into the snow, pushing it ahead of him like a plow as he made his way to the car.

"You don't have to do that," Abby said quickly, following in his wake.

"Somebody needs to."

Her defenses prickled. "I appreciate the gesture, but I'm perfectly capable of shoveling my own driveway."

His dark gaze roved over her. "But you didn't. And I'm guessing if you'd *had* a shovel in that little car of yours, you'd have already used it so you could get the car into the driveway."

Since that was true, she didn't really have a response. "My grandfather had a snowblower," she said. "I didn't really have a good way to move it here, so I sold it." Along with most everything else that her grandparents had owned. Except the crystal. Ever since Abby had been a little girl, her grandmother had said that Abby would have it one day.

And now she did.

The reality of it all settled like a sad knot in her stomach.

She'd followed her grandfather's wishes. But that didn't mean it had been easy.

They'd lost him when he'd died of a heart attack two years earlier. But they'd been losing her grandmother by degrees for years before that. And in the past year, Minerva Marcum's Alzheimer's had become so advanced that she didn't even recognize Abby anymore.

Even though Abby was now a qualified RN, she'd had no choice but to do what her grandfather had made her promise to do when the time came—place her grandmother into full-time residential care.

"So you'll get another blower," the man was saying. "Or a shovel. But for now—" he waggled the long handle "—this is it." He set off again, pushing another long swath of snow clear from the driveway.

She trailed after him. "Mr., uh—"

"Sloan."

At last. A name. "Mr. Sloan, if you don't mind lending me the shovel, I can do that myself. I'm sure you've got better things to—"

"—just Sloan. And, no, I don't have better things to do. So go back inside, check the fire and unpack that crystal of yours. Soon as you can pull your car up in the driveway, I'll leave you to it."

She flopped her hands. "I can't stop you?"

"Evidently not." He reached the end of the driveway, pitched the snow to the side with enviable ease and turned to make another pass in the opposite direction. At the rate he was going, the driveway would be clear of the snow that reached halfway up her calves in a matter of minutes.

She ought to be grateful. Instead, she just felt inadequate. And she *hated* feeling inadequate.

Short of trying to wrestle the shovel out of his hands— which was a shockingly intriguing idea—she could either stand there watching or do something productive.

Like checking the fire and unpacking.

She went back inside. The fire had already started warming the room. Dillon had shed his coat and was sitting on the beige carpet, setting his video games neatly inside the cabinet. "When're we gonna visit Grandma?"

Abby stepped around his plastic crate and went to the fireplace. "I thought we'd go next weekend." She moved the fire screen aside and took a piece of wood from the stack. She jabbed the end of it against the burning logs, sending up a blur of sparks before tossing it onto the top. Then she replaced the screen and straightened. "We can't go every day like we used to."

"I know." He pushed out his lower lip, studying the cover of his video game. "Would she 'member us if Grandpa hadn't died?"

Abby sat down on the floor next to him, pulled off her coat and put her arm around him. "No, honey. Losing Grandpa has nothing to do with it. But we remember her." She ignored the tightening in her throat. "And we'll visit her every chance we can, just like I've told you. Okay?"

She felt his nod against her cheek.

"Okay." She pressed her lips to his forehead before pushing to her feet. "Why don't we leave the rest of our unpacking until later and get the television hooked up. I'm finally going to beat you at 'White Hats.'"

He snorted softly. "Yeah, right."

Which just eased the tightness in her throat and made her smile instead. She turned away from him only to stop short at the sight of Sloan standing inside the door. She hadn't even heard him open it.

"Driveway's clear."

She pulled at the hem of her long sweater. "Thank you. I'll have to figure out a way to return the favor."

His dark gaze seemed to sharpen. And maybe it was her imagination that his eyes flicked from her head to her toes, but then that would mean it was also her imagination that her stomach was swooping around. And she'd never been particularly prone to flights of imagination.

"That might be interesting." Then he smiled faintly and went out the door again, silently closing it after him.

Abby blinked. Let out a long breath.

If Mr. Just-Sloan *did* have a wife, he had no business making new neighbors feel breathless like that.

"Come on, Abby," Dillon said behind her. "I wanna play 'White Hats.'"

"I know. I know."

And if he doesn't have a wife?

She ignored the voice inside her head and pulled the television out of the box.

Whether the man was married or not didn't matter.

All she wanted to do was start her new job at the elementary school and raise Dillon with as much love as her grandparents had raised her.

Nothing more. Nothing less.

So she carried the new television over to the cabinet and began hooking it up. In minutes, the distinctive music from Dillon's video game was blasting through the speakers. He handed her a controller and she sat cross-legged on the carpet next to him as she set about trying not to be bested yet again by a seven-year-old.

She was no more successful at that than she was at not thinking about the man next door.

Chapter Two

"Sloan, it's New Year's Eve. You shouldn't be spending it alone," his sister, the voice of reason, said through the phone at his ear.

"I'm not interested in crashing your evening with Axel." Even though Tara had been married to the man for a few years now—had two kids with him, even—it was still hard for Sloan to say his brother-in-law's name without feeling a healthy dose of dislike. Axel Clay was part of the darkest time of Sloan's life. His sister being happily married to him made the situation tolerable. Barely. If not for that, Sloan could have gone the rest of his life hating the man. No more than he hated himself, though.

"You wouldn't be crashing anything, Bean." Tara laughed. "Most of the family's going to be here. It's not like Axel and I will have a chance to be romantic while there's a half-dozen kids chasing each other around."

Bean. The nickname she'd called him when they were

kids. Considering everything that Sloan had put her through—the disruption he'd caused in her life by the choices he'd made in his—it was a wonder that she could even recall the days when he'd been her Bean and she'd been his Goober.

They were twins. And they'd grown up in a family that never stayed in one place for more than a few months at a time. As an adult, all Tara had ever wanted was a stable place to call her own. While Sloan had kept right on with the rootless lifestyle.

Which was why he was living here in Weaver at all. Trying to make up for the acts of his past. Trying to make things right with the only female left in his life that he loved.

"Fine," he said. "I also don't want to crash your evening with the entire Clay clan." He looked out the front window of his house again. Abby had finally moved her car into the driveway. "Maybe I have plans of my own."

He could almost hear Tara's ears perk. "What plans would those be? Sitting in the dark, staring morosely into a beer while you dwell on the past?"

Almost guiltily, he set aside the frosted beer mug he was holding. "You don't know everything, Goob."

She sighed noisily. "Oh, all right. But you're not getting off the hook tomorrow. Dinner at the big house. You've already agreed, and if you try to back out, I'll call Max and sic him on you."

"My boss may be your cousin-in-law, but that doesn't mean he's gonna let you tell him what to do." In Sloan's estimation, nobody told Max Scalise what to do, not even the voters who put him in office term after term.

"We'll see," Tara countered. "Squire's expecting everyone for New Year's dinner, and nobody wants to cross *him*. Not even the mighty sheriff."

Squire Clay was Tara's grandfather-in-law and the patriarch of the large Clay family. He was older than dirt. Cantankerous as hell. And one of a few people in Weaver that Sloan could say he genuinely liked.

"I said I'd be there tomorrow and I will." A flash of red caught his eye, and he watched Abby bounce down the porch steps. But instead of heading toward her car, she started crossing the snow separating their houses.

"But tonight is mine," he finished. Up close, Abby had looked even younger than he'd expected, but she'd also had the prettiest gray eyes he'd ever seen.

"Okay. Happy New Year, Sloan," his sister said. "I'm glad you're here."

He pinched the bridge of his nose. He wished he could say the same, but he didn't know what he felt. If anything. "Happy New Year, kiddo."

Then he hung up and watched Abby cross in front of the window where he was standing. A second later, she knocked on his front door.

He left his beer on the table and answered the door.

"Hi." Those gray eyes of hers looked up at him, carrying the same cheerfulness that infused the smile on her soft, pink lips. "Sorry to bother you."

"You're not." He leaned his shoulder against the doorjamb. He ought to feel like a letch, admiring her the way he was. But he didn't. He felt…interested.

The first time he'd felt interested in longer than he cared to remember.

"What d'you need?"

"Wood, actually."

The devil on his shoulder laughed at that one. No problem there. The angel on his other shoulder had him straightening away from the doorjamb. "It's back behind the house." He pushed the door open wide. "Come on in."

The tip of her tongue peeked out to flick over her upper lip. "Thanks." She stepped past him into the house, and he saw the way her gaze took in the sparsely furnished living room. "Hope I'm not interrupting anything."

"Nope." He led the way through the room to the kitchen at the back of the house and outside again. He gestured at the woodpile stacked next to the back steps, protected from the weather by the overhang of the roof. "Help yourself."

She went down the steps, her shiny hair swaying around her shoulders. He shoved his fingers into the pockets of his jeans and tried not to think how silky her hair would feel.

"Thanks again." She stacked several pieces of wood in her arms. "I'll restock as soon as I can."

"No need." Thanks to his connection to the Clay family and their gigantic cattle ranch, the Double-C, he had a ready supply of firewood, whether he wanted it or not. "House warming up okay over there?"

She nodded. Her hair bounced. Her eyes smiled.

She'd have the boys at the elementary and junior high schools sticking their fingers down their throats just to have a chance to visit her in the nurse's office.

The devil on his shoulder laughed at him again. *Wouldn't you do the same?*

"Your brother live with you all the time?" Sloan was betting the "brother" story was just that. The boy looked just like her. He was probably her son. Which would mean she'd had him very, *very* young.

"Yes." She lifted the load in her arms and started backing away, making fresh tracks in the snow. "Thanks for this. Hope you and your wife enjoy the rest of your evening."

Interesting. "Who said there's a wife?"

Her gaze skipped away. "Just assuming." She smiled again. Kept backing away. Right until she bumped into the side of her house. She laughed and began sidestepping instead.

"Assuming wrong."

She hesitated. Just for a moment, before continuing right along. But it had been long enough for him to notice.

Definitely interesting.

"Ah. Well." She clutched the logs to her chest. "Hope you enjoy the rest of *your* evening, then." Her smile never faltered.

He wondered if it ever did. She had a face made for smiles.

"You, too."

She reached the end of the fence and finally turned away, crossing into her front yard.

Her hair swayed and bounced.

Sloan shook his head and went back inside. Whether or not the boy was her brother or her son, a young woman like Abby Marcum didn't need something temporary in her life.

And temporary was all he had to offer.

The car was unloaded. Most of the boxes unpacked.

Abby sat on the wooden barstool at her breakfast bar and looked at Dillon. He was sprawled on the couch, a fleecy blanket pulled up to his chin, sound asleep. He'd had his triumph at 'White Hats.' Had his popcorn. Had the casserole she'd managed to throw together.

It was nearly midnight. She could have gone to bed herself.

She sighed and poked through the box of chocolates, selected one and followed it up with a chaser of milk. She doubted her girlfriends would approve. They'd also sent her away with a bottle of champagne. It was sitting, unopened, in the refrigerator.

No champagne and no horizontal entertainment for her,

both of which they'd insisted it was high time she finally experience.

She held up her grandmother's delicate crystal flute and stared at the milk. "Happy New Year," she murmured just as the lights flickered twice then went out completely.

With the television silent, all she could hear was the ticking of the clock that she'd hung on the kitchen wall and the faint hiss from the log burning in the fireplace.

By firelight, she leisurely finished her milk and waited for the electricity to come back on. When it didn't, she retrieved the lighter from the mantel where Sloan had left it and lit several candles.

Then she headed back to the barstool and the chocolates.

There was a loud knock on her door as she picked up the gold box. And at that hour it was certainly unexpected. But it wasn't alarm that had her hurrying to the door; it was the fact that she didn't want Dillon waking up. He was sleeping so soundly, and she didn't want to ruin it. It was a rare night that passed without him waking out of a bad dream.

She cracked open the door and looked out. Sloan stood there, a sturdy flashlight in his hand, and she opened the door wider. The air outside felt bracingly cold in comparison to the warmth slipping through her at the sight of him.

"Everything okay here?"

"Fine." She poked her head out the door, looking up and down the darkened street. "Why?"

"Just making sure."

"It's only a power outage." She smiled. "Did you think I'd be over here shaking in my boots?"

The beam of his flashlight shifted, moving across her bare feet. "You're not wearing boots."

She curled her toes against the carpet. "You caught me." She realized she was still holding the gold box and extended it. "Care for one?"

"I don't know." His deep voice was amused. "There was a time when my mother told me not to take candy from strangers."

Abby grinned. "Wise woman. But it's your loss. These aren't just ordinary chocolates." She held the box up a little higher. In the glow from the flashlight, he couldn't fail to notice the distinctive box. "You sure? I promised the friends who gave them to me that I'd share them with someone other than Dillon."

"I see. Can't have you breaking a promise, then." He raised his flashlight and took one.

"No point in standing out in the cold. Come on in. I'll get you something to drink." And then she held her breath, because she was pretty sure that he wouldn't accept her invitation.

But he stepped past her.

Her stomach swooped.

She noticed that Dillon still hadn't moved as she quietly closed the door before crossing to the bar again. "Have a seat." She waved at the second barstool and set the chocolates on the counter.

He shut off his flashlight and shrugged out of his jacket. "Looks like you're putting your grandmother's crystal to good use."

"Trying." She got a second flute from the cupboard then pulled open the refrigerator and snatched the champagne. She set the glass and the bottle in front of him. "You'll need to open it, I'm afraid." She didn't even know how.

He tilted his head slightly as he picked up the crystal flute she'd been using. Candlelight danced over it. "Definitely doesn't look like you're drinking champagne."

She felt silly. Grown women didn't drink milk out of champagne glasses. "I'm not."

He lifted her glass to his nose. The old crystal looked shockingly delicate in his long fingers. "You mind?" But he didn't wait to see if she did; he simply took a sip. Right from her glass.

Her mouth suddenly felt very dry, and she sat down weakly on her own barstool. The width of the counter separated them, but she still felt dwarfed by him. It wasn't just that he was tall. His shoulders were massive. And up close like this, she was pretty sure she could make out a tattoo of some sort on his neck, not quite hidden by the neckline of his long-sleeved T-shirt.

"Milk always goes well with chocolate," he murmured. He set her glass down on the counter and slid it toward her. "That's what I'll have if you've got enough to share."

She nodded, afraid that if she tried to speak, her voice would just come out as one long squeak. She went back to the fridge, blindly snatched the milk carton and filled his glass.

"Anything else your friends say you're supposed to do besides share the chocolate?" He kept his voice low, and even though she knew it was because of Dillon, it still felt unbearably intimate.

She picked up her own glass. She couldn't lie to save her soul, and there was no way she'd share what they'd told her about finally having sex, so she just grazed the side of her glass against his. "Cheers," she whispered instead.

"Not exactly an answer, Abby."

"I guess it isn't. What'd you say your name was?"

His teeth flashed in the dim light. "Sloan McCray," he finally offered.

And just like that, she realized why he'd seemed familiar. Because she'd seen his face before in the newspapers. On the television news. On the internet.

He looked different from the clean-cut man in the snapshots she remembered, but she was certain he was the undercover ATF agent who'd brought down the horrendous Deuce's Cross gang a few years ago. She remembered watching the news stories on the television in her grandfather's hospital room. Sloan had succeeded at something no one before him had been able to do. He was a hero.

And he was sitting right here, watching her with narrowed eyes, as if he were waiting for some reaction.

She got the sense that if she gave one, he'd bolt.

So she didn't.

"So, Sloan McCray," she said softly. "Why aren't you out celebrating New Year's Eve somewhere?"

"I am out celebrating." He tilted the glass and drank down half of the milk.

She couldn't help grinning, even though she was afraid it made her look like a cartoon character.

He set the glass down again and pulled the gold box closer so he could study the contents. He'd folded one arm on the counter and was leaning toward her. "Anything besides the job bringing you and Dillon to Weaver?"

"No." She realized she'd mirrored his position when he looked up from the box and their heads were only inches apart. Her heart raced around fiendishly inside her chest. "We lived in Braden, but working at the school here was too good an opportunity to pass up. I'll have essentially the same hours as Dillon." Her grandfather had planned well, but that didn't mean Abby could afford to spend money on after-school care if she didn't need to.

"And you want to stay close to Braden," Sloan concluded. "For your grandmother."

"You did overhear that."

He nodded once. Took another sip of milk, watching her over the rim of the flute.

"What about you? What brings you to Weaver?"

"Maybe I come from here."

If she recalled correctly, the news stories had said he'd hailed from Chicago. "*Do* you?"

He didn't answer immediately. He selected a chocolate. Studied it. "My sister lives here," he finally said. Then he turned his back to her and stood.

Disappointment flooded her, but all he did was walk across to the fireplace and quietly place another piece of wood on the dying embers. Then he returned to his barstool. He held up his nearly empty glass. "Unless you've got more, we might need to open that champagne after all."

"I have more," she said quickly and retrieved the milk carton. She filled his glass, emptying the carton.

"You're not going to have any left for Dillon in the morning."

She curled her toes around the wooden ring near the base of her barstool. "He likes brown sugar and raisins on his oatmeal anyway."

His lips twitched. "That's the way my mother used to fix oatmeal for us. What else did you leave behind in Braden?"

Her mouth went dry all over again at the way he was looking at her, his eyes so dark and hooded. "I tried to bring everything that mattered."

"Grandma's crystal." He held up his glass.

"And Grandpa's shotgun." She smiled. "Safely stowed away in a cabinet, well out of Dillon's reach. Plus his video games. Dillon's that is, not my grandfather's." She was babbling but couldn't help herself. "Photographs. Clothes."

"You're not answering my real question. You have a boyfriend waiting for you in Braden? Some nice kid as fresh-faced and wet behind the ears as you?"

She didn't know whether to be charmed or insulted. "I'm neither a kid nor wet behind the ears."

He gave that slight half smile again. "How old are you?"

She moistened her lips. "Twenty-three."

He made a face. "I've got ten years on you."

She managed to hide her surprise. He was ungodly handsome, but his face held far more wear than any man in his early thirties should. She guessed that was the price for the kind of work he'd done. "In any case, no, there is no one waiting for me to come home to Braden." She plucked a chocolate from the box and shoved it into her mouth with no regard for its fineness. "No boyfriend. No husband. No nothing," she said around its melting sweetness. "Been too busy raising Dillon for the past two years. Even if there had been time, I'm still a package deal."

His eyebrows rose. "Where are your parents?"

She lifted her shoulders. "Who knows? He's my half brother. We share the same mother, but she was no more interested in raising him than she was me. Which is why—"

"The grandparents," he concluded.

She nodded. "What about your parents?"

The devil laughed mockingly in Sloan's ear. That was what he got for showing some curiosity about Abby. She naturally showed some curiosity in return. "They died when my sister and I were twenty," he said abruptly. Tara had turned into a homebody after their childhood, and he had been the opposite. But he knew they shared the same distaste for talking about that childhood.

"That must have been hard."

Not any harder than growing up without parents at all, which seemed to be the case for her. He folded his arms on the counter again, leaning closer. Close enough to smell the clean fragrance of her shining brown hair. "You start work when the holiday break is over?"

"In two days. At least it'll be a short week."

"Nervous?"

She shook her head. Made a face. "Guess it shows, huh?"

"You'll be fine."

She toyed with her glass for a moment. "What do you do?"

"Deputy sheriff. For the next few months, anyway." He didn't know what the hell had him offering that last bit. Maybe a thin attempt to lay some groundwork. Some *temporary* groundwork.

"What happens after that?"

He hesitated and wasn't sure what he would have said if the electricity hadn't kicked on just then. Light from the overhead fixture flooded the kitchen, and the television came to life.

"Look," she whispered, leaning to the side to peer around him. "The ball in New York is nearly down."

He glanced over his shoulder. Sure enough, the TV showed the famed crystal ball inching its way down while a mass of people around it cheered and screamed.

"Three." He turned back to watch Abby, whose gray gaze was focused on the countdown.

"Two," she whispered on a smile.

"One," he finished.

Her pretty eyes lifted to his. "Happy New Year, Sloan."

Maybe it was the devil. Maybe it was the angel.

Maybe it was just him.

"It is now," he murmured. And he leaned the last few inches across the counter and slowly pressed his mouth against hers.

Chapter Three

Shocked, Abby inhaled sharply.

He tasted like dark chocolate. Cold milk.

And things that she'd never experienced and suddenly wanted to, so very badly.

But just when she was adjusting to the notion that Sloan McCray's lips were brushing across *hers,* he was lifting his head. "Next time you talk to your friends, you can tell them that you lived up to your promise."

He meant sharing the chocolate, of course. But she couldn't do a single thing except sit there and mutely nod.

The lines arrowing out from the corners of his dark eyes crinkled a little. "You pour a helluva cocktail," he murmured before turning away and walking silently to the door.

A moment later, he was gone.

And Abby was *still* sitting there as mute as a stump of wood.

"Izzit New Year's?" Dillon's sleepy voice startled her so much she jumped off her stool as if she'd been stung. She rounded the counter and went over to the couch where he was knuckling his eyes.

"It is. And time for *you* to go to bed, Mr. Marcum."

He giggled a little, the way he always did when she called him that. "I stayed awake the whole time, didn't I," he boasted as he slid off the couch, dragging his blanket after him.

"Sure thing, honey."

He padded barefoot into the first bedroom. "I think Mr. Sloan is a White Hat," he said.

She folded back the comforter for Dillon to climb into bed. It was noticeably cooler in his room than in the living room, but the comforter would keep him warm enough. "Why's that?" The video game was the classic story of good against evil. White Hats against Black Hats. Of course in this instance, it was geared for children, so the hats were worn by animated dinosaurs. Dillon loved all things dinosaur.

Her little brother shrugged as he climbed onto his twin-size bed. "'Cause."

"Sounds like a good reason to me." She brushed his dark hair off his forehead and kissed him. "Go to sleep. Oatmeal with raisins in the morning."

He threw his arms tightly around her neck. "You're not gonna leave, too, are you, Abby?"

Her heart squeezed. He didn't mean leave his bedroom. He meant *leave*.

"I'm not ever going to leave," she promised. She smacked a kiss on both of his cheeks and settled him against his pillow. "Ever," she added.

He let out a long breath as if her answer had actually

been in doubt then grabbed his fleece blanket up against his cheek and turned onto his side.

Abby left his room, pulling the door halfway closed so that he'd still be able to see the light from the bathroom next door.

Then she returned to the living room, blew out all the candles and cleaned up, washing and drying the crystal glasses carefully before putting them back in the cupboard.

Seeing that the fire was burning low and steadily, safely contained by the screen, she shut off the lights in preparation of going to bed herself.

Instead of going to her own room, though, she found herself at the front window, peering into the darkness.

She touched her fingertips to her lips.

Felt her stomach swoop around.

It was a first for her.

Oh, not the kiss. She'd been kissed before. Just never at midnight. Never on New Year's Eve.

But she needed to remember that to Sloan McCray, the kiss was probably nothing more than a simple gesture.

She looked at the house next door. Wondered where his bedroom was. Wondered if he was thinking about her, too.

But then she shook her head. He'd called her "wet behind the ears." And the way she was standing there, gazing at his house in the darkness, would only prove that she was. So she turned on her heels and went into her bedroom across the hall from Dillon's.

Her bed wasn't the narrow twin that Dillon's was, but it was just as innocent. She peeled off her leggings and her sweater and pulled open her drawer. Her pj's were about as seductive as Dillon's, too. Soft cotton pants with pink-and-green polka dots and a matching T-shirt with a grinning skunk on the front of it.

She made a face as she changed and threw herself down on the middle of her full-size bed.

Her room was even chillier than Dillon's, but she felt hot. Flushed. It didn't take a genius to figure out why.

Even before learning that the man next door was a true-life American hero, he'd made her stomach swoop.

She stared into the darkness and pressed her fingertips to her lips again.

Then she groaned and flipped onto her side, hugging the pillow to her cheek.

The mattress springs squeaked slightly when Sloan flipped restlessly onto his back for the tenth time.

Dawn was finally relieving the darkness seeping around the blinds, and instead of lying there, tossing and turning pointlessly for another few hours, he pushed off the bed and went to the window. He tilted the blinds just enough so that he could look down on the house next door.

Did the window on the side of the house belong to her bedroom or Dillon's?

He muttered a low oath. Kissing her had been stupid.

Sweet as all get-out.

But still stupid.

Abby Marcum was a nice girl. And, sweet lips or not, she was not what he needed in his life.

He didn't know what he needed. But he knew it was not a girl like her. A girl with responsibilities. With ties. The kind of girl who'd expect ties.

As well she should.

If there was one thing Sloan was not good at, it was ties. He was trying where Tara was concerned, but even with his own sister he wasn't winning any awards.

He turned away from the window, dragged on his running gear and went outside. The air was frozen, sending his breath into clouds around his head as he stretched. He usually ran in the middle of the night. Maybe that was crazy, but it was better than tossing and turning while sleeplessness drove him nuts.

Last night, though, he'd been busy looking into Abby's open, innocent face.

He shut down those thoughts and set off down the street in the opposite direction from the one he usually went, just so he wouldn't pass by her house.

Instead, he ended up passing the school where Dillon would be going in a few days, and where she'd be handing out bandages and ice packs, and he thought about her anyway.

He picked up his pace and headed around to Main Street. Light was already streaming from the windows of Ruby's Café. New Year's Day or not, Tabby Taggart was obviously already at work in the kitchen, probably making the fresh sweet rolls that people came for from miles away. He knew that she'd already have hot coffee brewing and if he knocked on the window, she'd let him in.

He kept running and passed the darkened windows of his sister's shop, Classic Charms. Even though she'd taken on a partner now, he still thought of the shop as Tara's. He finally slowed as he reached the sheriff's office and went inside to the warmth and the smell of coffee there.

The dispatcher, Pam Rasmussen, gave him a look over the reading glasses perched on her nose. "Surprise, surprise. Some of us come into the office because we're scheduled on duty. Others, namely you, come in because you have nothing better to do."

"Happy New Year to you, too. And I'm not here to work. I was just out for a run." He reached across her desk and flipped the book she was reading so he could see the cover. "Suppose that's another one of those romances you like."

"What if it is? *Romance* isn't a dirty word. If you realized that, maybe you wouldn't go around so grumpy all the time. I know plenty of women who'd—"

"No," he cut her off bluntly. The last thing he needed was a setup by her. Or by his sister. Or by anyone.

The taste of dark, creamy chocolate on Abby's lips taunted him, and he ruthlessly closed his mind to it. "Quiet night?"

"Except for a call out at the Pierce place." She grimaced. "Neighbors called in the disturbance."

Sloan filled his mug and glanced around the office. All of the desks were empty. "Who took the call?"

"Ruiz. Just before he got off shift. Report's still on his desk if you want to read it."

Dave Ruiz was one of the other deputies at the Weaver office. There were more than twenty of them in all, covering the county.

"Dawson's out on an accident toward Braden, and Jerry's checking an alarm that went off at the medical offices next to Shop-World," Pam added, without looking up from her book.

Sloan picked up the report on the Pierce disturbance, read through it and tossed it back down again. "Lorraine Pierce needs to leave that bastard," he said.

"Yup." Pam turned a page in her book. "But she won't. Not until he puts her in the hospital. Or worse."

Sloan sighed. He figured Pam was probably right. And there wasn't a damn thing they could do because Lorraine refused to admit that her husband, Bobby, had hurt or threatened her in any way. Every time they'd locked him up, she'd taken him home again. "She ought to put some thought into that kid of hers, then," he muttered. Calvin Pierce was about Dillon's age.

Which only had him thinking about Abby yet again.

He gulped down the coffee, scorching the lining of his

mouth in the process. But not even that managed to eradicate the image of Abby's soft eyes staring up at him over a crystal glass full of milk.

"When're you gonna tell Max you'll stay on for good?"

He looked over at Pam. She was still reading her book.

The sheriff had asked him to stay on permanently, but Sloan wasn't ready to agree. "Guess that's between me and Max."

She tilted her head, eyeing him over the top of her reading glasses. She just smiled slightly. Pam was not only the department's dispatcher, she was also one of the biggest gossips in town, and he didn't want to provide the woman with any more fodder than necessary.

He took his coffee, went into the locker room and grabbed a shower. Then he dressed in jeans and an old ATF sweatshirt, signed out his usual cruiser and drove back home through the thin morning light.

Abby's house was still dark when he turned into his driveway a few minutes later. No signs that they were up and about or that the oatmeal with raisins was in progress.

He went inside and started a pot of coffee and tried to pretend that the house next to him was still sitting empty and cold and unoccupied.

He was no more successful at that than he was trying to decide what to do with his life.

"Abby, come *on*." Dillon was dancing around on his snow-booted feet, impatiently waiting for her to finish putting away the breakfast dishes. "You promised we'd make a snowman. With a carrot nose and everything."

Her brother was a lot more enthusiastic about trudging around in the snow for a few hours than she was. But she'd promised, so she rounded the breakfast counter and tugged his stocking cap down over his eyes, making him giggle. "You can get started while I put on my coat."

He pushed his hat back and raced out the front door, so anxious that he didn't even pull it shut behind him. She followed and stuck her head out. "Stay in our yard," she started to warn needlessly. Dillon was already crouching down next to the porch, balling up a handful of snow in his mittens to begin the snowman.

Her gaze shifted to the house next door.

It was completely still, not even showing a spiral of smoke from the chimney like most of the other houses on the block. She would have assumed he was gone, if not for the SUV emblazoned with Sheriff on the side parked in his driveway.

"Hurry *up,* Abby!"

Dragging her eyes away from the house next door, she noticed that Dillon's snowball had already grown to the size of a pumpkin. She retrieved her own coat and boots and, when she was bundled up almost as much as her brother, went outside.

The pumpkin had nearly doubled in diameter by the time she joined Dillon in the middle of the yard. "How big are you planning to make that?"

He threw his arms wide. "This big."

She couldn't help laughing. "You want a *fat* snowman, then. All right." She bent over and put her gloved hands against the big ball. "Let's roll, bud."

Even between the two of them, by the time they managed to push the growing ball across the yard twice more, they could barely manage to budge it. "This is big enough," she told him breathlessly as she straightened. Her breath clouded around her head, but warm from their exertions, she pulled off her knit cap and shoved it into her pocket.

"No, it's not," Dillon argued. He threw his arms wide again. "*This* big."

"Dillon—"

"Kid's right," a deep voice said behind them. "It's nowhere near big enough."

She whirled to see Sloan standing on his front porch watching them. Pleasure exploded in her veins.

He'd kissed her.

On New Year's Eve at midnight, he'd kissed her.

Maybe it meant nothing to him, but it sure had meant something to her.

"Happy New Year," she said brightly. Despite the frigid temperature, he was wearing only a long-sleeved black sweatshirt with his jeans. "Aren't you cold?"

There was at least fifty feet separating their houses, but she could still see his wry smile from where she stood. "Watching all that work you're doing's keeping me warm enough."

Not entirely sure what to make of that, she felt herself flush. Dillon was bouncing around his snowman base, and she focused on that. "We can't make this any bigger," she told them both. "It's already too heavy to move."

"Mr. Sloan'll help," Dillon said. He peered up at Sloan. "Wontcha?"

"Dillon," Abby cautioned quickly. She was still surprised at Dillon's unusual openness where their new neighbor was concerned. "Mr. *McCray* might have other things to do right now. It's New Year's Day, remember? It's a holiday. People usually spend holidays with their families or friends."

Dillon's lower lip pushed out. "We're not with our family. And maybe he's a friend."

She didn't dare glance at Sloan. "We just met Mr. Mc-

Cray yesterday." Kiss or not, it was too early to tell just what Sloan McCray was to them, besides their neighbor.

"Every time you say Mr. McCray, I want to look around my shoulder for my old man."

"I suppose it really should be Deputy McCray, anyway."

"You're a *deputy?*" Dillon's voice went up a notch. "Do you got a gun and a badge?"

"I do, though I don't much care for the gun part." Sloan had come down his steps. He was carrying a silver thermal cup in one bare hand, and his eyes narrowed slightly as he took a drink of its contents while he crossed the yard. "And I think just calling me Sloan will do."

Considering the heat rising inside her, Abby wanted to unwind the scarf from around her neck and ditch it, too, but she resisted the urge. Dillon would think he could do the same, and he was plagued with winter colds. "You need a coat," she told Sloan. She also didn't want Dillon thinking he could emulate the tall man from next door, either. "At least some gloves."

"I didn't get to come out without *my* coat," Dillon said. With his stocking cap, his puffy down coat, his scarf and his mittens, his skinny little body was nearly round.

"And we've got to do as Nurse Marcum says," Sloan drawled. He pulled a pair of black gloves from his back pocket. "Think these'll do?"

She knew she was blushing. "Not unless they're on your hands."

His amusement turned to an outright smile, confirming what she already knew. Spectacular. Definitely spectacular.

And she felt entirely caught in the spell of his brown eyes.

"Hold this." He handed her the thermal mug and pulled

on his gloves, his gaze finally sliding away to focus on Dillon.

"Your sister needs to see what the men can do," Sloan was saying to Dillon, who beamed in response. He crouched next to the boulder-sized snowball. Dillon did the same, and they began rolling the ball, not stopping until it was even more enormous.

Abby dragged her gaze from the view of Sloan's backside before he straightened. "Good thing you finally stopped," she offered. "Or there wouldn't be enough snow left on the ground to make the other two parts of Mr. Frosty, here." She held out the mug, but Sloan waved it off.

"Dillon, you start on the head," he suggested. "Your sister and I will work on the middle."

"He's gotta have a *fat* belly," Dillon warned.

"I think we can manage," Sloan assured him. His gaze met Abby's. "Or did you just want to sit on the porch looking pretty while the men slave away?"

"I was working hard enough on the base before you appeared." She set the mug on one of the porch steps.

Did he really think she was pretty?

Embarrassed by her own thoughts, she scooped up a handful of snow, packing it down tightly to start the midsection. Sloan added to it until it was so large she needed both hands to hold it. Then they rolled it around on the ground until it was almost as big as the base and they had to wrestle it into place. Once they had it where they wanted it, Sloan lifted Dillon so he could put the head he'd formed on top.

When they were done, Abby stood back and laughed. Dillon's snowman head was woefully small in proportion to the rest of the monster.

"I'm gonna get the carrot!" Dillon raced into the house.

Sloan moved next to Abby, and she went still when he unwound the scarf from her neck. "What are you doing?"

"Not trying to undress you in the middle of your front yard," he murmured dryly.

Her cheeks went hot. "I didn't—"

"Not that undressing you doesn't hold plenty of appeal."

Her lips snapped shut. She feared her face was as red as her coat.

He smiled slightly. "But a snowman needs a scarf, doesn't he?" He finally turned away and wrapped the scarf around the snowman's neck. The candy-cane-striped knit fluttered cheerfully against the enormously oversize mid-section.

Dillon's boots clomped on the porch as he returned. He clutched a long carrot in his fist and reached up to jab it squarely in the center of the snowman's face. "What're we gonna use for eyes?"

"When I was a kid, we always used buttons. But we don't have any spares anymore." Abby thought about the old jelly jar her grandmother had once used to store spare buttons.

Even though she looked away quickly, Sloan still caught the sudden shimmer in Abby's eyes.

Fortunately, Dillon hadn't noticed because he was too enamored of his snowy creation. Sloan gestured at his house. "I have a bag of cookies on my kitchen counter," he told the boy. "Run over and grab a few. They'll work for eyes."

But the boy didn't race off the way Sloan figured he would. He sidled next to Abby. "Should I?" he heard him ask under his breath.

She brushed her fingers over the cap on his head. "Do you want me to go with you?"

The boy ducked his chin into his coat and gave Sloan a look from the corner of his eye. "He's really a *deputy?*"

Abby nodded. She smiled at Sloan, but it didn't hold a fraction of the brilliance that he knew it could. That it should.

"Look at the truck in his driveway," she told her brother. "It says Sheriff on the side and everything."

Dillon looked. After a moment, his chin came out of his coat. "I can go myself," he announced. Evidently, *deputy* and *sheriff* were the encouragement he needed.

"Bring a couple extra cookies," Sloan suggested. "I think we need to eat a few after all this hard work."

Dillon nodded and headed across the yard with the care of someone crossing a minefield.

"He's pretty serious for a little kid."

"You would be too if you'd had a mother like ours." Abby didn't look at him but fussed with the scarf around the snowman's neck. "I was lucky. She dumped me off on her parents when I was a baby. She chose to hold on to Dillon until he was four."

"And then she booked."

Abby nodded. "Don't know where. Don't care why." Her face was open. Honest.

"But you care about buttons."

"Dillon's too serious, and you're too observant."

"County pays me to be observant."

Her lips curved sadly. "This is the first New Year's that I haven't spent with my grandmother. Every year before she got sick, she'd make black-eyed peas for good luck and roast a turkey with all the fixings." She looked past him toward the door that Dillon had disappeared through. "She used to save her buttons in a jelly jar. When I was little, I'd string them into necklaces and bracelets." She shrugged. "Probably sounds silly."

"Sounds like good memories."

Her expression softened. And he had a strong urge just to fall into the soft, gray warmth of her eyes. "They are good memories. Thanks for reminding me of that."

He took a step toward her, not even sure what he was after, but Dillon returned with all of the speed that had been missing when he went into the house. He was holding up a handful of chocolate sandwich cookies. "We gotta put the eyes in! Otherwise, Deputy Frosty can't see anything."

Abby caught the corner of her lip between her teeth, and her eyes smiled into Sloan's. "He's been promoted to deputy already? What are we going to do for a badge?"

"I'll draw him one." Stretching, Dillon worked the cookies into the snow above the carrot nose. They were a little uneven but seemed to suit the small-headed, big-bellied guy.

"What about his mouth?" Abby asked.

"He don't need a mouth."

"Sure he does," Sloan argued. "What if a pretty snow-girl came by and wanted to kiss him?" He enjoyed watching the pink color bloom in Abby's cheeks.

Dillon, however, wrinkled his nose. "Kissing's gross."

Sloan hid a smile. "Depends on the snowgirl, kid."

"Now I see why you're not still hanging around the office on your day off."

Sloan looked over his shoulder to see Pam Rasmussen sitting in her SUV, the window rolled down. She was grinning like the cat who'd gotten the cream. "Looks like y'all are having fun."

He didn't want to imagine the speculation going on inside the dispatcher's busy mind as he started to provide the briefest of introductions.

But they turned out to be unnecessary when Abby crossed the lawn and shook Pam's hand through the opened window. "I think we actually know each other through an old friend of mine from high school," she told her. "Delia Templeton?"

Pam clapped her hands together. "Of course!" Her gaze went past Abby to Sloan. "Delia's my cousin," she told him. "Well, my husband Rob's cousin, anyway. And now here you are, playing in the snow with one of our very own deputy sheriffs. What a small, small world."

Sloan could practically see the wheels turning inside Pam's head. "What're you doing here, Pam?" She and Rob lived on the other side of town.

"Doing a favor for my mom. She's been keeping an eye on her uncle's house while he's been gone." She gestured toward the house on the other side of Abby's where old Gilcrest lived. "He's coming back tomorrow, and she wanted the heat turned up for him. Told her I'd take care of it when my shift ended. Never expected to find a little romance brewing right next door." She smiled slyly as her SUV began slowly rolling forward. "Better get that heat going."

Sloan managed not to groan. "Don't pay her any attention," he told Abby as Pam drove a little farther and stopped in front of her uncle's house. "She's always like that."

"I know." Her head bobbed quickly. "Delia has shared loads of stories about her family. Everyone is into everyone's business." She looked over at Dillon, who'd lost interest in what the adults were doing and was sitting on the porch steps holding two chocolate cookies in front of his face as though they were his eyes. She grinned at the sight and looked back at Sloan. "Do you have plans for dinner today? I'm not fixing anything fancy—nothing like a turkey or black-eyed peas, but—"

"I do have plans," he cut her off abruptly then felt like a heel. He was aware of the way Pam was watching them as she walked up to the old man's house. "I promised my sister. Family dinner."

"Abby, I wanna make a badge for the snowman."

Her gray gaze cut away from his face to look at her brother. "Sure thing, honey." She glanced at Sloan again as she started toward the house. "Thanks for your help with the snowman. Hope you have a good time with your sister."

Given a choice, he'd have been happy to stay right where he was, with or without Pam's unwanted attention. There wasn't a romance brewing for the simple reason that he didn't do romance. No point.

But the heat? That was definitely already on.

Chapter Four

"Here." A longneck bottle appeared over Sloan's shoulder, and he looked back to see his brother-in-law standing there.

He wanted nothing from Axel, but he could see Tara watching them from across the living room of the Double-C's main house, where they'd all congregated after the New Year's Day feast. He accepted the bottle and clinked the bottom of it once against Axel's and turned his attention back to the football game playing on the wall-mounted television.

His hope that the other man would move along was blown when Axel sat down on the couch, too.

"Tara's worried you're going to book when your stint with Max is up."

He already knew that. But he was damned if he knew what to do about it when he couldn't even figure out what *he* wanted to do. He thought a little longingly of Abby's dinner. He wouldn't be having this conversation if he'd canceled on his sister and stayed with Abby and Dillon. But if he'd canceled, he'd just have another thing to regret where Tara was concerned. "Whether I stay or not doesn't have anything to do with Tara."

Axel grimaced. "Right, 'cause it has to do with me."

Sloan picked at the bottle label with his thumb. "I don't want to talk about this."

"Neither do I. But I love my wife. And she loves you."

"I've told her she needs to stop worrying about me."

Axel laughed shortly. "Yeah. That's going to happen. She's finally got you back. She doesn't want to lose you again."

"Whatever I decide, she's not going to lose me." He kept his focus on the television, even though the first half of the football game had just ended. "Undercover work for me is in the past." He hadn't merely worked undercover. He'd been deep undercover. So deep, and for so long, that the line between reality and fiction had gotten way too blurred.

Some days—most days—it still felt that way.

The record books would show a successful conclusion to the operation. A deadly gang had been dismantled. Murdering thieves had been imprisoned.

But in the end, Sloan's ATF career had been toast and the woman he'd loved—whom Axel Clay had been brought in to protect—had been dead.

He knew he couldn't lay the blame for Maria's death at Axel's door even if he wanted to. Sloan was the one who'd set that into motion when he'd told her the truth about what he was really doing. He hadn't wanted to lose her. But he'd lost her anyway when she'd tried going back to her old life once he'd taken his years of evidence to his bosses. If she hadn't known the truth about Sloan, they'd have left her alone. She wouldn't have been a possible witness in their eyes; she'd have just been the cocktail waitress they'd never had reason to distrust.

All she'd wanted to do was keep her life intact, but she'd paid a fatal price for it. Then it all seemed to be repeating itself when Sloan's sister suddenly found herself in the same sort of danger. It was Axel who'd succeeded in keeping Tara safe. Sloan was grateful for that, but he still knew it was his fault that she'd needed protecting in the first place.

He gave his brother-in-law a steady look. "Whether I stay or go doesn't have anything to do with you, either," he said evenly. "Or Maria," he made himself add. For his sister's sake. "Tara's good at putting down roots. I'm not."

"You're good at it when there's something that matters enough to you." Axel's tone was just as deliberate. "You spent a lot of years riding with Johnny Diablo and the Deuces." He scooped up his two-year-old son, Aidan, who was chasing full tilt after one of his older cousins. "Seems to me the question is what does matter that much to you?"

Sloan caught his nephew's wildly swinging foot before it connected with his face and tickled the bottom of it, making Aidan squeal. The little whirlwind managed to climb from his dad's lap to Sloan's back, where he clung like a monkey. "Ride! Ride!"

Glad for an excuse, Sloan rose from the couch. "Duty calls." He turned on his heel to give Axel's son his requested ride.

They went as far as the basement, which was as crowded as the upstairs living room. The main house was big, but so was the extensive Clay family. They had every age covered from babies to octogenarians.

"Gampa, Gampa, Gampa," Aidan yelled when he spotted Squire sitting amid a trio of young teenagers.

The old man handed his video-game controller to the

only girl in the trio. "Infernal game," he groused. But considering the way his face was creased with a grin, there wasn't a lot of bite to it.

Tristan Clay, who was the youngest and wealthiest of Squire's sons—and as far as Sloan was concerned, the wiliest—roused himself from his napping sprawl nearby. "That infernal game's putting a new wing on the hospital," he pointed out without heat.

Squire harrumphed. "Folks have always been willin' to throw good money away."

Tristan just smiled faintly, letting the jab pass.

It wasn't often that Sloan saw Tristan looking so relaxed. He ran his insanely successful video-gaming company, Cee-Vid, but he was also the number two man behind Hollins-Winword, an international firm that dealt in private security and covert intelligence. And it was in that role that Sloan had first dealt with the man and his nephew, Axel. Before he'd gone undercover with the Deuces, he'd asked Hollins-Winword to watch over Tara. She still hadn't quite forgiven him for not informing her of that particular fact, but since she was as happy as a clam now with Axel, she didn't beat him up with it too often.

"Give me my great-grandson," Squire told Sloan, and he was happy enough to push aside the memories as he detached the kid's fingers from his hair to set him on the floor. The kid immediately bulleted toward the gray-haired man, who scooped him up and blew a raspberry against his neck. Aidan's laughter filled the spacious room and immediately, young cousins began appearing, clamoring for similar treatment from the old man.

"I thought he was bad with his grandchildren," Tristan commented, leaving his spot that was no longer peaceful at all to follow Sloan back up the stairs. "He's twice as bad with his great-grandkids. The man was hell on us when we were growing up, but given the chance, he'll spoil the daylights out of them."

Sloan wondered if Abby's grandfather had been similarly inclined, or if her grandparents had been stricter because they'd taken on a parental role.

They made it to the top of the stairs and turned into the kitchen. The enormous table there was covered with a dozen desserts in varying stages of demolition, sidetracking both of them. Tristan studied his choices while Sloan helped himself to a hefty wedge of the chocolate cake he knew his sister had brought. It was the same cake his mother used to make for their birthdays when they were kids.

The cake was incredible. The memories that came with it weren't.

"Max sending you to that conference coming up in Cheyenne?"

Max had tried working on him to attend, but he couldn't see the point. Not when he wasn't even sure he was going to be around in a few months. "Dawson and Ruiz are going."

His sister entered the kitchen. "There you are." She was carrying Hank on her hip.

"Wasn't exactly hiding," he pointed out and watched the way his nephew eyed the cake on his fork. He knew better than to give the boy any, though. He'd made that mistake once already and quickly learned that Tara didn't want him having anything sugary until he was older.

Not that Hank the Tank was looking particularly deprived. The kid wasn't a year old yet, but he was already showing signs that he'd inherited the Clay genes when it came to size. He sure hadn't gotten his height from his petite mama. Tara was nearly a foot shorter than Sloan, and he and her husband were pretty much eye to eye.

"This is the first time I've had a chance to talk to you," she returned.

"Could've come talk to me earlier instead of sending your husband."

Tara's brown eyes flashed. "I didn't *send* Axel to do anything! As if the man ever does something he doesn't choose to do in the first place." Tristan made a noise and buried his attention in his pecan pie as he escaped. So much for the big-shot secret agent.

Sloan wished he could follow. He pushed his fork into the cake again and ignored the hopeful gleam in Hank's eyes. "He'd take a bullet for you."

She rubbed her cheek against Hank's bald head. "You're the one who took a bullet," she reminded him.

A graze. And it had been more than two years ago. She'd been pregnant with Aidan and on the verge of marrying Axel.

"But he has walked through fire for me," she allowed. "Literally."

"Which was my fault, too."

She shook her head. "I've never blamed you for what happened at the church that day when Maria's brother set that fire. He wanted to get back at you for her death by getting to me. He was insane with grief."

"You have more pity for him than I do." And more pity than the courts had. The lunatic had been convicted and would be locked away for a good long time.

"It's all water under the bridge, anyway," she dismissed. "If you really want a fresh start, don't you think that should include letting go of the past?"

He wished he could give her the answers she wanted to hear. "I don't want to promise something I'm not sure I can deliver."

She studied him for a moment. "Would you go back to the ATF if you could?"

He let out a humorless laugh. "Goob, they don't *want* me back." They'd made that plain enough when he'd been fired after the Deuce's trial had finally ended. They hadn't taken kindly to him drawing in anyone from Hollins-Winword to protect Maria or Tara. They'd told him it had shown a strong lack of faith in his own agency and conveniently ignored the fact that they hadn't been willing to provide any sort of protection themselves.

"But if you *could?*"

Would he? Nearly his entire adult life had been wrapped up in his ATF career. "I don't know. Maybe. Probably." He shook his head. "I don't know."

"Well," she said after a moment, "that's not what I wanted to talk to you about, anyway." She shifted Hank onto her other hip. "What's this I hear about you and your new neighbor? She's the new school nurse, right?"

He stared. "What do you know about her?"

"*She* was your mysterious plan last night, wasn't she?"

"She, who?" Max and his wife, Sarah, chose that moment to wander into the kitchen, and her blue gaze bounced from Sloan to Tara and back again. "Pretty little Abby Marcum?"

Sloan eyed his boss, but Max just shrugged. "Don't look at me. I might be the sheriff, but I don't know anything."

Sarah poked him in the side, and he jerked away, grinning. Then he frowned. "No more pecan pie?"

"Tristan finished it off."

"Figures." He took the last slice of chocolate cake. "This'll do just as well."

"Even after all these years together I do *not* know how you can eat the way you do and never gain a pound," Sarah complained. "You had a piece of Gloria's cheesecake an hour ago."

Max swatted her lightly on the butt. "My wife keeps me well exercised."

She rolled her eyes. "Here I thought you were going to help me get started on some of these dishes. Go on, then. Go back to your football game. I know that's what you really want to do."

"Always figure it's smart to get while the gettin's good." Max looked at Sloan. "You coming? Half time's over."

Sloan finished off his cake in a single bite and tossed the paper plate in the trash. "Just like Mom's," he told his twin, and then he did what any smart man would do and escaped while the escaping was good.

The house was cold again when Abby waked early the next morning. She pulled on a thick sweatshirt over her flannel pajamas and checked on Dillon, who was still sound asleep, before starting a pot of coffee. With the water gurgling and the scent of coffee beginning to fill the kitchen, she pushed her feet into her boots and let herself quietly out the door. She didn't like having to take more wood from Sloan's pile, but they'd burned through the last of what she had during the night, and she didn't want Dillon getting up to such a cold house.

Deputy Frosty's fat belly was just as fat as it had been the day before, but the striped scarf had fallen onto the ground. She stopped long enough to wind it around the snowman's neck, making sure the cardboard badge pinned to the knit was visible. Dillon had spent considerable time making the thing, and he'd certainly want to see it there today.

When she was finished, she balled her cold hands in the pockets of her sweatshirt and hurried across the yard.

"You're an early riser."

She nearly jumped out of her skin at the sound of Sloan's voice. The sky was gray and heavy, but it was still light enough to see him standing on his front porch.

And it was more than a little alarming the way pleasure engulfed her at the sight of him. Particularly considering the way he'd bolted the day before, after Pam Rasmussen had come by.

"So are you." Her voice sounded breathless but she couldn't help it. Seeing him made her feel breathless. "You're looking very official." He was coatless, too. But whereas she'd been caught in her flannel jammies and an oversize sweatshirt, he looked downright glorious in his uniform. He wore sharply creased khaki-colored pants with a dark green, long-sleeved shirt and black tie, complete with badge pinned to his insanely wide chest. She also noticed that, with a collared shirt, there was no hint that he had that intriguing tattoo that started on his neck and dipped beneath his clothing. "On duty today?" She cringed since it was pretty unlikely he would wear his uniform if he weren't.

"In a while." He lifted the mug he was holding. "Want some coffee?"

Even though she had her own pot brewing, she very nearly nodded. She pushed her fists deeper into her pockets, hoping to stretch the sweatshirt a little lower over her stupid pajama pants. "No, thanks. I was just going to grab some more wood. Dillon's still sleeping."

He straightened away from the post he'd been leaning against, set his mug on the rail and came down the steps toward her.

Her ability to breathe normally evaporated entirely.

All she could think of was the way he'd kissed her.

And the way he'd bolted.

Admittedly, he *had* been headed for a family dinner, but it still had felt as if he couldn't wait to escape.

He kept going when he reached her, though, angling toward the back of the house. "Half expected to see another snowman keeping Frosty company in your front yard."

She skipped to catch up with him and wished again that she'd taken the time to change into jeans. "If we get more snow out of those clouds, I expect he'll have company soon enough." She pulled one hand out of her pocket to tuck her hair behind her ear, only to realize she hadn't taken the time to brush her hair yet, either.

Lovely. Plaid pajamas, morning breath and a rat's nest of hair.

She ducked her chin into the collar of her sweatshirt and twitched the hood up over her hair.

"Cold?"

She smiled and shrugged, even though she was sure he was the cause of her shivering rather than the cold morning.

When they reached the back of the house, she quickly gathered several pieces of firewood. When he started to help her, she protested. "You're going to get your shirt dirty."

"Sweetheart, I've gotten worse things on my uniform before than a few wood slivers."

Sweetheart.

She shivered again and headed back around the side of the house, crossing diagonally to her front door.

Sloan followed her inside, and they stacked the wood next to the fireplace. "Looks like you did some more unpacking. Are they your grandparents?"

She glanced at the framed photographs he'd noticed on the mantel. "Yes."

"This you?" He tapped one in particular of Abby and her grandparents.

"We were pheasant hunting." She added a split log to the fire and jabbed the embers before adjusting the screen.

"How old were you?"

She didn't have to look at the photo to remind herself. "Seventeen." She and her grandfather had gone out hunting only one more time after that. It hadn't been the same without her grandmother coming along, but she hadn't been healthy enough at that point to accompany them.

"You look about thirteen."

And even more wet behind the ears, no doubt.

She pressed her hands against her flannel-covered thighs and straightened. "Maybe so," she said, "but he taught me to shoot almost as well as he could." She headed into the kitchen.

"You like hunting?"

"I liked going out with my grandparents. Without them?" She shrugged and filled a coffee cup. "I can't really see myself going out again. I don't think I have the heart for it." She took a sip, watching him over the brim of the cup. Not even the width of the living room was enough to dim the sheer wattage of him. "I'll get enough wood today to replace what I've used."

"I told you not to worry about that." He leaned on the breakfast counter. "Every time you talk about your grandparents, you look sad."

She started to tuck her hair behind her ear again, ran into that rat's nest of tangles and opened an overhead cabinet instead, pulling out the cardboard container of oatmeal to occupy herself. "I miss them. The worst thing about leaving Braden is not being able to visit my grandmother every day."

"It isn't that far away."

She smiled a little. "That's exactly what I keep telling Dillon." She realized they were in the same positions they'd been in when he'd kissed her and felt blood rushing into her face. She snatched up her coffee and took such a hasty drink that she almost gasped. "Aren't you on duty soon?" she asked abruptly.

His smile widened a little as if he knew exactly how he affected her. But he straightened and headed toward the door. She couldn't seem to help herself from following him out onto the porch. But the sudden shrieking of her name from inside the house had her racing right back inside, Sloan hard on her heels.

She met Dillon in the hallway, where he collided with her and grabbed on to her as though the world was ending.

Another nightmare.

Her heart squeezing, she sank down to the floor and pulled him right onto her lap. "I'm here, honey. Right here."

"I couldn't find you," he sobbed. "I looked everywhere, but—"

"Shh." She smoothed his hair back from his sweaty face and kissed his forehead. "I'm here, and I'm not going anywhere."

The hairs on the back of Sloan's neck slowly settled as he watched Abby sit there, comforting the boy.

"It was just a bad dream," he heard her say in a soothing voice. "And it's all gone, but I'm still here." She pressed her cheek to the top of the boy's head, her glossy brown hair blending with Dillon's.

He knew he should leave them to their privacy.

But walking out when the kid was so upset went against every grain in his body. He took a cautious step forward, and Abby focused on him.

"Look who else is here," she murmured to Dillon. "Deputy McCray came to say good morning to you."

It wasn't true, but Sloan didn't care. Particularly when the little boy peered around Abby at him. "You did?"

He took another step closer and crouched down. "I also wanted to say that you did a great job making Frosty's badge out there."

"It's not like yours, though."

Sloan unfastened his badge and held it up. "I think it was pretty close."

Dillon didn't unlatch himself from Abby, but he sat up a little straighter. "Abby helped me cut out the star."

"You drew the star first," Abby said.

She was watching him as closely as Dillon was, and Sloan wasn't sure whose gaze unnerved him more. "Do you want to wear it for a minute?"

Dillon's eyes went as wide as saucers. "Can I?"

Sloan knew Max well enough to know his boss wasn't going to sweat him being a little late for his shift. Not considering the situation. "You bet." He attached the badge to the boy's dinosaur-print pajama shirt. "How does it feel?"

Dillon scrambled to his feet and darted into the bathroom that opened onto the hall. Sloan could see him stretching as high as he could to see himself in the mirror over the sink.

Abby gave Sloan a grateful smile and pushed to her feet, as well. She followed Dillon into the small bathroom and lifted him higher. "Pretty cool, huh?"

"The coolest," Dillon breathed. He wriggled, and Abby set him back on his feet. He came back out into the hallway, his thin chest puffed out. "When I'm big, I'm gonna be a deputy, too."

Abby's pretty eyes met Sloan's. "Thank you," she mouthed silently.

Then she touched Dillon's shoulder. "Deputy McCray

probably needs his badge back now, Dillon, so he can go to work."

"Okay." But before Sloan could unfasten the badge, the kid was already doing it, the tip of his tongue sticking out the corner of his mouth as he looked down to see what he was doing. When he'd unpinned it, he held the badge out on his flattened palm. "Watch your back out there," he said solemnly.

Sloan managed not to smile.

Abby wasn't so successful. The smile that her lips seemed created to wear was back on her face.

He took the badge and pinned it in place. He gave a quick salute and headed toward the front door.

"He's a real White Hat," he heard Dillon whisper behind him. "Isn't he?"

Sloan didn't wait to hear Abby's answer as he let himself out through the front door. Whatever the White Hats were that the kid was talking about, Sloan knew that he'd never worn one.

White Hats were for the good guys.

They weren't for the guys who'd only ever hurt the ones who least deserved it.

Chapter Five

Even though Sloan had told her not to worry about it, when Abby and Dillon went out later that afternoon and visited the big-box Shop-World on the far side of town, she added a few extra bags of firewood to their shopping cart. When they got back to the house and unloaded their purchases, she carted the bags to the rear of his house, pulled off the plastic and stacked the wood neatly on top of his pile.

By then, it had started snowing again, and she and Dillon spent the rest of the afternoon inside. They unpacked the last few boxes, played a game of 'White Hats' and baked a batch of chocolate cookies while the repairman she'd called fixed the furnace. And even though they were busy pretty much all day long, Abby was hyperaware that the SUV with Sheriff on the side didn't reappear in the driveway next door all day. It wasn't there when she caved to Dillon's constant begging and let him take a covered plate of the cookies to leave on Sloan's front porch. It wasn't there, even after she'd read a story to Dillon and tucked him into bed, and it wasn't there when she hustled him out of the house the next morning for his first day at his new school. *Their* new school.

Mercifully, she didn't have any extra time to think about the handsome deputy as Principal Gage gave her a tour of the school and she settled into the office that was now hers. She checked supplies, read through the files of the students who had continuing health-care needs and by lunchtime had seen a half-dozen children for everything from an earache to a girl having her first period. She was so busy, in fact, that she ate her peanut butter and jelly sandwich in her office and didn't leave it at all until she went with the rest of the teachers and administration to attend the assembly being held in the gymnasium.

There, she stood in the back of the room while the students noisily claimed their patches of gym floor and sat down. They were arranged by classes with the youngest in front and the oldest in back, and Abby didn't even realize how nervous she was for Dillon until she spotted him sitting cross-legged next to a little blond-haired girl who, judging by the way she was chattering away, didn't seem too put off by Dillon's apparent silence.

Then the genial principal moved to the front of the room, efficiently gathering the children's attention while the teachers began moving to the back of the room where a few rows of folding chairs were set up.

"Come on." Dee Crowder, one of the first teachers Abby had met that morning, nudged Abby along the row of seats. She taught third grade and was short like Abby with wildly curly blond hair and an infectious smile that reminded her of Delia's. "There's room for you to sit, too."

So Abby scooted along the row of chairs to the end and dutifully sat down. "How often are there assemblies?"

Dee shrugged and pulled a tube of lip gloss from the pocket of her red sweater. "Couple times a month. They don't always have all the grades at once, though. Today it's just because of the presentation."

Abby knew that safety and drug-abuse prevention were the topics this afternoon. While she certainly supported the cause, she hoped the assembly wouldn't drag on too long. She still had a stack of student files to get through.

"I don't know why I thought moving to one of the condos out near Shop-World would come with better pickings where men are concerned," Dee whispered. She bumped her shoulder against Abby's. "You buy the old Downing place that's been empty for a year and basically hit the lottery."

Abby dragged her thoughts from the unread files waiting for her to the teacher next to her. "Sorry?"

"I'm stuck in a lease, living between newlyweds on one side and a lady who has four cats on the other, and you move in next door to the hottest guy in town."

She realized that Dee's avid gaze was glued to the front of the gymnasium and followed it.

There stood Sloan, alongside Sheriff Scalise and two other officers.

And even though she was sitting in the back of a very crowded gymnasium, when his attention traveled across the audience, it seemed as if his gaze honed right in on her.

She moistened her lips and shifted in her seat.

The sheriff had taken over the microphone at the podium after the principal finished his spiel about home emergency plans, but she barely heard a word of what he said.

Sloan looked as magnificent in his uniform now as he had the morning before.

Dee leaned close again, her whisper barely audible. "You might know he'd be good-looking. He's not a Clay, but his sister married one, and there's not a dud in the bunch."

Abby had grown up in Braden, but anyone who lived in the state had heard of the Clay family. There was the cattle ranch they owned, the Double-C, which was one of the largest in the state. There was Cee-Vid, the company that put out games like 'White Hats.' It, too, was run by one of the Clays and was located right there in Weaver. There was also the hospital—the only one in the region. From the stories her grandparents had told, building it had come about mostly because of the Clays' efforts.

"Even Sheriff Scalise fits the mold," Dee was saying. "He married Sarah Clay."

Abby had met Sarah that morning. She was the other third-grade teacher. And Dee had a point. Sheriff Scalise definitely qualified as tall, dark and handsome. But there was nothing about the married father of three that made Abby's mouth run dry.

Unlike his newest deputy.

Sloan and one of the other deputies—a slender woman with dark blond hair—had begun moving along the rows of students and were handing out stacks of flyers.

"Half of those flyers are going to end up as paper airplanes," Dee whispered. "Mark my words."

"What are they about?"

As the deputies went row to row, the noise level in the cavernous room was rising, and Dee didn't bother to keep her voice down. "They have a drawing contest every year for their drug-abuse resistance program. The winners from each grade get to do a ride-along in a car with an on-duty officer—all geared appropriately toward their level, of course—and then from those drawings, they'll choose a final winner. The drawings will be used on all the flyers and brochures about the program for the next year." She suddenly popped out of her seat. "Calvin Pierce." Her voice, surprisingly loud for someone so small, rang out across the room. "That shoe belongs on your foot, not on your neighbor's head."

Abby saw a towheaded little boy near Dillon sink guiltily onto his bottom and shove his foot back into his shoe.

Dee sighed and sat back down herself. "It's a popular program with the kids," she went on as if there'd been no interruption whatsoever. "And anything that keeps the message going about saying no is a good thing as far as I'm concerned. It was Joe's—Principal Gage's—idea. They are trying to come up with something similar that would be just as popular at the junior-high and high-school levels. But they're a tougher audience." She sighed a little then crossed her legs and looked at Abby. "Don't you think he's hot? You know," she prompted when Abby hesitated. "Your neighbor."

For a moment, Abby had thought the other woman meant Principal Gage. "I don't know Deputy McCray all that well." She just knew what his lips tasted like. How he smelled. How his smile was too long in coming…

"That's not what I hear."

Abby started. "Hear from whom?"

"You're from Braden, right?" Dee barely waited for Abby to nod. "Then you know how word gets around."

"Not always an accurate word, though." She felt flustered right down to her bones, and it wasn't helped by the fact that Sloan had reached the back of the room where they were sitting.

"Ladies." He handed Abby, who was at the end of the

row, the rest of the flyers he'd been holding, and his fingers brushed against hers.

"Deputy McCray." Dee smiled brilliantly and took the stack, save one sheet, out of Abby's nerveless grasp. She kept a few for herself before passing them along to the teacher beside her. "It's so nice to see you taking part today."

Sloan barely glanced at the curly-haired teacher as he gave a noncommittal smile. "Part of the job."

He did, however, do more than glance at Abby, and she could have melted into her metal folding seat when his smile seemed to warm for her alone. "Thanks for the cookies," he told her. "You make them yourself?"

Much too aware of Dee's attention, Abby lifted her shoulders. "Dillon thought you needed some." It was only half the truth.

Her little brother *had* thought Sloan needed some since they'd used his store-bought cookies for both the snowman's eyes and Dillon's stomach. But while she'd mixed up the chocolaty dough, Abby hadn't been able to forget that her grandmother always claimed she'd caught Abby's grandfather with that very same recipe. Since they'd married only a month after a young Minerva had offered an equally young Thomas one of her cookies at a church bake sale, and had stayed married for the rest of their lives, Abby figured the story had some merit.

"Then I'll have to thank Dillon, too." He began making his way back up to the front of the room where the principal was making an effort to quiet the crowd.

Dee bumped her shoulder again. "Make cookies for everyone you barely know? Your other neighbors, too?"

The woman was grinning with such good cheer that Abby couldn't help but like her. "My other neighbor has been out of town," she said blithely. "But, yes, I'll have a plate for him." She'd have to make another batch, but that was moot.

Dee laughed soundlessly and turned her attention back to the principal.

Soon after, the gymnasium was once again a madhouse as the students were dismissed back to their classrooms. Abby slowly folded her chair and stacked it against the rest. She knew she was lingering, watching Sloan as he stood at the front of the room talking with the principal and the sheriff.

But he didn't look her way again, and rather than being the last person to leave, she made her way back to her office and the files awaiting her. She didn't have a chance to finish studying them, though, because a boy came in with a bloody nose, and then she needed to see several students at the junior high next door to administer their regular medications.

When she collected Dillon at the end of the day, he had a stack of work sheets clutched in his hand that he was supposed to finish at home, and she had a stack of district policies to read. "We both have homework," she told him as they set off for the short walk home. "What do you have to work on there?"

He pushed the papers into his backpack then hitched it over his shoulders. "Spelling. And we gotta turn in a report about our 'mergency plan at home."

Two things he would fly through, she knew. Dillon was all about what to do in an emergency. She'd already shown him how to open all the windows in the house in case there was a fire and they couldn't get out the front door. "What about the drawing contest the sheriff talked about? Do you want to enter?"

He ducked his chin. He took her hand as they crossed

the street that had gone quiet again after the last of the students had departed. "Dunno."

Surprised, she looked down at him. "You love to draw. Why not?"

"Calvin says only weenies enter the contest."

Abby squelched the first response that came to her mind where Calvin was concerned. "Who is Calvin?"

"Calvin Pierce," he muttered, his chin even deeper in his coat.

The same towheaded boy that Dee had called out during the assembly. "Calvin is in your class?" The growing school had two classes each for most grades.

Dillon nodded. They followed the sidewalk around the corner onto their street. "I gotta sit at the same table as him." He sounded morose. "In the *front* row."

"Well, maybe you won't be in the front row all the time," she said encouragingly. "And you shouldn't listen to nonsense from any of the other kids about entering a contest that I know you must be interested in. Don't you want a chance to see what it's like to be a deputy like Deputy McCray? You would get to tour the sheriff's office and ride in one of their official vehicles."

"I prob'ly wouldn't win anyway." He tugged his mitten-covered hand free of hers and hitched up the straps of his backpack again.

Abby hid a sigh. "You don't know that unless you try." She decided to drop the matter for now. "How did you like your teacher?"

"Ms. Normington's okay. She's got a goldfish on her desk."

"And the other kids in your class? Besides Calvin?"

"They're okay."

She chewed the inside of her lip and watched him as

they reached the edge of their yard. "Who was the girl you were sitting next to during the assembly?"

"Chloe."

"She looked pretty friendly." Talkative, at any rate, from what Abby had observed.

"She's at my table, too." He suddenly looked up at her. "Is Deputy McCray gonna be your boyfriend?"

She stopped in her tracks. A squiggle of something worked around inside her chest, messing with her breathing. "Of course not!"

He peered at her. "Wouldn't he be a good one?"

Thoughts of just how good Sloan might be in all sorts of roles swirled inside her head, nearly making her choke. "I have no idea," she managed to say with a reasonable amount of calm, all things considered. "Deputy McCray is a nice man who lives next door to us. That's all." She moistened her lips. "Why would you even ask that question?"

But he seemed to have lost interest in the subject just as quickly as he'd brought it up. He hitched his backpack up again and set off across the snow, stopping only long enough to reposition the snowman's sagging carrot nose. "Can we have skeddi for supper?"

"Sure," she said faintly and wished her own thoughts could be so easily switched.

What would Sloan be like as a *boyfriend?*

The term was almost laughable, because there was nothing boyish about him.

He was a man. All man.

And while she had no personal experience being *with* a man, her imagination where Sloan was concerned worked just fine.

Too fine.

Warmth flowed through her, making her feel a little weak.

She swallowed, glancing over at the two-storied house next door as she unlocked her front door and waited for Dillon to go inside. But when she saw the familiar SUV turning onto their street at the end of the block, she jumped as if she'd been caught doing something wicked and rushed inside after her little brother, closing the door harder than necessary.

"What's wrong?"

"Not a thing. The wind caught the door." She blamed the heat in her cheeks on the lie. "Why don't you sit at the counter to do your work sheets? I'll get you some milk and a cookie to hold you over until spaghetti. Okay?"

He nodded as he started unearthing himself from his coat. She left him to it and hurried into her bedroom, where she dumped her briefcase on her dresser and ignored her flushed reflection in the mirror as she pulled off her own coat and gloves. Then she exchanged her navy suit for jeans and a sweatshirt from nursing college and yanked her hair up into a clip on top of her head. The person looking back at her in the mirror now was the one she felt more familiar with than the RN who wore a suit and carried her grandfather's ancient leather briefcase.

She headed back out to the kitchen. Dillon was sitting at the breakfast counter, hunched over a work sheet with his pencil clenched in his fist. The tip of his tongue was caught in the corner of his mouth.

She smiled, resisted the urge to smack a kiss on his head and poured him the promised glass of milk. She set two of the chocolate cookies they'd baked together on a napkin beside his milk and began pulling together the makings for spaghetti sauce. When the doorbell rang a few minutes later, she didn't even have a chance to set down her knife before Dillon hopped off his perch. "I'll get it!"

It was so out of character for her usually shy brother

that she hated to caution him, but she still followed him. And then she went dry-mouthed all over again after Dillon pulled open the door to reveal Sloan standing there on the step.

When his eyes met hers, her stomach swooped and her riotous imagination went completely berserk. She was glad for Dillon's presence, because she could only imagine what the good townspeople of Weaver would have to say if the new school nurse tried to jump their deputy sheriff's bones right there on the front porch.

"We're having skeddi," her little brother announced, grabbing Sloan's hand and pulling him right inside. "You want to have some, too?" He shut the door hard, as if he could keep Sloan from leaving by that act alone.

Abby opened her mouth. Closed it again.

She knew she was blushing and there wasn't a darn thing she could do about it.

Sloan was still eyeing her, his expression amused—hopefully because of Dillon's enthusiasm and not because he could read her X-rated thoughts. He was holding the empty cookie plate. "He say that to every guy who comes to your door with plate in hand?"

She managed a smile. Very few guys had ever come to her door once they knew about Dillon. And none at all with an empty cookie plate from her. But she had no intention of telling him that or about anything else that was currently in her head. "You're welcome to join us for dinner. Spaghetti with marinara," she translated and gestured vaguely toward the kitchen. Her hand was shaking. "Although it's going to be a while."

"Abby makes her own skeddi sauce," Dillon said, sounding boastful. "She doesn't pour it out of a jar."

She'd never thought she'd be the center of a public-relations spin, much less one offered by a seven-year-old boy. "Your homework isn't going to get done by itself." She nudged him toward the breakfast counter.

"They give homework to second-graders?"

She looked back at Sloan and, with nothing to occupy her nervous hands, tucked her fingers in the back pockets of her jeans. "He had homework even in kindergarten."

"Only things I remember from kindergarten are graham crackers and nap time. Didn't matter which school, they were all the same." He touched her shoulder as he stepped around her to head into the kitchen with the empty plate.

All he'd done was touch her shoulder and she wanted to shiver. "You went to more than one school while you were in *kindergarten?*" She'd known the same kids from kindergarten right through high-school graduation.

He turned on the hot water and ran the perfectly clean plate under it. "Three." His voice sounded short, and he didn't look at her as he set the plate in the sink and turned toward Dillon.

Abby's breath came a little easier with his focus no longer on her. She poured olive oil into a pot and set it on the stove. Breathing might have been easier, but the man still occupied the kitchen with her, and the room had never felt smaller.

He picked up one of the papers spread across the counter, glanced at it and set it back down. "What're you going to draw for the contest at school, champ?"

"I dunno."

Abby hesitated, ready to jump in, but Sloan leaned on the counter until he was down at Dillon's height. "Figured you'd already have a lock on it."

Dillon didn't even look at Abby. "Really?"

"Sure," Sloan said easily, as if he'd dealt with inse-cure, wishful children every day. "You made that badge for Frosty and it was great."

She slowly scraped her diced onions and celery into the pot, holding her breath as she listened. Dillon's attitude toward the contest was considerably more positive with Sloan than it had been with her, and she didn't want to mess with progress.

"But I gotta draw more 'n a badge," her little brother was saying.

No mention whatsoever about Calvin Pierce and his weenie theory. She chewed the inside of her lip to keep a smile from forming.

"Says who?" Sloan challenged lightly. "You heard what Sheriff Scalise said, didn't you? If a badge means doing the right thing to you, then draw a badge." He lowered his voice a notch. "You think Abby has any more of those chocolate cookies hanging around?"

"Yup!" Dillon hopped off his chair again and dashed around the counter, dragging down the plastic container holding the cookies. "Deputy McCray says I can draw a badge for the contest," he told her in a loud whisper.

"I heard," she whispered back. It was almost impossible to keep from glancing at Sloan, but she managed.

While Dillon set the cookies on the counter and flipped off the lid, she reached in the cabinet and pulled out a squat crystal glass. She filled it with milk and set it in front of Sloan.

"Thanks." His long fingers slid around the glass.

She returned to the stove and stirred the softly sizzling contents with a wooden spoon. It was a much safer occupation than imagining how his fingers would feel sliding over *her*.

"Golly." Dillon drew out the exclamation. "Abby never lets us use Grandma's glasses."

"And you're still not using Grandma's glasses," she said, sending him a wry smile. Dillon had an entire selection of plastic glasses patterned with dinosaurs. "One day, they'll be yours, but only if they stay unbroken until then."

He wrinkled his nose. "I don't want no fancy glasses. They're for *girls*."

"Then someday you can give them to the girl you marry."

Looking even more horrified, he leaned over and made a loud retching sound.

Sloan's gaze caught hers, and she rolled her eyes. "Little boys," she dismissed, as if that explained it all.

"I'm not so ancient that I can't remember being one myself." His lips crooked and his gaze seemed to rove over her.

She went breathless all over again, her hand tightening spasmodically around the spoon's long handle. And when Sloan took a step closer, she froze altogether.

"Good thing he doesn't know all the things he has in store for him one day." He lowered his voice a notch, and his breath whispered against her temple. "Kid would be taking cold showers in the middle of the night like I've been doing since you moved next door."

Her jaw loosened as she stared at him.

Then the radio attached to his belt crackled noisily and she jumped. The spoon slid out of her fingers, falling into the pot.

He looked from her face to the stove as he spoke into the radio, responding to the gibberish that she couldn't begin to understand. In the span of seconds, he'd returned the radio to his belt. "Going to have to take a rain check on the spaghetti." He reached around her to fish the spoon out of the pot and set it aside. "Better be careful." His voice was low. "Don't want to burn yourself."

Then he turned out of the kitchen, fist-bumping Dillon on the way to the door.

She exhaled shakily.

His warning came too late.

She was already burning, and the cause of it had just walked out of her house.

Chapter Six

Sloan sat in the Pierces' shabby living room with Lorraine after Max took Bobby away in handcuffs.

There was no smell of fragrant cooking filling this house.

He'd left that behind at Abby's.

In fact, it seemed to Sloan that he'd left behind everything warm and comfortable at Abby's to spend the past four hours in a house that was cold and a helluva lot worse than *un*comfortable.

Even though he wanted to shake some sense into Lorraine, he didn't. She was the victim here no matter what she claimed to the contrary. She was too thin. More ragged than any female her age should ever have to be.

He remembered thinking the same thing about his mother when he was young. She hadn't been an abused wife, but she damn sure hadn't known what sort of life she'd be in for when she'd married Sloan's dad.

He blocked out the thoughts the way he always did and wished the counselor they'd called to come and talk with Lorraine would hurry up and get there.

"Lorraine." This was a close community. No point for *Mr.* and *Mrs.* when you were just as likely to sit next to the people you were serving and protecting at the local bar on Saturday night as in the church pew on Sunday morning. "You have more power than you think." He sat forward on the threadbare chair, wishing to hell that he could convince her and knowing just as well that he probably never would.

The Pierce home had been the first call he'd gone out on when he'd signed on with the sheriff's department, and not a month had passed since when he hadn't had to repeat the visit. Six months in Weaver. Six months of trying. Six months of failing.

"You don't have to keep taking this sort of thing from your husband," he continued. "You'll have support."

Lorraine looked away. Her arms were folded tightly across her thin chest. "Bobby takes care of me and Cal. And you and the sheriff got no right busting in here again just 'cause we got a couple of nosy neighbors."

He pinched the bridge of his nose. "The neighbors called because they were worried." He gestured at what had once been the front picture window but was now covered over with the large sheet of plywood that he'd had put up to keep out the cold. "*Somebody* threw that kitchen chair out that window." They'd found the chair stuck in a snowdrift glittering with broken glass. "It didn't happen by itself. We've got probable cause, Lorraine. We don't need for you to say Bobby's a danger to you when we can see it for ourselves."

She angled her bony jaw and looked away. "I told you Calvin was the one who threw the chair. That's why I sent him to his room."

Sloan grimaced. "Blaming it on your kid? That's a new low, Lorraine."

She blinked a few times. But she didn't recant.

He rose, feeling hemmed in by the depressing aura that filled the room. He didn't move too fast because moving at all seemed to make Lorraine even more nervous.

He wanted to shake her. But mostly, he just wanted to protect her. Get her to protect herself *and* that boy of hers she seemed willing to throw under the bus to save her husband's sorry hide. When he'd spoken with Calvin, the boy had been sullen and full of attitude. If he *had* tossed the chair through the window, he'd have bragged left and right about it. But Calvin had said nothing.

There was a small collection of photos in cheap picture frames hanging crookedly on the wall, and he studied them. No school pictures of Calvin. No family portraits. Just snapshots of Bobby, arm looped over the shoulders of one buddy or another. In all of them, the men were astride their Harleys. Like the Deuces, Bobby put more money into his ride than he did his home.

He blocked the memories again, staring restlessly up the narrow staircase leading to the second floor, where Calvin had been banished to his room by his mother. The counselor was coming as much for the boy's benefit as Lorraine's.

Again, Sloan wished that Dr. Templeton would hurry. When they'd called her, she'd been over in Braden dealing with an emergency there, but she'd promised to be there as soon as she could.

"Bobby loves me, you know."

"Maybe he does, Lorraine—" a twisted version of it, in Sloan's estimation "—but you shouldn't have to go around being afraid in your own home of someone who loves you."

The doorbell rang then, and since he was close he answered the door himself and let in Dr. Templeton. She apologized for being so long as she unwound her knit scarf and peeled off her gloves. The doctor was about Sloan's age, though she looked a lot younger, and if she felt the same stifling depressiveness inside the Pierce home that he did, she hid it well. She sat down next to Lorraine as if they were two girlfriends getting together to dish about their day.

Sloan didn't care what her approach was as long as it worked.

With no official reason to remain, he left them to it and returned to the office, wrote up his report and headed back home.

It was getting late, and golden light was shining from the front window of Abby's house when he pulled into his driveway next door. If he went over and knocked on her door, he knew that she'd let him in. That her pretty eyes would be soft, and her lips would curve into a genuine smile.

And they'd taste sweeter than anything he'd tasted in a long, long while.

She was a lot more of a mother to Dillon than just a sister. Just as much a mother, in fact, as Lorraine was to Calvin. But there was no other comparison he could draw between them. Sloan, though, could have been looking at himself in those pictures on Lorraine's wall.

He'd helped take down the Deuces. He'd infiltrated them with the sole purpose of doing so. He'd befriended their leader, Johnny Diablo, until the man thought of him like a real brother. He'd prepped for his cover for more than a year then rode with them for more than three. And it had been another two after that before the case ever made it to court. Two years when he'd remained underground still, just to keep the Deuces from finding him.

Nearly his entire adult life had been consumed by the deadly gang.

But even now, after it was all said and done, Sloan wasn't sure how much of himself he'd left behind with them.

He sat there for a long while looking at the golden glow spreading over the front of Abby's yard where the snowman stood sentry. He sat there until the still engine no longer ticked and the truck's interior went cold.

Then he climbed out, feeling stiff and older than his years, and went inside his own dark house.

"How's life with Deputy Hottie?"

Abby looked up from the first-aid supplies she was inventorying to see Dee Crowder strolling into her office. There was no point pretending she didn't know who the teacher meant.

Nor was there any point in pretending that Sloan hadn't been avoiding her. It had been an entire week since he'd returned the cookie plate. A week since he'd implied that she'd been the cause of some sleepless nights for him.

He did more than imply it.

She ignored the voice inside her head and closed the metal supply cabinet. "I told you. We're just neighbors." She couldn't even say they were neighbors who flirted. He may have made that comment, but he hadn't so much as glanced toward their house during his comings and goings since then.

She knew this because she'd spent a lot of her time surreptitiously watching for *him*.

Dee set a foam cup on Abby's desk. "Fresh coffee from the teacher's lounge." She leaned her hip on the corner of the desk. It was the middle of the afternoon, and she'd made a habit of stopping by Abby's office during her prep period.

Abby had quickly realized that Dee's excuse for dropping by with coffee was just as much an excuse to smile and wave at the principal, whose office was next door to hers.

The curly-haired teacher had it bad for Principal Gage but hid it behind impish smiles and a wolf whistle for any male beyond the age of consent.

Abby pulled out her squeaky desk chair and sat down, gratefully taking a sip of the coffee. She grimaced, though, and looked up at Dee. "This is *fresh?*" The most she could say about it was that it was hot.

"Made it myself." Then Dee grinned. "Of course, the coffee maker in there probably hasn't been cleaned in a decade. A bunch of us spinsters get together once a month for Friday-night poker. If you're really just *neighbors* with Deputy McCray, then I guess you're almost one of us. Tomorrow night at my place. Want to come?"

"I would," Abby said truthfully. "But I can't leave Dillon."

"I can recommend a half-dozen sitters," Dee coaxed.

Abby didn't doubt her. The other woman seemed to know every name in town. "I still wouldn't want to leave him. He's—" how could she describe her brother? "—still settling in here." Dillon was the only one that Sloan didn't seem to be avoiding. He'd done more than share the time of day with her little brother; he'd even helped Dillon make another snowman to keep Deputy Frosty company. But the second that Abby had gone out to join them, Sloan had made an excuse to leave.

Dee looked thoughtful for a moment. "How 'bout if we meet at your place instead?" Then she grinned again. "Or is that too pushy of me?"

It was, but Abby could only laugh. Dee's good humor had that effect. And maybe with the distraction of a girls' night—even a girls' night *in*—Abby wouldn't dwell so much on Sloan. "What time?"

"Seven. You got a good table, or should we pack a few card tables and folding chairs?"

"Chairs, I guess," she started. "But what else—?"

Dee waved her hand, hopping off the desk. "Nothing else. All the necessities will come to *you*." She suddenly tugged a curl out of her face and hurried into the corridor. "Hi, there, Principal Gage," she greeted.

Abby sank her teeth into her lip, trying not to giggle.

But really, was she any different than Dee? Dreaming about a man who didn't seem to be all that interested after all?

Joe barely looked at Dee and turned into Abby's office instead. The serious look on his face ended any desire whatsoever that she had to giggle. "Ms. Marcum, would you mind coming into my office?"

Alarm climbed up into her throat. She nodded and quickly stepped around her desk and followed him. Behind the man's back, Dee caught her gaze, lifting her eyebrows, and Abby shrugged a little helplessly.

"Call me," the other woman mouthed.

Abby nodded and turned into the school's main office. Joe's secretary, Viola Timms, was sitting at her desk. She looked thin-lipped and humorless, but since that was the way she always looked as she guarded the doorway to her boss's office, Abby couldn't take any clue from her. Feeling as if she'd done something wrong, and not knowing what, she passed by the older woman and went through the doorway.

Then she stopped short.

Dillon was sitting in the chair in front of Joe's wide

desk, hunched over and looking too small. "Dillon?" She hurried toward him and gasped when he turned to face her. He'd obviously been hit in the face. His nose and eye were swollen. She crouched next to him, lifting his chin with her fingers. "Who did this to you?"

"Nobody," Dillon mumbled. "Can't we just go home now?"

Abby gaped at her little brother. "Dillon!"

Joe closed his office door and moved around to lean against the front of his desk. "Mr. Rasmussen found him in the boys' room," he told Abby. "Dillon." His voice went a shade sterner. "I can tell your sister or you can."

More alarmed than ever, she squeezed Dillon's cold hands. Rob Rasmussen was one of the sixth-grade teachers. "What happened, honey?" This was the hour that his class was supposed to be in chorus.

Dillon flicked a gaze at the principal then ducked his chin again. "Was in a fight," he said, almost inaudibly.

Abby absorbed that. Dillon never acted out. In Braden, he'd been so introverted that she'd worried about him. Since coming to Weaver, though, he'd started to come out of his shell.

Mostly with Sloan.

"Who were you fighting with?"

His lips clamped shut, and she looked up at Joe.

"Calvin Pierce," he provided.

She looked back at her little brother. "Honey, if he's picking on you, you need to tell me about it!"

Joe stirred at that. "Dillon, I want you to go sit by Mrs. Timms's desk and wait for your sister while we talk."

Without looking at her, Dillon slid off the chair and shuffled out of the office, dragging his coat and backpack behind him. Joe closed the door after him.

"I don't know what to say." Abby felt bewildered and

knew it sounded in her voice. "Dillon doesn't like sitting at the same table with Calvin in class, but I had no idea it was this bad between them."

"Calvin is a challenge," Joe said quietly. "I won't deny that. But I'm not sure he was the one who started the fight. Not this time."

"What do you mean?"

"Mr. Rasmussen saw Dillon throw the first punch."

She stared. "I don't believe it. That's just not like him."

"And it is entirely like Calvin," Joe agreed. "But it's not like Rob to get the details wrong." He gave her a regretful look. "Dillon won't tell me what instigated the scuffle."

"Did Calvin?"

His lips tightened a little. "Calvin actually claims he was the one who started it," he allowed. But he still shook his head. "Forgive the expression, but he's protecting his reputation as a hard-ass."

"He's *seven!*"

"Eight, actually. And he comes from a family I wouldn't wish on my worst enemy. Look, Abby. I'm not trying to say Calvin is a saint. There've been more than a few times when he's been at fault in similar situations, and maybe he is this time, as well. But I've been doing this job for a long time. I recognize that neither of those boys is being truthful with me, and I'm going to trust that my teacher is accurately describing what he saw. Dillon and Calvin *were* fighting. And that's not allowed. So I'm suspending them both until Monday."

Abby swallowed. Suspended. She'd never been suspended in her life. And now, in the second grade, Dillon already had been.

"It's only for a day," he added, sounding sympathetic. "And I know you're new in town, so you'll probably need to take the day off to stay home with him, as well. I don't want you to worry about this affecting your position here or anything. I'll call in a backup for you here for the rest of today and tomorrow."

She hadn't even gotten so far as to think about that. "I appreciate it. Did you tell Dillon he's been suspended?"

"Yes."

She closed her eyes for a moment, sending a silent apology to her grandparents for the rotten job she was apparently doing. Then she blew out a breath and stood. "I'm sorry about all this," she told Joe.

He accompanied her to the door and opened it for her. "It happens, Abby. Talk to Dillon. Find out why. Let's try to keep it from happening again." He sounded more encouraging than judgmental, and Abby could see a little more clearly why Dee was so taken with him.

With Dillon in tow, she stopped at her office, collected her things and locked up. Then they headed outside and began walking home.

It was quiet and felt strange without the usual end-of-day chaos. And it seemed entirely fitting when she realized it was starting to snow again. "Principal Gage said you were the one who started the fight," she finally said. "You want to tell me why?"

Dillon walked on, silently.

She tried another tack. "Was Calvin making fun of you entering the sheriff's contest?" Dillon had been drawing badges for a week now. They were pinned up all over the walls of his bedroom.

But Dillon just shook his head.

"Honey, I wish you'd tell me why it happened. I'm going to have to come up with some sort of punishment, and if I knew why, maybe it would help."

He looked at her as though he wanted to argue. But still he said nothing.

She exhaled. "I guess I'll have to take away my permission for that field trip next week." The second- and third-grade classes were going to tour Cee-Vid, and Dillon had talked of little else since he'd brought home the permission slip.

"No! That's where they make 'White Hats'!"

"I know. So tell me *why* you were fighting."

His mouth clamped shut. He pulled up the hood of his jacket and kept walking.

Abby dashed a snowflake from her face and kept walking, too. She was so frustrated, worried and focused on Dillon that she didn't even notice at first the sound of an engine until Dillon stopped on the sidewalk and looked.

Sloan was pulling up beside them in his SUV. The passenger window rolled down, and he looked across at them. "You two look like you're in need of a ride. You heading home?"

It was pointless to deny it, though Abby was tempted. He just looked so darned *good*. And she felt so darned miserable.

Without a word, she pulled open the door, gesturing for Dillon to get in. He scrambled up into the front seat. She closed the door and got in the back, which was separated from the front by a see-through grille. She shuddered a little. Dillon was getting a taste of a ride-along regardless of the drawing contest, but Abby wasn't enjoying it one little bit. She felt like some sort of criminal.

Maybe her crime was moving her brother from everything he knew in Braden. If they'd stayed, none of this would be happening.

"You going home sick or something?" Sloan asked Dillon. "Your face looks swollen."

"Nuh-uh."

"Dillon's face looks swollen because he got punched,"

Abby said bluntly. "He was fighting and got suspended. *That* is why we're going home."

Sloan looked over his shoulder at her. He looked as poleaxed as she felt.

She turned away and stared out the window. At least he seemed to genuinely care about Dillon. Not that she knew him well enough to know anything for sure.

"Why were you fighting, bud?"

Good luck, she thought. That was the million-dollar question.

"'Cause Calvin Pierce called me a liar."

She snapped forward on the seat when Dillon answered as if he'd only been waiting to be asked. "What?" She latched her fingertips through the cold metal grille. "*Now* you're in the mood to explain?"

Sloan shot her a look through the mirror.

She pressed her lips together and subsided.

"What did he say you were lying about?" Sloan asked calmly.

It was probably easy for him to be calm. Dillon was an ordinarily shy seven-year-old. Sloan was used to dealing with a treacherous motorcycle gang full of murderers and gun runners.

"I told him I wore a real deputy badge, and he said I didn't. That I was a liar *and* a weenie."

"Oh, Dillon," Abby said, sighing. She sat forward and started to put her fingertips on the grille again but stopped just in time. "It doesn't matter what someone else says to you. You can't start a fight because of it."

"He said I was a liar," Dillon repeated. His agitated voice rose. "I never been a *liar.* That's what Black Hats do!"

"Take it easy, bud," Sloan said. He turned onto their street and a moment later was parking in his driveway.

"Let's go inside and you can tell us about it." He turned off the engine, and he and Dillon opened their front doors to get out. Abby tried, too, but the handle on her door did absolutely nothing, and she had to wait for Sloan to come around and open it for her.

"Back doors don't open from the inside," he pointed out needlessly.

She quickly climbed out, feeling no small amount of relief. "Thanks for the ride," she told him. "But I think I've got it from here on out." Without looking at him again, she grabbed Dillon's hand and headed across the yard. "You and I are going to have a little talk," she warned when they reached their front steps.

"Abby. Wait."

She unlocked the door and nudged Dillon inside before she turned and faced Sloan.

He'd followed them across the yard. Snowflakes glittered in his hair, and he was so freaking beautiful that it was almost painful to look at him.

"This isn't your problem," she told him huskily.

"It is if it all started because I let him wear my badge for a few minutes." He looked genuinely pained.

"It doesn't matter if Dillon did or didn't wear your badge. He's old enough to know right from wrong. And he knows that fighting is wrong."

"It's not always wrong."

She exhaled roughly and tugged the door closed behind her before stepping next to the wooden railing of the porch. "Fine. Maybe there are situations when fighting is the right thing to do. But the situations that call for it are a lot more serious than a little bully egging on my brother. I said I'll handle it and I will, even if I have to deal with Calvin's parents to do it."

"Don't go anywhere near Calvin's parents."

Something rippled down her spine. She'd never been particularly good at having someone tell her what she could and couldn't do.

She'd had the same reaction the first time someone had told her she was too young to take on raising Dillon. But her grandfather had believed she could, and that was what had mattered. She closed her hands over the rail. "There's no law I'd be breaking, Deputy. I'm perfectly free to have a civil discussion about their son and Dillon. For heaven's sake. They're little boys!"

"Abby." He covered her hands with his. Neither of them wore gloves, but his palms felt like hot irons in comparison to her cold fingers. "There's not much that ever stays civil where Bobby Pierce is concerned. I have a lot of experience with that family, and I'm *asking* you, for your sake, to keep your distance." He squeezed her hands.

Maybe if he wouldn't have done that—pressed his fingers so warmly, so familiarly against hers—she would have just taken his words for the advice they were. But he did, and she leaned forward until her face was barely a foot from his. She searched his eyes, wishing she knew what was going on inside. Wishing she knew if her attraction to him was so great that she'd only imagined he might feel the same. "I don't know what to make of you," she said huskily. "Is this just the deputy speaking, Sloan? Or is it someone else?"

"It's just me," he said evenly. "I wouldn't want to see anything happen to you or Dillon."

It was an answer, but a singularly frustrating one because she knew nothing more than she ever had. Which was a big fat zilch.

"For whatever reason, Dillon has taken to you," she said finally. "He's telling you things he won't tell me. And while I appreciate that, *I* don't want him hurt. Not by Calvin Pierce." She moistened her dry lips. "And…and not by you." Sloan had already told her he was with the sheriff's office for only a few more months. He'd never said what he intended to do after that. She wasn't so wet behind the ears as to think he'd be around for Dillon forever.

His gaze turned even more inward. "You're a smart woman, Abby. Dillon's lucky to have you."

And that was it.

That was all he said.

Because he turned and walked back across the yard, got into his SUV and drove away.

Chapter Seven

"Remind me when we play again not to bet against you," Dee said the next night as they carried the folding chairs she'd brought to Abby's back out to her car and stacked them in the trunk. There'd been eight of them playing, and though the competition was fierce, there had been just as much gossiping, pizza eating and margarita drinking going on as there had been shuffling cards. "You're a shark in sheep's clothing. Who taught you how to play poker?"

Abby set the last chair in Dee's trunk and stepped back so the other woman could shut it. "My grandfather. He also taught me how to shoot and how not to spit into the wind."

Dee was wearing her usual mischievous grin. "The man did too good of a job. I can't afford to lose like that. Don't earn enough teaching." She looked past Abby toward Sloan's darkened house. "Was hoping to catch a glimpse of Deputy Hottie."

Abby didn't have to look over her shoulder to know

that Sloan wasn't there. His SUV hadn't returned since he had given them a ride home from school the day before. "And here I thought you were the last to leave because you wanted to help me clean up the mess." She hadn't pulled on a coat before bringing out the chairs, and the night air was cold through her long-sleeve turtleneck. "Why do you care so much about Deputy McCray, anyway, when Principal *Gage* is the one you want?"

Dee peered at her. "Who told you that?"

"Nobody had to tell me. I have eyes."

The other woman's lips twisted. "Wish Joe Gage had eyes."

"Ask him out." She knew the principal wasn't married or otherwise involved. "Open his eyes for him."

"Easier said than done. He's the boss. Dating one of his employees is against the rules."

"Some rules are meant to be broken." Only as soon as she said the words, they reminded her of Sloan telling her that it wasn't always wrong to fight, and even though she'd vowed not to, she glanced back at his house.

"The school board also has some pretty strict rules," Dee was saying. "And I need my job. So…" She trailed off and lifted her shoulders. "I can't have his body, but I can have the pleasure of watching the man's backside whenever he's walking down the hallway at school. It's a poor substitute," she lamented with a wicked smile, "but it's all I've got."

Abby couldn't help but laugh. "You're terrible."

"I am. Everyone in town will tell you so." Dee gave her a quick hug and then pulled open her car door. "Sorry if we were too noisy for Dillon once he went to bed."

"It was fine." She'd checked on her brother a few times throughout the evening. He'd fallen asleep reading a book. She hoped he managed to make it till morning without a bad dream. He'd awakened twice with nightmares the night before. So even though she'd been horrified about his school suspension, it was just as well, because they'd both fallen asleep for a few hours in the middle of the afternoon as a result of their disturbed night. "And I had a lot of fun. So thanks again for inviting yourselves to my place."

Dee chuckled. "Anytime." Then she got inside her car and drove away.

Abby rubbed her hands up and down her arms. The sky was clear again, black and studded with stars. Only two of the houses on the street had lights on inside at this late an hour: hers and Mr. Gilcrest's next door. She'd met the elderly man the week before when she'd taken over a plate of chocolate cookies. It had been the neighborly thing to do. Just as it had been the neighborly thing to do to bake cookies for Sloan. It meant exactly the same thing.

On the surface, it worked. Underneath, though, she knew that was plain malarkey.

She sighed and turned around, her boots crunching through the snow as she headed back across the yard. The scarf around Frosty's neck was looking decidedly bedraggled, and his cookie eyes and carrot nose had disappeared days ago. She stopped in front of him and his smaller companion, who was scarfless and faceless because Abby had interrupted Dillon and Sloan while they'd been making him.

"Well, guys. I'd invite you inside for hot chocolate, but I don't think you'd survive it."

"They say the first sign is when you start talking to snowmen."

She nearly jumped out of her skin, yelping as she whirled to see Sloan standing in the middle of the street. "*Must* you do that?"

"Do what?"

"Sneak up and startle the life out of me!"

He came closer, and she realized his dark clothing wasn't his uniform at all, but running clothes. He looked more like a wide receiver geared up for a workout than an off-duty deputy. "Sorry."

"No, you're not," she countered. "You're like little boys everywhere who enjoy sneaking up on little girls just to see them jump." He was so far from boyish that it was ridiculous, but the assessment made her feel better. "Do you always go out running in the middle of the night? Where's your truck?"

"Sometimes. And it's at the office." He came a little closer. His head was bare. "I don't always bring it home, and I'm off duty until Monday morning. I've got my own wheels, too."

She'd been living there nearly two weeks and had seen him drive nothing other than that sheriff's SUV. "Where are you hiding them? In your attic?"

His teeth flashed. Just for a moment.

Or maybe that was her wishful thinking.

She'd told him to go away, and he had. It was still the smart thing to do, so she had no business having wishful thoughts where he was concerned.

"In my garage."

"Are you talking about that dinky shed behind your house?" If he was, his car would have to be even smaller than her little sedan. It was hard to picture.

"None other." He stepped over the chunks of grit-filled snow at the edge of the street. "It's nearly midnight. Little girls shouldn't be out so late."

She'd been the one to use the term first, but when *little girl* came from him, it reminded her how young he really considered her. "Maybe I had a date," she said blithely.

"A threesome with Frosty and his snow-bro?" He came closer. "I'm thinking probably…no date."

She shivered. Lifted her chin. "You don't know everything."

"I know you wouldn't leave Dillon."

Caught, darn it all. Her chin lowered. "I had some friends over."

"Girlfriends."

Her breath escaped on a puff. *"Friends."* She was completely out of her depth with him. Didn't even really know what they were doing talking in the middle of the night on her front lawn.

"*Girl*friends," he pushed again.

She pressed her lips together. Shivered some more and crossed her arms tightly. It was mid-January, and the temperature was hovering below freezing.

So why did she feel so hot inside?

"Why does it matter to you if they were *girls*—" she drew out the word the way Dillon would "—or not?"

"It shouldn't." He took another step. Stopped within arm's reach of her. "But it does."

Her spurt of bravery disappeared. Her heart thumped hard inside her chest, as if she'd been the one out having a midnight run.

"I don't like thinking of you with another man."

She dug her fingertips into her arms. Her nails poked hard. She wasn't dreaming. "Dee Crowder from school," she said faintly. "And some friends of hers. We…we played poker. I won."

Again, a brief flash of white teeth. "That's my girl."

"I'm not your girl." She shifted her feet, and the snow creaked under her boots.

"Half the town keeps telling me that you are."

She swallowed. Moistened her lips. The heat inside her

was rising up her neck, and she wanted to claw at the snug turtleneck that felt as if it was strangling her. "I'm not your girl," she whispered.

He took another step. It was either stand her ground or back up into the snowmen. Sloan didn't touch her, but she still felt the heat radiating off him as he lowered his head until his mouth brushed against her ear. "If you were—" his deep voice was soft "—we wouldn't be standing out here freezing." His gloved hand slid against her neck. Curved beneath her jaw. Her knees felt like melting wax. "I'd have you in bed…." His lips grazed her earlobe.

She moaned a little, knowing she ought to protest, even if she suspected he was right. "Sloan—" She twisted her head until her mouth found his.

And then it didn't matter that he'd been avoiding her for days. It didn't matter that they were standing alone in the middle of the night in the middle of her front yard. And it didn't matter whose girl she was or was not.

There was only the taste of his mouth. His tongue. The ridge of his teeth. There was only the feel of his chest, warm and hard against her as she wrapped her arms around him.

When he tore his mouth away, far too soon, she made a protesting sound. "Don't stop." She kissed his jaw. Tried to reach his lips again. "Sloan—"

He caught the back of her head and tucked it against his chest. His mouth brushed her ear again. "We have to stop. Or I'm not going to be able to."

"Would that be so bad?"

His chest moved with the groan he let out. "I'm pretty sure it wouldn't be *bad*." He kissed the top of her head, and his voice turned serious. "You were right to want to protect Dillon. And you should want to protect yourself. You don't need a man like me in your life."

She turned her head. Listened to the fast beat of his heart. "Why not?"

"Too many reasons to count." He ran his hands down her spine. "I'm not a good man, Abby."

"You're a hero."

He went still.

"I recognized your name when you first told me," she admitted softly. "Braden isn't cut off from the rest of the world. I know what you did. How you brought down the Deuce's Cross and that guy, Johnny...whatever his name was."

"Diablo." His chest moved with the deep sigh he let out. "Not everything about that situation made it into the newspapers. I might have done my job, but it was everyone around me who had to pay the price for it. Believe me, sweetheart. That is not what heroes do. I hurt too many people, and I don't want you to be another. If I were a better man, I'd have never touched you."

She couldn't feel the cold from the outside anymore. This time it was slowly seeping from the inside. "Then why did you?"

But he didn't answer. "First time I saw you, I thought Dillon was your son," he said instead.

She let out a short laugh even though she felt more like crying. And that wasn't something she was going to do because it would just be one more thing he'd feel responsible for causing. "That would be a challenge since I—" She realized what she was about to admit and broke off. "Nope. Not my son."

"But you're the only mom he's got, whether you carry the title or not."

She exhaled. "The only one who really believed I could do it was my grandfather."

"I believe you can do it."

Which just sealed the deal on tears stinging her eyes, no matter how much she wanted to keep them at bay.

I could love this man. The realization filled her head. *If only he'd let me.*

His hands slid to her shoulders, steadying her, even as he took a step back. A step away.

"It's late. You should go inside. Go to bed."

Where she'd lie, alone, and wish for him. A man she knew so little about. "What about you?"

"I'll keep running."

"Until you can sleep?"

His lips twisted. "Sure."

Something about the way he hesitated caught at her. "Do you have nightmares, Sloan?" He just looked at her and cocked his head slightly. "Dillon does. That morning that you were there wasn't the first, but at least they're coming less often. When he wakes from them he runs to me."

"He's a smart kid." He jerked his chin toward the house. "Go inside, Abby."

That was the smartest course. It was cold. It was late.

Sloan didn't want things to go further with her, and she ought to be grateful that he had the self-control that she didn't.

Everyone *she'd* ever loved had left her, too. Her mother hadn't wanted her. Her grandfather had died. Her grandmother had forgotten. Dillon, too, one day would grow up and go out to live his own life, and that was how it should be.

"Don't run too far," she said softly. And then, before she lost what little sense she had and begged him to come with her no matter what the consequences, she circled around Frosty and his friend and went inside.

She closed the door quietly and leaned back against it, closing her eyes.

There was no sound of Sloan following her up the steps. He wasn't standing on the other side of the door, prepared to knock softly and tell her that he'd changed his mind.

There was nothing but silence.

She moved away from the door and turned off the lights, one by one. When the house was dark, she went to the front window.

Sloan stood in the middle of the street. Tall. Broad shouldered. But still little more than a shadow in the moonlight.

She'd never really wondered before what loneliness looked like. But now she knew it looked like him.

And even though she knew he couldn't see her through the window, it was as if he did, because he turned then and disappeared into the night.

She wiped her wet cheeks and went to bed.

The sun was streaming across his bed when Sloan waked the next day. He rolled onto his back, throwing his arm over his eyes. Since he hadn't gone to sleep until well after the sun had come up in the first place, the presence of sunlight didn't say a helluva lot about what time it was.

The television was still on, reruns of headline news droning in the background. He could hear the sound of high-pitched laughter coming from outside, though, so he shoved aside the blankets and walked naked through his second floor until he could look out the window overlooking the front of the house. He didn't worry about being seen. The window was too high.

But it was just right for looking out.

Dillon was running around both his yard and Sloan's with the mangiest-looking dog he'd ever seen, and he wondered where it had come from. The fact that Abby was there, too, her shining brown hair bouncing around the shoulders of her bright red coat, told him there was no cause for worry.

And seeing the smiles on both of the Marcums' faces made it all worth watching.

So he did, until his phone started ringing and he had to go and answer it.

He was off duty for the next two days, but that didn't mean he couldn't get called in if the necessity arose. He grabbed the extension in his bedroom. "McCray."

"Clay," his sister responded with a laugh. "Nice way to answer the phone, Bean."

He raked his hand down his bristly cheeks and tucked the phone against his shoulder while he pulled on his jeans. "What's wrong?"

"Nothing!" She sighed noisily. "You're too quick to think the worst. I'm just calling to let you know that Sunday dinner is here at our place tomorrow. We're having pizza from Pizolli's. *Please* consider coming."

Sunday dinner to the Clays—which now included his sister—meant a weekly family dinner where they all got together as though it was a damn holiday or something. In the months that he'd been in Weaver, he'd succeeded in missing most of them.

"I know you're not on duty," she went on. "Because I had Sarah ask Max."

He grimaced. "Your being cousins-in-law with my boss's wife has a real downside."

"Bring your friend Abby and her brother along," she went on as if he'd never spoken.

"We're just neighbors." The lie was blatant. He didn't much care.

Neither did his sister, evidently, because she ignored him. "Mallory's on duty at the hospital, but Ryan came into the shop this morning to buy Chloe a new dress, and he said they'd all be there. I know that Chloe and Dillon are in the same class at school. She'll have someone to play with if you bring Abby and her little brother."

God help him. There were just too many freaking members of this family that his sister had married into. Ryan was yet another one of Axel's cousins. "And if you can't succeed with me, you'll make me feel guilty because of Ryan's little girl."

"Whatever works," she said blithely. "We're just having pizza. I'll expect you around three."

As if it were a done deal, she hung up.

He listened to the dial tone for a moment. Then he stared at the receiver before replacing it on the cradle and shaking his head.

Marriage and motherhood had made Tara downright sassy.

He pinched the bridge of his nose, willing away the pain that was there courtesy of too little sleep, and went into the bathroom.

The mirror showed what it always did. The same gray in his dark hair that his dad had also had at Sloan's age. The same lines radiating from his bloodshot eyes that he'd earned riding with Johnny Diablo and the Deuces. The same tattoo he'd gotten the first year he'd rode with them. The scar from the gunshot courtesy of Maria's crazy-assed brother two years ago was still on his biceps, a long, narrow trench of white, puckered tissue.

He looked the way he always did.

Like hell.

He heard the laughter from outside again, sounding closer, so he headed to the bedroom again and peered through the blinds to see a streak of red dart through the snow between his house and Abby's.

He went back into the bathroom and flipped on the

shower. The rush of water at least drowned out the sounds from outside. It didn't do a thing, though, to drown out the memory of kissing her. And it didn't do a thing to stop his imagination from conjuring more, not even when he turned the water stone cold and it felt as if he were being pelted with bits of ice.

Sexual frustration was easy enough to cure. All he'd have to do was find a woman who wanted nothing but sex. Easy enough to accomplish. He'd done it before.

But she wouldn't be Abby.

Feeling about as cheerful as a junkyard dog, he pulled on warm clothes, grabbed his helmet out of the hall closet and stomped out the back door of his house.

God had some mercy on him, because the only sign of Abby behind his house were her footprints in the snow.

He rolled his bike out of the garage—which really was nothing more than a glorified shed—and swung his leg over the seat, kicking the engine to life. Despite the fact that he rode the thing only a few times a month these days, the engine roared and he felt an almost guilty pleasure from the sound.

He rode over the snow-covered alley behind the houses to the end of the short block and turned out onto the street.

And then he just rode.

Chapter Eight

Abby watched the black monster of a bike disappear around the corner while she tried to clip the leash onto Rex's collar.

Sloan's wheels, she realized.

The scary-looking bike suited a man who went running in the middle of the night in the dead of winter.

"Was that Sloan? I didn't know he had a motorcycle." She hadn't thought it possible, but Dillon sounded even more reverent about their neighbor.

"I didn't know, either." She turned her attention to the leash. The overexcited dog wasn't having any part of it; he wriggled out of her grip and bounded over to Dillon again, jumping against him with such enthusiasm that he lost his balance and landed on his butt in the snow.

Her brother's laughter filled the air as he rolled around on the ground with the dog. It had been an impetuous decision to bring the dog home from Shop-World, where a rescue organization had set up camp for the day. She simply hadn't been able to resist. Dillon had been so taken with the two-year-old mutt, whose wiry coat had too many colors to count or define. He'd fallen in love with Rex on the spot. And maybe it was only because she needed something else to love, but Abby had, too.

So despite the fact that she was trying to impress on Dillon the importance of not fighting at school, back into the big store they'd gone, where they'd purchased dog food and a leash and a dog bed that Abby hoped she'd be able to get Rex to use instead of Dillon's bed.

She caught up to the dog and finally managed to click on the leash. He immediately managed to tangle it around her legs, nearly taking her to the ground as effectively as he had Dillon. She succeeded in unwinding herself and handed the end of the leash to Dillon. The swelling on his face had gone down, only to be replaced by a bluish bruise in the corner of his eye. "Let's see how he does walking to the park."

They got to the park fine, though Abby wasn't sure if Dillon was walking Rex or if it were the other way around. Then she held the leash while Dillon played on the swings for a while. They creaked loudly in the cold, but they worked, nevertheless.

She sat on the bench nearby, enjoying the welcome warmth of the sun. All in all, it should have been a perfect day, and it would have been if she didn't have such an ache inside her.

"Pretty hard to get a decent suntan when we're covered up to our ears with coats and scarves, isn't it?"

Abby smiled with delight as she recognized the woman who plopped on the bench beside her. "Hayley! What are you doing here?"

"Trying to get in a little exercise," Hayley Templeton

said ruefully. "A friend of mine is supposed to meet me here." She stretched out her legs and wiggled her running shoes. "I heard through the grapevine that you'd moved here from Braden. How's everything going?"

That particular grapevine, Abby knew, would be in the form of her talkative high-school mate Delia, who was Hayley's cousin. "It's new," she said, glancing at Dillon. He'd taken to jumping out of the swing when it was at its height, and Rex barked every time. "We're settling in. I haven't talked to Delia in a while. I didn't know you were here in Weaver."

As quickly as she'd sat, Hayley rose and propped her foot on the bench, stretching. "A little over a year ago I took over a practice here from a psychologist who was retiring. I do mostly family counseling right now." She switched legs. "I was sorry to hear about your grandfather. He was a good teacher. I wouldn't have made it through any of my math classes in high school if it hadn't been for him. And now, even as a nurse, you're working at a school, too."

Abby smiled ruefully. "I am."

"What about your grandmother? How's she doing?"

"She's at Braden Bridge full-time now."

The psychologist straightened. Her eyes were kind. "Alzheimer's is such a cruel disease. How are *you* doing?" She looked over at the little boy playing on the swings. "And your brother? It's Dillon, right?"

Abby nodded. "We're managing." Aside from her being dangerously close to falling for her neighbor, and Dillon's fight at school, everything was just dandy.

"Well." Hayley pulled her foot down from the bench. "If you ever need to talk, just let me know." She waved at the other jogger who'd just entered the park before leaning over to pet Rex on the head, much to his delight. "You're a cutie."

Abby laughed at that. The dog was homely in the extreme with a head that didn't fit his body and a body that didn't fit his short little legs. "We adopted him this morning from a rescue."

The other jogger reached them. "Do you know Sam Dawson?" Hayley asked.

Abby shook the other woman's hand, recognizing her from the school assembly. "You're with the sheriff's department."

Sam smiled. "Guilty as charged." She was jogging in place, and she gave Hayley a wry look. "You're already thinking about wimping out for a cinnamon roll over at Ruby's, aren't you?"

"Maybe," Hayley allowed. She grinned at Abby. "The disadvantage of having Sam as a running partner is that she never wimps out."

"Would lose my job pretty quickly if I did," Sam said dryly. "Nice meeting you, Abby," she said as she started off along the path.

"Exercising is such a *chore*," Hayley admitted. But she dutifully set off after the other woman.

Dillon jumped off his swing again and trotted over to kneel next to Rex. "Can *we* go to Ruby's and have a cinnamon roll?"

She might have known that he'd overhear that. But since it was lunchtime and she didn't have any real desire for peanut butter and jelly sandwiches at home, she agreed. "You have to have some real lunch, though, too."

"Can we take Rex?"

"We'll tie him up outside the diner." She pushed to her feet and handed Dillon the leash again. "Rex needs to mind you," she said. "Not the other way around."

Fine words. Rex dragged Dillon—and then Abby, too, when she took over the leash—all the way to the diner. She latched the leash around the light post that was outside the diner door, and they went inside. It was already crowded, the booths and tables filled, but there were several stools at the counter that were free, so they sat there.

Dillon got a kick out of that. He liked seeing everything that went on behind the counter. He took forever reading through all the specials that were written on a board before he decided on a grilled cheese sandwich.

As soon as the girl took their order, Dillon twirled on the padded red seat and faced the crowded diner behind them. He kicked one leg absently. "If Deputy McCray's not your boyfriend, how come you was kissing him last night?"

It was as if every person in the restaurant went silent, just so they could hear Dillon's high, boyish voice.

Abby's face was on fire. She gave Dillon a stern look, even though it wasn't *his* fault that he'd seen what she'd been doing the night before. "Turn around and eat your lunch."

He looked over his shoulder at his place mat. "I don't got any lunch."

"You don't *have* any lunch," she corrected. "Turn around and drink your milk, then."

He sighed noisily and turned around. "Why are you mad?"

"I'm not mad."

"Then why do you got a—*have*—a frowny face?"

Abby stifled a groan and mentally smoothed out her expression. "I'm not frowning. And what were you doing up in the middle of the night last night, anyway?" She'd looked in on him the way she always did, and he'd been sound asleep. "Did you have a bad dream?"

"Nah. I was thirsty."

"Gotta love kids," a voice said beside her. Abby looked over to the petite brunette who was standing at the counter paying her bill. "They say the darndest things, don't they?" The woman stuck out her hand. "Tara Clay," she introduced herself. "And you're Abby."

Abby managed a weak smile and shook her hand. "Yes. Abby Marcum. Nice to meet you."

Tara had eyes as dark as chocolate, which crinkled slightly at the corners as her smile widened even more. "I'm Sloan's sister," she said meaningfully.

"Oh!" Abby's stomach dropped. "I…suppose you heard my brother."

Tara laughed softly. "Honey, everyone in here heard your brother. Don't look so upset, though. We've all survived people in this town talking about us." She looked past Abby to Dillon. "Your dog's doing a good job greeting everyone who comes in here. What's his name?"

Dillon stared shyly at Sloan's sister. "Rex," he whispered.

Abby sorely wished he'd have whispered earlier.

"Good name." Tara tucked her change into her purse as the waitress settled Abby's and Dillon's lunches on the counter. "I told Sloan earlier that he should bring you two along for dinner tomorrow," she said after the waitress had gone again.

"Oh, but—"

"We're getting together for pizza. Nothing fancy. Pizolli's. They're new but good."

"Pizolli's *is* good, but—"

"That's settled, then." Tara smiled brightly. "I'd stay to chat longer, but I've got to get back to the shop." And just like that, she hurried out the door.

"Sloan's sister looks like Snow White," Dillon commented, catching a melting string of cheese from his sandwich with the tip of his tongue.

Her shoulders sagged. "I guess she does." Dillon didn't know how embarrassing his question had been. But she didn't want a repeat of it, either. Not in the crowded diner. So she hurried him through his lunch and had his cinnamon roll wrapped to take with them. When he started to protest, she reminded him of poor Rex, tied up and waiting outside in the cold.

He needed no further prompting and barely waited long enough for her to pay the check before going outside. He stopped short, though, at the sight of the woman and boy crossing the street toward them.

Abby recognized Calvin and assumed that the thin, tense-looking woman with him was his mother.

There was no point in pretending they hadn't all seen one another. Not right there on the sidewalk outside of Ruby's.

She put her hand on Dillon's shoulder. Even through the puffy coat, she could feel the way he'd gone tense. Rex, leash twisted around the light post, thumped his tail, whining excitedly as he waited for Dillon's attention. "Untangle Rex," she suggested softly.

Calvin—with a bruise on his eye nearly identical to Dillon's—was glaring at her brother, and Calvin's mother looked as if she wanted to be anywhere other than where they were.

When faced with an uncomfortable situation, Abby's grandmother had always suggested heading straight on into it. Better to meet it with some control, Minerva used to say.

And this was a distinctly uncomfortable situation.

Abby stuck out her gloved hand, walking toward Calvin's mother. "Mrs. Pierce," she greeted calmly. "I'm Abby Marcum. Dillon's sister. It's nice to meet you."

The other woman looked a little confused. A little fearful. As if she didn't quite know what to do about Abby's extended hand. But after a brief hesitation, she extended her own hand, awkwardly shaking the tips of Abby's fingers before quickly pulling back. "You, too," she said half under her breath.

"I'm sorry about the trouble between the boys at school," Abby forged on despite the wholesale lack of encouragement coming from Calvin's mother. "I just want to assure you that nothing like that will happen again." She looked at her brother. "Will it, Dillon," she prompted.

He was crouched down hugging Rex as though the dog was his last friend in the world. His gaze flicked to Calvin. Then his face turned mutinous. "Will if he calls me a liar again."

"Dillon!"

He didn't look at her; he just ducked his head against Rex.

Her grandmother hadn't given her any words of wisdom to prepare for situations like *this,* and Abby wished she'd have just followed Sloan's advice to keep her distance from the Pierce family.

She gave Calvin's mother an apologetic look. "I'm sorry. I don't know what's gotten into—"

"Figures you'd have the ugliest dog in the world," Calvin sneered, interrupting.

"Hush your mouth." His mother swatted his shoulder. "Don't mind him," she told Abby. "He's wanted a dog forever."

"If I *did* have a dog, it wouldn't be no dinky excuse like that."

"Rex *isn't* dinky," Dillon defended, hopping to his feet. Rex, still tied to the post, bared his teeth and growled.

"Rex, be quiet." Abby casually sidestepped so she was

standing between the dog and the Pierces. "There's a rescue group with all sorts of dogs out at Shop-World today," she shared. "The only fee we had to pay for Rex was for the dog license. Which was a good thing, because that's about all I could afford," she added lightly, just in case Mrs. Pierce took offense.

"Calvin's daddy doesn't much care for dogs."

Abby managed not to wince. She felt as if she were digging herself in deeper. Despite her effort to be a barrier between Rex and Calvin, the little boy was still managing to antagonize the young dog, kicking bits of gravel-ridden snow toward him. "Well." She smiled warmly. "I didn't mean to keep you out here in the cold." Calvin's mother's coat looked threadbare, and while Dillon's coat was too big for him, Calvin's was definitely too small. "I just wanted to say how sorry I was for everything." She reached down and unfastened the leash from the light post and kept a tight grip on it when Rex took a little lunge, growling again.

She couldn't really blame the dog when Calvin was deliberately taunting him. She took Dillon's hand. "Hope you enjoy the rest of your weekend," she told Mrs. Pierce as she tugged boy and dog with her away from the diner.

She waited until they were well out of earshot before she looked down at Dillon. "What were you thinking, telling Calvin that you'd fight him again?"

Dillon didn't answer. He was focused on something else. Some*one* else, she realized quickly when Sloan stepped into their path.

"What were you thinking, talking to Lorraine Pierce in the first place," he asked.

She felt frazzled. First his sister in Ruby's, then the Pierces. And now him? "What are you doing here?"

He glanced over his shoulder at the building next to

him, and she realized she'd walked Dillon right past the sheriff's office. "Lying in wait for you," he said blandly.

Her lips tightened. "We ran into Calvin and his mother outside of Ruby's. I wasn't going to be rude and just ignore her. We ran into your sister inside Ruby's, too," she added before he could get on his soapbox about the Pierces.

His eyes narrowed. "Tara."

"Do you have another sister?" Her spurt of smart-i-tude fizzled. "Yes. Tara. She's very nice."

"She is," he agreed.

She'd considered warning him about Dillon being overheard inside the diner. But heading straight on to that particular awkwardness was a lot more difficult than facing Calvin and his mother.

So she focused on the least explosive thing she could. "She must be the official welcoming committee for Weaver. She invited us out for pizza tomorrow afternoon."

He didn't show any sort of reaction, but Abby still sensed his sudden unease.

"We can't," she added as if she hadn't noticed his reaction. A girl had her pride, after all. "We're going to Braden to visit my grandmother."

That got Dillon's attention in a hurry. "We are?"

She squeezed his hand, hoping he'd get the message.

"Not that your sister gave me a chance to tell her that."

"Sounds like Tara."

She moistened her lips, searching her mind vainly for some safe topic. But it turned out she didn't need one because Sloan's brown eyes mercifully focused on Dillon as he hunkered down to pet Rex. While her brother chattered on about how they'd adopted him that morning, Abby surreptitiously studied Sloan.

She knew his hair was thick and felt as slippery as satin

through her fingers. Knew the shadow on his jaw felt sexily abrasive against her palms.

What she didn't know was what made him tick. What he believed and cared about.

What caused his restlessness.

Even though she knew it was better to remain uninvolved, she couldn't help wanting to understand him. It was a desire that came dangerously close to need.

Which would get her nowhere. Inexperienced or not, she wasn't a fool. She wasn't looking to get hurt. Even though she couldn't imagine ever forgetting how it had felt to be in his arms.

"You could come, you know," he said abruptly. "After you visit your grandmother."

All her sensible thoughts screeched to a halt, and she stared at him.

"Tomorrow afternoon," he added, as if she needed clarification. "Unless you were planning to spend the entire day in Braden. Dillon would have a few kids to chase around with, too."

Dillon tugged at her arm. "Can we? I wanna chase around."

She let out half a laugh that sounded as helpless as she felt. Just when she started to think she had a course set, had her path laid out clearly before her where I'm-No-Hero Sloan was concerned, he tossed a wrench in the works.

"I do like Pizolli's," she finally said. It was a small family restaurant, and Sloan was right: there were usually a few kids for Dillon to play with. "Your, uh, your sister told me that's what the plan was. I suppose we could be back from Braden in time." Plenty of time. It would take only a few hours coming and going. And Minerva didn't tolerate visitors well for any length of time. It distressed her when she knew she ought to recognize them but didn't.

"Good." Sloan straightened and his eyes roved over her, which had the usual result of making her knees feel wobbly. "It's settled, then."

The comment was exactly like his sister's. As if whatever concerns or questions Abby might still have were moot.

"Will you give me a ride on your motorcycle?"

Abby closed her hand over Dillon's shoulder. "Honey, you can't just ask people things like that."

Sloan's lips twitched. "It's okay." He lifted the helmet he was holding. "You can wear this. It'll be too big for you, but we're not going much farther than around the corner to your house. Long as Abby says it's okay."

Dillon looked as if Christmas had just come all over again. He looked up at Abby. *"Puhleeze?"*

She pointed her finger toward Sloan. "Straight back to the house."

He lifted his palm. "Swear it."

She was such a sucker, swayed by the amusement lighting his expression. "You'll have to mind him for a few minutes until I catch up with you."

He looked even more amused. "Think we can manage not to burn down anything. Take your time."

Dillon eagerly handed her Rex's leash and latched his hand around Sloan's as if he were afraid the man might change his mind.

Abby caught the flicker of emotion on Sloan's face and ached inside. It seemed so obvious to her that he was a man who cared. Who *wanted* to care. So why wouldn't he let himself?

She stifled a sigh and eyed her brother. "Hold on and do everything that Sloan tells you to do."

Dillon nodded so hard the hood on his coat bounced.

"It's just a motorcycle ride," Sloan murmured. "We're not going skydiving."

She made a face. "Might as well be."

"Never been on a bike?"

"Sure. The two-wheeled kind that depends on pedaling for power." Feeling oddly bereft now that Dillon was holding Sloan's hand and not hers, she scooped Rex off his feet and cuddled him against her chest. The dog trembled with delight and tried to lick her face. She lifted her chin out of range, and he transferred his adoration to her wrist.

"Deputy McCray would give you a ride, too," Dillon said. "Wouldn'tcha?" His young voice was filled with utter faith.

She focused on Rex, rubbing his head. It was safer than looking at Sloan, since she was afraid her face probably showed the same bare emotion as her seven-year-old brother's. "I don't have any desire to ride on the back of that thing, so it doesn't matter anyway."

"Think your sister's afraid," Sloan told Dillon, sounding very man to man.

"You don't have to be afraid, Abby," Dillon assured her earnestly. "You won't fall or nothing."

"Or anything," she corrected faintly. But she was afraid. Not of falling off but of falling, period.

And a few minutes later, as she watched Sloan ride slowly down the street on his big black monster with Dillon attached to his back like a little limpet, she was afraid it might already be too late.

Chapter Nine

Sloan was still kicking himself the next afternoon as he checked out his usual cruiser and drove over to pick up Abby and Dillon.

He could have left things as they were. Abby and Dillon would have spent the day in Braden visiting their grandmother, just as she'd planned. No harm. No foul.

He'd told her he needed to keep his distance.

How was asking her to his sister's—for their weekly family dinner, for God's sake—keeping his distance?

He'd thought that taking the bike out would clear his head. And it had. It had cleared his head of every bit of sense he'd ever possessed.

The second he pulled into Abby's driveway, her front door flew open and Dillon raced out. Abby, coatless, followed hard on his heels but only to catch Rex, who'd darted out, as well.

In a competition between Abby and the homely little

pup, she was outmatched. Whenever she zigged, the dog zagged, bounding over the snow as though he had springs in his short legs.

Sloan got out of the SUV to join the chase. It helped him stop thinking about his insanity, at least. He pointed at the corner of the yard. "Dillon, keep Rex from getting past you over there."

Dillon ran toward the area, snow kicking up under his heels. Then he turned, bracing his feet wide apart and crouching a little.

He looked like a miniature linebacker. A very thin, very short linebacker, maybe, but if the determination on Dillon's face was any indication, he was going to stop Rex, come hell or high water.

Sloan didn't know where the urge to laugh came from. It was just there. Same way his head went clear when he rode. He stifled the sound with a cough, though, and gestured for Abby to take the opposite corner, between the back of his SUV and the street. Sloan took a third corner, between her yard and his. Rex, caught in the middle, bounced toward Dillon, yipping with excitement at this latest game.

"Don't let him get past you," Abby called out. "He'll head for Sloan's backyard like he did yesterday." Her eyes were bright and shining as she looked at Sloan. "He climbed behind your woodpile, and I would've never gotten him out if he hadn't chosen to chase after Mr. Gilcrest's cat instead."

"That grumpy old man's got a cat? Since when?"

"He told me he's had Marigold for years. And what do you mean by *grumpy?* As long as you don't make the mistake of bringing up the federal government, he's perfectly friendly." She danced around a little when it seemed as if Rex was going to turn her way. But the wily dog tore around in a circle, heading off to the center of the yard, where he lifted his leg and did his business at the base of Deputy Frosty.

Sloan had lived in the neighborhood for half a year. He'd never seen Gilcrest's cat, much less heard of her.

Abby had been there less than a month and she found the old coot friendly.

He wanted to blame it on her youth—on naïveté. But he suspected it was simply *her*. Something about her that brought out the best in people.

"Oh, Dill—he's heading for you again!"

Dillon launched himself at the dog and landed face first. He got an armful of snow and not much else. Rex pounced on Dillon's back and ran up the slice of ground between their houses.

"Nuts," she muttered as she ran past Sloan, grabbed Dillon and set him on his feet and followed the dog toward the backyard. "Just call his name and see if he'll come back to you," she yelled.

Sloan walked over to Dillon and finished dusting the snow off his back. "You ever have a dog before?"

Dillon shook his head. "You?"

Sloan shook his head. "Nope."

"But you're old!"

Sloan winced. "Sometimes it seems that way," he allowed dryly.

Dillon's forehead crinkled. "How come?"

He figured the boy was still on the topic of dogs and not Sloan's state of decrepitude. "Because we never lived anywhere we could have one."

"How come?"

"Because we moved around a lot."

Dillon still looked curious. "How come?"

"You give *persistence* a new name, sport."

"Huh?"

He roughed up the boy's hair. It was as dark a brown as his sister's and just as soft. "Nothing. Run inside your house and get a handful of dog food or something."

"He's got treats!" Dillon darted over to the house and up the porch steps.

Rex wasn't going to go unloved, obviously. "A treat sounds good," he said, even though Dillon wasn't there to hear him.

The dog wouldn't be able to resist temptation.

He heard Abby's boots crunching on the snow as she returned. Her cheeks were as pink as the sweater she was wearing and her shiny hair was tousled.

It would look the same way if he ran his fingers through it.

Homely dogs weren't the only ones swayed by temptation.

Sloan had to shove his hands in his pockets to keep from reaching for her. "No luck getting the hound?"

"He went straight behind your woodpile again. I don't know what's back there that's so interesting to him. Where's Dillon?"

"There." He nodded toward the boy, who was racing out of the house waving a bone-shaped dog biscuit.

Abby made a face. "Silly I didn't think of that in the first place." They trooped to the rear of Sloan's house, and Dillon crouched next to the woodpile.

"That space doesn't look big enough for a rat to get through."

"Now there's a lovely thought." She grimaced. "You don't suppose there's something dead back there, do you?"

Sloan wished he would've kept his mouth shut. "Nah," he lied. How the hell would he know what kind of creatures dwelled or died behind the wood?

Dillon called the dog's name. "I've got a treat for you," he crooned. As if by magic, Rex gave a woof.

They all turned to see the dog standing behind them, his head cocked as if they were the ones doing something strange.

"Rex!" Dillon pounced on him, feeding him the biscuit at the same time. "Where'd you go, buddy? Huh?"

Abby looked from the woodpile to Rex and back again. "It's a mystery to me." Then she scooped up the wriggling dog herself. "I'll shut him in the house, and we can get going."

Sloan rubbed the dog's head. He had the face of a beagle, the body of a terrier and the short legs of a dachshund. Altogether it was quite a combination. "You could just bring him, you know."

"Tie him up outside Pizolli's?" Her brows pulled together. "I suppose so, but it's just as easy to leave him here. He's potty trained already—"

"Not at the restaurant. At Tara's."

Her lips parted and some of the rosiness seemed to drain out of her cheeks. "We're…going to your sister's house?"

"That's where they're getting together this week for Sunday dinner. Thought she told you."

Abby looked even more alarmed. "She invited us for pizza. Pizolli's. I assumed she meant at the restaurant."

Not with that crowd, he thought. They'd overrun the place. "Is there a problem?"

Her eyes were wide. "No," she said quickly. "I… We… just don't want to intrude." She moistened her lips, leaving them shiny and unintentionally inviting.

"Tara invited you," he reminded her. "Pretty sure she knew where she was inviting you *to.*"

Her cheeks flushed again. "That's true, of course. But we can't show up with a dog in tow." Rex sighed heavily as if he felt disparaged. "It's bad enough I didn't offer to bring something." Panic had started to creep into her eyes again. "I don't have anything in the house to take. I should have dressed up nicer."

He couldn't help it. He grinned and slid his hand around her neck, tugging her close to kiss her forehead. "She's going to consider your presence gift enough. And believe me, sweetheart. There's not a damn thing wrong with the way you're dressed." She had on jeans that fit her perfect butt like a glove.

He let her go only to remember Dillon, who'd watched the brief exchange with his mouth open. "You *are* her boyfriend! You called her *sweetheart*."

Abby looked pained. "Dillon, that doesn't mean anything."

The little boy ignored her, his eyes narrowing in on Sloan's face. "Grandpa used to call Grandma *sweetheart*," he challenged. "And even though she doesn't 'member us, she still has a picture of him in her room."

"That's different." Abby handed him the dog. "Take Rex inside and make sure his water dish is full. You can give him another dog bone but be sure you close the front door before he gets out again. And bring my coat, please."

For a moment, Sloan wondered if the kid would argue. But he didn't. He just gave Sloan another close look then carried Rex back to the house.

Abby, on the other hand, looked anywhere other than at him. Her embarrassment was plain. "Sometimes he gets an idea that he just can't let go of." She laughed awkwardly. "A few months ago, he was convinced that there was a, uh…well, an alien…living in the attic. You know. Not-from-this-world sort of alien. Nothing I told him changed his mind."

He managed to keep a straight face. "Can't fault the kid for a lack of imagination. What finally worked?"

She lifted her shoulders. "Nothing. When the new owners moved into my grandparents' home, I had to keep Dillon away from them so he wouldn't let them know they weren't—" her voice dropped a register "—*alone*."

"So you're saying I'm not going to be able to convince him I'm not your boyfriend."

Her cheeks turned even redder. "No! I'm just saying that— Oh, criminy." She all but stamped her foot in the snow. "I'll talk to him. That's what I'm saying. So don't worry about it."

The more uncomfortable she got, the more he relaxed. He was pretty sure that didn't say much about his character. "Do I look like I'm worried?"

Her gaze flew to him and skedaddled away just as quickly. Her soft lips compressed. She shook her head even as she lifted her shoulders.

A less decisive gesture didn't exist, and it made him want to scoop her close and kiss her crazy.

If you're going to be accused of being Abby's boyfriend anyway, why not take advantage of it?

He kicked the devil inside him to the corner.

"Didn't know all it took to be someone's boyfriend was to call her *sweetheart*," he commented dryly, trying to steer things back on course. "Might have tried it a time or two when I was a kid."

Her cheeks were still red, but she gave a reluctant smile. "I'm sure you needed no help in that area."

"You'd be surprised." He closed his hands over her shoulders and steered her toward the driveway. "Pretty sure I've never qualified as anyone's boyfriend." There'd never been enough time when he'd been young. And then he'd gotten in with the ATF, and the stakes had turned too high. He'd loved Maria, and they'd been lovers. But not even during that relationship had anyone ever thought of him as her boyfriend. It would have been too normal.

Abby dug in her boots, and she gave him an incredulous look. "You're saying you've never been...you know, *with*—"

He realized where her mind had gone and nearly laughed. "I don't mean I haven't slept with a woman before."

"I know," she said defensively.

He brushed his finger down her nose. "Don't lie to a cop, sweetheart. We can always tell."

She exhaled noisily and marched to the driveway. "Why don't we take my car," she suggested. "I don't really want to ride behind the grille, where the doors don't open from the inside."

"I do," Dillon said, racing up to her and handing her the red coat. "I wanna ride in the back."

"Problem solved." Sloan reached past her to open the back door of the SUV, and Dillon climbed up inside.

Abby just looked stymied as she pulled on her coat. "I hope this isn't some indicator of the future," she muttered.

Sloan grinned and opened the passenger door for her. "I think you're safe. That boy's sense of right and wrong goes bone deep."

"Not deep enough to keep him from fighting with Calvin Pierce again. Threatening to, anyway." She didn't look at Sloan as she climbed inside, taking with her that fresh scent her hair always carried.

He rounded the vehicle and got behind the wheel. Old Gilcrest was sitting on his porch next door and actually had a benevolent-looking smile on his face. He held a fat orange cat in his arms and returned Abby's wave.

Sloan shook off his bemusement and backed out of the driveway.

After fastening her seat belt and making sure that Dillon had done the same, Abby sat facing forward, her arms crossed over her chest. "Where does your sister live?"

"Little ways out of town." It was an understatement. "First time I went out there, the road wasn't even paved. They've done some improvements since then." Nevertheless, the *cabin,* as they called the spacious house, was still off the beaten track.

"Do you catch a lot of bad guys back here?" Dillon sounded excited at the prospect.

He turned at the corner. "I've transported a few."

"Like on *Star Trek?*" Dillon giggled. "Beam me up, Scotty."

"Old television reruns," Abby offered, looking resigned.

"Captain Kirk and Mr. Spock were reruns when *I* was a kid. Didn't matter where we were living, I could always count on those old episodes." He smiled a little, thinking about it. "Tara and I would fight over channel control. She was more the *Brady Bunch* type."

Abby stirred. "He discovered *Star Trek* last year. Our grandmother was watching it one time when we visited, and he was hooked. Did you live in a lot of different places?"

"Thirty-some, I guess." He glanced at her and saw her shock.

"That explains the kindergarten classes," she said faintly. "The only place I've ever lived was in my grandparents' house in Braden. Well, other than here, obviously."

"Tara would have envied you. She hated all the moving around. Never having friends for more than a few months at a time. Never feeling settled."

Abby had relaxed her arms and turned slightly toward him. "But not you?"

He slowed automatically as they drove past the Pierce place. The sheet of plywood was still fixed over the broken picture window, but everything looked quiet; there was no indication at all that a troubled family was living inside. "I was always restless." He picked up his speed.

"And now?"

He could have given her a pat answer. Taken the easy way out. But he glanced at her, and the earnestness in her pretty eyes made it impossible. "It's something I'm trying to work out."

She pursed her soft lips in thought. "Is that why you haven't agreed to stay on permanently with the sheriff's department even though Max Scalise has asked?" She lifted her hands a little when he shot her a look. "Can't live in this town for more than a week without hearing someone mention it. It's not exactly a secret, is it?"

"A good reason *not* to live in this town," he muttered.

Her lashes swept down, and he turned his attention back to the road as Weaver became a reflection in his rearview mirror.

Dillon's voice popped up again. "I lived in Cheyenne."

Abby looked over her shoulder, obviously surprised at the admission. She caught Sloan's questioning look. "That's where he lived with his mother," she said under her breath.

Not our mother, but *his*. As if the woman hadn't had anything to do with Abby's existence at all. "And he usually doesn't talk much about living there," he concluded, just as quietly. "Reading your face is as easy as reading a book," he added.

"*That's* a comforting thought."

"And then I lived in Braden," Dillon continued blithely. "And now we live in Weaver."

"Where we'll be staying for a long time," Abby said firmly. "So if you're thinking you want to be like Sloan and live in another twenty-seven towns, you can just forget it. I *like* being settled in one place." She glanced at Sloan. "What did your parents do, anyway, that kept the wheels always rolling?"

"My dad was in the CIA."

Again, she looked shocked. "That sounds like something out of a movie."

"It wasn't anywhere near that interesting." He didn't want to get into their nightmarish childhood. He caught Dillon's gaze in the rearview mirror. "What's your favorite *Star Trek* episode?"

Beside him, Abby groaned a little.

"'The Trouble with Tribbles,'" Dillon said immediately. "We had a Tribble in our old house, you know. It lived in the attic."

Abby covered her face with her hands, and her shoulders shook slightly.

It took Sloan only a second to realize she was laughing, and soon he was, too.

It had been so long since he'd laughed—really laughed—that he laughed some more.

It seemed as though no time at all had passed when he turned off the highway onto a graded road full of curves and pulled up in front of his sister's place.

Abby stared at the half-dozen vehicles already parked in front of the big log house and felt alarm nudge its way into the pleasure she'd gained from hearing Sloan's deep laugh. "Looks like there are a lot of people here."

Humor still lurked in his dark eyes. "Astute detective work."

Rather than wait for Sloan to open her door for her—which seemed much too datelike—she pushed it open herself, leaving him to open Dillon's door instead. Then he led the way through the congestion of vehicles toward a wide porch.

There were two rocking chairs sitting on the porch, and judging by the blanket draped over the arm of one of them, they were actually being used even though it was the dead of winter. "My grandparents used to sit on their front porch in a glider. They were always holding hands."

"And Grandpa called her *sweetheart,*" Dillon added, stomping up the stairs behind them.

She gave him a look. "Please don't start that again."

"It's the truth," he challenged.

"Yes, but—"

"You're here!" Tara had opened the front door and was smiling hugely over the head of the toddler she was carrying. "I was beginning to think big brave Deputy McCray had chickened out on me again." She waved them into the foyer, where she set the boy on his feet, only to redirect him when he tried to bolt out the front door. "Daddy will take you outside later, Aidan."

She was more successful at catching her son than Abby had been at catching Rex. The toddler went running back inside yelling for his daddy.

"It's my fault we ran late," Abby admitted.

"Our dog got out," Dillon added. He seemed to have forgotten his shyness with Sloan's sister as easily as he had with Sloan. "You look like Snow White."

Tara laughed, delighted. "And you look like Prince Charming," she returned, holding out her hand for him. "Let me show you our castle." She didn't glance back at them as she drew Dillon deeper into the house. "Show some manners, Bean, and take Abby's coat," she said.

Abby waited until Tara was out of earshot. "Bean?" She turned and tried not to shiver when his hands brushed her shoulders as he helped her out of her coat.

"Old nickname. Hers is worse."

Free of the coat, she turned to face him. He stood much closer than she'd expected, and she felt short of breath. "What is it?"

"Goober."

The glint in his eyes was so appealing it was all she could do to smother her laughter. "That *is* worse. But why Bean?"

"Nothing exciting. Mom used to harp on me to eat my beans." He grabbed her hand and pulled her in the same direction his sister had gone. Before she could make too much of it, he'd released her hand again as they entered a soaring great room dominated by enormous windows with a spectacular view of distant mountains. Vying for equal billing was a stone-fronted fireplace, where a welcoming fire crackled.

And in the middle of all of that were a dozen people sprawled around, plates of pizza on their laps. Abby felt herself flushing to the roots of her hair when their attention turned to her.

"Fortunately, we're a small group today," Tara said from across the room, where the pizza boxes were spread over a wide table. "So there's still some food left." She handed Dillon a plate, directing him to choose whatever he liked.

This was a small group? Abby hated to see what they'd consider a large one.

"Don't just stand there like a bump, Bean," Tara chided. "Introduce your girlfriend, already."

"We're just neighbors," Abby said, wishing the floor would open up and swallow her. "Friends."

Tara had a mischievous smile on her face, but she said nothing. She didn't have to.

"That isn't what I hear," a very slender blonde said from the corner of a chair where she was curled. "I'm Lucy, by the way. It's all over town how you two were getting all cozy on the front porch the other night." Her eyes danced merrily.

"And he calls her *sweetheart,*" Dillon chimed in.

"Well, then," Tara concluded. "That seals the deal for me." She held up a plate in invitation. "Pizza?"

Chapter Ten

"So…" A few hours later, Tara stood next to Sloan at the kitchen sink, watching the rest of the family chase around outside in the snow with a football. "I like her."

No point pretending he didn't know whom she meant. Despite the trial by fire his sister and her family greeted them with, Abby managed to rise above it simply by wading right into the group, extending her hand to one person after another as she introduced herself. She didn't offer a single explanation about kisses or sweethearts or anything. Just was her usual friendly self as if the notion of being his girlfriend wasn't worth the breath of denying or confirming.

Now she was running around with the others, a grin as wide as Dillon's on her face.

"Abby's a likable person," he said, taking the wet plate his sister handed him and swiping the towel over it. "She's a good neighbor. Not like that guy who lived next to us when we shared that brownstone back in Chicago. The guy who was always stealing the paper. What was his name?"

"Mr. Quinlan, and stop trying to change the subject."

He stacked the plate with the others he'd already dried. "Don't make more of this than there is."

She pulled the stopper on the drain and leaned her hip against the sink. "Don't make less of this than there is," she countered softly. "I see the way you look at her."

He tossed down the towel, struggling for patience. "You know better than anyone why I'm not going down that path. I'm not cut out for it."

"Because you think you're too much like Dad was, or because of what happened with Maria?"

Trust his twin not to mince words.

"Just drop it." He turned to leave.

But she grabbed his arm. "I put my life on hold for five years for you," she reminded him tartly. "I gave up the only home I'd ever had until then and moved from Chicago to Weaver—started over *again*—just to satisfy your overprotective nature while you wormed your way into the Deuces."

"I get it. I owe you. I'm here, aren't I? I'm trying. I warned you I wouldn't be any good at it."

She gave a huge sigh. "Sloan, you don't *owe* me. I love you. I want to see you happy. And you know that my coming to Weaver turned out to be the best thing that ever happened to me, because this is where I found Axel. Why can't you just be hopeful? Go with your emotions for once?"

"Emotions never managed to get me anywhere I wanted to be."

"That's the past," she reminded him softly. "Abby's not Maria. Working for Max is not the same as pretending to be in league with a bunch of criminals. You lived long enough in the shadows. We did it when we were growing up because we had no choice, but things are different now. We're different."

"Are we?" He jerked his chin toward the window over the sink. "You're living exactly the sort of life you always dreamed of having."

"What sort of life did *you* dream of having?"

He chucked her lightly under the chin. "We're twins, Goob, but we're pretty damn different. *I* didn't dream."

She just shook her head. "Everyone has a dream. And you're only hurting yourself by pretending otherwise." She dried her hands. "And I still like Abby."

He stifled a curse. "She's too young."

Tara laughed at that. "She's raising a seven-year-old boy. She bought a house on her own, has an education and a good job. What she is is a young woman making a life for herself. She's not someone you need to rescue, and *that* is what probably scares the daylights out of you. Means you don't get to call all the shots and try to control everything. For the majority of us, that's what real life is." She patted his arm as she headed for the back door, grabbing a jacket off a hook on the way. "Whether Abby is in your future or not is up to the two of you. Just don't let what's happened in the past make the decision for you."

It took all of Abby's self-control not to watch Sloan too carefully when he followed his sister outside to join the football game.

Of course calling it a *football game* was playing fast and loose with the term. There *was* a football, and there did seem to be some sort of scoring. But mostly it was just a chance to run off too much pizza and—according to Chloe's father, Ryan—wear out the kids well enough that they went to sleep on time for once.

The success of which was proven later when Dillon dozed off on the drive home.

When they got to her house, Sloan offered to carry him inside for her.

"Thanks." She went ahead of him to unlock the door and then followed him down the hall to Dillon's room. She'd managed to keep her emotions in check since she'd waded into Sloan's sister's family and began introducing herself as if everything were perfectly normal.

But watching him settle her little brother so carefully in his bed now was more than she could take.

She turned on her heel and went out to the kitchen, kicking off her boots along the way. Needing something to do, she filled the coffee maker and started it up. The caffeine would keep her awake later, but it seemed smarter than pulling out the margarita mix left over from poker night with the girls. After those margaritas, she'd made out with Sloan in the middle of her front yard.

And look where that had led. He'd kissed her only to end up pushing her away.

She heard him when he came out from the bedroom but couldn't bring herself to look at him. "I'm making coffee." She stated the obvious. "Would you like some?"

"I'm sorry about all that crap at Tara's."

"We had a very nice time. Dillon particularly. Did you see him and Chloe? Like two peas in a pod."

"About *us*," he said.

As if she didn't know. "They were just poking at you the way families do." She pulled a mug from the cabinet and held it up. "Yes or no?"

He sat down on one of the barstools, tossing his leather jacket onto the empty stool beside him.

She took that as a yes and set the mug in front of him then got down a second one for herself. The scent of coffee was starting to fill the room, but the coffee maker still had plenty of gurgling to get through before it would be finished.

Which left her with nothing to keep herself busy, so she opened the container of cookies and set it on the counter. They were left over from the second batch she'd made, most of which had gone to Mr. Gilcrest next door.

"Dillon's shiner is really coming in."

She snatched up a cookie and broke off a corner, trying to keep her eyes from him. It was hard when he looked so darned good. "It's nothing to sound so pleased about. Calvin's is equally awful. It's no wonder his mother could barely stand talking to me."

He hesitated for a moment. "How was your grandmother when you visited today?"

She had the sense that hadn't been what he'd wanted to say. She plucked a paper napkin from the holder next to the toaster, folded it in half and set her cookie on it. "The same."

"Which means what?"

She sighed. "That she usually thinks I'm one of the nurses who works there and that Dillon is the grandson of the janitor."

"That's rough."

She chewed the inside of her lip and lifted her shoulders. "Thinking about it makes me want to cry," she admitted, "so I'd just as soon not think about it." Tears burned behind her eyes anyway.

"How long has she been sick?"

She turned to face the coffee maker, wishing the thing would hurry. "She was diagnosed six years ago. My grandfather took care of her, though, until he—" Her throat tightened. The machine spit out its last gasp of coffee, and she grabbed the pot, turning to fill Sloan's cup. "He had a massive heart attack two years ago."

"Then who took care of her?"

"I did at first."

"Weren't you still in nursing school?"

She nodded. "I hired someone for the days that I couldn't be there because of school. She watched Grandma, and then one of our neighbors helped get Dillon to and from school."

"Couldn't have been easy."

"That's just the way it was. My grandfather was always a planner and he'd planned well. Their house was paid for, plus there was insurance. In his will he made it plain that he wanted me to have guardianship of Dillon." Her throat tightened again. "And to do whatever I needed where my grandmother was concerned. He didn't want me feeling guilty when the day came that I wouldn't be able to care for her anymore. He'd already made arrangements for where she would go. Braden Bridge is a wonderful place."

"He sounds like quite a guy," he said after a moment. "What'd he do?"

"High-school math teacher. My grandmother was pretty great, too. This is her favorite cookie recipe, by the way. She was as quick with a kiss as she was a kick in the butt if she thought you needed one. I never once felt like I'd missed out on not having a mom. They loved me so much. I want Dillon to grow up feeling that same sense of security."

He nudged her fingers away from the handle of the coffeepot and filled her mug, since she'd clearly forgotten to. "Why wouldn't he?"

"That fight with Calvin doesn't shout success. He's never done such a thing at home in Braden, and we've barely settled in here, and *wham*."

"How often did he have nightmares in Braden?" he challenged. "Damn, but these things are good," he murmured, taking another cookie for himself and popping it into his mouth whole. He shoved the long sleeves of his dark gray T-shirt up his sinewy forearms. "You've only been here a few weeks. You can't judge anything by that."

"Maybe. I just don't want my decision to move here to have been a mistake." She pressed her fingertip into the crumbs from her cookie and absently sucked off the chocolate.

His sudden stillness penetrated the air, and she realized he was looking at her mouth.

"You haven't made a mistake." His voice was deeper than usual. His gaze jerked up to meet hers as if he'd realized where his focus had been.

Or maybe that was her imagination again, working overtime where he was concerned.

"You're in a new job," he continued, sounding a little gruff. "He's in a new school. You've both had a lot of changes, and that might make it rocky at first, but that'll smooth out in time."

She dabbed more crumbs onto her fingertip, only to wipe them off again on the napkin when she realized her hand was trembling. "Comforting words from a guy who can't commit to anything beyond the next few months."

His eyes narrowed slightly. "Sweet Abby Marcum has claws."

She blew out a noisy breath and shook her head. "Not really." She wiggled her spread fingers. "Just an occasional tendency to say inappropriate things. My grandfather used to call it my smart-i-tude."

He caught her fingers in his hands, and she froze. "If there's anything inappropriate around here, it's me."

She made a face, prepared to deny it. But her words

dried when he guided her fingertip back to the crumbled cookie and slowly pressed down, picking up crumbs the same way that she had. And when he pulled her finger to his mouth and closed his lips over the tip, her throat closed altogether.

Then he turned her hand, spreading her fingers flat, and kissed her palm.

Shivers danced down her spine. Something was working overtime inside her, and it definitely was not her imagination. "Sloan." It was barely a whisper.

His eyes looked into hers. "Inappropriate."

She swallowed hard. "Why? Are you hiding a wife somewhere after all?"

"I'm trying to be serious here, sweetheart."

But his lips had twitched again, so she grew a little braver. She'd encouraged Dee to open Joe Gage's eyes. Why shouldn't she try her own advice? She leaned her elbows on the counter, bringing herself closer to him, and turned her hand in his to slide her palm slowly against his. His eyes narrowed and he drew in a slow, careful breath.

The reaction made her feel heady.

"Do you actually have fuzzy aliens living in your attic?" she whispered seriously.

He waited a beat before chuckling softly. "You do make me laugh."

"Is that all?"

His jaw canted to one side. His eyes met hers again, and she felt the impact right down to her toes.

"We've already established that isn't all."

"And *that's* inappropriate. The fact that I—" She pressed her tongue against the edge of her teeth, steadying herself for a moment. "That you—"

"Yeah," he murmured. *"That."*

She leaned even closer, unintentionally crushing what was left of her cookie. She barely noticed. "Why?"

"You know why."

She slowly shook her head. "All you said was I didn't need a man like you."

"You're confusing the stories from the news with reality."

"I'm not confused." She inched closer until her lips were so close to his that she could feel the warmth of his breath on them. "I think you feel safer thinking that I'm confused."

He pulled back a few inches, one eyebrow lifting. "Is that a fact."

Her heart beat so hard in her chest, she felt dizzy from it. "It's not the guy in the news who built a snowman with my brother," she whispered. "Who gives him a ride on his motorcycle and encourages him. It's *you*. Dillon doesn't even know about what you did with the Deuces." His hero worship would know no bounds once he did.

"I'm not doing anything that anybody else wouldn't do," Sloan dismissed. "He's a good kid."

"He is," she agreed. "But you're wrong thinking everyone would treat him the same as you do. Just because I didn't leave behind a boyfriend in Braden doesn't mean I didn't have the opportunity."

His gaze sharpened. "What sort of opportunity?"

"Nothing I cared to explore. Not every guy has the patience to put up with having a little boy around." She shrugged. "And I don't have any interest in someone who doesn't understand how important Dillon is to me." Because she couldn't resist, she traced her thumb over his lower lip. "No matter what you say, you'll never make me believe you're not a good man."

"I want to sleep with you."

Her breath eked out. "I want to sleep with you, too," she managed to say, striving for calm and falling shudderingly short.

His gaze roved over her face, hesitating on her lips. "Just sex," he added flatly. "It's not about anything else but that. Still think I'm a good deal?"

Something about the way he said it penetrated her lightheadedness. His eyes were pinning her in place, oddly remote and divulging nothing in return.

This is the man who convinced a horde of thugs he was one of them.

The realization calmed her, and her hand shook only a little as she laid her palm along his jaw then trailed her fingertips down the hard column of his neck to the swirling edge of his tattoo, feeling him stiffen when she touched him there. "It's not going to work," she warned. "You won't scare me off by pretending you don't care." Then, before she lost her nerve, she leaned forward and brushed her mouth slowly over his.

Again.

And again.

Until she felt his lips soften, and he made a low sound that danced across her nerve endings. Then he moved suddenly, his fingers sliding through her hair, twisting gently as he pulled her head back.

The gaze that burned over her face was anything but remote. She didn't know what he was looking for, but he must have found it, because he gave that low groan again that thrilled her and fastened his mouth over hers. Hot. Hard. Deep.

She leaned closer, trying to wrap her arms around him, but the counter was in the way, and he seemed to realize it about the same time she did, because his hands left her hair and slid beneath her arms, and he pulled her right up onto the narrow surface.

She gasped.

"Don't wake your brother." He pushed aside the coffee mugs and the container of cookies. "Pull your legs over."

She shifted onto her rear, swung her legs around until she was sitting on top of the counter and tried not to gasp again when he closed his hands around her ankles and tugged her across the smooth surface until her chest hit his. Her heart raced and she was so afraid he'd stop that she caught her legs around his hips.

His expression turned unholy. "Have some experience with kitchen counters, do you?"

Her mouth opened; she almost blurted that she had no experience with anything at all, but he took advantage of her parted lips, kissing her again, even more deeply. And then she couldn't think about anything at all. Couldn't worry. Couldn't plan.

She could only feel.

Feel the heat of his fingers sliding beneath her sweater, slowly dragging it upward. He pulled away from their kiss so he could work the sweater over her head and toss it aside. Her own fingers flexed, desperate to get their own skin time, but his lips touched the side of her neck then burned their way down to her heartbeat that pulsed madly inside her chest.

Her head swam, and her hands fisted in his hair as he dragged his mouth over the lacy cups of her bra, dipped a finger inside and slowly drew it down until an aching nipple sprang free for him to taste.

Heat streaked from that wet warmth surrounding her to her center and she jerked, biting back a groan.

He drew in a hissing breath and straightened again,

crushing her against him. She could feel his pounding heart almost as well as she could feel her own.

"Tell me you're on the pill, sweetheart." His voice rasped against her ear as he kissed her cheek. Her neck. "Because it's been a long time since I've needed to carry around a condom."

She froze.

She was a *nurse,* for crying out loud.

Why hadn't she thought this far ahead?

"I, uh, I—" She tried to speak, but her throat was too tight. Every nerve in her body felt perched on a jagged edge, ready to splinter. "No," she managed to say and moaned a little when his teeth grazed the point of her shoulder as he drew the strap of her bra over it.

At first she wasn't sure he'd even heard, but his roving hand slowly stopped. He lifted his head. His eyes were hooded, even darker than usual, and filled with heat. "Not on the pill? What do you use?"

"Nothing," she whispered.

His eyebrows rose.

"There was never a need," she added, feeling shaky inside. "Before." Why wasn't there a how-to book somewhere that gave tips for situations like this?

His hands went from her hips to press flat against the countertop on either side of her. His eyes searched hers. "Abby?" He said just her name, but the way he drew it out, there was a wealth of questions in it.

She could either let him come to his own conclusion or she could head straight in and admit it first.

"I didn't need the pill," she said huskily, "because I've never…never done this before."

And then she flinched as he let out an oath and let her go as if she'd suddenly grown horns.

Chapter Eleven

Sloan stared at Abby. "You're a virgin," he said flatly, wanting clarification even though he didn't really need it. He should have realized. Should have figured that her aura of innocence went deeper than the surface.

Her lips were swollen and red from his kisses; her hair tumbled around her bare shoulders; her breasts lifted rapidly against the lacy bra barely confining them. Then her lashes lowered, hiding the clouds that her gray eyes had become. "I'm sorry."

He raked his hand down his face and stifled another oath. He started to move away from the counter, only to stop. He was hard as hell but at least the counter provided some shield. "There's nothing wrong with being a virgin."

"Really?" She didn't look at him as she pushed off the counter and bent to retrieve her sweater. "Then why are you looking at me with such horror?"

"It's not horror. It's surprise." He turned his back on her

because watching her put on her sweater was torment. He wished he could rewind time and undo the past hour or so.

Hell, if he was wishing for the impossible, why not rewind the past ten years?

The devil on his shoulder laughed maliciously. *She'd have been thirteen.*

He blew out a long breath and slowly looked at her. Thankfully, the sweater was back in place. Now he only had the vision of her body underneath to torture him for the rest of his days. "The only one who should apologize here is me."

Her chin crumpled slightly, and he braced himself for tears. But they didn't come. "I think you *should*," she said, angling her chin instead. "Stopping like that was…rude." A fresh tide of red flowed through her cheeks.

Not the reaction he'd expected. Nothing about Abby was turning out like he'd expected. "A little smart-i-tude, Abby?"

She lifted her shoulder, but she didn't lower her chin.

He knew better than to smile, but something inside him felt lighter. "I don't have any experience with women like you," he admitted slowly.

The shadows in her eyes—shadows he'd put there— flickered. "I don't have any experience with women like me, either."

The bark of laughter escaped him.

She pressed her soft lips together. She didn't look quite amused, but at least she didn't look as if she were going to cry. He wasn't sure he'd be able to take it if he made her cry.

"Why didn't you tell me?"

She lifted her hands. "It's not like it's a natural topic of conversation, and I never thought we'd—" She broke off and shook her head, looking away.

He let out a long breath. "We're not going to solve this problem tonight."

"Is that what my virginity is? A problem?"

"The lack of condoms is a problem," he said bluntly and watched the way her eyes widened.

Then he watched a swallow work down her slender throat and tried not to think about the way it felt pressing his mouth against her creamy skin and the pulse thundering beneath.

"You're not turned off?"

The devil on his shoulder was cackling so merrily he fell right off his perch. Sloan closed his hands around her hips and pulled her close, rocking her toward him. "Sweetheart, there is nothing about you that doesn't turn me *on*."

She inhaled audibly. Her hands roved over his shoulders, fingertips kneading. "I didn't mean to start something I couldn't finish," she whispered.

"I believe you. This is not your fault, so don't tell me you're sorry again." Then he kissed her. Well and thoroughly.

And when he couldn't take it another second, he set her from him. "That's a poor substitute for everything else I want," he said huskily, "but it's going to have to do for now."

"It's not a kiss-off?"

He shook his head, amused despite himself. "You don't have a clue what sort of hold you have over me, do you. Things are nowhere near finished, Abby. And next time, I can promise you I'll be prepared." He scooped up the two remaining cookies that had escaped their countertop antics and gave her a long look. "You won't have any reason to call me rude for stopping…*like that*."

Her eyes turned smoky.

Before he could lose his remaining sliver of self-control,

he grabbed his jacket and headed for the door. "Thanks for the cookies."

She just gave him a bemused look. "You're welcome."

Abby didn't catch a glimpse of Sloan the next morning. His SUV was already gone when she hustled Dillon out the door for school.

But that was okay. She knew she'd see him soon enough. Things were working out.

Sloan hadn't looked at her as if she were a space alien when he'd learned she was a virgin. If he had cared about that, he wouldn't still want to see her.

It was all she could do not to grin like a buffoon when she left Dillon outside his classroom and headed to her office.

She hummed her way through three hours of vision screenings at the junior high, doodled through a conference call with the education board and realized she'd forgotten to pack her own lunch when Dee stopped by her office, brown bag in hand.

"Come and share my misery," Dee begged. "I have ten minutes to eat and then playground duty."

Abby chuckled. "It can't be *that* bad."

Dee clucked her tongue. "You really are young. The Pollyanna luster hasn't had a chance to wear off. Give it a few more years." She gestured. "You coming or not?"

Abby had nothing else she needed to take care of, and it was her lunch hour. "Why not?" She pushed away from her desk and retrieved her coat.

The lunch bell had rung, and the hall was filled with children boisterously leaving their classrooms behind. "You want to pick up something to eat from the cafeteria?" Dee asked over the chaos.

Who needed food? She was floating on air. "I'm fine."

They reached the heavy metal doors that led outside, and Dee gave her a sideways look. "It's a Monday, for God's sake. But you're even more chipper than usual. Why?"

She pushed open the door and led the way to the playground. "No reason."

Dee narrowed her eyes but didn't say anything until they reached one of the benches. So far, the space was quiet since the children were inside for lunch, and they sat down.

Abby stretched out her legs and lifted her face to the sun.

"Oh my God," Dee muttered softly. "Are you sleeping with Deputy Hottie?"

Abby jerked and stared at Dee. "What? No!"

Dee just pursed her lips knowingly. Her eyes danced. "Don't tell lies to your elders."

Abby rolled her eyes and looked away. "Give me a break."

"Well, *something* has gotten into you. If it's not your hot neighbor, who is it?"

"Dee!" Despite her embarrassment, Abby laughed. "Someone's going to hear you."

Dee made a point of looking around them at the entirely empty playground. "Come on. Dish."

"There's nothing to dish about!"

"He was bad in the sack, huh?" Dee tsked. "Well, just because a guy looks great doesn't always mean he'll *be* great. Learned that lesson a time or two myself."

Abby covered her face, shaking her head. "Too much information, Dee."

Her friend laughed. Then she bumped her shoulder against Abby's. "So it *was* good, then."

She flushed and looked away. "I'm not going to talk about this with you."

"Oh, come on." Dee's laughter died away, but she was still amused. "You really like him?"

She nodded. "I do."

"Oh, well, shoot," Dee grumbled. "Now I'm *really* jealous. Although, the next poker night won't be so costly if you're not among us spinsters."

"None of you are spinsters," Abby said with a laugh. "I still can't believe you call yourselves that."

"Honey, most of us are over thirty and not a one of us is tied up with a man." Dee's expression turned devilish. "Rope ties being the exception."

"Dee!"

"Just kidding. It is *way* too easy to shock you." Dee looked over her shoulder to make sure that the doors to the school building were still closed. "So is it serious? This thing between you and Sloan?"

Abby thought about it. "I don't know."

"Has he decided to stay in town after all?"

"I don't know," she said again. And she didn't really want to think about it because when she did, it had a particularly dampening effect on the happiness bubbling inside her.

"Not that there's anything wrong with just enjoying the moment," Dee added. "As long as you know that's what you're doing."

She knew that Dee was trying to watch out for her. "I know."

Dee studied her for a moment. Then her eyes filled with mischief again. "I'm still jealous."

Abby laughed, and soon, the metal doors behind them clanged. Children spewed out into the sunshine, propelled by a morning's worth of cooped-up energy.

Dee put aside her lunch on the bench. "Brace yourself,"

she warned, pushing herself to her feet. "Now the real fun of the day begins."

Abby rose, too, even though she had no particular responsibility as a playground monitor the way the teachers who shared the job in rotating shifts did. Dee wasn't alone, either; she was soon joined by Rob Rasmussen, the teacher who'd caught Dillon and Calvin fighting in the bathroom. Two of the student teachers whose names Abby couldn't recall came out to supervise, as well.

She wandered among the children as they clustered in their obviously familiar groups. Some headed off onto the snowy baseball field, some climbed on the jungle-gym equipment and some sat huddled on the cement pads that were painted with lines for activities. She tossed a bouncing red ball back to a foursome of chattering little girls and spotted Dillon and Chloe Clay heading for the swing set.

When the bell rang a half hour later, Abby felt almost as much disappointment as the kids did. She returned to her office and a ringing phone, which she grabbed as she shrugged out of her coat. "Nurse's office."

"Do nurses ever wear white uniforms and caps anymore?"

Pleasure flooded her at the sound of Sloan's voice, and she smiled as if he were there to see it. "Is your fantasy showing, Deputy?"

He laughed softly. "Might bear some thinking about."

She very nearly shivered. She glanced at her empty doorway as she sat down behind her desk. "How do you feel about sturdy white shoes with rubber soles that squeak against the floors?"

"Now whose freak is showing?"

She giggled. The only fantasy she had was *him;* hearing his voice was enough to have her squirming in her chair. "How's your day been?"

"Long. One of the other deputies is going to be out for a while. Ruiz. He had an emergency appendectomy yesterday."

"That's too bad. Is he all right?"

"He will be. But I have to take his spot at a conference in Cheyenne. Leaving this afternoon."

Disappointment swamped her. Then she shook herself. He was just doing his job. "How long will you be gone?"

"We'll be back on Friday."

"Who else is going?"

"Max and Dawson."

She ignored a quick jab of jealousy. Dawson, the one who jogged in the park and never wimped out. "What's the conference about?"

"It's a national thing once a year. Combined agencies, a bunch of workshops. Ruiz's appendectomy is a pain in my ass," he added wryly. "I hate sitting in meetings."

"Maybe you'll learn something valuable."

"Maybe I'll be thinking about you in a cute little nurse's cap and nothing else."

He laughed softly when she caught her breath, and she knew he'd said it just to shock her. "Maybe I'll be waiting for you on Friday wearing exactly that," she managed to say smoothly and enjoyed the way he choked a little on his laughter. "I'll miss you," she admitted.

"Find someone to watch Dillon Friday night."

Her stomach swooped, and her mind seemed to fizz. "Okay." A movement at her doorway had her sitting up straight, though. "Thank you for calling," she added primly.

His laughter was low and knowing. "Friday, sweetheart." Then he hung up.

She swallowed, trying to look at least vaguely professional as she replaced the phone and gestured for the student who was clutching a hall pass to enter.

That student was the first in a stream of them, not leaving Abby with a lot of time to dwell on the call. She made up for it that night, though, after Dillon was sound asleep, and she couldn't close her eyes without images of Sloan overwhelming her.

But even that was okay, she realized, as she turned her head into her pillow. Because she went to sleep and dreamed of him.

The next day, after Abby left Dillon at his classroom she headed to Dee's room. Her friend made her way around the children hanging up their coats and met Abby in the doorway. "What's up?"

"Can you watch Dillon for me Friday night?"

Dee's eyebrows went up. "Deputy Hottie?"

Abby rolled her eyes, but she couldn't very well deny it. And there wasn't much time before the final bell would ring, signaling the start of classes. "Try not to announce it to the world, okay? So can you?"

Dee grinned. "Sure. Second and thirds get dismissed late that day, you know. Because of the Cee-Vid field trip."

Abby wanted to slap her head for forgetting. "I already told Dillon he couldn't go because of that fight." She shifted to allow a little girl lugging a backpack that was half her size to get past.

"He'll probably be the only one not going," Dee said seriously. "The tour is one of the highlights of the year." The bell buzzed over the last of her words, and she looked over her shoulder. "Seats," she called out, and the kids began scrambling. "Just think about it," she told Abby as she reached for the door and started to close it. "Either way, you can count on me for Friday night." She grinned quickly. "But if it spills over onto Saturday morning, I've got a pole-dancing fitness class at eleven."

Abby tried not to choke on her laughter as she stepped into the hall so that Dee could close the door. All up and down the corridor, she could hear the similar sound of other doors closing, and then she was alone, and the sudden silence nearly echoed.

She turned on her heel, and the sole of her shoe squeaked loudly on the tile.

She hurried to her own office, where she wouldn't be caught grinning like a fool.

"Sheriff's looking for you."

Stifling a yawn, Sloan glanced up from the report he was reading on trends in crime in rural areas to kill time between conference sessions. "Where is he, Dawson?"

"Coffee shop."

Glad for a reason to move, he handed the dull report to her. "Better than prescription sleep aids."

She eyed the thick report ruefully. "I'll bet." She tucked it in her bag. "See you at dinner." Without a second glance, she headed off as he worked his way through the crowded hotel lobby to the coffee shop. It, too, was teeming with conference attendees, but Sloan spotted Max easily enough and wound his way through the tables to reach him.

"What's up?"

Max gestured toward the chair opposite him. "Glad you're here. Gives me a chance to talk to you for a second."

They'd been in Cheyenne since the previous afternoon. Max had had ample opportunities to talk to Sloan if he'd wanted. "About?"

"Your plans." Max stuck his mug out for the harried-looking waitress, and she splashed coffee into it without slowing her stride. "If you've been thinking about the offer I made."

"I've been thinking," Sloan allowed. "You in a hurry for an answer all of a sudden?"

Max toyed with the coffee mug. "Do I need to sweeten the pot?"

Sloan grimaced. "I'm not angling for anything, Max. I just don't know if—"

"—if you want to stay in Weaver." His boss's fingers flicked off the idea. "You've been clear about that from the start." He glanced toward the door. "I need a chief deputy."

Sloan went still. "Ruiz has the most seniority. He'll be back on his feet before long."

"It's not a matter of seniority. In any case, Ruiz has already told me he's not interested. Doesn't want the stress."

Sloan snorted. "Does anyone?" The chief deputy would be second in line only to the sheriff. "How much is administrative?"

"Not as much as I've got to deal with."

"I don't have the experience."

Max snorted.

Sloan shifted. "Supervisory experience," he added.

"A man's gotta start somewhere." He glanced toward the door again. He didn't seem to see what he was looking for and sat forward. "I have to get my butt reelected every four years. But I get to hire who I want. And I want you."

"Why?"

"Because you're good at what you do," Max said bluntly. "I know the job is a helluva lot more staid than running undercover with the Deuces, but it's still important. The department covers a lot of territory. Lot of people count on us."

"Why'd *you* decide to make the change?" Sloan knew that Max's history was with the DEA.

The older man's lips twitched slightly. "Sarah."

Max was talking about his wife. But it was Abby who popped into Sloan's head way too easily.

Then his boss glanced at the door again and muttered an oath. "Just keep it in mind, okay?"

Sloan frowned but nodded. And then he stiffened when he recognized the man approaching them.

Max had risen, his hand extended to the other man. "Sean. Good to see you again." He gestured toward Sloan. "I agreed to get him here because I owed you one. Now we're even." He tossed a few bucks down on the table for the waitress as he stepped out of the way. "Deputy Mc-Cray." He pinned Sloan with a look. "We'll finish this later."

Sloan nodded once, but he didn't look away from the interloper's face. He did wait, however, until his boss had walked away before he let his feelings show. "Didn't know the ATF was sending special agents all the way out here from the Chicago field office," he drawled. "Or are you just slumming, Sean?"

Sean Cowlings smiled thinly. "Good to know there's still no love lost between us." He took the seat that Max had vacated, pushed aside the thick white coffee mug and folded his manicured hands on top of the table. "Think you're the one slumming it. You happy playing traffic cop in the middle of nowhere?"

He let the insult slide. He and Sean had come up in the academy together, but to say they'd been friends would have been seriously overstating it. "What do you want?" There wasn't any question that Sean had maneuvered to see Sloan. Max had made that clear.

Sean smoothed his hand down his silk tie. "We've got intel that Tony Diablo is trying to reestablish the Deuces."

Sloan's jaw tightened. "Tony's a punk. He'll never succeed at replacing his cousin."

Sean shrugged, not giving away whether he agreed. "I'm in charge of the investigation. ASAC."

Assistant Special Agent in Charge. Old Seany-boy had been promoted. "You always did have your eye on the ladder."

"You're in a unique position to understand all the pieces where the Deuces are concerned."

"The Deuces don't exist anymore," Sloan said flatly. "Without Johnny, it's a dead deal."

"Johnny's dead, too."

Sloan looked away. He'd known about the man's death in a prison fight. The day after he'd heard the news, he'd decided to give Weaver a try. "What's your point, Sean? I've got a gripping seminar on internet crime to get to."

"We want you back."

Sloan laughed. "As what? You running confidential informants?" He couldn't exactly go undercover anymore. His face had seen too much airtime.

"Officially," Sean clarified. He looked none too pleased at the attention Sloan's bark of laughter had garnered. "Full benefits as if you'd never left."

Sloan's laughter dried up. "I didn't choose to leave," he reminded him flatly. "I was escorted out the door by an armed guard."

"Standard procedure."

"Screw standard procedure." He wanted to say it much more bluntly, but there was a little kid who reminded him of Dillon sitting with his dad on the other side of the aisle. "The agency treated me like I was an embarrassment at the least and a freaking criminal at the worst."

Sean's lips thinned. "And they were wrong. You think *I* wanted to be the one sent to deliver their mea culpa?"

"You've always been someone's lackey, Sean." Sloan pushed to his feet. He'd had more than enough of the man's company. "If it weren't for you, they'd have never known I'd made my private deal with Hollins-Winword to protect Maria and my sister. The suits would have never been able to use that as an excuse to fire me."

"You broke protocol," Sean said tightly. "You knew it and you did it anyway."

"Damn straight," he said flatly. "And I'd do it again in a second." He turned on his heel and began working his way out of the restaurant.

"Like it or not, McCray—" Sean's voice followed him "—nobody can stop Tony better than you. You'll never be able to walk away from that!"

Chapter Twelve

"How was your day?"

When she heard Sloan's voice, Abby tucked the phone against her shoulder and sat up in bed. "It's nearly midnight."

"Were you sleeping?"

"Yes."

"Dreaming?"

She smiled into the darkness. "Yes."

"About what?"

She curled her bare toes into the sheets. "Something very…naughty."

"You've never been naughty in your life."

"A person's gotta start somewhere. Why not in their dreams?"

He gave a low laugh. "What was it? Leaving school fifteen minutes before you're supposed to?"

Her smile widened. "Riding on the back of your motorcycle, actually."

"Now I know you're screwing with me."

She tucked her chin over her drawn-up knees. She wasn't about to tell him that it had been vividly erotic having her arms clutched around his rigid midriff with the throaty engine rumbling beneath them. "My day was an entirely ordinary Tuesday," she said, answering his original question. "Finished up vision screenings with the junior-high kids this morning. Then back to my office for two fevers and an asthma attack. What about you? Learning anything fascinating?"

"Learning that sitting on my butt watching PowerPoint presentations is no more interesting than it ever was. How's Dillon?"

"He's nearly done with the poster he wants to enter in the sheriff's contest. He asked if Chloe could come home with us from school tomorrow to play 'White Hats.' I said she could."

"What is this whole White Hat thing, anyway?"

"Video game. His favorite." She told him the premise behind the game.

"And he wants to play it now with Chloe Clay. Romance is starting younger every day."

She laughed softly. "I'm not going to worry about that unless I see him deliberately losing the game to her."

"You get him taken care of for Friday night?"

She hadn't expected that he'd forget, but having him mention it sent excitement through her. "Yes."

"Good. Then I'll get everything else taken care of."

She could only imagine what that meant. "Okay."

"Sorry I waked you."

"I'm not."

He was silent for a moment. She imagined him smiling slightly. Hoped he would be, anyway.

"I wish you were here, though," she added.

"Get some sleep, Abby." His voice deepened. "I wish I were there, too," he added before he hung up.

She was smiling when she fell back asleep to dream, yet again, of Sloan.

She was still smiling the next day, until Calvin Pierce appeared in her office doorway clutching a hall pass. The bruise beneath his eye was fading, but it still stood out against his pale skin just like Dillon's did.

She gestured him inside. "Calvin? Are you sick?"

He shook his head and continued hovering in front of her desk. He looked around to see if anyone was in the back part of her office where two cots were positioned, and his shoulders seemed to fall when he saw that they were both occupied. "Are they sick?"

"Fevers." The flu had begun making its annual rounds. "They're waiting for their parents to come and pick them up." She pulled the sliding door between the rooms nearly closed and rounded her desk to press her hand against Calvin's forehead. It was little-boy warm, but nothing worse. "What's wrong?"

He angled away from her. "Ms. Normington said I hadda come and get a bandage." He held up his hand, showing her a wicked gash on his palm.

"Sit down." She nudged him onto one of the chairs in front of her desk before going to her sink to wash her hands. "How'd you get the cut?" When he didn't answer, she looked over her shoulder at him. "Calvin?"

He hunched his shoulders. "My dad broke sump'n."

It wasn't exactly a detailed explanation.

She dried her hands and pulled out supplies to clean him up, too, since there was no point in bandaging the wound if his hands were still filthy. She sat down next to him with gauze and antiseptic wash and spread a clean towel over her lap before taking his hand and spreading it flat. "How's your eye feeling?"

"Fine." He didn't even flinch when she carefully washed his hand and irrigated the cut, though she knew it had to sting. He thumped the front of her metal desk rhythmically with his tennis shoe.

She studied him as she worked. His clothes were shabby and worn, but they were clean. His socks were mismatched, and his tennis shoes barely had soles left. She remembered how his coat had been two sizes too small when she'd spoken to his mother and him outside Ruby's.

She finished cleaning his hand then calmly began working on his wrist, which was covered in fading bruises.

"Did you cut yourself this morning?"

"Last night."

She'd suspected as much, just from the state of the wound. "No bandages at home?"

He looked down again. Shook his head.

The sight of two violently purple finger-sized bruises on the back of his neck made her close her eyes. She had to hold back a shudder.

"Well," she managed to say, though her throat felt tight. "We'll take care of that now." She dried his hand and taped it up then dropped some supplies into a plastic bag that she gave to him. "You can take those with you," she said. "You have to keep the cut clean and covered, or it might get infected."

"So?"

He was the little bully of the school. He'd been tormenting Dillon from day one. But she still wanted to pull him close and hug away his hurt.

Because there was no doubt in her mind that he was definitely hurt.

"It takes longer to heal if it gets infected," she said smoothly. She signed his hall pass and returned it to him. "Go back to your class, Calvin."

He took the pass and turned to leave.

"Calvin?"

He looked over his shoulder. "What?"

"Everything's going to be okay."

"Whatever," he muttered as he left.

She realized she was shaking and badly wished that she could call Sloan.

She cleaned up the supplies and checked on the students still resting before she went next door. "Mrs. Timms, would you mind waiting in my office for a few minutes? I have two students whose parents are supposed to pick them up anytime now, and I need to speak with Principal Gage."

Mrs. Timms gave her a look brimming with disapproval. "Principal Gage is a very busy man."

She peered at the older woman. "And it's imperative that I speak with him *now*," she said flatly. "Are you willing to go next door and supervise my office for a few minutes or not?"

"Abby?" Joe appeared in his doorway. "What's going on?"

Tears were burning behind her eyes, but she was damned if she was going to let them fall and prove how unequipped she was for the job for which she'd been hired. "I need to talk to you about C-Calvin."

His brows pulled together. He extended his arm. "Viola. Go next door."

The woman sniffed, clearly put out, but she rose and swept past Abby into the hall.

"Come on in," Joe said.

Swallowing hard, Abby entered his office and waited until he'd closed the door. "Someone is beating Calvin Pierce." Just saying the words nearly choked her. "I'd bet my license on it."

He nudged her onto a chair and pushed a box of tissues toward her. "How do you know?"

She grabbed a tissue, but she was too upset to sit, so she stood up and paced around the office as she told him about Calvin's cut. "He has old bruises on his wrist. And yes—" she looked at the principal "—I know kids get bruises for a host of perfectly innocent reasons. Dillon's usually sporting a variety of them himself." She bunched the tissue in her fist. "But it's pretty hard to get a pair of fingerprints on the back of one's neck by accident, and that's what I just saw on Calvin!" Her breath shuddered out of her. She held up her hand, fingers spread. "The bruises were twice the size of my fingers, Joe. An adult did that."

He exhaled, swearing ripely. "Sorry."

She shook her head. "Nothing I don't want to say myself." She pressed her lips together. "I have to report it to the sheriff."

"Yes. You do." He looked grim. "This'll likely get worse before it gets better, but Calvin's the important one."

She nodded and waited while he picked up the phone and made the call. It took only a few minutes before he was done. "They're sending over an officer now."

"Have, uh, have you ever had this happen before?"

"Once." He ran his hand over his thinning hair. "And that was one time too many." He looked out the window behind his desk. "They'll take your report. Get one from me and likely Olivia Normington, as well. Someone from protective services will come and talk to Calvin. His parents will be interviewed. They'll make the determination whether Calvin is in immediate danger."

"Would there be any doubt?" Her voice rose again. She raked back her hair, composing herself. "Sorry. It's just—"

"—upsetting. I should have seen something before now."

"If it weren't for Mrs. Normington sending him to me because of his cut, I wouldn't have seen anything, either."

"Crazy to be grateful a kid got a cut on his hand," he muttered.

A few minutes later, one of the deputies from the sheriff's office arrived, and Joe left them alone in his office so Abby could make her report.

By the end of the day, the entire school buzzed with the news that the sheriff's department had been there and that little Calvin Pierce had been taken away by a lady in a suit who'd come all the way from Gillette.

"Hey." Dee came by Abby's office just as she was closing it up for the day. "How're you doing?"

She dropped her keys in her purse. "What's a little exhaustion compared to what Calvin's going through?" She shook her head. "Who knows how long it's been happening."

"I heard Viola Timms was bawling her eyes out in the bathroom," Dee murmured. "Guess she has a heart lurking in her skinny chest after all."

"Everyone's upset." They turned in unison and walked toward the exit. Abby knew that Dillon would already be outside waiting for her, Chloe undoubtedly with him, since those particular plans hadn't changed just because Calvin's world had been tilted off its axis. "Have you ever had to make a report like that?"

Dee shook her head and tucked her arm through Abby's. "You call Sloan and tell him?"

"Yes." He hadn't been able to talk long. Just sighed when he heard the news and asked if she was okay.

"Who took the report?"

"Jerry Cooper. Do you know him?"

"Yeah." Dee smiled, though the news about Calvin had dimmed her spirit, too. "He pulled me over for speeding once. Besides that he's okay." She pushed open the exit door. "Call me if you want company tonight," she said before turning toward the parking lot.

Dillon and Chloe were waiting exactly where they were supposed to be, and his eyes were wide. "Calvin got *arrested*," he told her.

"He wasn't arrested," she corrected and smiled at Chloe. The little girl was cute as could be with her brown hair pulled up in pigtails and her blue eyes as bright as buttons. "You ready to play some 'White Hats'?"

Chloe's pigtails bobbed as she nodded. She grabbed Dillon's hand then grabbed Abby's with her other. "I'm ready to *win* some 'White Hats.'"

"You're not gonna win," Dillon scoffed, tugging his hand away to wipe it on the front of his coat.

And for the first time since that morning, Abby felt a real smile tug at her lips.

Romance indeed.

She flipped his hood up so it fell over his nose. "You can go on the field trip on Friday," she said.

His jaw dropped a little.

Then he let out a whoop and grabbed Chloe's hand. They jogged ahead, their backpacks bouncing.

Thankfully, the rest of the week passed without any additional traumas, and the mood at the school settled some.

By the end of the day on Friday, Abby locked up her office with indecent haste the second she could.

Dee had agreed to drive Dillon home when their classes returned from the field trip and then stay there with him while Abby and Sloan did…whatever. Which left Abby with about an hour and a half of entirely free time, and she didn't intend to waste a moment of it.

She practically jogged home and tossed her briefcase on her bedroom dresser. She let Rex out long enough to do his business then gave him a dog biscuit, grabbed her keys and closed the door on his imploring face. She drove downtown to Classic Charms, which according to Dee was "the" place to shop for anything decent in Weaver. The fact that the shop was owned by Sloan's sister couldn't be helped. Not that Abby didn't like Tara. She did. But she didn't necessarily want to shop for something pretty to wear for Sloan under the knowing eye of his twin sister.

But Tara wasn't there anyway. A friendly girl who looked a few years younger than Abby was manning the old-fashioned cash register, and she was happy to direct Abby through the eclectic shop to the women's clothing.

She quickly rummaged through the hangers, wishing she had more time to go through the plethora of unusually nice things. It was certainly a better selection than what she'd ever find out at Shop-World. She grabbed a long, ivory cowl-necked sweater that she could pair with tights and boots, and dithered longer than she had time for over a display of outrageously priced, outrageously pretty panties only to pass on them all because every time she thought about wearing them—about Sloan *seeing* them— she lost her nerve.

She quickly paid for her purchases then raced back home and was glad that Jerry Cooper wasn't watching for speeders or she'd have been caught for sure. She showered in record time and was drying her hair when she heard the door open and Dillon's young voice yelling her name.

She tightened the belt of her robe and went out to greet

him. "Hey there!" He had a plastic bag clutched in his fist. "What do you have?"

"Video games," he said reverently and dumped them out right there on the hallway floor. "Everyone got a whole bag!"

"Exciting." Abby stepped around him to meet Dee as she came inside. "Thanks for bringing him back."

Dee's gaze ran over her. "If that's the attire for the evening, guess I don't have to ask what you'll be doing."

Abby flushed. "I have clothes."

Dee just grinned wickedly, and Abby was glad the other woman didn't pursue it. "How long before Deputy Ho— McCray gets here?"

"He said by six."

"Know what he has planned?"

She flushed even harder.

"Never mind," Dee said dryly. "I can figure that one out." She glanced at her watch. "I'm just gonna run back over to the school and grab some papers I need to grade. I'll be back in time."

"Thanks, Dee."

"What're spinster friends for?" She grinned and left.

Abby quickly looked over the games that Dillon had brought home, just to make certain they were appropriate for his age. "Sure you're okay with Ms. Crowder watching you this evening?"

He shrugged, clearly more interested in his bounty than either her or Rex, who was bouncing around trying to steal the discarded plastic bag. She roughed up Dillon's hair and hurried back into the bathroom to turn on the blow-dryer once more. As long as she focused on one thing at a time and didn't think too far ahead to what the evening would hold, she could function. More or less.

When she heard pounding on the front door a short

while later, she gulped. Not only was Sloan early, he sounded impatient. She dashed her hands down her robe again, hurried toward the front door and nearly jumped out of her skin when it crashed open before she could reach it.

Rex yipped and raced past the intruder's legs, bolting for freedom.

They weren't Sloan's legs.

A complete stranger was standing there, eyeing her with cold-blooded loathing. He pointed at her. "They took my boy 'cause of you."

Horrified realization rolled through her. She grabbed Dillon and pushed him behind her. "Go to your bedroom and lock the door," she ordered. "Now!"

Looking terrified, he scrambled down the hall, and she waited tensely until she heard the door slam. Then she eyed Bobby Pierce and completely, fully understood why Sloan had been so adamant that she keep her distance.

She edged toward the kitchen, wondering what her chances were of getting to her grandpa's shotgun before Bobby got to her and figuring they weren't stellar considering he was about as close to the kitchen as she was. "You shouldn't be here, Mr. Pierce."

"Why not?" He stepped farther into the house, eyeing her up and down. "Got no place else. Can't go home. Can't see my wife. Can't see my boy."

Thank God for that, she thought, but wisely didn't voice it. "Breaking in like this won't help your case to get them back."

"Wasn't locked."

"You entered without my permission." She sidestepped a little more. The breakfast counter was the problem. She had to go around it to get into the kitchen, which would take her closer to Pierce. "But if you open up that door again and leave now," she suggested reasonably, "we can forget this ever happened." *Like hell.*

He took a long step into the room, ending any hope she had of making it into the kitchen, and she changed course instantly, backing instead into the living room.

He smiled gruesomely, clearly pleased with her retreat, particularly when she had to stop abruptly because of the fireplace at her back. He advanced. "Afraid, little girl?"

Desperately.

"You're loathsome," she hissed. The iron fireplace poker felt wonderfully solid as she reached behind her and silently wrapped her hand around it. The closer he drew, the stronger the stench of liquor became. "Does it make you feel big and powerful to beat up a little boy?"

"You bitch." He raised a fist, and she braced herself, prepared to swing the poker. "You don't know nothing about me."

"She doesn't. But I do."

Abby's knees nearly went out from beneath her at the sound of Sloan's voice.

"Take another step, Bobby," he warned as he stepped through the front door. "Give me a reason to shoot you."

There was no question Sloan meant it.

The gun he was aiming at Pierce made that more than clear.

"Abby." His gaze never strayed an inch from the man he was watching with deadly calm. "Dillon's outside waiting for you. Go on now."

The fireplace poker clattered noisily as she dropped it and fled around Bobby, stopping only to snatch up her snow boots that were lying by the door before running outside.

Dillon was, indeed, standing next to Sloan's cruiser, huddled alongside Mr. Gilcrest. She shoved her feet into the boots and ran down the steps, not caring that she was wearing a robe and little else. She lifted Dillon in her arms, also not caring one whit if he thought he was too old and too big for such things. "You're supposed to be in your room!"

Her brother just hugged her tightly around her neck and hung on. She looked around, wondering where Rex had run off to, but didn't want to say anything. Dillon was already upset enough.

"Climbed out his window," Mr. Gilcrest offered by way of explanation. His lined face was proud. "Said you needed help." His words were drowned out by the screaming siren of a SUV like Sloan's. It stopped in front of Sloan's house, and two uniformed deputies quickly emerged. "Dep'ty Mc-Cray got here before I finished calling 911."

Abby rubbed Dillon's back. "You brave boy." She kissed his cheek and willed the other deputies to move faster. Sloan had a gun. But he was still in there alone with a crazy person.

The other neighbors were coming out onto their porches, venturing onto the street to see what the commotion was all about. One of the deputies who'd just arrived broke off and started waving at everyone to keep back. Abby buried her head against Dillon's, controlling the urge to scream at them all, because as long as the deputy was watching out for *them,* he couldn't watch out for Sloan.

"Everything's fine," she whispered to Dillon. "It's all going to be fine." She repeated it, again and again, like a litany.

Sloan waited until he was sure that Abby was gone before he spoke. "You are the dumbest son of a bitch to ever walk this earth, you know that, Bobby?"

The other man craned his head around, his lips twisted in contempt. "You're not gonna shoot me."

"Might." The image of Abby's terrified face wasn't going to leave him anytime soon, and it filled him with the kind of rage he'd never wanted to feel again. He lifted his firearm and sighted on Bobby's forehead only because he knew, even as angry as he was, he'd never pull the trigger. He didn't know what he was, but he wasn't a killer. Not anymore. "This close? No possible way of missing." His arm shifted and he aimed lower. "Course I could just shoot you somewhere else. Nobody'd care much if I gelded you."

The fool actually paled and took a faltering step back. "You wouldn't."

Moving faster than he remembered he could, Sloan holstered his weapon and slammed the man up against the brick fireplace, his arm on Bobby's windpipe. "Or I could just put you out of your misery like this," he gritted. "What d'you think, Bobby? You want to take me on? See what it's like with someone who isn't smaller?" He pressed a little harder, hearing Bobby wheeze. "Who isn't weaker?" He waited a beat. "I *ever* see you around Abby or Dillon again, I'll finish this," he promised. "You understand me?"

Bobby's eyes were filling with panic. His wheezing was coming harder, and his hands scrabbled against Sloan's immovable arm.

"You're going to leave Lorraine alone. And you're gonna leave Calvin alone. Got it?"

Bobby couldn't nod but he blinked furiously. Sloan figured it was close enough. He flipped him around and cuffed him while Bobby was still gasping for air.

"You're crazy," Bobby yelled hoarsely as Sloan searched him for weapons.

"Yeah. I was a Deuce, you jerk. We were all crazy." Finding nothing on the man but a thin wallet, Sloan shoved him toward the front door and pushed him out into the cold, where an indistinguishable streak of color flew at him. Rex growled and snapped at Bobby's legs, and the guy howled when the dog found some purchase. He kicked Rex off him, but the dog didn't back off. He continued snarling ferociously, and while it was tempting to let him go at Bobby again, Sloan didn't. "Rex, sit."

The dog's butt hit the porch deck. He whined once, watching Sloan hand Bobby over to Max, who must have just arrived.

"He tried to kill me," Bobby screamed as Max yanked him toward his waiting vehicle. "You gonna do anything about that?"

"Ask him why he didn't finish the job," Sloan heard his boss respond mildly.

Sloan wasn't interested in hearing anything more, though. He pulled off his coat and headed for Abby and Dillon, wrapping it around them before pulling them both into his arms. His throat felt tight, and his head was pounding the way it always had from too much adrenaline. "You okay?"

Abby nodded against him. Even though she was already holding Dillon in her arms, she managed to wind an arm around Sloan's neck, too. "Welcome home." She laughed thickly then promptly burst into tears.

He pressed his cheek to her head, wanting to kill Bobby all over again. He brushed back Dillon's hair until he could see the kid's eyes. They were still dilated with fear. He rubbed his thumb over the tears on Dillon's cheeks. "You're both pretty brave, you know that?"

"Is that man gonna be gone forever now?"

"I sure hope so, Dillon." Sloan slid his arm around the boy, taking his weight off of Abby as best he could, considering the awkwardness of their positions. He watched over their heads as Max drove off with Bobby. Pierce wouldn't be gone forever, he knew.

But maybe he'd be gone long enough that his family could find some peace.

Abby shifted. Her cheeks were wet, her eyes a drenched sea of gray. "So much for our Friday night, huh?"

The night wasn't going to end up anything like what he'd anticipated. But he couldn't care less.

"You're safe," he said roughly. "That's the only thing that I care about right now." Then he kissed her on the lips, not caring in the least what conclusions Dillon or anyone else who saw them would draw.

Chapter Thirteen

Even though Max had taken Bobby away, it wasn't long before it seemed as if half the town was crowding onto their short street.

Sloan took Abby and Dillon over to his place, since the idea of going back into their own house leached the color right back out of both their drawn faces.

"Get a little crowd control going," he suggested as they passed Jerry Cooper, who'd also arrived. Sloan managed not to yell the instruction, so he figured maybe he had more self-control left than he thought. Then he remembered Rex and gave a sharp whistle. The dog came running.

Once inside, he left Abby, Dillon and the dog huddling together on his couch in his sparse living room and bolted upstairs long enough to drag the blanket from his bed and take it back down to them. "You want something hot to drink?" His coat was still draped around her shoulders as he spread the blanket across them.

Abby shook her head. She'd dried her tears, but she was still clearly upset as she pulled the blue blanket up to her shoulders. "Don't you have to go in and make a report or something?"

He did. "Right now the two of you are my priority."

Her eyes went soft.

Dillon's hand emerged from the blanket and worked the fabric down until it was beneath his chin. "I can't breathe under there, Abby," he complained. A second later, Rex's nose popped out, too.

She laughed brokenly and pressed her cheek against the top of his head. "Sorry." She let out a shaking sigh. "Are you thirsty? Do you want something to drink?"

He shook his head. His gaze seemed to be glued to Sloan. "Told you he was a White Hat," he whispered to Abby, though Sloan could hear him well enough.

"I know, sweetie." Abby's eyes met Sloan's, and the trust in them was strong enough to shake him. "He's even more of one than you know."

Sloan tugged at his collar and was vaguely surprised to remember that he was still in his dress uniform. He yanked his tie loose, but it didn't seem to ease the vise tightening around his throat. "I'm going to go change."

Abby nodded. She closed her eyes and leaned her head back on the couch as if all she wanted to do was sleep, even though it was barely past six o'clock.

He headed for the stairs again but veered off for the front door when he heard someone knocking.

Both Dee Crowder *and* Tara were standing on the porch, looking equally wild-eyed. "I was at the bank when I heard," Tara said. "Are you all right?" Her gaze raced over him as if she were looking for proof otherwise.

"*I'm* fine."

"Some nice timing you have, Deputy," Dee said, moving past them to cross the room toward Abby. She sat on the couch next to her friend and put her arm around her shoulders.

Sloan exhaled, knowing whatever time he was going to have alone with Abby and Dillon had just ended. It would take an explosion to unseat either Tara or Dee now. He squeezed his sister's shoulder. "Will you stay here with them while I go over to the sheriff's office?"

She nodded immediately. "Should I call Axel?"

He shook his head. "No need. Max isn't going to let Bobby go anywhere. Everyone's safe."

"Thanks to you, from what I've been hearing."

"You didn't see Abby," he murmured. "She would have taken the guy's head off with the fireplace poker if I hadn't gotten there when I did." He didn't wait around to hear what his sister had to say about that. He just grabbed his keys and left to take care of business as rapidly as he could.

Rapidly, though, turned out to be a relative term, and it was several hours later before he was able to return. When he pulled up in his driveway, light was spilling from the front windows of his house, and something tightened inside his chest.

He ignored the feeling and went inside, immediately spotting Dillon where he was sprawled sleeping on the couch. The blanket from Sloan's bed was gone, but the kid was covered by Sloan's jacket, and Rex was on top of that. The dog opened his eyes and watched Sloan. But Rex didn't budge, and Sloan rubbed the dog's head as he studied Dillon.

He wondered if Calvin and his mother were sleeping just as soundly, knowing they were safe from Bobby for at least a little while.

He could hear the soft voices from the kitchen, and he gave Rex a final pat before moving silently in that direction. The three women were sitting around his kitchen table, but as soon as they heard him, they looked up. Dee was the first one to hop to her feet. "Gotta go!" She scurried past Sloan, giving him a wink.

His sister was almost as quick. "Dinner's at Jefferson and Emily's this Sunday," she told him. They were Axel's parents. "Do I need to twist your arm?"

He gave her a resigned look, though he was more interested in looking at Abby. She had dark circles under her eyes and had his blanket wrapped around her like a shawl. "We'll be there," he told his sister.

She blinked once, obviously noticing the *we* part. "Well, hallelujah," she murmured as she reached up to kiss his cheek. "Get some sleep, Abby," she ordered softly before hurrying out also.

A few seconds later, they heard the distinct click of the front door closing.

"And then there were two," he said quietly.

Her eyes searched his. "What happened?"

"Max is sitting on him. There won't be a judge available for an arraignment until Monday morning. He's got him until then, at the earliest."

"I'm going to need to make a statement."

He nodded once, not surprised that she'd reached the conclusion on her own. "You've got all weekend," he assured her. "You won't have to see Bobby—"

"I'd *like* to see him sitting in a jail cell," she interrupted, sounding fierce. "Preferably in shackles and chains."

"I should have gotten there sooner."

Her brows pulled together. "Why? You had no more reason to expect him to show up at my house than I did."

"I knew about the report you'd made about Calvin. I should have suspected."

She slowly pushed the blanket off her shoulders. She was still wearing only her robe. "Everyone in town probably knew about that report as soon as I made it."

"It's supposed to be confidential. If I find out Pam had anything to do with the news getting out, I'm going to—" He broke off when Abby reached out and pressed her fingers to his lips.

"Stop," she whispered. "This is nobody's fault but Bobby's. He's the one who abused his family. He's the one who invaded my house. How anybody finds out anything in this town doesn't matter. What matters is that he's been stopped."

"We should've been able to stop him before this." He pinched the bridge of his nose and turned to pace the kitchen. "Family protective services has been at that house more times than I want to think about. I should have seen that he'd started in on Calvin, too."

Abby hated hearing the blame in Sloan's voice that he directed squarely at himself. She walked up behind him and slid her hands over his tight shoulders, feeling the flinch he gave.

But he didn't move away, and she squeezed her fingers, kneading his back. "Bobby's the Black Hat here."

Sloan turned, his eyebrow lifting, and she realized she'd used Dillon's terminology. "You know what I mean. Bobby's the bad guy. Period." It seemed strange standing there with her hands digging into his shoulders while he faced her, and she slowly lowered her hands. "Do you know what's happened with Calvin?"

"Family protective services has him placed in a foster home for now."

"He wasn't at school yesterday or today."

"Not surprised."

"What about his mother?"

"They have to determine if she was part of the problem or a victim."

She thought of that poor, fearful woman she'd met on the sidewalk outside of Ruby's. "Victim."

"I think so, too, but Lorraine's got a terminal case of stand-by-her-man. I hope she'll choose to stand by her son this time." His lips twisted and he ran his hands down her arms with a frightening sense of finality. "You're beat." He stepped around her and moved toward the loaf of bread that was sitting out on the table. "Were you able to eat something?"

Feeling a little chilled, Abby nodded. "I can make you a sandwich."

"You don't have to make me anything." He twisted his head around as if his neck ached. "You can take my bed," he said abruptly.

It had been difficult not to poke around upstairs while he'd been gone, but she'd resisted the urge. If Tara hadn't been there, Abby wasn't sure if she'd have been able to keep Dee from egging her right into it. So she didn't know what sort of room or bed situation he had going on up there. "What about you?"

He shrugged. "I'll make do."

She chewed the inside of her lip. She truly had no desire to go next door to her own place, though she knew they'd have to soon enough. "There's no reason not to go back home. I'm being a ninny," she admitted. "But I don't want to go back in there unless it's during the cold light of day."

"You're not a ninny," he dismissed, sounding gruff. "You were going to bean the guy with an iron poker if you had to."

She swallowed, shuddering. It was still too vivid. All

she had to do was close her eyes and she could feel Bobby looming over her and looking crazed.

She heard Sloan curse. Then he slid his arm around her and pulled her against his chest. She couldn't keep herself from clinging to him. From pressing her ear against his chest where she could hear his steady heartbeat. Feel his steady breathing.

"I wanted to kill him," she whispered. "I never thought I'd feel such—" She broke off, not even able to articulate what she'd felt. "He hurt his own son. Scared Dillon out of his mind. God only knows what sort of nightmares he'll have now."

"Why does he have them in the first place?"

Sloan's hands slowly moved up and down her spine. He had never taken the time to change out of his uniform, and the fabric of his shirt felt smooth and crisp against her cheek. And beneath that, he was warm. Steady. Safe.

"His mother used to leave him alone for hours on end."

"You never refer to her as your mother, too."

She pulled back enough to look up at him. "It's hard to think of her as mine, though biologically she is. I have no relationship with her and don't want one." She thought about it for a moment. "It probably sounds shocking, but I really don't have any feelings toward her at all except for disgust at the way she cared for Dillon. The parents who counted for *me* were Minerva and Thomas Marcum."

He didn't look shocked, though. "And the parent who'll count for Dillon will be Abby." He said it as if it were already fact. Then he set her away from him and moved, looking suddenly restless. "Were her parental rights severed? Is it official?"

She tried not to think he'd put the granite-topped island between them as a barrier, even though it seemed that way. "I'm legally Dillon's guardian. I don't expect her to ever come back wanting him. She never did with me. But if she did, she wouldn't get anywhere. I have the assurance of several family-court judges on that particular score. Dillon's not going anywhere."

He studied her. His jaw was roughened by a dark shadow but not enough to mask its sharp angles. "You scare the hell out of me," he said abruptly.

Her stomach hollowed. "Why?"

He rubbed his hand down his face. Clawed his fingers through his hair. "You're twenty-three freaking years old."

"You want me to lie?" She smiled weakly. "Pad my age with a few years?" She pressed her palm against the cool granite, letting it steady her. "Shouldn't it matter less about the years and more about the life? There's ten years between us, not fifty."

"Might as well be," he muttered. His gaze drilled into hers. "You felt like you wanted to kill Bobby. Well, I *have* killed."

She swallowed hard. "Because you were doing your job?"

"While I was a Deuce."

"While you *rode* with the Deuces."

His lips twisted. "Don't romanticize it, Abby. I spent nearly a year closed up in a federal penitentiary just so my cover held water before I even got close to the Deuces, much less became one of them. There were whole years when there was no difference between them and me."

"Sloan." She spread her hands. "Of course there was a difference. If there hadn't been, you wouldn't be here now! You would have stayed with them. They'd have never known the truth. None of them would have seen the inside of a jail cell because of the evidence *you* brought to light."

His lips tightened. "The only reason I finished the job was because of Maria. She was a cocktail waitress where we'd hang." He went silent. The only sound came from the faint tick of the clock on the stove.

She pressed her tongue hard against the roof of her mouth, aching from the way he said her name. *Maria.*

"We got involved," he finally said. "And she hated thinking she'd fallen for a Deuce. She hated everything about them, but she couldn't get away from 'em because she already knew more about them than she should." He yanked off his loosened tie as if it were strangling him and balled it up in his fist.

"You loved her," Abby concluded softly. "So you told her the truth."

"And I got her killed because of it."

Her eyes burned. "I'm sorry."

"So am I." He turned on his heel and left the kitchen.

Abby's breath slowly eked out of her. She listened to the clock tick. Listened to the silence.

She could gather up Dillon and take him home. There was no bogeyman there. He was safely locked up in a jail cell for now. She could give Sloan space.

She ran her hand over the cool granite and heard a soft sound from above her. He'd gone upstairs.

She gathered up the blanket he'd given her—the one that smelled like him that she'd stayed huddled in for the past several hours—and balled it up in her arms, pressing her face into its softness for a moment.

Then she left the kitchen and padded silently past Dillon. He was still sleeping on the couch. Even Rex was snoring softly.

She reached the foot of the stairs and put her hand on the wooden newel-post. There wasn't much light coming from up there, but there was enough.

She put her foot on the first step and very nearly lost her nerve and turned around. But she didn't. She climbed the second step. And the third. And each one after that just got easier. At the top, she turned in the direction of the light and found Sloan sitting on the foot of a wide bed. It had no blanket. Only rumpled white sheets.

He was still in his uniform. His tie still balled in his fist.

She set the blanket on the bed and silently tugged the tie free from his hands. He didn't fight her. But she felt his gaze burning between her shoulder blades when she turned and smoothed out the tie carefully on the top of the chest of drawers across from the bed.

Then she turned back and crouched at his feet and began undoing the laces of his highly polished shoes. When they were loose enough, she pulled them off his feet then rolled off his socks and set them neatly aside.

Now the only thing she could hear was the sound of her own pulse clanging inside her head.

But she was here. And he hadn't told her to go.

She pushed to her feet and took his hands, pulling him up.

His eyes narrowed, but he stood, and she led him around to the side of the bed. She unbuttoned his shirt and tugged it off his shoulders. The white T-shirt beneath clung to his muscular shoulders, but that wasn't what made her breath catch in her throat. Nor was it the tattoo spreading below the short sleeve of his undershirt. It was the ugly scar tissue rippling over his right biceps. Maybe there'd come a time to ask about it.

But not now.

Reminding herself that she was a trained nurse didn't keep her hands from trembling as she undid his leather belt. It slithered from the belt loops when she tugged it free of his pants. She coiled it up and set it on the felt-lined tray sitting on top of the chest.

Nothing about Sloan moved except his eyes, which followed her as she came back and stood in front of him. She undid his pants, tugged them down his hips and willed herself not to pay too much attention to the dark gray boxer briefs he wore beneath as she kneeled and waited for him to step out of his trousers. Once he had, she shook them out and folded them over the back of the straight-backed chair in the corner.

She returned to stand in front of him once again. She started to lightly touch his shoulders, but she curled her fingers into her fists and reached around him instead to pull back the top sheet and smooth out the bunched-up pillows. The bed was as neat as she could make it in just those few seconds, and she looked at him. "Lie down," she said quietly.

His gaze flickered. The mattress sank a little when he sat down on the side of it. She waited, and after a moment, he let out a sigh and stretched out on his side, facing her.

She smoothed the sheet over him then turned off the lamp that was sitting on the nightstand next to him, plunging the room into darkness.

"Where are you going?" His voice was deep. A man's. But the question behind it could have come from her little brother.

"Nowhere," she soothed calmly. She walked around the bed, and her hand found the blanket where she'd left it. Then she climbed onto the mattress and stretched out behind him, spreading the blanket over them both. It was strange—her heart was pounding heavily, but she'd never felt more calm. She slid her arm over him, and her palm found the center of his chest. She pressed her cheek against the soft cotton knit stretched over his tense back. "Go to sleep, Sloan," she whispered. "I'm not going anywhere."

She didn't close her eyes. She didn't sleep. She simply

counted her heartbeats. Breathed slowly, knowing that he would feel the movement against him.

And a long, long while later, she felt a deep breath shudder through him, and he closed his hand tightly around hers.

Only then did she close her eyes.

Only then did she sleep.

Dawn was a silvery glow outside the slanted blinds at the window when Abby next opened her eyes. Sometime during the night, Sloan and she had turned over, and their positions had reversed. His arm was a heavy weight clamped over her waist.

She lay there for a long while, listening to his steady breathing; it wasn't quite a snore but obviously he was sleeping soundly. And while the idea of happily lying there with him for the rest of her days was lovely in theory, it wasn't exactly practical. Moving gingerly, she managed to slide out from beneath his arm without seeming to disturb his sleep and scooted off the foot of the bed. She glanced out the window as she passed it and realized it looked down on the side of her house and her own bedroom window.

Had he ever looked out, thinking of her?

She quickly turned away and silently slipped downstairs, where she visited the powder room tucked next to a room that could have been an office or a bedroom if it had possessed even one stick of furniture. She cracked the back door open long enough to let out Rex. For once, he cooperated beautifully, and in seconds he trotted back inside, where he immediately returned to the living room and hopped onto the couch near Dillon's feet. He circled a few times then settled in a ball and lowered his head on Dillon's leg. Her brother didn't even stir.

She adjusted the coat still draped over him like a blanket, and when he slept on, as peacefully as she'd ever seen him, she tightened the tie on her robe again and crept back up the stairs to Sloan's bedroom.

He hadn't moved, either, so she carefully worked her way back to where she'd been when she'd wakened, right down to the wonderful detail of his arm lying heavily across her waist.

She let out a long breath and closed her eyes.

Then Sloan's lax fingers tightened. They moved and spread and pressed flat against her belly, pulling her entire backside from shoulders on down solidly against him. "Wondered if you'd come back." His voice sounded rusty with sleep but that was the *only* thing that was sleeping where he was concerned.

That fact was glaringly noticeable, and the heat that collected deep inside her was instantaneous. She tried to speak, but only a garbled sound came out.

His knee crooked against the back of hers, and his hand ran possessively from her belly up over her hip. She could feel the heat of his palm even through her robe.

"Also been wondering what you had on underneath this thing." His fingers inched along the flannel, slowly drawing it up her leg. "If anything."

She let out a careful breath, thinking about the pretty panties she could have purchased at Tara's shop. If she hadn't chickened out, she wouldn't now be wearing her plain white cotton. "Nothing exciting."

"I don't know about that," he murmured. His palm slid beneath the flannel and curved over her upper thigh then slid behind it, gliding up over her hip, back down then up again. Gaining another inch with each pass, and making it increasingly difficult for her to remain still.

When he reached the narrow edge of her panties and

slid his fingers beneath, her lips parted and she hauled in a soundless breath.

His hand palmed her rear then tormentingly inched between her legs, where there was no mistaking her arousal. "That's pretty exciting," he murmured.

She moaned, shifting restlessly and much too quickly as his hand moved again but only to unknot her tie belt and draw the flannel away from her body. He kissed the shoulder he bared. "That's pretty exciting, too."

He shifted, his thigh sliding over hers and nudging her onto her back. His eyes roved over her as he slowly spread the robe, leaving her wearing nothing at all but her panties. "Ex." His fingers grazed oh-so-quickly over the juncture between her thighs again then trailed up the flat of her belly. "Cite." His fingertip circled one rigid nipple, then the other, then dragged over the hollow at the base of her throat, up her neck and stopped beneath her chin. He tilted it upward, toward his lips. "Ting," he whispered and kissed her softly.

And all the while he kissed her, his palm slid back down again, retracing its path. Lingering longer. Not teasing, but promising. When his hand glided over the center of her, she gasped. Then his fingers moved, swirled, and she shuddered, rocking needfully against him.

His breathing roughened. "Exciting, all right." He kissed her harder, only to pull back. His hands deliberately gentled. Slowed. His kiss turned sweet.

Her heart felt as if it were cracking open. She loved him. She knew she did. But his tenderness was almost more than she could bear, because she didn't know how she was going to survive it when he left.

And leave, he would.

"Don't stop now," she managed to say, pretending that her throat wasn't tightening and her heart wasn't breaking. She dragged at his T-shirt. "Wouldn't want to be rude, would you?"

He smiled a little. He pulled back enough to yank the shirt off, revealing the tattoo in its entirety. She caught her breath. The complicated design spread over his entire left shoulder and fanned out over his pec. "It must have taken days," she whispered. *"Why?"*

"Part of the job."

His hand slid along her cheek. "You want me to put my shirt back on?"

His thumb brushed over her lips, and she had to close her eyes against the tears that wanted to come. "No." She ran her hand deliberately over the tattoo. It was just ink. *He* was smooth and warm.

"If you want me to stop," he murmured, "just tell me. Something you don't like, you say so."

She let out a strangled laugh. Her body was humming, desperate for more, while he was only concerned that he might hurt her.

He would, too. She knew it. But it wasn't the hurt beyond his bed that counted here.

She rubbed her finger against the line between his brows. "I don't think that's going to happen." She shoved at his shoulders and pushed him flat on his back. She kicked off her panties and straddled him then leaned over until her breasts were flattened against the hard planes of his chest. Sensations buffeted her at every turn. Physically, there was nothing about him that wasn't hard. Honed. But inside, she knew he was even more vulnerable than she.

"I'm not going to break, Sloan." She kissed his bristly chin. Tugged gently at his lower lip with her teeth. "Please don't treat me like I will."

His hands closed over her rear, pulling her down against

him, and she gasped at the thrilling feel of him pulsing against her. His eyes searched hers. "Are you sure?"

She rocked her hips slowly, and her eyes nearly rolled back in her head with pleasure. "Never more."

His hand left her only long enough to reach for the drawer in the nightstand. He pulled out a foil packet. "You *that* sure?"

She took it from him and tore it open. "Still questioning?"

He gave a strangled groan. "You're killing me here, Abby."

She leaned over again, her lips hovering above his. "I'm a nurse, remember?" She felt the quick twitch of his lips, and it made her feel braver. "Show me, Sloan," she whispered. "Let me make it better."

His hands clamped on her head, and he kissed her deeply. Then he showed her. And when his fingers fisted around the bedding beside him rather than her, she tugged at his hands until he let go and guided them to her hips instead and slowly took him in.

"I don't want to hurt you," he gritted.

"You aren't," she promised, lying only a little. The pressure was immense, but he was inside her and she loved him, and soon the pressure was just pleasure that kept growing. And when she didn't think she could feel anything more, he groaned her name—*her* name—and he turned, tucking her beneath him. His palms slid against hers as he lifted their linked hands above her head, and he drove even harder, even deeper, and the bed squeaked softly.

Even though she'd promised herself that she wouldn't cry, helpless tears leaked from the corners of her eyes, because there were only so many ways her emotions could escape. And then his hands left hers and cradled her face.

"Look at me." His voice was low. Rough. "Abby. Look at me."

Everything inside her was tightening. Opening her eyes felt nearly impossible. But she dragged them open.

His face was tense, his jaw tight. But it was the tenderness in his eyes as he stared into hers that made it feel as if her soul were cracking wide. "It's okay," he whispered. "Let yourself go, sweetheart. I've got you."

He reached down, one hand clamping around her hip, tilting her, and she felt him even deeper. As if the blood pulsing inside him were her blood; as if her heartbeat had become his. Then there was no more except the ecstasy of exploding with him in a perfect shower of light.

Chapter Fourteen

"Abby! Can we have oatmeal for breakfast?" The sound of Dillon's voice was accompanied by the pounding of his footsteps on the stairs, waking Sloan. Abby, too, he noticed regretfully when her warm body shifted away.

"My brother," she whispered urgently.

Sloan's brain suddenly snapped into gear. Half the morning was already spent, he realized, as he bolted from the bed through the doorway of his bathroom. He shut the door just as Abby was yanking on her robe and shoving her tumbled hair out of her face.

"Good morning, Mr. Marcum," he heard her calmly say a moment later. "And, yes, I imagine we can have oatmeal. Why don't we go downstairs and see whether Sloan has any, or if we need to get it from our house?"

Sloan stared at himself in the mirror as he listened to their fading voices as they went downstairs.

Abby was calm, but his heart was thundering as though

he'd just escaped being caught committing the worst of crimes.

He'd never really subscribed to the notion that a man stole a willing woman's virginity. He also knew that he'd never taken a woman to bed who'd had less experience than he. And *his* first time, his partner had possessed considerably more.

But with Abby?

He rubbed his chest as if her fingers were still pressed against it.

He didn't know what the hell he was feeling, but he knew it wasn't familiar.

He looked at his reflection. For once, his eyes weren't bloodshot. Guess that was what happened when he actually slept the entire night through.

No nightmares. No insomnia.

Abby had put her arms around him and he'd slept like a damned baby. Last time he could remember sleeping so soundly, he'd been a kid.

He turned on the shower and tried not to wish too hard that Abby was there with him. Oatmeal was a good way to start the day. But making love with her was a helluva lot better. He'd already discovered that.

Twice.

Then he realized he was grinning like a damn fool and he didn't care.

Laughing at himself, he stepped into the water. The sooner he showered, the sooner he could go downstairs and join them.

"Is Sloan your boyfriend *now*?"

Abby hesitated only briefly before setting the empty cereal bowl she'd found in Sloan's cupboards on the table for Dillon. "No," she said calmly. She was excruciatingly aware of the sound of the shower from upstairs. "Why?"

Dillon wrinkled his face, studying her as if she was dim. "'Cause he rescued you and everything." *Duh.*

"You did some rescuing yourself," she reminded him. "I told you to stay locked in your room. I think maybe I should get after you for not doing exactly what I said and climbing out your window instead."

"It was a 'mergency," he pointed out. There was no panic in his eyes. He was simply stating a fact.

She smiled and reached across to tweak his nose. "Yes. It was an emergency. And you were very brave to get out that way and go for help."

Rex suddenly left his spot at Dillon's feet to run across the kitchen, his paws sliding on the smooth travertine. She turned to see Sloan.

His wet hair was slicked back, nearly black. He'd shaved and was wearing faded jeans that hung enticingly on his hips, with an equally faded blue waffle-weave shirt. His feet were bare, and the lines radiating from his dark eyes were crinkling with a smile.

Looking at him made her blood hum. But seeing that smile made her tremble with hope. She might as well have been Rex, pretty much shaking with delight.

She quickly turned to busy herself with the oatmeal on the stove and nearly shrieked when she felt Sloan slide his arm around her from the back and kiss her on the neck.

"G'morning," he murmured. His fingers slid wickedly inside the lapel of her robe where Dillon couldn't see and toyed with her breast. "Looks like it's getting hot."

She swatted at his forearm. He grinned, looking amused, and tucked her robe back in place before moving away. He leaned over to scratch Rex behind the ears, and the dog groaned with delight. "Dill, you want to go out on the motorcycle again?"

Abby stared into the oatmeal she was stirring. She felt as if she'd fallen down the rabbit hole or something. Everything appeared so...normal.

Yet it wasn't.

"Abby says you're not her boyfriend," Dillon informed Sloan, instead of answering.

She looked over her shoulder at her brother, giving him a warning stare. But he was focused singly on Sloan.

"But *I* think you are," he finished.

Sloan angled the chair opposite her brother and sat. He stretched out his long legs. Leisurely. As if this sort of thing were an everyday occurrence for him. "Does that idea bother you?"

"Only if you make her sad," Dillon replied immediately, as if he'd put quite a bit of thought into it.

"Well," Sloan answered seriously, "I'd better try really hard not to do that, then."

She realized she was gaping and turned back to the oatmeal. It was bubbling and spitting, and she quickly turned off the gas flame beneath it. She poured the hot cereal into two bowls and nearly tossed them onto the table in front of Sloan and her brother. Dillon made a face, holding up the empty bowl she'd already given him, and flushing a little, she returned it to the cupboard. "I don't know what you have to put on top of the oatmeal," she said vaguely, already turning to escape. "I'm going home. It's time I got dressed." She knew her little brother would be perfectly happy to stay there with Sloan and eat.

"Geez," she heard Dillon say as she practically skidded out of the room with about as much grace as Rex. "What's with her?"

She didn't wait around to overhear whatever Sloan

might answer. She just pushed her feet into her snow boots and fled.

She was halfway across the yard between their houses when she realized she had put her boots on the wrong feet, but she plowed on and hurried through her front door.

It had been left unlocked all night, and it wasn't until she made it to the relative sanctity of her own bedroom that she realized she hadn't given Bobby Pierce's threatening attack a single thought on her way over.

She let out a disbelieving laugh and scrubbed her hands down her face. She retrieved clean clothes—trying not to dwell on the fact that she'd left her panties buried somewhere among Sloan's bedsheets—and took the first cold shower she'd ever willingly taken in her life.

When she came out a while later, scrubbed and wearing goose bumps beneath her turtleneck and jeans, she stopped short at the sight of Sloan leaning against her breakfast counter. "Where's Dillon?"

"Outside talking to Gilcrest." His eyes roved over her. "You okay?"

Besides having mush for knees? She realized she was chewing the inside of her cheek and made herself stop. "Fine. You?"

The creases deepened at the corner of his lips. "Fine." His voice was mild. "When do you want to make your statement?"

"Does Dillon have to be there?"

"I don't think that'll be necessary."

"So he can stay here with you while I go and take care of it now?"

His eyes narrowed thoughtfully. "You don't need me to go with you?"

Yes! She focused on pulling on her boots, correctly this time. "It's just as well if I do it on my own."

"Why?"

She straightened and tightened the clip that she'd used to pin up her hair. "Because if I get used to depending on you, it's just going to be harder when you leave."

He studied her for a moment. "I'm here now."

As much as it stung, she appreciated his not pretending that he was going to be around for the long haul. She yanked open the coat closet and pulled out a short white jacket and a yellow scarf.

"Maybe *I* need to go with you," he added.

She looked at him. "Officially? Or because you're feeling weird about what happened?"

"Making love with you wasn't weird," he answered. "Don't look so serious, Abby. That's usually my job." He nudged her chin, tilting it up with his knuckle. "One of the first things I noticed when we met was that you had a face made for smiling."

"You're just saying that."

He held up his hand as if he were taking an oath. "Nope."

He made it too easy to like him. It ought to have made things easier. But it didn't. "Someone is going to have to watch Dillon, and as nice as Mr. Gilcrest is, he's ninety. I'd feel bad even asking him."

"What about Dee?"

She looked past him to see the clock in the kitchen. "She's probably on her way to pole dancing about now."

He grunted. "I'd be shocked, except I know that's the exercise class Pam Rasmussen's always going on about. I'll call my sister. She works at the shop on Saturday mornings, and it's just down the street from the sheriff's office."

"I don't want to put her out." She also didn't want Tara reading more into things between Sloan and Abby than she already did.

"She'll be pissed if she finds out I didn't ask her. Of course, you don't have to make your statement right this minute, either."

She shook her head. "I want to get it done." Before she could second-guess her decision, she went to the door and called to Dillon. He came running, and she waved at Mr. Gilcrest before shutting the door. "Go put on some clean clothes," she told Dillon.

"Are we going to see Grandma?"

"Sure," she decided suddenly. Visiting her would be a good way to remove the bad taste of having to officially recount Bobby's actions. "But first there's some business I have to take care of. So be quick."

Sloan called his sister while Dillon trotted down the hall toward his bedroom. A few minutes later, they were headed out the door. They dropped Dillon off at Classic Charms, where Tara greeted him with a wide smile and a cowboy hat that she plunked on his head. "Want to help me unpack some boxes?"

He nodded and didn't give Abby so much as a second glance.

"I think my brother is infatuated with your sister," she told Sloan as they crossed the street toward his office.

"Nah. He's got it bad for Chloe."

Abby shook her head. "Please. She trounced him at 'White Hats.'"

He reached past her to open the front door of his office. "Never underestimate the appeal of a woman who gives just as good as she gets." Then he lifted his hand, greeting the man sitting at the dispatcher's desk. "Max around?"

"I'm here." The sheriff's voice came from an office behind the cluster of desks arranged in an open area, and a moment later the tall man appeared in the doorway. He smiled and beckoned to Abby when he saw her. "Come on in."

She hadn't thought she'd be nervous. But she suddenly was.

Sloan seemed to realize it. He wrapped his hand around hers. "It's going to be okay."

She knew he was talking about the task ahead of her. But just then it felt as if he meant so much more. "Okay."

He squeezed her hand. His eyes crinkled with a smile. "Thatta girl."

While the frightening incident with Bobby Pierce had been mercifully brief thanks to Sloan's timely arrival, Abby quickly realized that making an official complaint about the entire thing was not, and by the time she finally signed her name at the bottom of the statement, several hours had passed. She felt as if every speck of energy had been wrung out of her.

"I know this wasn't pleasant," the sheriff said, looking kind. "But the better we're prepared with the charges for the judge, the longer Bobby is going to be out of everyone's life."

"He needs to be out of his son's life."

"I agree. And we're taking care of that as well, thanks to you." He took the papers she'd signed and set them on the credenza behind his desk. "In the meantime, if you want to speak with someone, a victim's advocate—"

She shook her head. "I'm good."

"Okay. But the offer stays open."

"So are we done?" She pushed to her feet. "My brother is probably driving Sloan's sister up the wall by now."

"We're done." He stood up and accompanied her through the doorway. Sloan was sitting at his desk but rose as soon as he saw them. "She's all yours, Deputy."

The sheriff had no way of knowing how badly Abby wished that she *were* all Sloan's. "Thank you, Sheriff."

"Max'll do." He smiled and returned to his office.

Sloan handed over her coat. "Doing okay?" His eyes roved over her as if he were looking for evidence that she wasn't.

She took the clip out of her hair and rubbed her fingers through it. "Pooped, actually." He'd been with her for the first hour before leaving her alone with the sheriff.

"You did great."

"Maybe. But Dillon's going to be disappointed when I tell him I just don't have the energy to drive to Braden this afternoon." The sun was bright in the sky when they left the office, and she squinted, looking across the street toward Tara's shop.

"I'll drive you if you still want to go," he offered.

"You'd do that?"

He laughed softly. "It's not exactly the moon, sweetheart. It's just Braden."

But to her, it wasn't "just" anything.

He was here now. He'd said it. And she wanted every bit of "now" with him that he was willing to give. So she nodded.

They collected Dillon. He chattered throughout the entire drive to Braden, pointing out the school that he'd gone to and their old house. Even though it was the middle of winter, there was a new tire swing hanging from the tree in the backyard, and Abby felt good knowing that the home where she'd grown up would still have children in it.

When they arrived at Braden Bridge, they found Minerva in the sunroom, fussing over the potted plants that she loved. Her hair was silver and her face was lined, but she had a beaming smile. The only thing missing was a spark of recognition in her gray eyes as she greeted them. She didn't seem shocked when Abby kissed her cheek or take much notice when she introduced Sloan. But Minerva sat right down and pulled Dillon on her lap, listening with appropriate awe as he told her how he'd climbed out the window to call for help when Abby needed it, and that right there made the visit worthwhile.

But she also knew they couldn't stay for too long. It was better to end their visit earlier than she wanted than to tire Minerva too greatly and cause her the distress that always followed. So they soon walked her back to her small suite, where Abby helped her grandmother settle into her favorite chair.

"Your young man reminds me of Thomas," Minerva whispered. "The way he looks you right in the eye when he speaks." She nodded. "A good choice." She picked up the framed photograph of Abby's grandfather from the little table beside her chair and showed it to Abby as if she'd never seen it before. "It was a whirlwind that lasted fifty years." Her narrow fingers brushed tenderly over the picture, and her gaze found Sloan. "He fell in love with my chocolate cookies, you see. We married a month to the day after that."

If Abby hadn't already fallen in love with Sloan, she would have now just from the way he smiled so gently at her grandmother. "I can understand why," he told her. "I believe I've had your chocolate cookies, too."

Minerva smiled again, but even as she did, Abby knew the moment had passed. She recognized the faraway expression, the suddenly restless movements of her hands, and knew that it was time to leave. She returned the picture frame to the table and brushed a kiss against her grandmother's soft cheek. "We'll come back soon to visit."

Minerva nodded politely. "Tell your grandfather that he's watering the begonias too much," she told Dillon.

Her brother nodded. "I will, Grandma."

As soon as they left the room, Abby quickly excused herself and hurried down the hall to the ladies' room.

"She's gonna go in there and cry," Dillon told Sloan. "But you can't go in there," he added when Sloan took a step toward the door. "I think it's against the law."

He almost smiled. "Not exactly." He hated thinking she was in there alone. He wasn't blind. Even though she'd had a calm smile on her face as they'd visited her grandmother, he'd seen the strain behind it. "She do that every time you visit?"

"Uh-huh." Dillon hopped from one floor tile to another. "She'll be okay, though."

"How do you know?"

"Because she told me sometimes a person needs t' cry. And she feels better after she gets it all out. Can I ride on your motorcycle when we get home?"

It would be dark by the time they got back to Weaver. Sloan figured Abby would be even less thrilled with the notion. "Tomorrow," he promised. "Maybe you can talk your sister into having a ride, too."

"You can ask her." Dillon crouched then leaped to another tile. "All you gotta do is say *please*."

"Please," Sloan wheedled the next day.

He was sitting astride his big black motorcycle, holding out the helmet that Dillon had already surrendered after riding around the block a few times with Sloan.

"No, thank you," she said for the third time. She'd been sitting on the front porch step waiting for them to return and her butt was cold. Dillon was doing his level best to start another snowman since Frosty was little more than a headless hump at this point, but the snow was too dry to cooperate. "I don't like motorcycles."

Sloan's lips tilted. He set the helmet on the seat behind him and leaned his folded arms over the handlebars. "How do you know you won't like it if you've never tried it?"

She flushed all the way through. He'd said the same thing that morning when she'd awoken to his kisses on her thighs and he'd worked his way up with wicked intention. Of course, he'd been right. She'd nearly gone out of her mind from pleasure.

"Aren't we supposed to be leaving for your sister's Sunday dinner soon?"

"Don't know that it's Tara's dinner so much as the Clays in general," he drawled. "It's a thing with that whole family, and we've got over an hour, anyway. What are you afraid of, Abby? That you might like the feel of a Harley between your legs? It's not really walking on the wild side, you know." His eyes were amused and oh, so appealing. "Not unless thinking that way gets you going."

She covered her face, trying not to laugh. "I'm not leaving Dillon unattended, even to just ride around the block!" She pushed to her feet and dusted off the seat of her jeans with her mittens.

"Eh, leave him be," Mr. Gilcrest called from his front porch. "Boy's not going to go anywhere, and I ain't dead yet. He can sit and play checkers with me."

"Cool." Dillon abandoned his efforts to build a snowman appallingly quickly and started to run across the yard.

"Dillon! I didn't say you could go."

He slipped on the packed snow but managed not to fall. "Can I?"

Abby looked from his bright eyes to Sloan's. She wasn't at all certain that the two of them—three, if they'd roped in Mr. Gilcrest—hadn't somehow prearranged this.

"Oh, fine," she grumbled.

And she knew she'd really been had when Dillon bumped

his mitten-clad fist against Sloan's knuckles as he trotted past him.

Sloan held the helmet out to her. "You might like it."

"Don't count on it," she grumbled as she took the thing from him and pulled it over her head. It felt heavy and too large as she awkwardly swung her leg over the bike. Sloan told her where to keep her feet then pulled her hands around his waist.

She wondered what he'd do if she let her hand drift lower. He'd managed to shock the stuffing out of her that morning. Seemed as though a little turnaround was due.

He shifted his body, and the engine growled to life. Dillon was waving at her, and she managed to unclench her fingers long enough to wave back before the bike swayed in a curve and Sloan roared away from the house. She gasped, grabbing on to him again, and, though she couldn't be certain, she thought she felt his shoulders shaking with laughter.

Then they turned the corner at the end of the street, but he didn't head around the block like she expected. He headed away from town. And a few minutes later, he turned onto a narrow road that she'd never even been on and picked up speed.

Alarm shot through her. She leaned over his shoulder as much as she could, which wasn't much. "Where are we going?" she yelled.

His smile flashed. "Does it matter?"

Since she was wearing *his* helmet, that meant that he wasn't, and the wind was ruffling his thick hair. He looked more carefree than she'd ever seen him. The sky was blue, the land around them iced with snow. It was a beautiful winter afternoon, and he was smiling.

"No," she finally yelled.

He squeezed her hands where they were clenched together over his belly, and a moment later, the engine gained even more speed as they flew along the empty road.

The truth was, she'd go with him anywhere, as long as he asked.

Chapter Fifteen

By the time they returned nearly an hour later, Dillon and Mr. Gilcrest were still bundled up and sitting on the old man's porch, playing checkers.

Abby slid off the back of the motorcycle, feeling as exhilarated as she felt shaky. "I'm still vibrating inside," she admitted.

Sloan's eyebrow arched. "Intriguing."

She flushed. "It wasn't an invitation."

He laughed. "I'm going to put this back in the shed, and we can head out for dinner." He started the engine again and slowly steered the bike right across their snowy yards toward the back of his place.

"It was fun, huh," Dillon said when she retrieved him.

"Yes." She smiled up at Mr. Gilcrest. "Thanks for minding him."

He just waved his hand dismissively. "Boy plays a good game." Then he looked over his glasses at her. "If you want t' bring me some more of them cookies sometime, I guess that'd be all right."

She chuckled. "It's a deal."

"And tell that deputy of yours someone was snooping around his house lookin' for him."

Abby stiffened, her mind too quickly going to Bobby Pierce. But the man was safely in jail. "When?"

Mr. Gilcrest shrugged. "Thirty minutes ago or so. Drove one of them *government* cars." His tone made it plain what he thought of that. He pushed to his feet, looking stiff as he shuffled to his front door. "Keep an eye out for Marigold, will you? Damn cat's disappeared on me again."

"I will." She watched until he'd gotten safely inside then turned and hurried Dillon to their own house. While he cleaned up in the bathroom, she tended to Rex and changed into the new sweater that she hadn't yet worn. She brushed out her own hair, smoothed on some lip gloss and tried to pretend that going with Sloan to the Clays' family dinner wasn't a big deal even though it was.

"Abby." Sloan called her name, and she left her bedroom. When she came into the room, his eyes ran over her. "Dillon," he commented to her brother, "you've got yourself a pretty sister."

Dillon made a face as if he was gagging, but he giggled too much for it to have any effect.

"Thank you for that vote of confidence," Abby told him dryly. She retrieved her red coat and slid into it. "Someday you're going to need me to teach you how to drive so you can take a girl out on a date. And I'll remember how you just acted."

Dillon just giggled harder. "Sloan'll teach me how to drive, wontcha?"

Abby felt a pang. That was years down the road.

Sloan held back Rex even as he nudged Dillon out the door. "Sure thing, bud."

He saw the black sedan sitting in front of his house at the same moment that Abby did.

"Oh, right. Mr. Gilcrest mentioned..." She trailed off when she saw the way Sloan's jaw had whitened. She looked from him to the vehicle. A blond-haired man had gotten out. He was wearing a suit but no overcoat, and as he glanced around, his hand smoothed down his tie. "Do you know him?"

"I worked with him." His tone was flat. "On the Deuces case. Wait here."

He strode down the porch steps and crossed the lawn. "What the hell are you doing here, Sean?"

Abby closed her hands over Dillon's shoulders to keep him from following. She wanted to hear more of what they said, but Rex was barking inside the house, and Sloan had reached the other man near the car. Their voices were too low to make anything out.

Then the guy gave Sloan an envelope, and he looked back toward Abby.

She felt something clang shut inside her.

She could see it in his face. Read it in his posture.

Now had come to an end.

She couldn't even pound her fists and scream at the unfairness of it all. At the shortness of the time she'd been given.

"Dillon," she managed to say hoarsely. "Go back inside."

"But—"

"Go!" She winced when his face fell, and she touched his cheek. Swallowed. Rex could hear them and was nearly howling. She wished she could. "Please. I'll be there in a little bit."

His smooth brow crumpled, but he went back inside. Through the door, howls immediately became yips of joy.

At least someone was happy.

The black sedan was driving away, and she watched Sloan walk toward her. He stopped next to what was left of poor Deputy Frosty.

"They want you back," she said.

She'd expected it, but it still felt as if she'd been kicked in the stomach.

Sloan hated the look on Abby's face. A look he was responsible for. He wasn't any different than Bobby Pierce; he just hadn't raised his fists to deliver the blow. He lifted the envelope. "Travel arrangements."

Her eyes went dark, but they were unflinching. "Chicago?"

He shook his head. "Florida." He rubbed his eyebrow and wanted to look away. But he didn't deserve a respite. "I leave tonight."

"What's in Florida?"

"Tony Diablo," he said. "Johnny was his cousin." He told her what Sean had said about the signs that the Deuces were reestablishing themselves.

"And they want you to stop him?"

"The agency fired me. Before." He saw the fresh shock in her eyes.

"You never said."

There were a lot of things he hadn't said. "I don't want to leave you, Abby." He took a step closer. "But—"

"But." Her lashes finally fell, hiding her gray eyes. "They want you back," she finished. "And you want to go."

"I want to know I ended things on *my* terms."

"Then you should go," she said huskily. "You should go get what you want."

He took a step closer and thought about the other time,

when he'd stood in her yard, and she'd clung to her porch rail. He could count the days that had passed since then, so how could so much have changed? "What do *you* want?"

Her lips twisted. He thought she wasn't going to answer. But that wasn't Abby's way.

Her lashes lifted. Her pretty gray eyes met his. "I want what my grandparents had." Her voice was husky. "I want fifty years with the man I love. I want forever." She squeezed the porch rail then let it go and turned to the door.

"Abby!"

Even through the red coat, he could see her shoulders stiffen. She didn't turn, but her head angled until he saw the fine line of her jaw.

"I…care—" God, it shouldn't be so hard to say the words "—*more* than care."

He saw her swipe her cheek. "I know you do." She still didn't look at him. "It's okay, Sloan. You don't have to worry about me. I've worn big-girl panties for a while now."

"Smart-i-tude."

She finally turned enough to look at him. Her eyes were wet. "Don't knock it," she said. "I always knew you would leave, Sloan. I just…just didn't think it would be this soon."

"I'm not leaving *you*."

Her lips twisted. "The result is the same."

Come with me. The words rang around inside his head like a gong reverberating. But come where? Tony Diablo was in Florida at the moment. There was no guarantee he'd stay there; it was highly likely that he wouldn't. Nothing was stable about where he was going; and everything about Abby shouted stability. Dillon needed it. Her grandmother needed it. Abby had moved to Weaver, but there was no way she'd put even more distance between her and where Minerva lived in Braden.

And he'd never put another woman he loved in danger because of his work.

"It's okay, Sloan," she said again, as if she knew exactly what was going on inside his head. Inside his heart. Hell. Maybe she knew better than he did.

She pushed open the door and stepped inside.

His foot lurched forward seemingly of its own accord. "Dillon—"

"It's better if I handle my brother," she said, looking protective.

Which just hurt that much more, knowing that Dillon needed protecting from *him*.

"I told you I was no hero."

"The only one who ever cared about that was you, Sloan. We just cared about *you*." She pushed open the door. "Be safe," she whispered.

And then she was gone, the door closing quietly, finally, behind her.

"Come on, Dillon," Abby coaxed. Just because their hearts were breaking didn't mean that it wasn't a Monday and that they didn't need to leave for school. "You've worked on that poster for weeks."

Since she'd told him that Sloan had to leave, Dillon had barely spoken a single word. The fact that he'd had a nightmare hadn't come as a surprise. His world had been shaken up.

But she'd gotten him through the rough patches before and she would again. At least with him to focus on, she wasn't falling apart completely herself.

But now he didn't want to enter the contest at all.

She brushed her fingers through his hair and kissed his forehead. "I know you'll miss Sloan, honey. But he'd want you to turn in your poster, too."

His lips twisted, but he grabbed the poster and carried it with him to the door.

She exhaled silently, and they left. She avoided looking at Sloan's house. The driveway was empty. It would stay that way.

One Monday morning down. Only a lifetime more to go.

She told Dee about him leaving when she popped her head in during her prep hour. "Well, that bastard!"

Abby shook her head, trying not to cry. "He's nothing of the sort."

Dee tossed up her hands and shook her head as if Abby were crazy. Maybe she was.

She didn't have to tell Mr. Gilcrest that he'd gone. When she took him over a fresh batch of cookies, he'd already known. "Saw for myself when he left with that suitcase of his," he'd said and patted her hand. "Boy'll be back."

Abby didn't have the heart to tell him that *he* was the crazy one, too.

January slid into February, and Principal Gage announced the winners of the contest from each grade. Dillon didn't win, and neither did Chloe, though he'd been convinced she would. February slid into March and March into April. Calvin Pierce finally returned to school now that his father had been transferred to a jail over in Gillette and was well out of reach. Calvin and his mother had left their house and were living in one of the apartments by Dee. Lorraine had started taking college courses online and was looking like a new woman. When she and Abby ran into each other outside of Ruby's one afternoon, Lorraine smiled shyly, and they shared a cup of coffee.

She continued playing spinster poker and took up the pole class on Saturdays, where Pam Rasmussen gossiped the whole while about everything from the rash of petty thefts the sheriff was certain were being perpetrated by teenagers, to the hot romance she was convinced her great uncle was secretly having, because there was no other explanation for his good humor of late.

Though she couldn't seem to stop looking at Sloan's house every time she walked by it, as if one day he'd miraculously be standing there, she did stop looking every day for the inevitable for-sale-or-rent sign to show up in the yard. And she stopped avoiding going to Classic Charms for fear of running into Tara. She learned more details about Sloan's life during the conversations she had with his sister than she ever had learned from him.

Life, as she had learned more than once, did move along whether she wanted it to or not.

May arrived, and she set out flowers for Mr. Gilcrest. She helped Dillon plant a little garden in the back of the house and surrounded it with wire so that Rex wouldn't dig in it. But he dug, anyway. And when she discovered a groundhog burrow that extended all the way to the woodpile behind Sloan's house, she understood why she couldn't keep Rex from clawing at the wood and barking at it every chance he got.

The school year ended, and Abby signed Dillon up for the same day camp that Chloe attended, and she took a part-time job at the hospital that would last until school began again in the fall. She even went out on a date with one of the doctors there. He was charming and fun. But he wasn't Sloan. She didn't go out with him again.

And one day, in the middle of June, she came home after her shift at the hospital and noticed the window in the front of his house was open.

Her heart climbed into her throat.

No sheriff's SUV in the driveway. No vehicle at all.

Just an open window. And it was much more likely one

of the break-ins that Pam talked about than Sloan suddenly returning.

She hadn't heard a single word from him since the day that black car had stopped in front of his house, and her life had lost its luster. Tara had promised to tell her if she ever heard that he was hurt. But not even Tara had heard from him.

Sloan had left Weaver and he hadn't looked back.

She ignored the open window and went into her own house. She changed out of her scrubs and pulled on denim shorts and a red tank top. She glanced out her bedroom window up at his bedroom window. Saw nothing but the closed blinds, the same way they'd been for months.

She whistled for Rex, and the dog trotted outside with her, obediently plopping his butt on the sidewalk as she walked down to stand in front of Sloan's house again and study that open window. She'd feel silly calling the sheriff because of it.

For all she knew, a Realtor had come by to look things over. It was a warm summer day. Why *not* open the window and let in some fresh air to a house that had been left, neglected and alone, for months?

"Come on, Rex." She headed back toward her house, but he suddenly bolted down the side yard, furiously barking the way he always did whenever he thought there was a chance of catching that groundhog. She followed. So far, she'd resisted Mr. Gilcrest's suggestion of shooting the rodent, but every time she went back to her garden and found he'd managed to get over or under the chicken wire she kept putting up, the more tempting the idea became.

Rex was going nearly crazy, barking with the ferocity of a canine who believed he was twice the size that he actually was, and she quickly realized it wasn't the groundhog that had him so agitated.

It was the fact that the door of Sloan's shed was ajar.

She grimaced and went a few steps closer. "I've already called the sheriff," she lied loudly. "And I've got my granddaddy's shotgun," she added for good measure. "I'm a mighty good shot, so you'd better think twice about what you're doing in there."

The old wood door creaked, and she hastily grabbed for Rex's collar and missed when he lunged for the opening.

"See you're still having trouble catching the dog," Sloan said as he scooped Rex out of midair. He pushed the shed door open the rest of the way with his shoulder, avoiding the dog's slathering tongue.

Abby could only stare.

His hair was shorter, the flecks of gray more apparent. They were echoed in the short moustache and goatee he wore. His T-shirt had a line drawing of a skull on the front, and his jeans hung on his hips. He was tan. Leaner. And he hadn't had any fat to spare before. The scar on his right biceps and the tattoo on his left seemed to fit right in.

He looked dangerous. He looked hard.

Except for his eyes.

She slowly straightened and wished she were wearing something a little more presentable than the cutoffs that she'd had since high school.

He angled his head and considered her. "If you're packing a shotgun, I'm not sure where you're hiding it, sweetheart. Those shorts are pretty short."

She crossed her arms. "What are you doing here?"

He set Rex down, much to the dog's disappointment. "I came to get something I wanted."

Pain rolled through her, so much sharper than it should have been after all this time. She could see behind him to his big black motorcycle. It took up nearly the entire space inside the shed. "I wondered when you'd make arrangements for the Harley." He hadn't taken it when he'd left. And nobody had come for it since.

He didn't even glance at the bike. "Your hair's longer."

She self-consciously touched her hair. Annoyed with herself, she dropped her hands. Pushed them in the back pockets of her shorts. "Yours isn't. Looking a lot grayer, too."

His lip tilted. "Missed that smart-i-tude. How's Dillon?"

"Good." She left it at that. If he wanted to know more, he was going to have to be specific. It had been five months since he'd said a word to her. She wasn't going to make the mistake of thinking he was there for any reason that had anything to do with her.

"Your grandmother?"

Her jaw tightened. "Her condition hasn't deteriorated."

"And you?" His eyes seemed to bore into hers. "Found anyone who has the next fifty years available?"

She turned on her heel and walked away.

"Abby, wait." He caught up to her and closed his hands around her arms, turning her to face him.

She couldn't look at him. It hurt too much. "I can't do this." She stepped back and his hands fell away. "Just take what you came for and go. Dillon's going to be here soon, and I don't want him seeing you. He's finally stopped asking when you'll be home."

He looked pained. "I know I hurt you. Both of you."

She wasn't going to deny what was so patently obvious. "Are you…seeing anyone?"

"A resident from the hospital," she said without a shred of regret for exaggerating her one date.

"A doctor." Sloan's lips twisted. "Guess that stands to reason."

She smiled coolly. "He has a thing for girls in a nurse's cap. You? Anyone new you're tatting yourself up for?"

"Is it serious?"

"Terminally."

His jaw slanted. "Guess that's nothing more than I deserve. Probably giving him your grandmother's chocolate cookies."

"I bake a batch every week." He had no need to know they went to Mr. Gilcrest. She waved her hand at him. "You don't look like you're spending a lot of time wearing a suit and sitting behind a desk. What's the ATF have you doing? I guess the goatee is a little bit of a disguise, but—"

"I'm not with the ATF. Haven't been for four months."

She absorbed that. He hadn't raced back to Weaver, that was for sure. If she'd needed some sort of proof about the way he felt, that would seem to be it. She turned again to go.

"Not interested in what I *have* been doing?"

She stopped. Looked at him again. "Working on your tan by the looks of it."

His lips twisted. "I've been in the sun," he allowed. "Digging ditches, among other things."

"Why? Get yourself on a chain gang in preparation for something else undercover?"

"Getting my head clear," he said quietly. "Finally."

Her eyes suddenly prickled. "I'm glad for you," she managed to say.

"I'm sorry it took me so long."

Her chest ached. And standing there pretending was simply more than she could take. "You don't have to be sorry where I'm concerned."

"Right. Big-girl panties and all that."

She cleared her throat. "You should at least take a few minutes to see your sister."

"I will. I wanted to see you first."

"Why?"

"Because you're the reason I came home."

Home? She closed her eyes. "Sloan."

"I love you, Abby. I didn't want to. And I thought if I left, maybe it would go away. But every time I closed my eyes, you were there. Inside my head. Inside my heart."

She sank her teeth into her tongue, but not even that stopped a tear from escaping.

"But I also knew I was still carrying the same crap inside me that's been there for years, and if there was going to be any chance at all for us, I had to go back and deal with it."

She finally looked at him. "The Deuces?"

"Even before that, I was screwed up. Tara and I—we didn't exactly have a normal upbringing. I told you we moved a lot. About my father's job, but—"

"She told me what it was like," Abby interrupted huskily. "I know how you two would hide with your mother in closets and bedrooms whenever your father thought you were in some kind of danger. Was he really in the CIA? Or was he just suffering from paranoid delusions?"

"He was really with the CIA. And he was really paranoid. The way we grew up?" His eyes darkened. "It was a nightmare. And I'm a lot like him."

She twisted her fingers together. "Paranoid?"

He didn't smile. "Sometimes it seemed that way. But I have a clean bill of mental health."

"So what have you been doing, then?"

"Whatever I needed to do to keep some food in my stomach and a pillow under my head. Construction. Manual labor. Whatever was easy to pick up."

"And easy to leave?"

"I visited Maria's grave. My parents' grave." His gaze was hooded. "Johnny's. He wasn't a good man. But there were days when he was my friend. And I needed to face that."

She couldn't keep up with the tears rolling down her face, and she gave up trying. "You could have told me all this. You didn't have to leave. You didn't have to stay away and never even call!"

"Yeah. I did. Because I needed to realize that I did have a dream. That I'm not so different from my sister after all." He reached out and brushed his thumb over her cheek. "That I wanted this. Home. A life. A front porch." He looked down at Rex, who'd given up on getting his attention and had simply decided to lie across his scuffed biker boot. "A dog."

"He's not up for adoption," she said thickly.

He ignored that. "More importantly, I needed to realize that the only one I could have that with—the only one I wanted, *needed,* to have that with—was you."

She inhaled shakily.

"Love has never come easily for me, Abby. Or with any sort of—" he frowned, searching for the word "—grace," he finally said. "And then one day, there you were. Smiling at me over milk in a crystal glass, and nothing had ever seemed easier. Or more complicated." He touched her hair. His hands were shaking. "You made me laugh again. You gave me peace. And you deserve a lot more than I can ever be."

"Sloan—"

"I want forever." His voice was raw. "And I want it with you. Max has a job for me. A permanent one. So this other guy—"

She caught his face between her hands. "There is no other guy. How could there be? There's only you. There will only ever be you."

His eyes searched hers. "You'll marry me?"

She let out a choked laugh. "Are you asking?"

He reached into his pocket and pulled out a diamond ring that looked delicate and unreal in his long fingers.

"Dillon told me once all I had to do was say *please*," he said huskily. "Yeah. I'm asking. Abby, will you *please* marry me?"

She looked from the ring into his eyes. And she saw forever.

"Yes," she whispered. "Yes, I'll marry you."

"Are you *sure*?"

The diamond winked in the sunlight, and she realized his hands weren't steady. She slowly slipped the ring from his grasp and slid it onto her finger.

It fit perfectly.

"I'm sure."

His lips slowly curved. His eyes lightened. His hands slid behind her, and he slowly pulled her close, lifting her right off her feet until she could feel his heart beating against hers. She pressed her lips to his and twined her arms around him, finally believing that she'd never have to let go. "I've never been more sure of anything in my life," she whispered.

The whoop they heard gave them only a moment's warning before Dillon launched himself at Sloan's legs. "You came back!"

Sloan took a steadying step, managing to set Abby on her feet, though he couldn't bring himself to let her loose. Not completely. Not yet. He hugged Dillon with his other arm, but his eyes never left Abby's beautiful gray ones. "I came *home*."

Her fingers trembled as she stroked his face. She smiled back at him through her tears.

"So are you gonna be Abby's boyfriend *now*?"

"Buddy, I'm going to be a lot more than that," he promised.

Dillon thought about that for a moment. "Guess Grandma's cookies really work."

Sloan threw back his head and laughed. He scooped up Dillon in one arm and pulled Abby against him with his other. "Cookies, huh? So it was really all a plot?"

She lifted her shoulder, blushing almost as bright a red as her shirt. "They didn't work so well for me. It only took my grandmother a month to catch Grandpa. It took me one hundred and forty-six days."

"It's been that many days since I saw your face." He leaned over and kissed her slowly. "But it only took you one day to catch me," he said huskily. "All it took was that smile of yours." The smile he vowed to keep on her pretty face for the rest of his life.

Dillon squirmed and Sloan set him down. Rex immediately jumped against Dillon, and they were off, running around the yard. Sloan wasn't sure who was chasing whom.

Abby slid her arms around his waist and looked up at him. Her eyes were shining. "Welcome home, Sloan." She reached up and pressed her mouth to his.

This was the dream, he knew.

His Abby, who had a heart wide enough to include even a man like him.

* * * * *

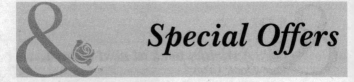

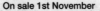

Join the Mills & Boon Book Club

Want to read more **Cherish**™ books?
We're offering you **2 more** absolutely **FREE!**

We'll also treat you to these fabulous extras:

- Exclusive offers and much more!

- FREE home delivery

- FREE books and gifts with our special rewards scheme

Get your free books now!

visit www.millsandboon.co.uk/bookclub
or call Customer Relations on 020 8288 2888

Come home this Christmas to Fiona Harper

From the author of *Kiss Me Under the Mistletoe* comes a Christmas tale of family and fun. Two sisters are ready to swap their Christmases—the busy super-mum, Juliet, getting the chance to escape it all on an exotic Christmas getaway, whilst her glamorous work-obsessed sister, Gemma, is plunged headfirst into the family Christmas she always thought she'd hate.

She's loved and lost — will she ever learn to open her heart again?

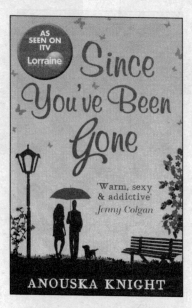

From the winner of ITV Lorraine's Racy Reads, Anouska Knight, comes a heart-warming tale of love, loss and confectionery.

'The perfect summer read — warm, sexy and addictive!'
—Jenny Colgan

For exclusive content visit:
www.millsandboon.co.uk/anouskaknight

The World of Mills & Boon®

There's a Mills & Boon® series that's perfect for you. We publish ten series and, with new titles every month, you never have to wait long for your favourite to come along.

Scorching hot, sexy reads
4 new stories every month

By Request

Relive the romance with the best of the best
9 new stories every month

Romance to melt the heart every time
12 new stories every month

Desire™

Passionate and dramatic love stories
8 new stories every month

What will you treat yourself to next?

Ignite your imagination, step into the past...
6 new stories every month

INTRIGUE...

Breathtaking romantic suspense
Up to 8 new stories every month

Captivating medical drama – with heart
6 new stories every month

MODERN™

International affairs, seduction & passion guaranteed
9 new stories every month

nocturne™

Deliciously wicked paranormal romance
Up to 4 new stories every month

MODERN™
tempted

Fresh, contemporary romances to tempt all lovers of great stories
4 new stories every month

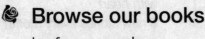